Parsippany-Troy Hills Library
Main Library
449 Halsey RD
Parsippany NJ 07054
973-887-5150

APR 2 3 2018

By Jasmin Darznik

The Good Daughter: A Memoir of My Mother's Hidden Life
Song of a Captive Bird

Song of a Captive Bird

Song of
a Captive Bird

A NOVEL

Jasmin Darznik

BALLANTINE BOOKS
NEW YORK

Copyright © 2018 by Jasmin Darznik

All rights reserved.

Published in the United States by Ballantine Books, an imprint of Random House, a division of Penguin Random House LLC, New York.

BALLANTINE and the HOUSE colophon are registered trademarks of Penguin Random House LLC.

Hardback ISBN 978-0-399-18231-0
International Edition 978-1-524-79766-9
Ebook ISBN 978-0-399-18232-7

Printed in the United States of America on acid-free paper

randomhousebooks.com

9 8 7 6 5 4 3 2 1

First Edition

Book design by Elizabeth A. D. Eno

For Kiyan and Sean

Remember its flight, for the bird is mortal.

—Forugh Farrokhzad, Iranian poet (1935–1967)

Song of a Captive Bird

Inspired by the life and poetry of Forugh Farrokhzad

PART ONE

I Feel Sorry
for the Garden

I.

There's a street where
the boys who were once in love with me,
the boys with tousled hair and lanky legs,
still think about the innocent girl
who was carried away by the wind one night.

—from "Reborn"

IT WAS THE END OF MY GIRLHOOD, THOUGH I DIDN'T know it yet. If I'd realized what would happen there, would I have followed my mother into that room in the Bottom of the City? If I'd guessed the purpose of our visit, would I have turned to run before my mother struck the brass knocker against the door? I doubt it. I was sixteen years old and by anyone's account already a troublemaker, but in those moments that my sister and I stood under the clear blue sky of Tehran's winter, I understood nothing about what would soon happen to me and I was much too frightened to break free.

My mother, sister, and I had set out from the house in the morning, wearing veils. This was strange and should have given me pause. My sister and I never wore veils, and the only time my mother veiled herself was at home when she prayed. She had a light cotton veil—white with pale-pink rosebuds—she wore for her prayers. The garments she handed my sister Puran and me that day were altogether different: black, heavy *chadors* I usually only saw old women wear.

"Put them on," she ordered.

We must be visiting a shrine to atone for my sins; this was the only explanation I could think of for why my mother insisted we cover ourselves up. I pulled the *chador* over my head and then stood studying my reflection. The girl in the mirror was thin, with pale skin and thick bangs that refused to lie flat under the veil.

I watched as Puran drew the garment over her head. She looked tiny with her body draped in the fabric and only a triangle open for her face. There were dark half-moons of sleeplessness under her eyes and, just beneath her left eye, a bruise.

So she's been punished, too, I thought.

"Don't step in the *joob*!" my mother called out as my sister and I jumped clear of the icy waterways that ran down the center of the street. A few blocks from the house, we passed the first of many hawkers and peddlers. His two swaybacked donkeys were laden with pomegranates, melons, eggplants, and an assortment of crockery and cooking tools. When we neared Avenue Pahlavi, my mother hailed a *droshky,* a small horse-drawn buggy topped with a black canopy.

We made a tight fit, the three of us, pressed together in the back seat. My mother drew her veil across her face, then leaned forward to speak to the driver. He looked at her curiously. "Are you sure you want to go there?" I heard him say. He looked very uncomfortable. "Begging your pardon, but it's no place for ladies such as yourself." My mother said something I couldn't hear. The driver tightened his necktie with one hand, took up his whip with the other, and with that, the horse lurched into the street.

"Where are we going?" I whispered, nudging my sister gently a few times, but she wouldn't look at me. She just sank back farther into her seat, staring miserably at her hands.

It was morning, just after ten o'clock, and the streets were crowded with people, many of them women on their way to the bazaar for the day's provisions. At the bakery the line snaked around the building and into an alleyway. Men carried trays of flatbread on their heads; a boy hustled down the street with two huge earthenware jugs. We traveled in silence, turning off from the main thoroughfare and onto a street I didn't recognize. The wheels of the *droshky* creaked and groaned and all the landmarks I knew disappeared until nothing was familiar. After perhaps another mile or so, we eventually passed a railway station. Here the sharp clap of the horse's hooves against the concrete gave way to the soft thud of packed dirt, which was how I knew we were now in the southern section of Tehran, the city's poorest district.

The streets turned shabby, and each corner we passed, each mosque, each row of houses and shops, seemed dingier than the one before. Whole families crowded around dung fires, rubbing their hands over the flames to keep warm. At the doors of a mosque, mothers stood with babies strapped to their chests, begging for alms as their children played at their skirts. Men slumped along the walls of the houses, while older children milled about barefoot in the streets.

Beggars, puddles, rubbish, stray dogs—I couldn't tear my eyes from any of it. Nobody I knew ever came here. I wanted to see everything. I wanted to understand.

"Tsss!" my mother hissed. "Don't stare like that!" She tugged at me and pulled me back.

At an intersection, we came to an abrupt halt while a man led two donkeys through the street. All the houses had mud walls and sloping tin rooftops, and the roads were rutted with bumps. This area was called the Bottom of the City, but it wasn't until much later that I'd learn that name.

"Are you sure you'll be all right, madam?" said the driver when the buggy jerked to a stop. My mother seemed nervous, but she nodded and quietly handed him the fare.

As I stepped from the coach and into the lane, a strange odor assailed me—a mixture of mud, manure, and smoke. All at once I felt clammy and weak-kneed, and I reached for my sister's elbow to steady myself. From the end of an alley came the sharp barking of dogs, and black plumes rose from the rooftops, smudging the bright January sky.

I followed my mother and sister a few paces, then stopped and planted my hands on my waist. "Why are we here? Where are we going?" I asked.

"It's a clinic," my mother answered. She spoke quietly, and now she, too, avoided my eyes. "For God's sake, just hurry up."

I was still confused, but I relaxed a little. The pain in my arm had worsened in the night, and my lower lip was swollen and throbbing. I'd be grateful for some pills to ease the soreness.

I gathered my veil around me, clasped it more tightly under my chin, and then followed my mother and sister down the lane. When we reached the last building, my mother gripped the edge of her veil with her teeth to free her hands and reached for the brass knocker. She banged on the door. She banged again. After a moment it opened a crack.

The vestibule was full of women. They stood in pairs and in groups, older women and several very young ones, from one end of the wall to the other. They waited with their heads tipped down, biting their lips and staring at the floor. No one spoke.

A worn, faded carpet had been strung up from the ceiling as a makeshift partition between the vestibule and the rest of the building. After some minutes, a girl of sixteen or seventeen drew back the carpet and led us down the corridor and into a cramped chamber lit by two small kerosene lamps. The air inside was laced with a strong, bitter scent—ammonia, I guessed. I squinted and scanned the room. There was a square window set high up in the wall and barred with a metal grate. Against one wall stood a table draped with a white cotton sheet. I glimpsed a washbasin in the farthest corner, etched with brown lines. The walls were bare, but as my eyes adjusted to the darkness, I saw that on one side of the room a crack reached from the floor to the ceiling in a single long, jagged line.

I glanced at my sister, but she still wouldn't meet my eyes. Was it then, in that moment, that I began to understand why we'd come to this place, or, rather, why I had been brought here? Perhaps—but by this time it was already too late. The door opened and a stout older woman entered. She had a sharp chin and she wore her hair parted in the middle and pulled into a low bun. She shut the door, issued a quick greeting, and looked from me to my sister and then to our mother.

"Which one?" she asked.

My mother nodded in my direction.

I watched helplessly as my mother and sister were ushered away. The younger woman stayed behind, standing with her arms clasped together in front of her. "Sit," the older woman ordered once they'd left, motioning to the table. I obeyed.

"Take off your underpants and then lie down," she said. With my mother and sister gone, her voice was suddenly harsh.

"My underpants?"

She nodded.

I shook my head. "I won't!"

The two women exchanged a look. That look—I'd never forget it and my own fear in witnessing it. I tried to stand, but before my feet reached the ground, the younger woman had already stepped forward. She was slight, slender as a reed, but her grip was astonishingly strong. She shoved me backward and, in what felt like a practiced gesture, jerked my legs up onto the table, dug her elbow into my chest, and cupped her hand firmly over my mouth.

"Lie still!" the older woman told me. She pushed up her sleeves and drew in a deep breath. She yanked my underpants down to my ankles and then placed one hand on each of my knees to force my legs open.

Whatever else I'd later forget about these next minutes,

or only pretend to forget, I can say I fought her—and hard. I pushed myself up onto my elbows and kicked my legs, but the younger girl only bore deeper into my chest with one elbow and then cupped a hand over my mouth to stifle my screams, and the older one held me by my ankles.

"Lie still!" they told me, this time together.

Working quickly, the older woman forced my knees apart again, thrust two fingers inside me, and hooked them in the shape of a "C." I jerked my legs back and kicked her, this time much harder. And that's when it happened, in that instant when I tried to free myself. All of a sudden I felt a tearing pain, quick and deep, and I sucked in my breath.

The woman drew her fingers from me and wiped them briskly with a cloth. Something gave her pause, and a deep crease sprang up between her eyes. "You're a stupid girl," she said, looking into my eyes for the first time since she'd entered the room. "I told you to lie still, but you wouldn't and now see what you've done." She shook her head and then pitched the cloth into a wastebasket behind the table.

"The curtain of skin is intact," she told my mother when she'd returned. "Your daughter is still a virgin."

I held my breath, too scared to say a word.

"Thanks be to God," my mother said, lifting her hands to the sky and murmuring a quick prayer. "And the certificate?"

"Of course," the woman answered breezily as she made for the door. "I'll sign it for you myself, *khanoom*."

"I had no choice," my sister sobbed afterward, when the others had left and it was just the two of us in the room. She buried her face in her hands. "Mother made me show her the letters Parviz wrote you. She turned up at the movie theater, you know, while you were alone with him. She must have guessed you were up to something, Forugh, because when we got home she made me do it. I had no choice, I swear. . . ."

She looked so pitiful with her tear-swollen eyes and her flushed cheeks. I could easily imagine how my mother had hounded her, and it made me miserable to see the bruise that had bloomed under her left eye since last night. I didn't blame her for showing our mother my letters from Parviz, not really anyway, but on that day in the Bottom of the City I couldn't muster a single word with which to answer my sister's pleas for forgiveness. And I certainly couldn't tell her this: When I stood to dress after the virginity test, my legs were shaking so hard and my head was so dizzy that I doubled over, and in that instant my eyes drifted to the wastebasket in the corner. What I saw there plunged my heart into my belly. A stripe of red on a white cotton cloth. My virginal blood.

For a long time I was afraid to tell anyone about what happened to me or even to let myself think about it at all, but I can tell you now that day was the end of my girlhood and the true beginning of my life. It always will be.

2.

My name is Forugh, which in Persian means "eternal light."

I was born in Iran, a country that stretches across a three-thousand-mile-high stone plateau and is bordered in every direction by tall mountains. To the north, forests of pine, birch, and aspen rim the Caspian Sea; to the south lie turquoise-domed mosques, villages sculpted from honey-colored rock, and the ravaged gardens and palaces of Pasargadae, Susa, and Persepolis. Vast deserts of salt and sand extend from east to west. On any day of the year, all four seasons take place within Iran's borders. Here, under a continually shifting surface of wildflowers, sand, rock, and snow, black veins of oil plunge to the heart of the earth.

By 1935, the year I was born, Tehran had long since been rid of the mud walls and shallow moat that once encircled it, but it was still an old-fashioned city of dirt roads, narrow passageways, and flat-roofed family compounds. It had nothing of the beauty of Isfahan or Shiraz, with their shimmering mosques and sumptuous palaces, but tall mountains encircled the city and even in summer the air carried the scent of snow.

It seems impossible to me now that my old neighborhood in Tehran, with its many houses, alleyways, and passages, has disappeared, but I know if I returned after all this time, after the war and revolution, I wouldn't be able to find it. Still, I only need to close my eyes to return to my father's house in Amiriyeh. For years, that house was my only country and the square above my mother's garden was all I knew of heaven's blue sky.

The rooms of my family's house were divided in the traditional manner, which is to say split into an *andaroon*, or women's quarters, and a *birooni*, men's quarters. A long, narrow corridor connected the two parts of the house, and high brick walls barricaded the compound on all sides. It was a house that turned from the world and cast its gaze inward, a house whose women believed the very walls listened for sin, a house where we whispered the truth or didn't speak it at all.

My father. When I was a child I never dared call him "Father"—he forbade it. To us children and also to our mother, he was only the "Colonel" or *ghorban*—"you to whom I sacrifice myself"—and to everyone else he was "Colonel Farrokhzad." I don't think I even knew his first name until many years later. I didn't have the courage to ask it, and even after I fled his house I still had no other name to call him but Colonel.

He was broad-shouldered and square-jawed, with piercing black eyes. No matter the day or the occasion, he always set out from the house dressed in military costume: a high-collared jacket with brass buttons, rows of gleaming medals, heavy black boots, and the tall, rimless hat of the king's army. Though he spent whole weeks away on military tours, leaving us in our mother's care, the house in Amiriyeh would always be his principal garrison and we children his foot soldiers.

The sound of his voice in the alleyway or the thwack of his black boots against the tiles in the foyer sent the seven of us children scurrying. For years, our sleep was freighted with fear of him. We could never be sure if he'd spend the night at home, but we always went to bed already wearing our next day's clothes, our shoes set carefully on the floor next to our mattresses, our bodies tense and expectant. When he did spend the night in Amiriyeh, he woke us the next morning one by one, girls and boys, youngest and oldest, with a single hard kick of his boot against our ribs. We jerked up, hastily combed our hair, and slipped on our shoes. Fumbling and tripping and rubbing sleep from our eyes, we filed out of our rooms, proceeded down the corridor, and descended the curved staircase. The servants were still asleep in their own quarters and our mother hadn't yet risen for her morning prayers; the house at that hour was therefore completely quiet and still.

The Colonel stood waiting for us in the hall. He was dressed, as ever, in full military regalia, his hair oiled, combed, and meticulously parted, and the tips of his mustache tweaked up with wax. He stood next to his prized gramophone. Its huge brass funnel gleamed in the dark. With one hand, he held the gramophone needle aloft; with the other he grasped the handle of a silver-tipped cane.

We assembled before him and he inspected us one by

one. "Stand taller!" he ordered. "Backs straight! Chins up!" Tousled hair, untucked shirts, and yawns earned us pinched ears—or worse.

"Now!" he called out, rapping his cane against the tiles three times in quick succession. He lowered the needle, and military marches boomed from the gramophone. We commenced our morning drills. We bent and straightened our legs, lifted and flexed our arms, marched in place. Always, we kept our eyes fixed on an imagined point beyond him; one look directly in his eyes and he whipped his cane against our thighs or our buttocks. We knew if we cried he'd only bring the cane down harder until we stopped. We didn't cry.

You see, the rules of the Colonel's house would always be the rules of our king, the shah: Strike first, show no mercy, and trust no one.

In his determination to shape his own destiny, the Colonel had much in common with the shah. One day in 1926, nine years before I was born, a former peasant and illiterate soldier named Reza Khan drew a blue pearl-trimmed cloak over his military uniform, marched into the great mirrored hall of Golestan Palace, and crowned himself king of Iran. The spectacle was the latest in an already extraordinary sequence of events. Over the previous decades, as the Qajar monarchs married Oriental opulence to European splendor, Reza Khan, a commoner from one of the remotest and most impoverished regions of the country, watched. He watched as they handed the British, the French, and other Europeans Iran's land, artifacts, minerals, and, most ruinously, the nation's lifeblood, its oil. He watched and he seethed. Uneducated and unsophisticated as he was, he had a sharp sense of both his country's past grandeur and his own destiny. He became a soldier, colonel, prime minister, and, finally, by force of his own extraordinary will, king of Iran.

Accustomed as they were to the elegance of the Qajar kings and princes, many who attended the coronation sneered secretly at the new king's gruff manners and provincial ways. It was said that even as he seized the country's most sumptuous palaces and fertile lands for himself, the shah hadn't given up his habit of unrolling a mat on the floor each night and sleeping on the ground like a peasant. But those who mocked him did so quietly, because while his manners might have been in question, by the time he crowned himself king no one doubted Reza Shah's temper or the brutality with which he expressed it.

At six feet four inches, my father, the Colonel, was one of the few men in Iran tall enough to meet the shah's eyes. The Colonel, too, had been born in a small village, Tafresh, one hundred miles southwest of Tehran. His people had something of a reputation for learning, but he didn't care to follow the well-worn tracks of his forebears. At an early age, he abandoned his ancestral home and enlisted as a soldier in the Cossack brigade. By this time, Reza Shah had assembled a massive army and equally massive civil bureaucracy, razed the country's weathered and derelict buildings, cut broad boulevards where there had once been only dirt alleyways, and, in his determination to eradicate every last trace of Oriental backwardness, proceeded to rid Iran of camels, donkeys, beggars, and dervishes. Through all this, the Colonel stood at the shah's vanguard, bound in service until death.

———

His first wife was my mother, Turan. She had thick black hair, full lips, and a slender figure. In previous generations, skinniness was considered undesirable in a woman, but by the 1920s, the years of my mother's girlhood, it qualified as an asset in certain quarters. Certainly, it proved so for my mother. Standing among her plump, pigtailed sisters in identical drop-waist cotton dresses in the courtyard of their girlhood home, she alone carried off the new style and smiled with a subtle but distinct awareness of her advantage.

Still, she didn't know if her figure was sufficient to overcome the handicap of her olive-toned complexion. If modernization had suddenly made skinniness desirable in a girl, it only increased tenfold the value of fair skin. When Turan passed her fourteenth birthday without a single decent suitor, her mother redoubled her efforts to lighten her daughter's complexion. She resorted to an array of tonics, lotions, oils, and tinctures, but Turan's skin only seemed to grow darker by the day.

To her family's relief, Turan eventually managed to secure not just an adequate suitor but one who was quickly ascending the ranks of the shah's army. It happened like this: After an absence of many years, the Colonel, now thirty-one, appeared in his family home in Tafresh to announce his intention to marry. He gave his mother curt but very specific instructions. "A slender girl," he said. With this, his mother set out at once for the bathhouse to make an inventory of the village's marriageable young girls. In the end, she chose my mother from a bevy of others she herself judged far prettier but whom her son was certain to reject.

My mother was fifteen when she married. "You're leaving this house in white," her own mother whispered in her ear on the eve of the wedding, by which it was meant she belonged now to her husband and should not return to her parents' home except in a white funeral shroud. She'd seen her husband just twice before their wedding, and both times she'd been accompanied by a chaperone, but this contact was sufficient to qualify in those days as a "love match." My mother would not have expected happiness in marriage (she'd been brought up expressly to dismiss the hope, much less the expectation, of this), but whatever fear or doubt she felt did not stop her from turning her face toward the future, which is to say toward her husband.

Her first test came soon after their wedding, when my father was sent to the foothills of the Alborz Mountains to guard the king and his family during their summer holidays. I once saw a picture of her from that time. The photograph had lovely scalloped edges and it carried the royal photographer's seal. In it, my parents stood two feet apart, sunshine dappling the beech trees and high mountains behind them. The Colonel was dressed in the costume of the Cossack brigade: a white tunic, black trousers, and tall leather boots. He was strikingly handsome, but it was my mother who transfixed me. She wore a pair of riding breeches, a white button-down shirt, and a silk scarf knotted prettily at her throat. I guessed she'd been horseback riding out in the foothills. The wind pulled tendrils of hair across her face, and with one hand she tucked a loose strand behind her ear. She smiled not only with her mouth but also with her eyes. That she might have known something of daring and pleasure was strangely fascinating to me.

Later, when Reza Shah outlawed the veil, a select contingent of his highest-ranking soldiers, ministers, and associates rounded up their wives and ordered them to appear, unveiled, before him. In the ensuing reappraisal of wardrobes, no accessory proved so telling an answer to the king's new law as the hats the women wore. The pious wives chose large feathered hats pulled low over their eyes—the closest approximation to a veil they could find without inciting the king's rage—while the less modest preferred tiny hats balanced at jaunty angles, and the downright brazen appeared with no hats at all.

With a blaring of car horns, the flotilla of unveiled women crept along Avenue Pahlavi at a slowness calculated to give the citizens of Tehran the longest possible view of their women's future. Soon, unveiled women would be showered with insults and, in some neighborhoods of the city, with fistfuls of stones. It wasn't only the mullahs who'd protest the shah's new law; thousands of women refused to set foot outside their homes once the veil was banned. But on that day, the people of Tehran were as yet too shocked to curse the king, stone the women, retreat to their homes, or even, perhaps, appeal to God.

I have no pictures of my mother from the occasion, but I imagine her sitting beside the Colonel as their black Mercedes proceeds slowly up Avenue Pahlavi. She's wearing a two-piece skirt suit and a cloche hat adorned with a single sweeping plume. Her legs are crossed at the ankle and her gloved hands are clasped in her lap. Even after the ban on veiling was lifted some years later, she never again wore a veil except when she prayed, attended a funeral, or made a pilgrimage to the holy shrine of Imam Reza in Mashhad. She dyed her black hair a reddish brown, wore corsets and seamed stockings, tailored her dresses to show off her narrow waist, and never stepped into the streets without a slash of red lipstick on her mouth.

But all of this was before I knew her, before she was my mother and I became the daughter who brought her so much shame.

In my first true memories of her, she stands in the walled garden in Amiriyeh, shielding her eyes from the sun with one hand and holding a watering can in the other. It's late summer and the garden is full of roses, nasturtium, and honeysuckle. Bees drone in the flower beds; sparrows and robins fill the pine and cypress trees. A long rectangular pool, or *hoz*, runs the length of the courtyard. Its tiles are a deep blue and the afternoon sunlight scatters diamonds across its surface.

My mother's joy was this garden. Here her face softened and her gaze turned kind. She set out huge clay pots of flowers in the courtyard, which she used to decorate the house, and also smaller pots for the mint, parsley, and basil she trimmed for her stews. In the mornings, she pumped water from the cistern and doused her plants one by one with a small tin watering can. For many years, water came to our house from a mountain spring by way of the Water Bearer, a wiry old man who piled giant earthenware jugs onto a horse-drawn cart and rode through the streets of Tehran selling fresh water. The contents of the jugs were stored in an underground cistern and carefully apportioned to last the whole week.

Come spring, with the first few warm days of the year, servants spread carpets under the loggia in the garden. There, under a canopy trained with thick, velvety roses, my mother and her friends took their tea. On long summer afternoons, as dusk gathered around them, they nibbled on cookies and cracked watermelon seeds, gossiping, bickering, and confiding. They talked until the sky turned dark and the time came to dust their skirts and plant noisy kisses on one another's cheeks. They always left with promises to resume their conversations the next day.

My older sister, Puran, and I played at the far end of the garden, spying on my mother and her friends or else lost to our own stories and games. We loved the garden but in the ways natural to children. I'd splashed about in that narrow, blue-tiled *hoz*, and so did all of my siblings. Mischievous as we were, we wouldn't dare pick even one of our mother's roses, but Puran and I freely plucked sprigs of jasmine and honeysuckle that grew so luxuriously along the garden's stone walls. We looped sour cherries over our earlobes and wore them as earrings; we stuck pink dahlia petals on our fingernails to imitate the women's pretty manicures. We knitted acacia blossoms into garlands for each other and wore the sweet white flowers on our heads like crowns. Sitting cross-legged under one of the many large fruit trees— quince, pomegranate, pear—I told my sister all my secrets, and she told me hers.

In the evenings, the garden belonged to our father and his military comrades. Servants spread silk carpets under the loggia and heaped up piles of brocade cushions. The samovar was filled with fresh water and set gurgling with a heap of coal; trays of sweets and fruit were assembled; and the air filled with the thick sweetness of smoke and rose essence rising from gilt-trimmed water pipes. Sometimes my father summoned my brothers to join the gathering, but we girls were strictly forbidden from showing ourselves to anyone. Yet the men's voices reached us even in the house, and we hid by a window along the upstairs corridor, cracked it open a few inches, and listened from there. Eventually, the men's talk of politics gave way to poetry. The recitations could begin with a quatrain from Omar Khayyam's *Rubaiyat:*

> I need a jug of wine and a book of poetry,
> Half a loaf for a bite to eat,
> Then you and I, seated in a deserted spot,
> Will have more wealth than a Sultan's realm.

To which a voice might answer with a poem by Rumi:

> My arrow of love
> has arrived at the target
> I am in the house of mercy
> and my heart
> is a place of prayer.

These gatherings went on for hours, with one guest after another reciting poems of the Persian masters—Rumi, Khayyam, Sa'adi, and Hafez. That my father, the Colonel, who could make us cower with a single sidelong glance, produced the most skillful recitations both bewildered and fascinated me. His voice had a deep timbre perfectly suited to reciting verse, and the frequent cries of "Lovely!" and "Exquisite!" roused him to ever more passionate declamation.

I listened from behind the window, enraptured by the music of a language that can sometimes sound like susurrations of a lover and sometimes like the reed's plaintive song. The words hooked into me and wouldn't let me go. Rivers, oceans, and deserts, the nightingale and the rose—the perennial symbols of Persian poetry first grew familiar to me through these late-night scenes in the garden, and even though I was still a young girl, only just a child, the verses called me away to different lands.

No one's thinking about the flowers,
No one's thinking about the fish,
No one wants to believe the garden is dying,
that the garden's heart has swollen
under the sun,
that the garden's mind is slowly
being drained of its memories of green,
that the garden's senses are
rotting in a distant corner.

—from "I Feel Sorry for the Garden"

"Make it more spacious, more open!" the Colonel ordered with a flourish of his silver-tipped cane one morning in the autumn of 1941.

For months the streets of Tehran had been filled with tall blue-eyed soldiers. Planes sputtered overhead. Tanks and trucks rumbled through the city. At night the Colonel retired to his study with a glass of *araq* to listen to the news on his wireless radio. A few times I listened from behind the door, but the broadcast was in English, and I couldn't make out a thing. If I'd dared ask what was happening (which I didn't), he would have said it did not concern me and what could I understand of such things anyway?

I put it together years later. We were an occupied country. To secure Iranian oil fields and ensure supply lines, the Allies invaded Iran. Forced to abdicate in favor of his young son, Reza Shah boarded the ship that would take him first to the island of Mauritius, then to South Africa. For nearly two decades he had ruled Iran with an iron fist; now he was forbidden from ever returning to the country. Month after month Reza Shah would sit, bitter, proud, and broken, in Johannesburg, his eyes trained thousands of miles away, beyond Africa and across the Persian Gulf, toward Iran.

As ardent a royalist as he was, the Colonel, I'm sure, thought the new shah, Mohammad Reza Pahlavi, with his timidity and his airs, was a sorry substitute for his father. In just a few years, when news came of Reza Shah's death, he would be grief-stricken. Still, through the countless abominations and humiliations that followed Reza Shah's ouster, the Colonel never ceased to walk in the streets wearing his military costume and his Pahlavi hat drawn low on his brow.

To us children, in our nearly absolute ignorance, his gait and his gaze seemed no less assured under the new king. We had no understanding of what was happening in Iran. What we feared were the Colonel's dark moods and rages, and these we knew well.

But then he destroyed the garden.

A band of workers descended on our house in Amiriyeh to transform our garden into a modern, Western-style one. My sister and I watched them from behind a small, darkly tinted window. They yanked out the trees and shrubs by their roots, the cypress, pine, and yew, the fig and the quince; they hacked away the shrubs, piled them high into a truck, and carted them away. In place of the rose beds and pots of geraniums, they laid sod for a lawn. They tore apart and hauled away the old hand pump and installed sprinklers, hoses, and sprays. They poured cement over the blue-tiled rectangular *hoz,* transforming this part of the garden into a parking space. They planted artificial acacia trees all around the yard, and then, finally, they departed.

In the coming years, thousands of gardens would be destroyed in Tehran, but it was only much later that I'd discover our garden in Amiriyeh, with all its gorgeous wild blooming, had been among the first. The old Persian gardens were quickly disappearing into oblivion, but despite all the changes that would take place in the coming years, the old walls between houses remained, and we therefore never witnessed the destruction of one another's gardens. We couldn't yet imagine what we had lost would be lost again and again.

The Colonel continued to entertain his comrades and other guests, except now they gathered around chairs and tables rather than carpets and cushions, and they drank imported whiskey and vodka rather than *araq*. If he missed the old garden, he never once let on.

But long after the workers had left, my mother lingered at the edge of the courtyard, twisting her apron in her hands, her face ravaged with grief. Afterward, she no longer took her walks through the garden in the mornings and early evenings, nor did she order the servants to spread carpets there for the afternoon tea. When visitors came, she always received them inside the house. Hassan, our manservant, dumped a handful of small goldfish into the few inches of water that remained in our pool. When the goldfish died, my mother didn't buy others to replace them, and soon the pool dried up completely and its tiles began to crack.

As for us girls, we would not be satisfied without re-

venge. We exacted it finally and secretly on the artificial acacias. One day we plucked their waxy plastic flowers until
there was nothing, not a single ugly, scentless petal or leaf,
left on those phony trees. Our garden had fallen to ruin,
and I would never forgive my father's sin in destroying it.

3.

—————

"GOD IS EVERYWHERE," MY MOTHER TOLD ME WHEN I was still a girl, narrowing her eyes and pinning me with a look. "He's everywhere and He sees everything you do."

Unveiled, corseted, and lipsticked though she was, my mother's life would always be a prayer rug spread at the altar of fear. She performed her *namaz* only at sunrise and sunset—not five times, as the truly devout did—and she often prayed in a hurried and abbreviated form. Still, she believed that everything, but everything, was in God's hands. When a piece of fruit fell from a tree, it was God's will; if it rotted and fell to the ground before ripening, that, too, was His will. To my mother's mind, there was no greater force in our lives than *gesmat*, fate. At birth, angels wrote our *gesmat* across our foreheads in invisible ink.

"You're powerless to alter God's inscription," she told me. "Powerless, Forugh, and also foolish to try."

The day after she lost her beautiful garden, two deep lines sprang up between my mother's eyes, furrows appeared along the sides of her mouth, and the corners of her lips turned down. Her temper had always flared easily and often, but there were now fewer intervals of calm than when she'd had her garden to care for, or so it seemed to me.

Nothing upset her as much as disorder. Our family was never wealthy, but my father's position as a colonel earned him a solid salary, and even through the worst of those years, even when Allied soldiers occupied the country and food was strictly rationed in the marketplace, we never lacked for necessities or even certain comforts. We definitely never lacked for servants. My mother could have delegated much of her housework to Sanam, our nanny and cook, the manservant, or one of the series of houseboys my father employed and housed in the *birooni,* the men's quarters. Instead, she spent her days in perpetual motion, hair pulled into a tight knot at the nape of her neck and a rag tucked into her skirt, grumbling about the idiocies of her servants, the misbehaviors of her children, and life's innumerable other cruelties.

"May God kill me!" she'd wail, shaking her head and lifting her palms and her gaze to the sky.

She now spent hours every day sequestered in the *mehmoon khooneh,* the large guest parlor in the compound. The most carefully appointed room of the house, it was decorated in the Iranian style of the period, that is, with an ostentation calculated to conjure seventeenth-century France. There was a maroon banquette, an assortment of gold-footed tables and chairs, and a marble-topped mahogany buffet. Crystal vases lined the mantel; velvet drapes framed the windows and pooled at the floor. In the *mehmoon khooneh,* too, lay the finest of our carpets, a large pale-blue silk Tabrizi, at once the single concession to native Iranian décor and the detail that lent the room its final touch of counterfeit European grandeur. When my mother finished dusting the furniture and mantel, she knelt on the ground and smoothed the carpet's tassels one by one by hand. A single stray string pitched her into a frenzy, and she began all over again, smoothing the strands until every one lay flat and straight.

On all but a few days of the year—holidays or important dinners for my father's comrades and associates—the *mehmoon khooneh* had no visitors apart from my mother. We children were strictly forbidden from setting foot in the room, and when her warnings and threats were no longer sufficient to keep us from trespassing there on occasion, she began to lock its doors with a key she kept tucked in the pocket of her apron.

She locked other doors besides these.

When Puran and I were little, just two and three years old, every day our mother would take us to the balcony of the interior courtyard, shut the door, and lock it from within. How long did she leave us out there? It seems to me whole days passed on that balcony. In the coldest weather she bundled us in our winter jackets, gloves, and woolen hats, and on the warmest days she dressed us in hand-sewn cotton frocks, but otherwise she made no provisions for our entertainment or comfort. That was our world, four feet across and two feet wide, with a high iron grille that blocked our view of the garden.

I don't think Puran and I minded our confinement so much when we were very young. We played with our dolls and told each other stories. That, for a time, was enough. We made our own world on the balcony, Puran and I, and only hunger could make us quarrel. But by the time I was five, I hated to be locked on the cramped balcony while my three older brothers played outside. They set out in the mornings with the other neighborhood boys and spent whole days away from the house, chasing one another in the streets, crouching on the side of the alleyways to shoot marbles, and playing soccer with a weathered cardboard box for a makeshift goal. From behind the walls of our house, I could sometimes hear them laughing and shouting to one another. It made me furious. I wanted to see farther, past the walls, past the alleyway, past my own reflection in the windowpane. At home, I often played with my brothers and took up their dares, but if they ventured into the streets and into the city, that world was closed and forbidden to me.

"Come on!" I called out one hot summer day. It was the hour after sunset. I was seven years old. I grabbed my sister Puran's hand and pulled her up the stairwell.

Outside, the heat rippled off the rooftops and forced a stillness over the streets and alleyways. Through the window came the scents of Tehran's long summer nights: black tea steeped with rose petals and cardamom pods; coriander and cumin wafting up from charcoal braziers; the scent of the city, pungent and dusty, rising from the sidewalks; and the heady mix of honeysuckle and jasmine released by the first hot days of the year. Down in the streets of Amiriyeh, peddlers folded up their trestles, placed their trays on their heads, and set off for home.

My mother and nanny emerged from the basement, where they always napped in the warmer months. Our

house filled with the sounds of their voices and the clank of
pots and pans as they heaped fresh coal under the samovar
for the evening tea and started in on the dinner prepara-
tions: trimming parsley, cilantro, and dill, browning onions
and lamb for the stew, rinsing and cooking the rice.

"Do you think they're still out in the city?" I asked my
sister in the stairwell. "They" were our three older brothers,
and they'd been gone from the house since noon. Maybe
longer.

She ignored my question and instead said, "I don't think
we should be doing this." She gripped my hand and tugged,
trying to pull me away from the door to the rooftop. "We'll
get in trouble if someone catches us up here."

As usual, I ignored her warnings. My sister was eight that
year, just barely a year older than me, and I could coax her
into some, but not all, of my schemes. "I bet they're playing
cards outside," I said. "Let's see if we can spot them down
in the streets."

The streets—the whole world was out there, in the city
streets. Whenever I thought about my brothers amid the
bustle of the *droshkies,* the rickety horse-led buggies that
crisscrossed Tehran, and the street vendors and their baskets
piled high with treats, my cheeks went hot with envy. Even
my little brother, Fereydoun, younger than me by three
years, was allowed to play in the alleyway with our older
brothers. "Why can't I go outside, too?" I'd ask my mother.
Each time she heard the question, she sighed, shook her
head, and wrung her hands—her only answer. But by the
time I was seven I understood something of my situation. I
was a girl, and girls were forbidden to play outside the
house. The streets, I was made to understand, might be a

boy's playground, but for girls it was a turbulent and dangerous place; home was our only refuge.

But I was bent on joining my brothers whenever and however I could. When they played in the house, I followed them, taking up their dares. One afternoon Puran and I had found them clambering up to the rooftop to shoot pigeons with handmade slings. I didn't at all care for those sorts of cruel games, but when I cracked open the door to the roof this time, I knew we'd caught our brothers in the middle of some truly tempting mischief.

I shrugged free of my sister's grip and studied them.

One by one, they stepped to the ledge, unbuttoned their pants, and peed into the alleyway behind the house.

"It's a contest!" I said, breaking into giggles. "They're having a contest to see which one can pee the farthest!"

"Come on," she said, "let's go back into the house before Mother finds us here!"

I shook my head. "Go back yourself!" I told her. "I want to stay."

Puran didn't leave, but she wouldn't let herself look, either, so she covered her face with her hands. I turned my attention back to the boys, and then, just as they were about to declare a winner, I broke away from my sister and stepped toward the edge of the rooftop. It was not easy to climb out so far—my feet had only the narrowest purchase on the roof's outer ledge—but once I got there I peeled off my underpants, lifted my skirt, thrust my hips skyward, and peed into the alleyway. Well, mostly.

When I finished, I hitched up my underpants and pulled down my dress. Then I turned around and walked back toward my siblings. My brothers stood before me, wide-eyed and openmouthed. My sister was now staring at me, but with her hands clapped over her mouth. Her cheeks were bright red.

"I won!" I hollered, skipping around my brothers in circles.

No one spoke. I stopped skipping and planted my hands on my waist. "I won!" I announced a second time, daring them to challenge me. None of them did.

The silence was interrupted by the sound of footsteps on the rooftop and my sister's frantic cry of "Hide, Forugh!"

But it was too late. Our mother had seen everything. She stepped toward me, her hand raised in the air, high above her head. "A *jinn*'s gotten into you again, has it?" she said. I ducked and raced toward the stairs, bounding down the steps two by two, my heart in my throat. Halfway down the stairwell she caught me by the sleeve of my dress and said, "Never do that again, never! Do you hear me?"

My cheeks burned, not in pain but in humiliation. I cried for hours afterward, but later at night, when Puran and I re-created the scene, we laughed until our sides ached. The contest, our brothers' faces, even my mother as she stood over me and beat me while my siblings watched—the details grew more dramatic with each telling.

I'd long since discovered the pleasure of breaking a rule, but that day I coupled it with an even greater pleasure: telling a story.

My willfulness was my mother's torment. An Iranian daughter is taught to be quiet and meek, but from earliest childhood I was stubborn, noisy, and brash. A good Iranian daughter should be pious, modest, and tidy; I was impulsive, argumentative, and messy. I thought of myself as no less than my brothers, with wit and daring to match theirs. When my sister and I played in the garden as children, my mother yelled at us for messing about in the dirt and ruining our clothes. Puran's sweet temperament and quick tears ensured she'd suffer only mild reproach, but one glance at a scuffed elbow, scraped knee, or soiled dress, and my mother swept down, grabbed my wrist, and smacked me on the bottom or across the face.

She spent hours speculating on the source of my rebelliousness, but mostly my mother ascribed it to a wayward *jinn*, or spirit. Every year at *No Rooz*, the New Year, I stole into the good parlor, filled the sleeves of my dress with sweets and fruits she'd set out for guests, chose a few for myself, and shared the rest with my siblings. When she discovered I'd filched the treats, my mother locked me on the balcony. I screamed so loudly and for so long that she had no choice but to open the door and let me back into the house, for fear the neighbors would hear me.

"A *jinn*'s gotten into her again!"

Jinn. I loved the word, and it thrilled me to think a wily spirit lived inside me. And who knows if there wasn't a *jinn* stirring in my blood? I definitely had a temper, and the force of it could startle even me at times. My clothes were perpetually soiled with ink, paint, or dirt. When I was angry, I tugged at Puran's braids until tears streaked her face, kicked my brothers in the shins, ran through the corridors, and tore down the stairs. "I'm more of a boy than any of you!" I shouted if my brothers taunted or teased me—and they often did.

When my mother threatened to punish me, I planted my hands on my waist, lifted my chin, and demanded, "Why?"

"Bite your tongue!" my mother ordered. Once, in answer, I plunged my teeth deep into the fleshy tip of my tongue until I tasted the sweet iron tang of my own blood. Then I stuck out my tongue to show her I'd done as she'd told me. "May God kill me!" she cried, clawing at her cheeks. But the worse my behavior, the less likely she was to mention it to the Colonel, since he'd only blame her for it.

Our nanny, Sanam, did her best to calm and quiet me. It seemed to me then that she was the only one who really loved us. She'd come to Tehran from the provinces as a girl of twelve. She never married, and I don't know if she longed to return to her village or to begin her own family, but she spent most of her life in the house in Amiriyeh, fussing over us as if we were her own children. Her complexion was quite dark, a warm cinnamon brown, and her cheeks were too thickly pockmarked for her to be considered beautiful, but her eyes were a lustrous black and she lined their rims with *sormeh*. She always smelled of basil and cloves, and when she laughed she threw back her head. I adored her.

To temper the *jinn* in me, Sanam dropped a tincture of valerian in my stew, another in my sour-cherry juice. At night, she tipped a speck of opium into my cup of boiled milk. I detested boiled milk, and anyway, I was much too clever for such a ruse. When she wasn't looking, I emptied the milk into a plant or the kitchen sink or else handed it over to my little brother, who always drank it hungrily and then slept for sixteen hours straight.

But neither my nanny's kind attentions nor my mother's rebukes could rid me of the *jinn*. Mother devised punishment after punishment. There was a game my siblings and I played as children. You'd sit with your palms facing up and the other person would try to slap them before you could draw them away. We called it "Bring the bread, take the kabob." When I was very little, one of my punishments went something like this game. "Hold out your hands!" my mother ordered. I held my palms out, as if playing a game, except my mother held a metal switch, and now there was no drawing my hands back.

As I grew older, she refined her punishments. She routed me from my hiding place in the attic, marched me down the stairs, and locked me in the basement, where the neighbors couldn't hear me no matter how loudly or how long I screamed. Even if the neighbors did hear, what would it matter? I was a disobedient daughter, and it was her responsibility to discipline me.

By the time I was fifteen, I'd made a vow to myself: I'd never beg anyone for anything. Each year I watched my mother more closely, perhaps even more closely than she watched me. At night I stood outside her bedroom door, too scared to enter but unable to turn away. I quieted my breathing, crouched low, and then, through the keyhole— an old-fashioned type, large enough for a heavy wrought-iron key—I watched her. She sat cross-legged on the floor, a pool of light on the embroidery set on her lap. Unbound, her hair fell in waves past her shoulders. Many nights, she didn't embroider at all but only stared at the wall or buried her face in her hands and wept.

One year, I watched as week by week her belly grew rounder and higher and her body finally betrayed what she herself would never tell me in words. "Don't cry," Sanam whispered in the kitchen that year, nodding her head toward my mother's belly. "Your tears will reach the baby!"

Maybe my mother's sadness really did seep into the baby, because when she was born, my little sister, Gloria—my mother's seventh and last child—barely made a sound, only gave a little cough when she was hungry.

When the Colonel was away, my mother ruled our house and all of us children, but in his presence she grew quiet, timid, and small. She didn't so much as lift her eyes to him when she spoke. She cowered. Fastidious as he himself was, the Colonel's hands touched neither white nor black, as the saying went, and his pride far outstripped his hunger or thirst. If my mother left the house to, say, run errands in the city or pay a visit to an acquaintance or an ailing relative, he sequestered himself in his library and wouldn't even walk to the kitchen for a cup of tea. As soon as she came home, she steeped a fresh pot of tea, and then she quickly carried a cup to his quarters along with a plate of soft cakes drenched in honey and rose water.

On the first day of each month, the Colonel placed exactly one hundred *tomans* for my mother on the mantel in the good parlor. From the hallway I sometimes overheard her begging him for more money. "The children's shoes are worn out," she said, or, "They need new notebooks for school." Then without fail this plea: "Won't you stay here tonight?" Her voice filled sometimes with sweetness and sometimes with despair, but she never, so far as I remember, raised her voice to him. She bit her lip, clawed at her cheeks, and wrung her hands, but she didn't complain outright about his absences or demand more money from him. Never.

That my mother could only beg—and for what she needed to run the house or, worse, for her husband's attention and company—was something I never forgot. Even though it was the Colonel's voice that rang out from behind the door, the thud of his fist against the mantel or sometimes the unmistakable sharp clap of his hand across her cheek, it was my mother whom I wished to take by the wrists and shake by the shoulders, my mother whom I judged and I punished, my mother whom I fought with a force nearly equal to love. And it was there, behind the door to the good parlor, that I would make this vow: So long as I lived I'd never beg anyone for anything.

I'd soon break this vow, it's true, but by then I'd already lost my name and belonged to no one at all.

4.

"THE PALACE," I WHISPERED IN PARVIZ'S EAR ONE AFTER-
noon in the alleyway behind our house. I'd just turned sixteen; I was still only a girl. "Friday," I added, rubbing my
arms to warm myself, and hustled away.

"Forugh!" he called.

I'd already reached the corner. I whipped around so fast
that I bumped into an old woman making her way down
the street. "Sorry!" I sputtered.

She grumbled something I couldn't make out, then
peered over my shoulder, looking quickly at Parviz and
then back at me. Did she recognize me from the neighborhood? Did she know my mother and where we lived? I
couldn't be sure, but all the same, I turned away quickly and
walked in the opposite direction.

As soon as she was out of sight, I returned to the alleyway. Parviz was still standing there, but his hands were now
buried in his pockets. He was pacing back and forth and

there was a helpless look on his face. *He won't meet me at The Palace,* I thought. It was risky—even I, in the thick of my infatuation, understood that—and he was scared of getting caught.

I was wrong. "What time?" he mouthed when he saw me approach.

I held up six fingers, smiled, and then, with my heart in my throat, I raced out of the alleyway and back to the Colonel's house.

Darband. It was here, in a village at the foot of Mount Damavand whose name in English means "closed gates," that my story with Parviz and also with poetry truly began.

That was 1950, the summer when a stupefying heat had clung to Tehran for weeks, thickening the air with dust and soot. In July, my father traveled north for a monthlong seaside holiday with his military comrades, leaving the rest of the family behind in the capital. The heat only worsened as the month wore on, driving us into the basement for whole days and nights, and the confinement made us restless and ill-tempered.

In August, when my mother couldn't bear the city anymore, we set out by automobile for my uncle's *bagh,* or landholding. Outside the city walls, the road led onto the foothills toward the Alborz Mountains, and the land unfurled, lush and fragrant with wildflowers. I'd lived all my life in Tehran, and I hadn't known the city could fall away and reveal such spaciousness and quiet.

My uncle's house was full of relatives that summer—his

many children, but also other family who'd come to escape the city's heat. While it wasn't without limits, our parents allowed us some measure of freedom with our cousins. In those days, cousins flirted with a flair and persistence that would have been unthinkable toward their other peers, and their flirtations often ended in marriage. I'd never had the faintest passing crush on any of my cousins; I thought of them as just another set of brothers, some more and some less annoying than the rest. But now when my brothers and our older male cousins gathered by the stream in the evenings to talk about philosophy and poetry, I was desperate to join them.

"Has anyone read Parviz's latest essay?" one of my brothers asked one night, holding up a magazine for the group to see.

"Yes, and it's brilliant!" someone answered.

Murmurs of praise and congratulation followed.

I stepped forward and grabbed the magazine from my brother's hand. Composing poetry was a common enough pastime, but I'd never known anyone who'd actually published a piece of writing. Sure enough, my cousin's name, Parviz Shapour, was printed at the top of the page in bold black letters. "Give it here, Forugh!" my brother demanded. I skimmed as much of the essay as I could before my brother snatched it back. As far as I could tell, it was a satire, but it was so thick with literary allusions and political references that I could hardly follow its meaning at all.

I'd left school when I turned fourteen the previous year. I now realized my brothers and cousins were reading books I'd never even heard of and studying languages I would never understand or speak. All that was nothing compared to the envy I felt now that I'd discovered my cousin Parviz had been making a name for himself as a writer.

It was a moment of reckoning, a moment I wouldn't forget.

I had been only too glad to be done with school, but the boredom of those days was awful. I spent whatever time I could in my father's library, a large room at the farthest corner of the *birooni*. The shutters were always half drawn, enclosing the library in perpetual quiet and darkness. Carpets were piled three deep in the corners, muffling every footfall. Here several dozen leather-bound, gilt-edged volumes of poetry, history, and philosophy reached from the floor to the ceiling.

The Colonel spent Fridays—the Sabbath—at home, and we were allowed to spend an hour in the library with him. Back when Puran and I were still in school, he quizzed us about what we'd learned during the week. He invariably questioned my brothers' lessons more pointedly than ours. I felt grateful to be the subject of less scrutiny, but increasingly I longed to distinguish myself among my siblings. I yearned for the Colonel's praise. Later, I'd hate myself for this yearning, but as a child I would have done anything to earn his esteem. If not that, I wanted to at least claim his attention. I soon discovered a way.

The Colonel frequently read aloud to us, either from the *Shahnameh*, the book of Kings, or the *Divan-e Hafez*, the two heftiest volumes in his library and the most treasured of all his books. He knew every poem in the *Divan*, or so it seemed to me. When he recited poetry, even if only a few verses, he ceased to be the Colonel and became, for those minutes we spent together in the library, my father. His features softened and his voice relaxed. When I was still little, he sometimes called me forward to turn the pages for him, and in those moments I lost nearly all my fear of him. I stood beside him, gazed at the pages, and felt his warmth. He smelled of brilliantine, cologne, and cigars. Often, he recited the poems by heart. He closed his eyes and lost himself to the words and, seeing this, I did the same.

On other afternoons, while the rest of the family napped, I crept into the library, pulled a volume from the shelf, and sat cross-legged on the floor with the book on my lap. The leather binding was cool and smooth to the touch. I would lift the cover, sinking into the private world of its pages. I traced the calligraphy with my fingers, following the slight swell of the ink against the paper. The letters looped and arched and stretched across the parchment, as if in flight from the page.

My reading exasperated my mother as much as my antics did. When I wasn't cloistered in the Colonel's library with my head bent over a book, I hid in the attic or the washroom with one of his discarded newspapers and read it front to back. Dinners grew cold, and my mother threatened to let me go hungry if I did not come at once. I preferred to go without eating, and I very often did.

"But what are you looking for?" my mother asked whenever she caught me reading. "What do you think you'll find in those pages?"

If I looked up at all, it was only to glare.

"More words to sharpen your tongue and keep away any husband who'd have you!"

She was right in her way, because it was my preference

for books and for the world inside my head that left me so incapable of accepting the usual and the ordinary. The more I read, the more I longed to let loose the words inside me.

At eleven, I'd composed my first poem. Paper was scarce, and so I'd write in the margins of my father's old newspapers, on discarded food wrappers, or only just in my head. At night before sleep and in the first moments of the day, in whispers and in silent chants, I practiced reciting my poem to myself until I learned it by heart. Then I screwed up all my courage and approached the Colonel.

"I wrote a poem," I'd announced one Friday in his study.

He raised his eyebrows and studied me for a long moment. "Have you indeed?"

I nodded.

He clasped his fingers over his chest and closed his eyes. "Recite it, then," he ordered.

My brothers sniggered. I ignored them and stepped forward. My throat felt tight and I was so nervous I could scarcely stand, but I steadied my voice and began.

I remember nothing at all about that first poem except that it was a *ghazal,* or lyric, composed in the manner of Hafez. When I finished reciting the poem, the Colonel opened his eyes, fixed me with another long look, as if assessing not the poem's value but mine, and then nodded. He said nothing more, but with this one gesture I knew I'd finally managed to please him.

Many years later I walked into a vast salon, where I was to read my poems aloud before a large audience, an honor rarely conferred on a woman. I was guided up to the front of the room and from there looked out to see a hundred people lifting their eyes to me. In that moment it was so quiet I could hear my own breath. I was a poet. I had written poems. I had published books. But however great my satisfaction that day, it was unequal to the pride I felt the first time I pleased my father with my writing. It was in me already: the desire to be a poet, to speak, to be heard.

I could hardly stop myself from writing other poems after that first one. If the Colonel had foreseen the shame it would bring our family, he would never have encouraged me—I'm sure of it—but for the time being I was free to write all the poetry I wanted. When I produced something I thought was especially good, I recited it aloud, and then waited, breathlessly, for the moment when my father fastened his gaze on me at last.

That night in Darband, I saw how little all my childhood aspirations had amounted to.

Crossing the dark courtyard back toward the house, it occurred to me I might be clever for a girl, but I still trailed pathetically behind my brothers and cousins, and unless I worked out some way of educating myself, I'd only fall further behind.

The next morning I began to study Parviz closely. He was several years older than me and we'd had little to do with each other at previous family gatherings. I couldn't even remember if we'd ever shared anything apart from the most ordinary passing exchange. The last time I'd seen him—a year ago, or was it longer?—I felt nothing. He wasn't particularly handsome; he had skinny legs, a narrow face, and slightly sad eyes. But now I saw how when he spoke, others leaned close to listen to his quiet, clear voice. And although he easily drew people's company and friendship, he had a certain gentleness that set him apart.

I often noticed him heading out for long walks on his own, but it would have been impossible to follow him without drawing the attention of the others. Besides, the more I studied him, the more nervous and awkward I felt around him.

Then, on the final day of our holiday, we met by chance on the footpath leading toward Mount Tochal. My sister and I had set out for a walk and he was making his way down the hillside by himself. Usually he dressed in a white linen shirt and tan slacks, but now he wore his slacks rolled up to his knees and his chest was bare. He'd been out for a swim, I guessed.

In all the time we spent in the countryside, passing each other many times each day, he'd scarcely lifted his eyes in my direction, and he was now staring so absorbedly at the distant hillside that I was sure he'd once again walk by me without a glance. What could I do to make him notice me?

Well, what I did was this: When we neared each other, I pretended to trip a little and then, as I steadied myself, I leaned toward him so that my forearm brushed against his. It was a silly ruse, one for which later I'd fall prey to Puran's mockery, without too much minding. Anyway, it worked. When our arms touched, Parviz looked up and blinked, as if confused, then he looked at me straight on, and he smiled.

It was nothing at all, that small, slightly lopsided smile. And of course it was everything and the only thing.

🌺

Those days of wonder at the body's secrets,
those days of cautious acquaintance
The blue-veined hand that beckoned

with a flower from behind a wall
to another hand, a small ink-stained hand.

And it was love, that quivering feeling,
that suddenly enveloped us
in the dark passageway
and enthralled us in the hot fullness of
breaths and beating hearts and furtive smiles.

—from "Those Days"

I returned from the countryside with a sickness whose first
but least dangerous symptom was a sudden compulsion to
study myself in my mother's mirror. "Vain," my mother
called me whenever she caught me looking at myself, and
also "shameless." So I had to be quiet and quick. I would
pull the bathroom door shut and begin my appraisal. My
arms and legs, I observed with a frown, were far too skinny.
Worse, my chest was flat. Though I hated the taste of it, I'd
taken to drinking cup after cup of boiled milk with pools of
fat glistening on the surface, but one look in the mirror and
I saw it had no effect at all; I was just as skinny and flat-
chested as ever. I drew my gaze up to my face. My skin was
fair, for which people called me pretty. I pulled my hair from
my forehead and studied my features more closely. I'd inherited my mother's full lips, but I had my father's square
jaw and also his eyes. And then there were my eyebrows.
They met in the middle, which gave my face a brooding,
old-fashioned look, but there was nothing for it. A girl's
eyebrows were plucked just before her wedding; one day

earlier and she'd cause a scandal the likes of which not even I was willing to risk.

I sighed, tilted my face in the mirror, lifted my chin, and looked at myself with heavy-lidded eyes. Next I smiled at my reflection with closed lips and then open lips, with my chin tipped down and then raised up. *Not bad,* I thought, unscrewing a small, round perfume bottle and dabbing a dot of scent on each of my wrists. As a final gesture I painted my lips with my mother's red lipstick, though I was always careful to wipe my mouth with the back of my hand and rub hard afterward.

I spotted him first.

It was in late October, a full two months after our holiday in Darband, when I finally saw Parviz again. My cousin Jaleh had recently gotten married, and my sister and I accompanied my mother to her housewarming party. On the chance that Parviz would be there, too, I wore a pretty new turquoise blouse with a pleated navy blue skirt and my favorite sandals, the ones with ribbon straps at the ankles.

He was standing among a group of young men who were talking loudly in the corridor, away from the main party. He wore a gray herringbone suit and a bow tie. The bow tie was slightly askew. He glanced in my direction, and there it was again, the sweet lopsided smile he'd shown me in Darband.

That night I helped serve tea alongside my cousins, a task for which I'd never before demonstrated the slightest enthusiasm. I grabbed the tray from my sister's hands, ignored her raised eyebrows, and headed for the parlor. I served the elders first, beginning with the men at the far end of the room, but when I stopped before Parviz, I lingered just a little. I stepped toward him and lowered the tray. When he reached for a cup of tea, I smiled. It was a smile I had practiced in the mirror many times, lifting just one corner of my mouth so the dimple in my left cheek deepened and then flicking my eyes up for the briefest moment.

This smile was a bluff. All the time I'd been serving the tea, my stomach was tight with nervousness. Even so, I managed to get his attention. Parviz was so flustered that he tipped the cup, and tea spilled onto the tray.

He mumbled an apology. I smiled again. His hands were shaking when he reached for another cup. He was nervous, which I took as a good sign.

I crossed the parlor and set down the tray. I took a cup for myself, tucked a sugar cube into my cheek, and sipped my tea, savoring the hot sweetness. Parviz's mother, Khanoom Shapour, was seated across the room. She had a hooked nose and long face, and unlike most of the women in the room, she wore a kerchief knotted tightly under her chin—a gesture of piety no less forbidding than her expression as she looked at me now. She lifted the tea to her mouth, puckered her lips, and set down the cup with a clatter. The appraisal was keen and measured, and it seemed to me the room grew immediately quiet, though of course this couldn't have been so.

I looked back at Parviz. He'd dropped his eyes to the carpet.

I remembered that in Darband some of my cousins, even a few very pretty ones, had fluttered about him, vying to capture his attention. Why, I wondered, hadn't he already chosen one of them to marry? He was twenty-six years old, an age at which a young woman would have long since been declared *torshideh,* or pickled. But for a man it was, of course, different; he could defer marriage for as long as he could deflect his mother's appeals.

I took a last sip of tea and then did my best to catch Parviz's eye from across the parlor. But it was no use. With his mother watching so closely, he was skittish and shy, and it was impossible to make progress.

I tramped out to the garden. A gramophone had been set up in the courtyard, the pool was covered with wide, wooden planks to make a dance floor, and electric lights—a novelty then—illuminated the leafy plane trees. There were dozens of young men milling about the garden, some of them cadets in the officers' academy, and my sister and I were allowed to dance because our brothers were there to watch over us. I had no use for the cadets, much less for any of the younger boys, but I knew all the dances at least a little, and I wouldn't give up a rare chance to practice.

When I found my sister, I grabbed her by the arm and we danced together, first the fox-trot, then the rumba, then the waltz, taking turns leading and following and stepping on each other's toes until we doubled over in laughter.

"You've got an admirer," Puran said, and gave my hand a quick squeeze.

I looked to where she was nodding. Parviz was standing at the far end of the garden by himself. When he caught my eye, I lifted my hand just a little and he looked away quickly. His sheepishness annoyed me, but at least he'd had the courage to follow me outside to the garden.

"Let's see if I do," I told Puran.

"Forugh! You can't—"

Before she could say any more, I was already making my way to him.

"Why don't you dance?" I asked him, planting my hands on my hips. "Aren't you enjoying yourself?"

He seemed surprised I'd spoken to him so boldly. "Well enough," he said after a moment, "I guess."

A silence fell, and as usual I could think of nothing but to fill it with words. "Do you like Dostoevsky?" I said, blurting out the first thing that came to my mind. I'd imagined this moment many times in the last weeks, but I'd spoken fewer than a dozen words, and already I could feel my cheeks reddening.

"Dostoevsky?" he asked.

I nodded.

"Sure, I like Dostoevsky. The Russians are masters of the form. I like poetry a lot more than novels, though."

"Do you read Hafez?" I asked.

"Of course; Hafez is—"

I cut him off. "I adore Hafez! I know lots and lots of his poems by heart!"

"By heart?" His shyness had eased and his voice now was light and teasing. "Hafez is wonderful, I agree. Just about the only one of the old guard worth reading anymore."

I must have look baffled, because the next thing he said was, "Haven't you read any *Sher-e No,* New Poetry? Nima, Shamlou?"

"Of course I have!" I answered quickly. It was an outright lie, and one he most certainly would have caught me in if my mother hadn't called my sister and me back to the parlor just then. "I've got to go!" I said, and didn't wait for him to answer.

In the stairwell, I fell in with Puran and some of the other girls. When I looked over my shoulder, I saw that Parviz was directly behind me, just a few feet back, and I could feel his gaze on me as I climbed the steps. I was relieved to have escaped without revealing the full breadth of my ignorance, but this thought was followed by the certainty that if I didn't make my intention clear now, I might not have another opportunity.

On the landing, I looked back over my shoulder again. "Write to me," I mouthed, and before he could question me further about New Poetry, or anything else, I bounded up the stairs and out of sight.

"Write to me," I had told Parviz, knowing full well it was an unreasonable proposition and one I might well regret. True, he'd visited our house in Amiriyeh before, but that was a long time ago. Even if he managed to find out my address without arousing suspicion, his letters would be intercepted before they ever reached me, and then there'd be no more letters. And meeting him someplace would be impossible. Since leaving school, I'd barely left the house except in my mother's company.

But we soon worked out a system. It started like this: Parviz cornered my little brother, Fereydoun, in the alley and bribed him into slipping me a letter. "I'll wait for you in the alleyway at four o'clock next Friday," it read. "Come meet me if you can."

Though he hadn't signed it, the note had nothing of the hesitation he'd shown when I'd served him tea that night at my cousin's house. Over the next days, I read his note again and again, as if it were a riddle and by studying it carefully I might somehow figure out how to solve it. How could I get away from the house long enough to meet him?

There was, I finally realized, a way, but it would only work with Puran's help. "We'll wait until the siesta, when they're all asleep," I explained. "You'll stand on the rooftop, and if you see anyone coming or hear noises from the house, toss a pebble down into the alley and I'll run back right away."

"I can't, Forugh! I just can't!"

I clasped her hands in mine. "Just once, Puran, I promise. Only this one time!"

I pestered her until at last she agreed to my plan. The following Friday, when everyone else went down to the basement for an afternoon nap, I slipped out into the alleyway behind the house, and Puran stood guard on the rooftop with a handful of pebbles.

Parviz was waiting at the corner of the street, holding a single pale-pink rose. "How'd you manage to get away?" he asked as I approached.

I cocked my head up toward the rooftop. "My sister's keeping watch."

He glanced up to the roof, then back at me. "You're sure she won't tell?"

"Of course not!"

This seemed to satisfy him. After another quick glance to the rooftop, he held out the rose and I took it. From a few houses down the alley there came the sound of a radio. It was Delkash, my favorite singer. Her voice, rich and pining, drifted from the window and filled the alleyway with an old Persian folk song.

Parviz reached into his breast pocket and drew out another gift, a bar of American chocolate—Hershey's—and also a small envelope.

I grinned.

He looked around nervously, then stepped toward me and brushed my cheek with a quick kiss. Without another word, he passed an envelope into my hands and turned from the alley.

I tucked the envelope into my shirt, under my chemise, and hurried back to the house. When I reached the attic, I sat cross-legged on the floor and pulled the envelope from my shirt. It'd gone soft with heat. I slit the envelope open with my forefinger and pulled out two sheets of cream-colored stationery. The first was a letter—a tender, innocent letter filled with compliments and longings: how pretty I looked the day we'd met on a hiking trail in Darband, how often he'd thought of me since then, how much he wished we could meet alone someplace.

I folded the letter, tucked it carefully back into my shirt, and began to read the second piece of paper. Here Parviz had copied out what looked to be verses of a poem. It was strange, though, like nothing I'd ever read. At first glance, it didn't resemble a poem at all. The lines were oddly broken, the phrasing was as simple as speech, and it had no rhyme and no meter. For all that, I could not help but read it again. After studying the poem, I pored over Parviz's letter a second, third, and fourth time, and then I tucked the two sheets of paper back into their envelope and hid it under my mattress.

That night, I went to sleep humming a tune by Delkash. For many years afterward, I only had to hear her voice and

I'd at once be enfolded in memories of the alleyway, of those days when my body was opening in innocent amazement and I had no other name for longing but love.

⁂

At about this time, my brothers had begun leaving Iran for Europe to continue their studies and earn professional degrees. My sister and I had both attended high school but only up to the ninth grade. There was no expectation that we would look for work. Actually, it would have shamed our family if we'd considered one of the few professions then opening to women: teacher, nurse, or secretary. "Only destitute women work outside the house," our mother told us darkly—the widowed, the ugly, and, although she did not say it, presumably also those depraved souls who practiced a profession so sinful its name could not be spoken aloud.

All this left me with little to do. For a time, I enrolled in an arts course at a technical school. Just as he'd done when I was a small child, my father's manservant walked me to class each day and waited by the gates of the school until class let out. The instructor, Monsieur Jamshid, had studied in France for a year, an accomplishment about which he reminded us regularly, some days hourly. *"Bonjour, mesdemoiselles,"* he drawled through a thick Persian accent, peppering his sentences with French words and phrases. The other students—all girls—came to class dressed in two-piece skirt suits and kitten heels, and they were incapable of laying down a single stroke of paint without first securing Monsieur Jamshid's approval.

I kept to myself. I dressed in trousers belted with a scarf, my hair piled into a messy knot at the top of my head. With painting, as with poetry, I routinely lost all sense of time. I spent hours priming my canvases and mixing my paints. I worked with no aim or ambition but to please myself. I covered my canvases in great messy whorls of blue and red, painting until my arms ached and grew heavy. Within a week, my smock was coated with a thick layer of paint splatters. I adopted only the methods that interested me; the rest I felt free to ignore. When Monsieur Jamshid insisted I shade a line here, add a figure there, I folded my arms over my chest and refused. "Incoherent and undisciplined," he sniffed, summoning the other students to delineate the flaws in my work. One day, I plucked my painting from the easel, tucked it under my arm, and marched out of the studio. I never returned.

I squirreled away whatever money I came by to buy my own books, classical Persian poetry mostly, but also the nineteenth-century European novels my brothers and their schoolmates were reading. Puran loved to read, as well, and for a while we'd pool our allowances to buy books to share. This worked out all right until she got tired of me always choosing the books and insisting on reading every new acquisition first. Left to my own devices, I could only afford poorly translated second- and third-hand editions, which I bribed Fereydoun into fetching for me from the bookseller near his school. Their pages were discolored and brittle to the touch; their spines were creased and split. I read chaotically, in great headlong rushes. One night, I picked up a battered copy of *Crime and Punishment* and cracked open the cover. Within the space of thirty-six hours, I'd turned the last page and begun to read it a second time through.

My other passion was the cinema. Once a month or so,

Puran and I trekked uptown to the movie theater on the Avenue of the Tulip Fields, with Fereydoun for a chaperone. At the concession stand outside the theater, we each bought a cup of sour-cherry juice and a cone of hot cashews. We sat in front, in the very center of the row, with our treats balanced on our laps. The films were American, mostly Westerns and musicals. They were dubbed, and clumsily at that, but it didn't bother us. In the cool darkness of the movie theater, Puran and I sank into our seats with grins and long sighs. We studied the actresses' clothes, their makeup, their gestures, and their voices. When we were children, America had been *yengeh donya,* the tail end of the world, so far and foreign we couldn't imagine it at all, but now America was Hollywood and the beautiful starlets we discovered inside the movie theater on the Avenue of the Tulip Fields.

I watched them, wanting what they had—their beauty, charm, and confidence, and also the places these things took them.

Back at home, I continued to study myself in my mother's mirror. I told myself that someday soon—very soon even—I'd sculpt my brows into a high, thin arch. I would perfect Ava Gardner's beguiling smile and Vivien Leigh's cool, confident stare. I'd go wherever it suited me and I'd write whatever I pleased. I admit my plan for accomplishing all this was hardly original, but within that bounded world my methods were entirely my own. I'd choose my own husband, and this way I'd finally escape the Colonel's house.

5.

"WE'RE HAVING GUESTS THIS AFTERNOON," MY MOTHER announced one morning at breakfast. Then, more pointedly, she turned to Puran and me and added, "You'll serve the tea."

Tea. To understand the dangerousness of my flirtation with Parviz and the punishments that followed, you need to know that in those days a girl's destiny wasn't settled through whispers and furtive gestures but over her mother's teatime pleasantries.

From the moment Sanam hustled into the kitchen in the early morning and lit the coals under the brazier, there wasn't a minute when a pot of tea wasn't steeping on top of the samovar. In our house in Amiriyeh, everyone—our father the Colonel, the servants, Sanam, and, most especially, my mother and her guests—drank tea all day. They drank tea to steel themselves for the new day, to air out grievances, to celebrate the slightest good luck, and to relax just before sleep. But no pot of tea would ever be prepared and served with greater ceremony than the ones intended for the grandmothers, mothers, aunts, cousins, and sisters of our prospective suitors.

"Three pinches!" Sanam said, waving three ringed fingers in the air. "No more, no less." She took her place before the samovar and we stood on either side of her. "Watch carefully," she continued, reaching for the iron canister filled with tea leaves. She dropped three pinches' worth into a little ceramic teapot, then tipped in a few cardamom pods and a single drop of rose essence. She filled water to the top of the pot, shut the lid, and then set it atop the samovar to steep for an interval of precisely ten minutes—any longer, she warned us, and the tea would turn bitter and we'd have to begin all over again.

"Now," she said, narrowing her eyes and pointing to the cabinet, "the cups." We pulled out the little gold-rimmed cut-crystal ones—Mother's best. We held the cups up to the light, one after another, wiped away the smudges and streaks with rags, and then arranged them in neat rows on a silver tray.

For days we practiced over and over, making it a game to please Sanam and outdo each other, until one day we were at last entrusted to prepare and serve our first afternoon tea.

All morning my mother scolded me, telling me to keep quiet, warning me not to make trouble. No sooner did the knocker hit the door to our house and the visitors repair to the *mehmoon khooneh* than she ducked into the kitchen and called out, "Forugh! Puran! Bring the tea!" Her eyes swept through the kitchen and then fixed on us: one quick, smiling glance at my sister and then a longer, vexed look at me.

"All-merciful God! Couldn't you bother to make yourself presentable, Forugh?" she said. "Go put on your good dress, and braid your hair neatly!"

I flicked my eyes up. "But there's no time. The tea will be ruined. . . ."

Of course, there was nothing she could say to that; a poorly prepared tea would completely spoil the visit. She threw her hands in the air. "Well, at least comb your hair!" she said, and hurried back to her guests. "And be quick!"

Puran and I took turns filling the cups. We poured an inch of the steeped tea into each one, followed by two inches of boiling water from the samovar. The tea turned from a deep brown to a warm amber. When we finished filling all the cups, Sanam threw us an approving glance and waved us out of the kitchen.

Now came the trickiest part: serving the tea to the guests. We each carried a silver tray down the corridor, pausing on the threshold to the guest parlor to scan the room for the eldest of the women. We lowered our eyes as we approached, then knelt slightly toward them with the tray so they could inspect the tea. We knew if we had steeped it properly and served it without spilling a drop, they'd smile; if we failed, they'd purse their lips and perhaps even refuse to take a cup.

That first time, Puran and I both managed to prepare a perfect tea. When we'd served all the guests according to age, we took our seats at the far end of the parlor. "Sit quietly," our mother had warned. "No laughing, no chattering."

I felt the weight of the women's eyes shift between my sister and me. Puran had a moon-shaped face, lovely arched brows, and very fair skin. Her silky brown hair was pulled back with two flowered barrettes, and her dress was simple but neat. Her cups of tea were invariably perfect, her deportment and manners impeccable.

"What a charming girl," the women purred as they took their cups from Puran's tray.

"It's your eyes that see her as lovely," my mother demurred.

"Not at all, *khanoom*. She's truly as lovely as can be!"

I didn't elicit any compliments. I might have envied my sister the attention, except I didn't wish to be praised. Not at all. That day I appeared in the *mehmoon khooneh* with my skirt wrinkled and my hair unkempt. Between chatting with her guests, my mother shot me sharp looks from across the room. The kinder of the women smiled at me as though I were feebleminded; the others lifted their eyebrows and clucked their tongues. I ignored them. When I smiled or laughed, I didn't hide my mouth behind my hands as a good daughter should. I swung my legs under the chair, ribbed my sister to make her laugh, and sighed loudly and pulled faces when she refused. And, in time, I prepared so many ruinously bitter and disastrously watery concoctions that I was finally relieved altogether of my duty of attending the afternoon tea.

***

The trouble started with a poem.

In these final months in the Colonel's house, I wrote scores of poems, though I did so in secret and destroyed most everything I wrote. This was because the Colonel's encouragement of my writing, however muted, didn't survive the poem I wrote soon after meeting Parviz in the alleyway. "My beloved came to me in an ecstasy of devotion," it began. "I spurned the false piety of my fear." The poem went on in this vein for several more verses. I'd written others much like it before, love poems in the style of Hafez, but there was, perhaps, something different in my recitation of this particular poem, some tenor of feeling that suggested I'd gained a new intimacy with the subject of love.

In any case, this time when I finished reciting my poem, the Colonel didn't nod his head. Instead, he got to his feet, crossed the room, and stopped just short of me.

"Tell me, Forugh, have you been meeting a boy?"

I looked up at him, confused. Parviz and I had so far only seen each other once in the alleyway, and that had been for less than fifteen minutes. I felt sure the Colonel knew nothing about my encounters with Parviz, and I was determined to keep my secret.

"N-No," I stammered. "I haven't been meeting anyone."

My father stepped closer to me, so close I could feel his breath on my cheek.

He gripped my shoulder and I dropped my eyes.

"Tell the truth!"

I opened my mouth to speak, but no words came out. I could only shake my head.

He turned away and began pacing the library with his hands clasped behind him. Then, for some minutes, he stood before the half-shuttered window, with his back to me. He didn't speak. My knees were quivering and I felt like I'd be sick. When he turned around, his gaze went straight to the sheet of paper I was holding. He strode toward me, freed it from my grip, and raised his hand to strike me.

Over the next weeks, the bruises on my face faded from dark gray to lavender to yellow. I didn't stop writing, but I was much more careful after that. I wrote my poems in secret and read them silently to myself to memorize them. Afterward, I tore them into thin ribbons and then tore the ribbons into confetti. At night, when everyone in the house was asleep, I climbed onto the rooftop and threw fistfuls of shredded poems into the alley behind our house. But the good ones—or the few I considered good back then— I folded into small squares and hid deep under my mattress.

For Puran, all those tea parties soon led to a marriage proposal. A band of women descended one afternoon on the house in Amiriyeh to make the formal offer. "You're part of our family now!" The eldest of them, the suitor's grandmother, beamed. She called my sister to sit beside her on the banquette, slid a ring onto Puran's finger, and kissed her, once on each cheek. Puran blushed a bright pink. *"Mobarak!"* the women cried: Congratulations! *"Li-li-li-li-li-li-li!"* Wedding trills filled my mother's good parlor. "We must sweeten our tongues!" someone called out. A plate of sweets was passed quickly from hand to hand. Our mother nodded and smiled from across the room. It was done. Puran was now engaged to be married.

My mother and Sanam immediately began to assemble the trousseau, though the wedding itself was many months off, as the groom hadn't yet completed his studies. Early marriages now gave the impression of backwardness in all but the most traditional families, but engagements were secured almost as quickly as ever to ensure a girl's chastity— and her family's reputation.

My sister had seen her suitor three times before their engagement, and all three times she'd only seen him across the vast distance of my mother's parlor. Still, his mere existence, coupled with the pretty ring she'd been given, now alternately plunged her into states of grinning torpor or frenzied bliss. In most ways her life didn't change at all, but she was now allowed leisurely afternoon outings in the city with her future grandmother, mother, and sisters-in-law. After visiting the boutiques on the Avenue of the Tulip Fields, they'd linger over *café glacé* and puff pastries in a posh new restaurant there.

"It's called The Palace, and it's got mirrored walls—can you imagine, Forugh!" she exclaimed. "And in the back there's a lovely sunken flower garden and a European-style band and it's full, I tell you full, of elegant foreigners!"

Whenever she left for one of these outings, I stayed behind in Amiriyeh, sulking until she returned. Already, our world was divided between girls with suitors and those without, and I most definitely belonged to the latter category. I didn't care to marry in the usual manner—I didn't want to wait about and be chosen by somebody's mother or grandmother—yet I felt a prick of jealousy whenever my sister recounted her visits to the Avenue of the Tulip Fields and The Palace.

All the same, Puran's joy in this time was infectious, and alone in our room we talked late into the night. Marriage to us back then meant wearing low-cut dresses, seamed stockings, and high heels. Bobbing our hair and plucking our eyebrows. Painting on red lipstick, rimming our eyes with a stick of kohl and darkening a mole with its tip. It was true that once they married, our older cousins weren't allowed to dance at family gatherings except with their husbands, but Puran and I chose not to dwell on such prohibitions.

We focused instead on the clothes and makeup we'd wear once we were married women—these and also the mysteries of the marriage bed.

One day our cousin Jaleh was dispatched to educate Puran about conjugal matters. Jaleh was three years older than we were and herself a newlywed. She wasn't the prettiest of our cousins, but with her marcelled hair, glossy raspberry lips, and black patent-leather high heels, she cut a thrillingly glamorous figure.

Jaleh and Puran retreated to the *mehmoon khooneh*. I was desperate to follow them, but my mother absolutely forbade me, so I had to make do with waiting outside and pressing my ear to the door. An interval of perhaps fifteen minutes passed. Jaleh and Puran whispered so softly that I couldn't make out a word. Then, all at once, the door flew open, and I tripped and nearly tumbled into the room.

"Well, well! The walls have mice and the mice have ears!" Jaleh exclaimed. She turned to Puran. "God is all-merciful, Puran. Maybe so merciful that He'll send even this *sheytoon* sister of yours a suitor one of these days."

Sheytoon—devilish. I'd heard the word often enough, though when my mother called me *sheytoon* it was always in a harsh tone. I started to answer, but then Jaleh flashed me a wink and smiled. She'd meant it as a compliment.

I replied with my most *sheytoon* smile.

"So what did she say?" I asked Puran as soon as we were alone.

"She said that a girl bleeds the first time. You know, when her husband . . ."

"Go on."

"When he does that thing."

I nodded. "What happens after that?"

"She said it wouldn't hurt so much, and that I'd have to show a proof of blood when it was done."

"And then?"

She bit her lip. "She didn't say, only that there'd be blood when he was finished and that he'd know what to do with it."

I considered this. "What else did she tell you?"

"She said it gives a man a wonderful feeling to be with his wife on the wedding night." She bit her lip again and furrowed her brow. "Forugh, what do you think that means?"

"I'm not sure. Didn't she explain it to you?"

"Well, not really, but she said it'll make him love me."

Now, here was something interesting. I could scarcely imagine what this "it" entailed, but that "it" had such awesome powers was totally new. I had to know more.

"But didn't she tell you anything more specific?" I asked.

Puran thought for a moment and then shook her head. The conversation with Jaleh had apparently gone no further.

We spent the following days poring over this new information, turning it this way and the other, setting it alongside the scraps of knowledge we'd picked up over the years. In the late afternoons, when the day's heat and cup after cup of tea at last loosened the women's tongues, my mother and her friends traded gossip, and we had sometimes contrived to listen in. Among the whispers were many stories about the wedding night. We knew that the Night of Consummation, as it was then called, could be the scene of scandal and shame: Brides who failed to show proof of blood could be turned from their grooms' houses, beaten by their brothers, and disowned by their fathers. Sometimes the girls disappeared on their own, never to return, and afterward their names were never spoken, not even by their families. Especially not by their families.

Banishment—it was a terrifying prospect, much more so for all we didn't understand about the circumstances that occasioned it, but for now my sister and I threw over such stories in favor of this: the promise of love and, through love, freedom.

"What did you think of the poem?" Parviz asked me the next time we met in the alleyway.

I'd barely managed to persuade my sister to keep a lookout on the rooftop so we could meet in the alley behind the house. I was turning sixteen soon. "Please, Puran!" I said. "It can be your birthday present to me this year . . ." She finally relented, but this time she swore that if more than fifteen minutes passed and I didn't return, she'd abandon her post and leave me to my own fate.

I pressed my lips together and thought for a moment. "Well, when I read it," I said slowly, "it was as if I was hearing a real person speaking to me."

"Yes," he said excitedly. "Nima does away with all that old-fashioned phoniness and posturing. No more overblown symbolism, superficial emotions, or hackneyed phrases."

"That's exactly it! He writes about what matters to him. About his life and the people he knows. And when it's ugly or strange, it's honest. True."

We were both silent for a minute.

"What would you write," he asked, "if you could write about what really matters to you?"

"I'd write about this moment," I said without hesitation, nodding toward the street. "This old alleyway, the cracked walls of that house over there, that rooftop up there, and I'd write . . ." Here I paused. "I'd write about you."

This last bit made his face redden. "You should write about those things, Forugh, all of them. And," he said, reaching into his jacket pocket and handing me a book, "you really should read this."

I read the book through that same night. Like the first poem he'd copied out for me by hand, the poems in this book had neither meter nor rhyme, but the speaker's voice and the simplicity of his images startled me. A fresh energy was at work in our country's poetry in those years, and it was this energy I encountered in Nima's poetry. These were poems about ordinary people, written with the cadence of ordinary speech. They cut right to the heart of the matter, to the essential facts of the world.

Reading Nima for the first time, I realized my poems hadn't really been mine at all; they were all imitations of one master or another, Sa'adi, Hafez, or Khayyam. It was a discouraging thought and it could've stopped me from writing altogether, and for some days, in fact, I wrote nothing but only read and reread Nima's poems. I pored over them, made notes in the margins, underlined my favorite parts.

In those days, I had a small black cloth-bound notebook left over from my school days, and I used it for all my compositions. One morning I pulled it from its hiding place beneath my mattress, took up a pen, and began to jot down some words. Faces, scents, old city scenes. My memories and my feelings. Then for the next hour or so, instead of writing, I went through and crossed out what felt unnecessary or untrue. I read the lines aloud to find the natural stresses, again and again paring away the words, images, and punctuation to get at the truth of what I meant. Of course, I was mimicking Nima, following his rhythms and conjuring his symbols, but at least now I could see what was weak in my poems and also what I could do to really make them stronger.

After several days of these experiments, I finally chose the poem I liked best and offered it to Parviz. All the next week, I wondered what he made of my writing. I was sure he thought it was awful—a feeble imitation by a silly, ignorant girl. On the day of our next meeting, I was so sure of my failure that I very nearly didn't go. But the first thing Parviz did when I stepped into the alley was to fix me with those wonderfully languid eyes and say, "They're good, Forugh. Better than good."

"Do you really think so?"

He nodded. "I really do. They're a little sentimental in places, sure, but there's something different to them. I think it's got to do with your being a girl, writing . . . well, from a girl's point of view. But it's more than that. There's an honesty in your poems. Anyway, you should write more. Write all you can."

I went dizzy with happiness—that's the only explanation I can think of for what happened next. Without even bothering to check if anyone might see me, I raised myself on my toes, threw my arms around his neck, and then kissed him full on the mouth. It lasted just a few seconds, but it was our first time kissing like that, on the lips. Afterward, he pulled away slightly and studied my face. "Sometimes you look like a mischievous little girl, and then there are moments when you are . . . something else."

"What do you mean?"

"Well," he said slowly, "the opposite of an innocent young girl."

"The opposite of an innocent young girl"—I puzzled over this phrase later. Did it please him or not? I couldn't be sure, but from how he'd said it, and from the way he'd looked at me afterward, as if he'd spoken too much and now regretted it, I gathered he didn't think it was altogether a bad thing.

"I'm going to meet him in the city," I confessed to Puran later that night.

We were lying in bed and the room was completely dark.

She pulled herself onto her elbows. "Forugh! You can't! Someone could see you together, and if anyone found out and told—" She stopped. The prospect of our father finding out was too awful to speak aloud. "Don't do it, Forugh! I'm begging you not to meet him again!"

I sighed and pulled the covers up over my head.

But Puran would not give up. She sprang over to my bed and leaned over me. "Please be careful, Forugh," she whispered frantically. "Promise me you won't go anywhere with him alone! The alleyway's bad enough, but promise me you won't go anywhere with him in the city where you might be seen together!"

I sank deeper into the sheets and ignored my sister. I'd always been the rebellious one, and now, as I plowed toward the consequences of my rebellions, things would change between us. Break us up in ways we couldn't stop. They already had.

I was sixteen and knew nothing. I thought, at that moment, my heart might burst from love.

6.

I SPENT HOURS PLANNING OUR RENDEZVOUS. OF COURSE, I could never leave the house on my own. Ten stolen minutes in the alleyway with Puran keeping a lookout from the rooftop was one thing, but a whole afternoon? I couldn't think how I'd manage it. And then it struck me: the movies. I'd go with Fereydoun and Puran, but just before the movie started I'd duck out on my own and make my way to The Palace. I knew it wasn't very far from the movie theater. It might take some work convincing my brother to keep his mouth shut, but I figured I could slip him a few *tomans* and that would do the trick. As for my sister, she continued to beg me not to meet Parviz, but I was sure she'd never betray me.

It was winter then, just after Yalda, the longest night of the year. The days were mostly temperate, suffused with sun, but that day a brisk wind blew through the streets and alleyways. I'd never gone so far into the city by myself.

There wasn't much time—just an hour and a half until the movie ended and I had to be back inside the theater—and I squandered half of it just getting myself to the meeting spot. I was too nervous to hire a *droshky,* and so I walked the whole way. I kept getting lost and I had to ask for directions three times. By the time I reached the red awning with *The Palace* written in black cursive letters, I was almost three quarters of an hour late and there was no sign of Parviz.

I paced the sidewalk. A breeze whipped at my skirt, and the perspiration on my neck chilled me. I'd come all that way on my own, and now he'd left. If he'd come at all, that is. *Stupid, stupid, stupid,* I chided myself. I'd borrowed a pair of white gloves from Puran's trousseau—for their prettiness, but also to hide the lack of a wedding band—and now I plucked anxiously at the pearls set at their wrists.

I felt a tap against my shoulder.

"Forugh!"

I spun around, and there he was. Parviz, with his sad eyes and his sweet, shy smile. His bow tie was perfectly even for a change. Smiling, I stepped toward him and gave it a little tug.

"I was waiting for you inside," he explained. "I figured you weren't coming, so I was about to leave."

"Of course I was coming!" I said, smiling broadly and cocking my head toward the entrance. "Now, let's go in, while we still have time!"

He took my arm under his and together we entered the restaurant. Once inside, I eased into my seat and looked around. The Palace was even better than Puran had described it, with a sunken garden full of gardenias and tuberoses; round, cloth-covered tables with candles and a single red rose at each one; and a gleaming parquet dance floor and a full European-style band.

"Café glacé," I told the waiter, with as much nonchalance as I could muster, to which Parviz smiled and ordered the same.

I was wearing a dress I'd sewn myself: white with a sweetheart neckline, capped sleeves, and a full skirt that just skimmed my knees. That day, I wore it with a red cardigan and bright-red kitten heels. "Cover yourself up!" my mother had ordered me before letting me out of the house, and for once I obeyed without a word of protest. The heavy black coat I'd pulled over my outfit now lay on my empty seat in the movie theater.

I'd felt very pleased with myself, setting out with my hair loose and glossy and my skirt swishing from side to side as I strode toward The Palace, but as I took in the scene around me, my confidence waned. The women all seemed so very sure of themselves in their silk day dresses and rouged cheeks and made-up lips. I glanced at the couple sitting at the next table. A blonde in a sateen sea-green dress with a full skirt and tight bodice was smoking a cigarette. A *farangi*, a foreigner. I'd seen foreign women in the streets before, but only rarely and always from a distance. This woman was so close to me, just a foot or so away. She smelled of lilacs and roses, as heady as spring. I couldn't wrench my eyes away from her. She slowly crossed and then uncrossed her legs. When she glanced up and caught me looking, her gaze told me she was wholly accustomed to being admired. What would it be like, I wondered, to go through your days like that?

Parviz interrupted my thoughts. "Are you sure your sister won't tell anyone you've come here?"

"My sister?"

He nodded.

"She'd never tell on me!"

"How about your brother? Can you really count on him not to squeal?"

I looked at him evenly. "Listen, if you're so worried, you could just leave."

"Oh no," he said quickly. "I don't want to do that."

"Why not? I mean, your mother's probably got a wife picked out for you, right?"

"No," he said, then added, "Not yet."

I'd touched a nerve—it was obvious from the way he looked away—but I wasn't pleased with myself for it. I didn't want him to look away from me. I wanted him to be how he was in the alley, sweet, teasing, and bold, and I wanted to be like that, too. I leaned toward him and lowered my voice. "So, you don't want to leave. Good. I'm awfully happy about that, but what *would* you like to do now that we're here together?"

His cheeks flushed a little and he flashed me a nervous smile. I relaxed and took a sip of my *café glacé*. A new song started up. I tucked my hair behind my ears and turned my attention to the dance floor and the band. I tapped my foot to the music, working out the rhythm. They were playing a rumba. Puran and I had danced it together many times before, and I figured I could dance half as well as any of the women there, so why not try?

"Well, I know what *I* want to do," I said. I got to my feet, smoothed my skirt, and held out my hand.

On the dance floor, I placed my arms on his shoulders and he reached for my waist and pulled me up toward him. We went round the room and back, my skirt swinging under me and brushing against his legs as we danced. He smelled wonderful—of soap, cotton, and cologne—and the whole time we danced, I could feel his warm fingers through the fabric of my dress.

I was still smiling when I returned to the movie house. I glanced at my watch. Five thirty-two. More than ten minutes to spare before the film ended! I bought a sour-cherry juice from the concession stand in the lobby and slipped back into the theater. I picked my way through the dark to join Puran and Fereydoun, ignoring hisses and sharp looks along the way. After stumbling a few times, I at last reached the front row, only to find all three of our seats empty but for my black coat and a half-eaten cone of cashews.

"Who is he and where did you go with him?" the Colonel demanded when I returned to the house alone that day.

I glanced over my shoulder into the alley. I could run, I thought. It seemed so easy. I'd run and I'd catch up to Parviz at the train station. I knew he'd be taking a six o'clock train to visit his parents in Ahwaz. But I was suddenly seized with a horrible thought: My father would follow me, and then he'd come face-to-face with Parviz. The way I saw it, I was more capable of handling the Colonel than Parviz was.

I stepped into the house and shut the door. My mother and Puran stood together at the foot of the stairs. My sister's eyes were wild with apology. But why had she and Fe-reydoun left the movie theater before the film ended? And how much did my father know about the day's events and about what had come before?

I guessed it couldn't be much or he wouldn't have asked me anything at all. I lifted my chin and crossed my arms over my chest.

"You tell me where you went with him, Forugh, or by God you'll regret it."

"What will you do? Hit me? Lock me in my room?"

We stared at each other. I was sixteen years old, but I'd never spoken to my father in such a tone. His eyebrows arched up and his face reddened. Three steps, low and even, sounded in the dark hall, and then he stopped just before me.

He turned to my mother. "Do you see what kind of daughter you've raised?" He gripped my arm, digging deep into the muscle, and pulled me toward her. *"Kesafat!"* he shouted—filthy!

She winced and lowered her eyes. "I knew nothing about it, I swear. . . ."

"Kesafat!" he shouted again, this time much louder than before.

He marched me up the stairs, still gripping my arm and his other hand clutching the back of my neck. When we reached the library, he shoved me inside and slammed the door shut. I inched toward the wall, but it was useless; there was no way out but past him.

When he struck me, I staggered and stumbled back. He hit me again, and that second time his ring must have caught the inside of my lip, because my mouth filled with blood. I lifted my fingers to my lips, then felt inside my mouth. One of my teeth had been knocked loose. I pressed my tongue lightly against it and it slipped free. Cupping a hand over my mouth, I spit the tooth into my palm. I was staring dumbly at it when he struck me again, this time so hard that my legs buckled under me and I fell to the floor.

When I opened my eyes, I met his black boots. I pulled my arms quickly over my head and screwed my eyes shut.

"Who did you meet in the streets, Forugh?"

I shook my head.

"Who did you meet and where did you go with him?"

"I didn't meet anyone," I said. My lower lip was throbbing and the words came out thickly. "I went alone, and I didn't meet anyone!"

"You are shameless and disgusting and you are lying to me."

For some moments, he stood over me with his boot still raised above my head. The pain in my arm was ferocious. I kept my arms pulled over my head, my legs drawn up, and my face buried between my knees.

"Out!" he said at last, and I struggled to my feet.

When I reached my room, I slammed the door shut and collapsed onto the bed. My lip was still bleeding heavily. I felt inside my mouth with my finger. There was a gap toward the back where my tooth had been. I yanked the sheet from the bed and stanched the blood with a corner of it. All at once a searing pain shot through my belly and bent me double. Sanam would give me a sliver of opium to quell the pain, but I'd have to go down to the kitchen to ask her for it.

I got up and crossed the room, but when I tried the door, it wouldn't open. I tried a second and a third time, rattling the knob and blinking back angry tears. It was no use. Sometime in the last minutes, the door had been locked from the outside.

✳

Two strangers waited for me the next morning in a room in the Bottom of the City. One of them was just a girl herself, a girl who held down other girls while her mother parted their legs and pried them open and looked at them there, in the place too shameful to be named. They had already worked in this way for years, this mother and daughter, having examined hundreds of girls together, and they would work together until the daughter became a woman and took her mother's place and her own daughter grew up and took hers in turn.

The door closed. The air hummed around us, the two strangers and me. It must have been clear from the awkward way I held it that I'd never worn a veil in my life, nor had I had reason to find myself in this place before. Like the others waiting in the vestibule outside, I'd been brought to this part of the city precisely because it was unfamiliar and there was at least a chance I wouldn't be recognized.

They were always frightened, the girls who were taken into such rooms—even the ones who knew exactly why they were there. Most often they were too stunned or too scared to do anything but submit, but however dim or precise their knowledge of sex, they were all intimate with shame, and so they closed their eyes and they waited.

But something different happened to me here. I fought. I fought to free myself, but the two strangers only forced me down harder, pinning me against the table. Still I wouldn't settle down. I wouldn't submit. I twisted and kicked and clawed. I surely wasn't the only one to fight back during this examination, but for me the cost wouldn't be a bruised cheek or scratched arm. No.

Fate or accident, call it what you will, but the truth was this: My hymen tore, I bled, and now my girlhood was gone.

Afterward, I was the one who locked the door.

When we returned from the Bottom of the City that day, my legs were still shaking so badly I could barely stand. I had told no one, not even my sister, what happened in the examination room—about the virginity test, about the sudden pain I felt between my legs when I jerked away and tried to free myself, about the blood-streaked cloth I'd seen in the wastebasket. A girl's virginity was the sum of her worth, and though she ascribed its loss to my stupidity and willfulness in resisting her, the woman who performed the test would never have divulged the truth to my family. It would have been not only my ruin but hers, and so she'd simply signed the chastity certificate and sent us on our way.

As for me, was it an instinct for self-preservation or the beginnings of a plan that kept me silent? I only know I was seized by a desperate need to be alone and to think through what had happened to me and what I might do about it now.

That night, when everyone in the house was asleep, I slipped into my mother's bedroom. I knew exactly what I needed, and I moved quickly and quietly in the darkness. At the foot of her bed stood a bench where she always laid her blue apron before sleep. I tiptoed over to it, reached inside the front pocket and pulled out the ring of keys. Then, closing my hand tightly over the keys so they would not clink, I crept back out of the room. Then I descended the stairs to the basement, shut the door, and pulled the heavy iron bolt closed; with the key in my possession, no one could get to me.

That night, I sat against the wall, just beside the basement door, with my legs drawn up and my forehead pressed against my knees, the key pressed between my palms. There was a small basin in the corner where I could relieve myself, but I had no food to eat and no water to drink. My arm was hurting even worse than before, and it was so cold that even after I found a blanket and pulled it over me, I couldn't stop shivering. Worse, my head was whirling with thoughts, and I couldn't make it stop. I had no idea what to do next or whom I could go to for help.

"Forugh!" Sanam called out from behind the basement door the next morning. "For God's sake, open the door!" she shouted, and then rattled the doorknob.

I refused to answer.

From behind the door I heard my mother say, "Even if she comes out, she'll be good as dead with all this shame and dishonor she's brought on us all."

Some time later, Sanam returned by herself. "I've brought your favorite pomegranate and walnut stew, Forugh," she said, "and a plate of crisped rice. I've died and come back to life ten times since last night. Please come eat something, sweetheart."

My stomach writhed. I'd eaten nothing since that glass of *café glacé* at The Palace, and that was two days ago, but I observed my hunger as from a distance.

All through my childhood, I was taught only to obey. I'd always considered myself daring and clever and different from other girls. Now I saw that all my rebellions had been nothing. No, worse than nothing. I'd done no more than exchange a handful of letters with Parviz in the alleyway and meet him just once in the city, but already I'd lost what little freedom I had. "Your daughter is still a virgin," the woman had told my mother in the Bottom of the City. Despite what had happened to me during the examination, my parents now had proof of my purity—a certificate that could be presented to any suitor who might come for me. The piece of paper offered no consolation, though; my flirtations with Parviz would only hasten, rather than forestall, my marriage. That much was certain.

On my second day in the basement, my mind grew sharp and clear. What I wanted was a home, somewhere, anywhere, that was not the Colonel's house. I still couldn't see how I'd get myself free and to such a place, but when I thought of the small, dark room in the Bottom of the City, that hand cupping my mouth to stifle my screams, and those fingers prying into me, my resolve tightened and it made me brave.

The next morning a peculiar lightness overtook me. Suddenly I didn't feel even a hint of hunger or thirst, only exhaustion accompanied by a total clarity of thought. I'd passed nearly three days in the basement by then. I lay on the floor, my cheek to the bare tiles, and I slept—deeply and soundly.

Once, I woke to the sound of metal scraping against the keyhole. Someone was trying to pry the lock open, though meeting with no success. I jerked my head up. "I'll die, I swear!" I shouted. "I'll kill myself if you don't let me marry Parviz!" After so long a silence, the force of my screams exhausted me, and I pulled my arms over my head and closed my eyes again.

All the next day I drifted in and out of sleep. One after another Puran, my mother, and Sanam banged on the door and begged me to open it and let them in. I refused. Eventually I must have fainted, because all at once their voices fell away and I heard nothing at all.

Then, sometime in the night, there was a hard, incessant rap against the door, and I woke. "Forugh," came a voice—my mother's—from the other side. It was so quiet in that moment that even from behind the heavy wooden panels I could hear her sigh. "Your father's arranged a match for you," she said. "You'll be married next Saturday."

7.

IMAGINE IT LIKE THIS. IMAGINE IT LIKE I'VE IMAGINED IT countless times. Before dawn one morning, on the fourth day after I locked myself in the basement and refused to eat or speak or open the door to anyone, the Colonel slid into the back seat of a black Mercedes. The medals on his breast shone; the creases in his trousers were knife-sharp. "Ahwaz," he told his driver, and laid his silver-tipped cane across his lap.

Usually, my father had no patience for gossip, dismissing it as "women's nonsense," but by the third day of my self-imposed confinement the whispers in the neighborhood had changed from rumor and speculation to statements of fact. "She's been meeting a man in the streets," they said of me. "When I saw her last," a neighbor reported, "she and her sister both had bruises on their faces, though they wore veils to try to hide it."

The Colonel set out from Tehran before sunrise. An hour outside the capital, the road opened onto a different country altogether. The trees became scattered and eventually disappeared, and the earth turned to sun-cracked clay. The age-old villages and caravanserai were indistinguishable from the desert that rose beyond it; all was a sea of gray and brown, except for the occasional turquoise dome of a distant mosque.

That day—the day the Colonel's boots crossed Khanoom Shapour's threshold and blackened her fate—was a Wednesday. At sunrise, after completing her first ablutions and prayers of the morning, she headed to the chicken coop behind the house, chose the plumpest inhabitant, and tucked it under the crook of her arm. Standing before the sink, she went to work with her strong hands. She snapped the chicken's neck with one hand and set about plucking its white feathers with the other. Its blood was soon hot and thick on her fingers and palms.

Parviz, she thought, and smiled to herself. Her only son, her *cheshmeh cheragh,* the light of her eyes. Three years ago he'd left the provinces to work in Tehran. Ever since then, on Friday afternoons Khanoom Shapour could be found, without fail, at the train station, waiting for her son. "May I die for you," she told him by way of greeting and, two days later, of goodbye.

Later that afternoon, Khanoom Shapour finished preparing the chicken, tossed back a small cup of bitter black tea, and set about peeling the mound of eggplant for the day's stew. When she finished, she glanced at her wristwatch: five. She still had two hours—plenty of time to prepare Parviz's favorite chicken-and-eggplant dish and maybe also the fresh *dolmehs* and stuffed peppers he loved. She pushed up her sleeves and began frying the eggplant. She was about to set in on the rice when the brass knocker sounded.

She stopped by the entry. The door had two separate brass knockers, one for men and another for women, each with a distinct sound. Khanoom Shapour listened again for the knock. The visitor was a man. She reached for the veil she kept in a small alcove. It occurred to her that Parviz might have borrowed a car and driven back home early to surprise her, but when she pulled the door open, it wasn't her son but the Colonel's unsmiling face that greeted her.

Manners forbade any show of surprise at this unexpected visit, much less any show of annoyance or displeasure. "You honor us with your visit, *ghorban,*" Khanoom Shapour said, bowing her head and averting her eyes. "My husband's resting, but I can call him if you please?"

"No, my business is with you, madam."

She couldn't at all imagine what business this might be, but the Colonel's clipped words told her it was best to ask him nothing here, on the threshold to the house, where they might be overheard by the neighbors.

She led the Colonel through the courtyard and into the modest guest parlor toward the back of the house, then retreated to the kitchen to make a fresh pot of tea. The Colonel waited with his silver-tipped cane firmly in his grasp. He'd traveled all day over rough roads and through thick clouds of dust, yet the creases on his trousers were still as sharp as when he'd set out from Tehran before dawn.

It was an unusual meeting and certainly an unexpected one. Marriage negotiations were women's work, though the final word rested with a girl's father. In this case—in my case—there was no time for custom, or for women's wiles, but the visit couldn't unfold without certain niceties. After all, the Shapours were my mother's relatives, and it wouldn't do to begin with demands or threats.

When Khanoom Shapour returned with a clinking tray, the Colonel took a cup of tea but refused the sweets. She bowed her head slightly, set down the tray, and assembled herself in a chair on the opposite side of the parlor.

It was time. Time for pleasantries to be cast aside in favor of the real business at hand. Just as Khanoom Shapour brought the cup to her lips, the Colonel cleared his throat, unbuttoned his jacket, and pulled several cream-colored envelopes from his jacket pocket. He deposited the letters on the table before her. He didn't retrieve the chastity certificate; there was no need of it—not yet, anyway.

Khanoom Shapour recognized her son's hand at once, but she was confused. She said nothing. The Colonel guessed she must be illiterate. Why else would she stare, openmouthed, at the letters? He'd have to read them aloud to her, he thought. It was a humiliation for which he hadn't prepared himself. He gripped the handle of his cane more firmly and reached for the letters, but Khanoom Shapour raised her eyes and lifted her left hand in a gesture that begged his patience. She'd had three years of schooling as a girl and was in fact modestly literate, and so she began to read.

"My sweet Forugh," each letter started. "Forugh," she knew, was the name of the Colonel's daughter. She remembered me well from the summer holidays in Darband: the wild girl tramping back to the house from the foothills with wet hair, dirt-streaked trousers, and sunburned cheeks. She remembered me, too, from the night of my cousin's party, remembered my brazen smile and how I'd made her son blush and spill his cup of tea before all the guests.

For some time Khanoom Shapour had been in pursuit of a suitable bride for her son. Too plain, too poor, too loose—

one by one, she'd dismissed all the girls in Ahwaz as unworthy of her son. She then set about surveying the girls of the surrounding villages, all of whom she'd also dismissed in turn. These efforts, however halfhearted, had been met with neither encouragement nor resistance from Parviz. "Whatever you wish for me," he told her whenever she brought up the subject of marriage. But here, in these declarations of love, she now found evidence of treachery and cunning of which she'd thought her son entirely incapable.

Calmly, coolly, she refolded the letters, set them on the table, and clasped her hands in her lap. She met the Colonel's eyes. He did not intimidate her. "What does it concern me," she said finally, "if you cannot control your daughter?" Her voice, as she said these words, was firm and her gaze steady.

The Colonel sat forward in the chair, leaning on his cane. "Your son, Parviz," he inquired with feigned curiosity, "is a man of what age?"

"Nearly twenty-seven," she offered.

He nodded. "Just as I thought. Your son is a grown man, not a boy, and by twenty-seven a man should have long since learned his limits. My daughter Forugh has only just turned sixteen," he said. After a pause, he added, "She's still a girl." He laid emphasis on the word "girl," a word that in Persian connotes "virgin" as well as "young woman." He held her eyes as he said this, and only when he was sure she understood his meaning did he continue. "I am a modern man. I had no plan for her to marry yet, but your son has attempted to seduce my daughter, and this gives me no choice."

"On the contrary," snapped Khanoom Shapour, "it's

your daughter who has thrown herself at my son. Everyone knows what sort of girl she is."

" 'What sort of girl'?" he echoed, raising an eyebrow.

"Surely, Colonel," she answered, smiling thinly, "you're not unaware of your daughter's reputation. It pains me to speak of it, *ghorban,* but she's an unsuitable match for my son."

The Colonel was unaccustomed to negotiating with women; in his dealings with my mother, as with me, he brooked no argument and resorted frequently, and without apology, to blows. He'd restrained himself so far, but Khanoom Shapour had now given him precisely the entrée he required to bring the visit to its conclusion.

"He'll go to prison," he said, stabbing the air with his silver-tipped cane. "They'll be married or I'll deliver him to the head warden of the Tehran police myself!"

Her son, the light of her eyes, shut up in a prison cell? At the thought of this, a trickle of sweat ran from Khanoom Shapour's neck down her spine.

"Fine," she said at last. She'd have years—decades, even—to plot her revenge, but she understood there was nothing she could do to stop the marriage, and she now had mere days to prepare for her son's wedding.

8.

BLOOD. FOR THE WEEK THAT THEN FOLLOWED, MY thoughts were only of blood.

From the moment I found out Parviz and I would be married, I started brooding over blood. Ignorant as I was back then, I'd listened at enough doors and overheard enough gossip to know that to sanctify the marriage, Parviz and I needed to show his relatives proof of my virginity on the wedding night. I knew what happened to me at the Bottom of the City would prevent my providing such proof. The certificate the woman had handed off to my mother would mean nothing if I couldn't support it with proof. And how could I tell my mother what had happened—the humiliation of it? Besides, I didn't think she'd believe me. Without proof, I'd be turned from my new husband's house and from my childhood home. What would happen to me then?

I suppose I was lucky in at least this respect: In the strange, frenzied atmosphere of those days, no one noticed my mood. Though the wedding itself would take place in Ahwaz, at Parviz's parents' house, there was suddenly so much to do that the whole household was pitched into chaos. The gossips of Amiriyeh were busy speculating about the reason for the quick marriage: "She was always a restless girl"; "she tried to run away"; "she lost her honor"; and so on. With all these rumors, we'd have to proceed with tremendous care, following the proper rituals precisely, or else Puran's impending marriage and even my younger sister's prospects might be compromised.

But first things first. To heal my battered lower lip, Sanam fashioned a pungent herb compress, which she pressed to my mouth. "To let down the swelling," she explained. She cooked me bowls of rice pudding ("To help you gather your strength," she told me) and fed me fistfuls of fat dates and pistachio nuts. She next turned her attention to the bruise on Puran's face, but for all Sanam's care it only seemed to grow more prominent. Eventually my sister became so distressed that she shut herself up in her room and refused to come out.

Then there was the problem of a wedding gown. With no time to hire a seamstress, I'd have to borrow a dress from my mother's closet. The only candidate was a plain ivory shift, which fell long and loose as a sack over my body. No sooner did I pull it over my head than Sanam began pinching and pulling at the fabric, sticking pins from collar to hem. "It won't be so bad when it's altered," she reassured me. "Not bad at all, you'll see!" I said nothing and let her think it was on account of the ugly makeshift wedding gown that I lifted my hands to my face and cried.

Later that night I lay awake, staring at the walls, begging them for an answer. I couldn't think of any possible solution to my predicament about the proof of blood. During those miserable hours, I would look over at my sister and wish I could shake her awake. More than anything I wanted to tell her what had happened to me in the Bottom of the City. The familiar shape of her skinny shoulders and the soft sound of her breathing made me feel strangely sad and lonely. Just a week ago, we'd lain awake for hours in our beds, whispering about her suitor and the mysteries of the wedding night. Now I'd be the first of us to marry, and there was talk in the house that she might not attend the wedding at all if the bruise on her face did not fade.

Despite everything, I still trusted her, and I would have gladly rid myself of my secret. But what, I reasoned, was the point of burdening her with troubles she could do nothing about? Troubles that would only make her confused and upset? Already she'd been punished, and all on my account, and if I were found out, it would not only ruin my own marriage prospects but compromise hers, as well.

I let her sleep and kept my worries to myself.

One morning, I sat in the kitchen with my chin in my hands, watching Sanam as she prepared platters of jeweled rice and trays of honeyed sweets. She flew from pot to pot, two circles of sleeplessness under her eyes and her brow sweaty from exertion. Yet for all her frenzied labors, it wasn't long before she glanced in my direction, pushed up her sleeves, and narrowed her eyes at me.

"You love him?" she asked. She was slicing oranges, cutting the rinds into thin ribbons for the rice.

I told her I did.

She set down her knife and threw her hands in the air. "Then why this sad look on your face? You'll be married and you'll have your own house and a brand-new life. It's all

a girl could want, to marry a man she loves! If you're ungrateful, God will snatch back all this good fortune, Forugh
jan."

I nodded. It was true. By marrying Parviz, I'd be luckier
than any girl I knew. After all, I'd chosen my husband myself, and at this I felt a rush of happiness and pride. When I
first learned it was Parviz I'd marry, I immediately imagined
myself sitting at his side during the ceremony, waiting for
him to lift the white lace from my face. Since then my mind
drifted again and again to this image, but always under such
happy fantasies lay the thought that if I didn't manage to
fulfill the proof of blood, everything would fall apart.

"You'll be a bride soon, Forugh," Sanam continued,
snatching me from these thoughts. She took up her knife
again and continued to slice the orange rinds with clean,
steady strokes. "Do you want your groom to see you looking miserable at your wedding?"

I shook my head. "No, but—" I was tempted to tell her
everything at that moment and very nearly did, but she
shook her head and waved her hands, silencing me.

"Then you mustn't worry about anything! Eat well and
rest, *azizam*," she said, leaning forward to give my cheek a
pinch. "You'll be a bride soon. An *aroos*! You have no worries now except to make yourself beautiful for your handsome groom!"

My head was aching the next morning as I made my way
through the *hammam*, my throat tight and dry. The bathhouse was noisy with the voices of women calling to one
another and the sounds of children splashing in the fountains and pools. I disrobed, wound a towel around myself,

and waited for an attendant to lead me to the private room in the back, an area I'd previously been forbidden to enter.

The wooden bench was cold and rough under my hands and bare thighs. As I waited, I followed the passageway with my eyes to where the hallway dimmed and curved away, and then I was suddenly overtaken by the certainty that I had been there before, that I'd stood in those very rooms. It was, in truth, my body that remembered, not my mind; my hand went to my cheek and I felt a searing heat as if I'd been slapped.

I saw it so vividly then. It was a day in this same bath-house, five years ago, when I was eleven years old. I'd stepped into a stall to undress and discovered a circle of blood in my underpants. My first thought was that I'd hurt myself—I was truly that ignorant then. But such was the custom in those days; our mother told us nothing at all, and we, in turn, asked her nothing, for fear our interest would be deemed perverse—an indication of waywardness. Any-way, I scarcely thought of myself as female. At eleven I was still lanky and extremely thin and had no breasts at all.

That day I stole through the dimly lit passages of the bathhouse, where I at last found my mother by the sound of her voice. She was sitting by the fountain, chatting with another woman and rubbing her forearm with a *kiseh*, a coarse washcloth. I tapped her shoulder and she turned around. "What is it?" she said, annoyed by my intrusion. I couldn't say a word, but my face must have betrayed my fear, because she stood up and led me to an empty corner of the bathhouse. When I showed her my bloodied under-pants, she pressed her lips into a tight line. Then, before I could duck, she slapped me—and hard—across both cheeks. Tears sprang to my eyes, and the only word I said was

"Why?" Her answer was to slap me again across both cheeks, this time even harder.

Later Sanam explained it to me: My mother's slaps were meant to keep the blush on my cheeks until I became a bride. "And now we must sweeten our tongues!" she'd exclaimed, clasping her hands before her and smiling broadly so that all her gold teeth shone at once. She pressed three chickpea cookies into my hand and took three more for herself. "You're a woman now! We must celebrate!"

I smiled weakly and popped a cookie into my mouth, but afterward I felt only confusion and, under this, a surge of humiliation and rage.

Now, sixteen years old and about to be married, I sat alone in the same hallway. I waited on the bench until eventually a woman appeared and led me through the corridors of the bathhouse, toward the area where only married women and brides were permitted, and then she left me before the door. As a child I'd wondered what took place in these rooms. I didn't know much more than that it was a place to which girls were taken just before their weddings, but I couldn't imagine what happened to them there.

I gathered my courage and knocked on the door.

A sweet-faced, portly woman of about sixty greeted me. A *dallak,* a bathhouse attendant. Her white hair had been gathered in a single long braid, which she coiled up on the top of her head, and she wore a brightly patterned smock. "Come in, dear one," she said, urging me inside with a warm smile.

Still wary, I followed her into the chamber.

"You poor girl, you're shaking! What do you imagine I'm going to do with you?"

"I don't know."

"Ah," she said, putting a hand on my shoulder. Her touch was gentle, her voice soothing. "I'll do no more than make you lovely for your groom!" she said at last, clucking her tongue and fixing me with a smile. "Like a peach you'll be, so smooth and ripe!"

I still couldn't make out her meaning, but I let myself be led to a table. "Let's look at you properly now," she said, bending closer. She smelled like basil and rose water. She took my face in her two hands and studied it from forehead to chin. Then, working quickly, she drew a length of thin cotton string from her pocket and began doubling and twisting it between her fingers. She started with my eyebrows, plucking whole rows of hair to the root, then rolled the thread over my whole face—forehead, cheeks, and, finally, my chin. Next she rolled the string the length of my arms and then from my ankles to the tops of my thighs. The pain was horrible—much worse by far than the pain I'd felt during the examination in the Bottom of the City. A thousand needles seemed to be pricking me at once.

The worst of it, however, was about to begin. The woman quickly drew the towel from my waist. I was naked. I tried to cover myself with my hands, but she pulled them away and pushed them to my sides. I turned my face to the wall, away from the *dallak,* and she began rolling the thread over my groin, plucking every last hair out with thread. When, out of an instinct to avoid the pain, my legs would clamp shut, she'd nudge them apart with her elbow and continue with her work. I bit my lip and willed myself not to cry, but soon I was sobbing—a messy, heaving, hiccuping cry that even the old woman's soothing words and kind encouragements couldn't quiet.

My only relief came when the *dallak* stopped to cut a

new piece of string. Every time she finished with one part of my body, she tossed aside the string, reached for the spool of thread, and cut a fresh length. I had kept my eyes shut for most of it, squeezing them tight against the pain, but toward the end of that awful hour, I opened them just in time to catch her slicing the thread with a sharp razor. The blade caught the light from her lamp—quick and sly as a wink—and suddenly I knew exactly how I'd manage to fulfill the proof of blood.

9.

———————

ON THE DAY OF MY WEDDING, I SHIVERED WHEN THE white lace-trimmed wedding canopy was unfurled above my head. The scent of wild rue, pungent, smoky, and sweet, threaded its way through the parlor and filled the room. Too nervous to meet anyone's eyes, I looked down at the wedding spread that had been laid on the floor before me. A plain mirror, a pair of silver candlesticks, one bowl filled with hand-painted eggs, and a smaller bowl filled with honey—it was the simplest wedding spread I'd ever seen.

Setting out from Tehran, I realized it had never occurred to me how far I'd have to travel for the wedding, how far away my new home would be from all I knew. Ahwaz lay south of Tehran, five hundred miles away in Khuzestan Province. I wasn't sure why we were moving to Ahwaz, only that Parviz had applied for a new position in his hometown, one I guessed would be more suited to life as a married man. We'd headed out just after breakfast, my mother and my sisters, and after crossing what seemed like an endless desert, stopping a few times for food and gasoline, we reached Ahwaz in the early hours of the next morning. Peering out the window, I saw that this was a scrubby land, without hills or meadows, a country of stones and stunted blooms. I'd slept for only a few hours in the car and awakened bathed in sweat, a headache thrumming behind my brow. My trousseau, like my wedding spread, was conspicuously modest; it fit into just one trunk set under my feet in the back seat of the car, and most of the dresses, jackets, stockings, and shoes, as well as bed linens, dishes, and tableware, had been plucked from the pile of gifts my mother had been collecting for my sister's wedding.

As I settled into a chair now, I didn't mind the simplicity of the wedding. I was relieved, really, to be free of all that phoniness, all that tired, obnoxious fuss. Besides, I had other thoughts to occupy my mind.

When I met my reflection in the mirror, set among the wedding spread, what I saw astonished me. With my newly plucked eyebrows, kohl-lined eyes, and painted lips, I barely recognized myself. Sanam had pulled my hair back from my face and pinned white peonies to my wedding veil—one large flower just above each ear. My wedding dress had also been completely transformed. Just yesterday the neighborhood seamstress had taken a hand to it, and the sack-like sheath was now something more than vaguely reminiscent of a wedding dress. I had the outlines of a waist, at least, and the sleeves and collar were trimmed with pretty lace. It was like this, looking prettier and primmer than I'd ever looked, that I waited for Parviz.

I sat up straighter, and for the first time I took a proper look around the room. The wedding party consisted of only my closest relatives and Parviz's. The women and girls had gathered for the ceremony in the good parlor, while the men waited together in an adjoining room. I spied my sisters, little Gloria in a pink organza dress and pigtails, and Puran with her cheeks painted with an orangey makeup and circles of rouge to cover what was left of her bruise. Wan and quiet, Puran stood in a corner with her arms folded over her chest. Along with my aunts and cousins, my mother was one of the several older, married women holding the wedding canopy above my head. She stood just behind me, so that for the length of the ceremony I could sometimes hear her voice but I couldn't see her face.

Parviz entered the room. I turned my attention back to the mirror, pressed my lips together, and studied his reflection. He looked nervous as he took his place before the wedding spread—the mirror was angled up and I could see him plainly enough—but there was nothing in his manner that suggested unhappiness or regret. On the contrary, as the *agha* began to recite verses from the Koran, Parviz gripped my hand in his and gave it a reassuring squeeze.

"In the name of the All-Mighty, the All-Merciful!" the *agha* called out, and with that the women grew quiet. Persian gave way to the Arabic verses from the Koran, and I could make out little meaning of what the *agha* recited, apart from our names and those of our families. One after the other, the married women holding the canopy stepped forward and took turns rubbing a cone of salt against a cone of sugar to symbolize how sadness and joy, the two constants of life, merged in marriage.

When the recitations ended and Parviz was at last asked in Persian if he accepted me as his bride, he answered with a clear *baleh:* yes.

Next the *agha* addressed me. "Does the bride accept this groom?" he asked.

From across the room, Parviz's mother, Khanoom Shapour, shot me an appraising look. A proper Iranian bride never replied on the first or even the second time she was asked; for a girl to reply at once suggested an eagerness to leave one's family or, worse, wantonness. Did Khanoom Shapour think me so reckless as to accept immediately? I lowered my eyes and made no answer.

"The bride's gone out to pick some flowers!" someone called out. It was my cousin Jaleh who spoke on my behalf. I lifted my eyes slightly, and through the veil, I again glimpsed Parviz's mother. Her lips were pressed together in a tight line, and her arms were crossed firmly over her chest.

Again the *agha* asked if I would consent to be Parviz's wife. Again I didn't reply.

"She's arranging the bouquet now!" another voice called out on my behalf.

It was only after the third time the *agha* asked if I'd accept Parviz as my husband that I finally said, "Yes." At this, the clamor of wedding trills filled the room. My mother stepped forward. All day she had barely looked at me or said a word, and now she was standing awkwardly before me. For a moment, the air was strange between us, heavy with unspoken words, but then she kissed me quickly on both cheeks and looped a string of small pearls around my neck. When Puran stepped forward, I saw her eyes were brimming with tears. We held our embrace for a long moment, my sister and I, until at last my mother nudged me on the shoulder to tell me it was time to let go.

I'd demurred as a proper bride ought to do, but it had little to do with shame or piety, or even with prudence. In those moments, I was sick with nervousness for what was to come next, for what I would soon have to do.

"Are you all right?" Parviz asked, shutting the door to the bridal chamber and walking toward me. The room was dark but for a small oil lamp, and from where I lay in the bed I couldn't see his face.

The women were chatting noisily on the other side of the door. Shortly after the wedding ceremony they'd gathered outside the bridal chamber. Their voices rose and fell to a hush, then rose again. What were they talking about? I could only pick out my own name and Parviz's, but their voices sounded shrill and mean.

I drew a deep breath and whispered, "Yes, I'm fine, only it feels strange with them standing out there."

"They'll leave soon enough. It's only until they see the handkerchief," he said, then added, "You know about the handkerchief? They told you about it?"

I nodded.

As he came closer, sliding beside me in the bed and removing his underclothes, I saw that his face was fixed with a serious look. No, not just a serious look, but a look of determination. No sooner did he arrange himself beside me than he lifted the hem of my nightshirt and pulled it up to my waist. His fingers trembled and his movements were so awkward that I suddenly understood he had little, and very likely no, experience. This might have eased my own anxiety, but then I realized I would have to make my way through these next minutes with little guidance from him. Should I move this way or that? Lift my knees or should I lie completely still? Thankfully, these awkward movements didn't go on for long. I felt no real pain, just a slight discomfort, but I was grateful he finished quickly, and I sighed in relief when he drew away from me.

On the bedside table lay a simple white cotton handkerchief, ironed and folded into a small square. Parviz pulled his tunic back on and smoothed his hair. I watched as he reached for the cotton handkerchief and then turned back to me, eyes averted. Wordlessly, I sat up and then opened my legs just slightly. He pressed the fabric quickly between my legs and then drew it back.

"Forugh . . ." he started. His voice sounded confused and also frightened.

He held the handkerchief up for me to see. I hadn't bled—not even a little. When I said nothing, he pressed the handkerchief between my legs again, holding it there longer than he had before. For a second time, the cloth came up without a drop of blood.

I couldn't put it off any longer. I pulled myself up onto my elbows. "Something happened to me, Parviz," I whispered. "My mother took me to the Bottom of the City for a test. A virginity test." The words came out jumbled, and I could tell from his expression that he didn't understand. "It was awful," I continued, "and I wanted so much to tell you, but I had no chance to speak to you in private. It hurt when the lady examined me. She said not to move, but I did something wrong and that must be why . . ." I said, nodding toward the handkerchief.

I wanted to tell him everything to make the look on his face soften, or at least explain the parts I understood, but there was no time for that now. I cleared my throat. "There's a way, Parviz. I've figured out a way to make it all right for us."

He stared at me with panicked eyes. "I don't understand you, Forugh. What way?"

The voices outside the door had grown louder; the women would only wait so long for the proof of blood. I had a few minutes, perhaps even less. If I hesitated now, I'd have no chance at all.

From under my pillow I drew the razor I'd stolen from the bathhouse and held it out to him in my palm.

"Where'd you get that?" he said, much too loudly.

"Shhh!" I said, lifting a finger to my lips.

He wasn't going to agree with my plan—from the look on his face I felt sure of it. But then, to my relief, he nodded, slowly comprehending, and took the razor from me. One prick and it would be done; the only question was where he should cut himself. But I saw at once that it was impossible; his hands were shaking so hard that he wouldn't be capable of cutting himself without doing real harm.

There was nothing for it. I grabbed the razor from his hand and scanned my body. I'd need to cut myself in a place where a scar wouldn't show, but where? I touched the edge of the razor to my stomach, to a spot just below my navel. No, that wasn't any good. If I cut myself there, everyone at the baths would see the scar. So instead, as Parviz watched, pale and silent, I sliced the blade quickly along the inside of my right leg, at the place where the soft flesh of my thighs met, and with my other hand, I pressed the white handkerchief against the cut, making sure it left behind a large red circle of blood.

There. It was done.

The women's voices grew suddenly louder, and then there was a sharp knock at the door. To my relief, Parviz stood, yanked his trousers on, and grabbed the bloodied cloth. Quickly, I pulled the sheet up to my chin. When he opened the door I saw them, a knot of women, ten or so, his mother, grandmother, aunts, and some of the younger cousins. He passed the handkerchief to them, then looked over his shoulder and caught my eye from across the room. For a moment I feared he'd betray me. I pulled the sheet over my head and sank deeper in the bed, and it was only when I heard the door shut that I felt myself breathe again.

Behind the door, the chattering gave way to silence. I thought the women had discovered the ruse, but all at once ululations broke out on the landing. The house filled with the voices of women, laughing and singing to one another, their trills of *"li-li-li-li . . ."* ringing out as, one by one, they lifted the cloth high above their heads and whipped it in the air with a flourish before passing it on.

"Mobarak!" came the women's cheers. "Congratulations!"

When the women at last abandoned their place behind the door, Parviz sat at the foot of the bed, his back turned toward me and his face buried in his hands. He didn't yell or strike me, as he might well have done, and I took solace in this. How, though, could I make him understand what had happened to me and that I'd had no choice but to do what I had done? I bit my lip, my mind racing. I could think of nothing else to say, and so I touched my hand to his shoulder and said only, "Parviz?"

He lifted his head. "My mother told me things about you, but I thought it was all rumors and lies." He drew a deep breath and began shaking his head. "But it's true what she said. You tricked me, Forugh."

"But I only wanted us to be married! And I thought you wanted it, too!"

When he didn't answer, I asked him, "Didn't you want us to get married?"

I sat up and edged closer to him as I said this, and when he felt me come near he gave a jerk, slapped my hand away, and jumped out of the bed. "Leave me alone!" he shouted.

I felt the sting of tears. He paced the room for a while, his head in his hands. When he returned to the bed, he lay down with his back toward me. After some minutes, he reached over and extinguished the lamp.

I don't know how long we stayed awake that night, how long I lay there willing myself to say nothing. The chamber still smelled strongly of the wild rue the women had burned behind the door while they waited. I wanted to cry, but I forced myself to stay silent and still.

That night I didn't yet know Parviz had secrets of his own. It was only later, many weeks after our wedding, that I learned the details of how the Colonel had gone to visit his mother and arranged our marriage. Until then I'd thought that by locking myself in the basement and threatening to kill myself, I'd managed to choose my own husband—to choose Parviz. I didn't know my father had threatened to send him to prison if he didn't marry me, nor did I know that without those threats or his mother's bitter blessing, Parviz and I would never have married.

It had all started so sweetly between us. A little more than two weeks ago we'd ordered *café glacé* and danced at The Palace. Those sweet, hasty meetings in the alleyway, our first furtive kisses, the poems he'd pressed into my hands and those I'd written for him in turn—now all of that had been made into something stupid, ugly, and wrong. I closed my eyes and it swam before me, the white handkerchief he'd handed off to his family a few minutes ago. It was the lie upon which my whole life now rested. All of it.

PART TWO

The Rebellion

10.

Empty house,
desolate house
house shuttered against youth's surge
house of darkness and dreams of the sun
house of loneliness, foreboding and indecision
house of curtains, books, cupboards,
and old photographs.

—from "Friday"

HE NEVER REALLY CHOSE TO BE WITH ME. NOT BEFORE
our wedding and not afterward.

A few times I tried to talk to Parviz about the wedding
night, but he refused to discuss what had happened that
night or the days leading up to our marriage. What I'd told
him seemed to count for nothing. I was furious and heartbroken. Did he really think I'd lost my virginity to someone
else? He knew better than anyone the restrictions my family
placed on me, and that alone should've been enough to

quiet his doubts. The more I thought about it, the angrier I felt, yet something surged through me in those days after our wedding, something that eventually made me abandon the explanation I'd been so desperate to offer. If Parviz could judge me so harshly, then I saw no point in begging him to believe me. Of course, this attitude did little to resolve our standoff, but I decided to say nothing more, not so much to punish him as to salvage some small measure of dignity.

And yet: I told myself I should be grateful for his silence. He could have sent me from the house. Even if I'd been a virgin before our wedding, it would take nothing for him to divorce me. Nothing at all. He could have cast me out like those girls I'd heard my mother and her friends talk about in hushed voices, the girls whose families wouldn't so much as utter their names once their husbands turned them away. But so far as I could make out, Parviz hadn't told anyone what happened on our wedding night.

We quickly settled into a routine. Parviz's new job was across town, at a government ministry. He left for work before morning's light, and in the evening he greeted me with a nod and quick hello, then headed to the parlor, where he knelt down and kissed his mother's hands. When he finished, she pulled him toward her and kissed the top of his head. They then spent an hour in each other's company, sharing news about the day, and my only role during this time was to serve them tea.

He'd reached beyond his limits by courting me, but he would never again move beyond them. I now realized that even our marriage, his one great rebellion, had been a concession to his mother's will. That was done, I'd say to myself, steeling myself against the hurt—but what angered me were the questions she'd clearly prompted him to ask, such as "Do you have to go into town so often?" He now put this question to me nearly every day, and he soon coupled it with "Do you have to wear your blouse unbuttoned so low and your skirt so short?" and "Could you wear less lipstick and rouge when you go into town?" Some cousin or neighbor had seen me out in the streets on my errands and told his mother he should keep better watch over me.

"Why do you go out so much by yourself anyway?" he would ask me.

"Do I have to stay home?" I would answer.

"I'm not telling you not to go out, Forugh," he said in an exasperated tone. "You misunderstand me. It's only that they say you're out in the streets by yourself too much."

"Who's been telling you this?"

"Mardom," he answered vaguely. People.

"And what's so bad about being in the streets?"

"It's just not safe for a woman to be out on her own. Now, if you were to wait and accompany my mother when she went to the shops—"

"But," I shot back, "I feel much safer alone in the streets than I ever do when I'm out with your mother or shut up in the house!"

"If you go out alone all the time," he continued, "they'll say it's because you're meeting someone in town."

"And who exactly is this 'someone' I'd be meeting?"

"A man," he said, lowering his eyes.

I laughed. "Who could I possibly meet in this place, Parviz? Do you think I'm carrying on with the old salt-seller at the bazaar? Or maybe one of those teenagers playing soccer in the streets? Do you honestly think I have an interest in any of them?"

"I'm only thinking of you," he said, "and of your name."

"It's your own name you're thinking of, Parviz, yours and your mother's, and you're as much of a coward as anyone in this town. No. You're more of a coward than anyone I know!"

He made no answer, only shook his head and walked toward the door.

For years I'd had to obey my parents, and I had no interest in obeying my husband or his mother. I was done with all that now. Still, I didn't want to hurt Parviz; I'd only meant to show him the absurdity of his mother's complaints and demands. "Stay," I asked, grabbing his shirt and pulling him toward me, but no matter how I pleaded or reasoned, in the end he always pulled away.

A sore silence wedged its way between us. At night, Parviz would turn off the light before he came to me and speak only in whispers. This was our only time alone together. Every day of our marriage was revealing to me how little I knew about him and how little he knew about me. The meetings in the alley outside my father's house in Amiriyeh, the letters, the poems, the furtive kisses—all that was much more than a proper courtship allowed, but we still had such little real knowledge of each other. For many nights after our wedding, we lay in our narrow bed, his back turned to me as I stared miserably at the ceiling. His parents' quarters were far away from our own small room, in a separate wing of the house, but if I talked too loudly, or what he considered too loudly, he pressed his hand over my lips with a "shhhh!" Enraged, I'd slap his hand away. Much later I'd forget many details of our arguments, but that one warning—"shhhh!"—

would always evoke the years in Ahwaz, our small, dingy room with its bare walls and dark shadows, the tangled ivy on the windowpane shutting out the sky, the explosive, echoing despair inside me. If I'd chosen to confide in anyone—and I didn't—there was no complaint that wouldn't sound trite. *"Besooz o bezaaz"* went the timeworn injunction to brides. Burn inwardly and accommodate. If I told anyone my troubles, I would have been met with exactly this phrase.

It wasn't desire but rather a terrible loneliness that at last made me reach for him one night. His body went rigid with my touch, and I thought he might refuse me—a mortifying thought. I hesitated for a moment and then I reached for him again, pulling gently on his shoulder. When he turned around and moved closer to me, I took his hand in mine and then placed it on my breast. I closed my eyes, and for a few minutes we were back in the alleyway, discovering each other again, and I felt happy and safe. He lifted the hem of my nightdress, pulling it over my head so that for the first time I was naked under him. Smiling, I opened my eyes, but already he'd turned solemn and quiet. That time and every time afterward, he turned his face from mine so that I couldn't catch his eyes and he couldn't catch mine. I was devastated. It was his worst betrayal, this looking away.

All day my mother-in-law watched me. She studied my complexion, my appetite, my walk. Most of all she appraised my religiosity. Morning after morning she greeted me by asking, "Did you go to the *hammam,* Forugh?" By this she meant to find out if I'd performed my ablutions. It was, you see, a sin to stand uncleansed before God in prayer, and among the devout an early-morning visit to the baths was also a sure sign of intercourse. Young brides like me were expected to appear at the bathhouse before dawn every day, though it was understood that their visits would lessen with the waning of their husbands' desires and the exigencies of childbearing and motherhood. In Tehran, where more and more homes were now outfitted with private baths, I might have been spared these exchanges, but here in Ahwaz I relied totally on the bathhouse and was thus the object of Khanoom Shapour's constant scrutiny.

It's possible that I could have loved her; I certainly didn't hate her when I first came to live with her in Ahwaz. In those first weeks of marriage, I was desperate for company. I'd grown up in a large family, and I especially missed Puran and Sanam. Here in Ahwaz I had no friends and knew no one apart from Parviz's family. So I think I could have loved my mother-in-law had she made the slightest overture of kindness toward me, but she didn't, not once.

I did feel close, in a way, to Parviz's father, Agha Shapour. He was a short man and wore thick glasses. A few years earlier he'd collapsed in the street from a heart attack. Khanoom Shapour treated him like a child and otherwise ignored him completely. His sole occupation was to survey the acre of land that stretched from the house to the neighbor's walls. Some mornings I walked out to the garden and sat down by the small pool and watched as he strolled among his fruit trees, thumbing his amber prayer beads and tilting his face occasionally to the sky. His eyes were covered with the milky white film of cataracts and he limped a little as he walked, but though he was half blind and crippled, he'd managed to coax figs, pomegranates, and sweet lemons from the hard silt of the land.

My escape was always short-lived. "Forugh!" Khanoom

Shapour called out. She emerged from the house with her hands on her hips, tucked one of the hens under her arm for the day's stew, and then gestured me back inside with a toss of her head.

My mother-in-law prayed five times a day, every day, and each time she retreated to her room to perform her *namaz* she threw a look over her shoulder to see if I would follow. I never did. My own mother observed her prayers and had taught us to perform the *namaz* when we were children, but my sisters and I had never been expected to perform our prayers daily, much less five times a day. The Colonel had forbidden my sisters and me to wear veils; following the shah's mandate, he considered such displays of piety back-ward.

Though they weren't commonplace in Tehran, such at-titudes were considered outright scandalous here. The Sha-pours' house was in Ahwaz's oldest neighborhood. Here, the call to prayer rang out five times a day, and custom was sacrosanct. I found the muezzin's voice beautiful and sooth-ing, but I didn't find God in these rituals and gestures. It was always in the garden or in the countryside where my heart opened and I felt myself in the presence of the divine. I couldn't pretend I felt differently, and so when my mother-in-law retreated to her room for her *namaz,* I never fol-lowed her.

"Didn't your mother teach you how to cook?" Khanoom Shapour asked me the day I prepared my first pot of rice.

"No," I said. It was an honest if curt answer. I'd been brought up with servants and with the expectation that I'd someday have servants of my own. True, I'd spent countless hours in the kitchen at Sanam's side, but I'd been so busy listening to her stories and songs that I'd paid little attention to her work. Which spice did she dust over her rice pudding? Cardamom, or was it cinnamon? Did she layer her rice for this or that dish with spinach or dill? I had no clue.

"Well, then," she said, "it's time for you to learn." She dumped my rice into a slop jar for the chickens. "A proper rice needs to soak in salted water for at least six hours before cooking," she instructed as she picked out small pebbles from the grains. "This is the only way the grains lengthen," she continued. "The rice should be boiled once briefly, then drained and rinsed with cold water before you put it back onto the stove. When it's done cooking, the rice should fall from a spoon in individual grains, each one infused with the scent of saffron and oil, and the crust should be crisp, golden, and thick."

I thought that if I pleased his mother by improving my cooking, things might get better between my husband and me. And so I bit my tongue. I washed and soaked the rice. I picked the pebbles from the grains. I boiled the water, drained the rice, and stirred saffron and oil at the bottom of the pot. But it was no use. The grains were never long enough, my crisped rice too thin or too soggy or horribly burnt. Worse, in the wake of each attempt at cooking, I left piles of charred pots in the sink. My mother-in-law cast a critical eye over the proceedings. Her arms crossed, her lips set in a thin line of disapproval, she scolded, "You're hopeless, Forugh!"

One night I managed to cook a perfect pot of rice, but the triumph brought me more misery than all my failures. Khanoom Shapour usually served the evening meal, but this time I reached for the plates, heaping thick slices of crisped rice for Agha Shapour, Parviz, my mother-in-law, and, finally, for myself. I took a seat at the table and lifted my spoon to my mouth, savoring the tender, buttery grains. I think I expected surprise and even praise for my efforts, but when I looked up I saw that my mother-in-law hadn't eaten a spoonful. I couldn't imagine what fault she'd found with the dish, and then, suddenly, I understood: I hadn't performed my morning ablutions or prayed before setting the food before her. It made no difference how well I cooked this pot of rice—or any other in the weeks to come. My touch, I realized, was *najes*.

This was a word my mother often used when I was a girl. It meant "unclean" and also "unholy." I'd never forget the first time I heard it. I was six years old and a mangy dog had come around the house, limping and begging for food. My mother kicked it so hard that it had hobbled out of the alleyway. *"Najes!"* she called out after the dog. Tears filled my eyes. I begged her to let me help it, but she forbade me from touching the dog, and in this way I was made to understand my own touch could become *najes* and I myself impure.

As the memory of that day brightened, then faded from my mind, I understood that my mother-in-law wouldn't accept food from my hands because they were *najes*. I was furious, but what upset me most was Parviz's refusal to eat the food I'd prepared, a refusal that owed less to religious piety than to his unwavering deference to his mother. Except on those rare occasions when she was away from the house and we dined alone, Parviz ate only his mother's dishes. By the blind logic of pride I continued to cook, but it was only old, sweet-tempered Agha Shapour who ate the food I prepared—Agha Shapour and I myself, though very often I was so angry I felt no hunger and ate nothing at all.

There was only one solution.

"When can we move to our own house?" I asked Parviz one day in the second month of our marriage.

We were in our bedroom. The smallest and least furnished room of the house, it contained a wooden daybed, a small table, two chairs, a carpet, a copper basin, and the leather trunk I'd brought with me from Tehran. The first time I saw it, my heart constricted. This was my home now, I thought, this small airless room, and the weeks that had passed had only intensified my feeling of entrapment.

"That isn't the way things are done here, Forugh. You know that."

"But I can't stand it, Parviz! I want to live in my own house."

"Well," he said slowly, "I'd have to save up some money first."

"How long until we have enough?"

"A year," he said, rubbing his chin. "Maybe two."

"Two years! But we only need a small apartment! Just two rooms would do—even one room, just so long as it's our own. And I could work, too, Parviz. I could help us save up money for a house."

He lifted an eyebrow. "What kind of work can you do?"

I bit my lip and then after a minute I said, "I can sew. I've always been good at that. Maybe I could open a small shop." I paused, warming to the idea. "I could sew party dresses and skirts, that sort of thing."

"You want to open a fancy shop in Ahwaz? The women here all sew their own clothes or hire seamstresses."

"But that's just it! They have to travel all the way to Tehran to buy modern clothes. If I opened a shop I'd have no competition. It's worth a try, isn't it?"

His only answer was silence and a slow, sad shake of the head.

I spent hours sitting at the small table in my bedroom, writing long letters to Puran. Neither she nor my mother had the means to visit me in Ahwaz. She would be married soon, and unless Parviz drove me to Tehran, my sister would celebrate her wedding without me. In my letters home, I was careful not to give away my feelings about my new life, which had less to do with shame than with pride. Puran sent me letters in return, as well as little parcels of candies and small gifts—an embroidered shawl, some silk stockings, a pair of silver barrettes. "Are you happy?" she asked, and "How are you and Parviz getting along?" But that wasn't the worst of it. "When are you coming to Tehran?" my sister asked at the end of each letter. Six words, impossible to answer except with the pathetic line: "I'll come visit you when Parviz can bring me there."

As the days wore on, I didn't especially want to visit my family, since I knew I'd have to endure my mother's sharp looks and my sister's curiosity. Still, I felt desperate to leave Ahwaz, and Tehran was the only place I could imagine traveling to.

"Can we go next week?" I'd ask Parviz.

"I've only just started this job. I can't ask for a vacation already, can't you understand? We have to be practical."

"Well, can we go for my sister's wedding? For just two days?"

"I'm very sorry, Forugh, but we can't. Maybe we can go

for the New Year. By then I should be more established, but right now it could cost me my position. I'd come off looking lazy."

In those days, Ahwaz was a full day's travel from the capital. We had no car and, anyway, I didn't know how to drive. For a while I let the subject drop, but then I remembered that Parviz had always traveled to Tehran by train. When I discovered that trains ran daily from Ahwaz to Tehran, I thought I'd found a solution to at least this one predicament.

"I'll go by myself, then," I said.

"And what will people think about you going all the way to Tehran without me?"

"What do I care what they think!"

He shook his head. "Why can't you be patient, Forugh? When I save up some money, we'll go to Tehran together. I promise we will."

It was in Ahwaz that I was first called *kharab*. Broken, bad. Behind their windows and veils, along the streets and alleyways, on the banks and bridges of the Karun River, the wives, mothers, and daughters of Ahwaz followed me with their eyes. I could easily imagine what they said of me: My skirts were too tight and too short, my heels were too high, my pleasantries and compliments merely cursory. "Tehran," muttered those inclined to trace every vice among them back to the capital—and there were many people like that in those years, in that town where I was once a bride. "She's been trouble since she got here," they said. "She doesn't do her *namaz* or lift a finger in the house." "Crows," I called them (but only to myself), these women with their *ta'arof,* their phony manners, their "yes, *khanoom,*" their "may I die for you," their thousand muted but unmistakable cruelties.

In Ahwaz I was known only as "the Shapours' bride." I was a bad wife. Shameless and wayward. In the bazaar, at the public baths, and in the alleys where they passed one another, the women dropped their voices and shared stories about how I was always running off to do God-knew-what with God-knew-whom. In answer to their stares and their whispers, I hemmed my skirts even shorter. When I walked in the streets, I exaggerated the sway of my hips. To keep from going crazy, I drew out my errands. I went alone, with no chaperone. One day I'd walk to the marketplace to buy a bolt of cloth; the next day I'd set out for a sack of lentils. And so on.

For the first time in my life, I dressed to please only myself. I owned a single pair of high heels—round-toed with straps at the ankle. I'd found them in the marketplace in the first weeks of my marriage and bought them because they matched the idea I had of myself as a fully grown-up woman. I imagined myself wearing them to parties with a pair of sheer stockings—a delicious thought—but in Ahwaz there were no parties apart from visits to Parviz's relatives, all those aunts, cousins, and elders who clucked their tongues and pressed their lips in tight lines at the mere sight of me. So one day I just decided to wear my round-toed heels to walk to the marketplace. They clattered noisily as I made my way down the streets, drawing all eyes to me, but I pretended I saw nothing, and I refused to feel a trace of shame.

Most weeks, there wasn't much left over from the housekeeping money Parviz gave me, but my sewing was more than passable, and I could always take an old, simple dress and make it pretty with a hem or a tuck or a pleat. It was a good thing I was clever in these ways, because I had few clothes and no jewelry at all apart from my thin gold wedding band and the rope of tiny pearls my mother had placed around my neck on my wedding day. I now wore those pearls long on one day, double looped on another, or knotted at the hollow of my throat. Once I wore them in my hair like a headband, and another time I wrapped them around my wrist three times like a bracelet.

At first I could trick myself into moments of happiness, but more and more I found I could barely summon the enthusiasm to get dressed and go out. I now lived hundreds of miles from my childhood home, but even across this distance I heard the echo of my mother's voice in my head, as clear as if she were in the room speaking to me. "Ungrateful," she called me, and also "selfish" and "shameless." Often, I was genuinely sickened by my ingratitude. I'd consider the women around me and wonder what it was about me that made it impossible to share their devotion to the simple comforts of family life. Why couldn't I be more like them? What was wrong with me? These thoughts would linger a day, sometimes longer, and I would try to make myself content with my marriage and the rituals of the house, but these intervals of self-recrimination were invariably followed by a succession of black days.

I remember Ahwaz as it was on those Fridays of the Sabbath, choked and desperate. The house was always quiet and empty, the doors locked and the windows shuttered. Alone in my room, the days went by like sleep—a long, deep sleep punctuated by a list of senseless dictates I issued to myself.

Find your fortune in swirls of cigarette smoke
or the thick black grains
at the bottom of your coffee cup
or the carpet's faded flowers. . . .
Hide your beauty like an old black-and-white
photograph in the bottom of a trunk. . . .
Place images of the condemned, the conquered,
and the crucified
in the empty frame of your days. . . .
Like a doll with two glass eyes,
sleep for a thousand years
in a felt box lined with tinsel and lace.

—from "The Windup Doll"

My desperation led me back to poetry.

When we married and moved to Ahwaz, Parviz brought the books he'd collected during his bachelor years in Tehran, as well as copies of the journals that had published his essays and satiric sketches. He'd dreamed of a literary career, and before our marriage he'd enjoyed some success as a writer, but all that had been cast off now. He'd taken a job in a government ministry in town, and he'd stopped writing altogether. If he regretted any of this, he never confessed his disappointment. So far as I could tell, he'd given up writing altogether, and he also read less and less, not even the books by Nima and Ahmad Shamlou that he'd once shared with such enthusiasm.

Those books saved me. I dragged the old wooden daybed in our bedroom over to the window that looked out onto the orchard. Mornings I pulled on a dressing gown, eased into that bed, and read my way through Parviz's books and literary journals. I still read very little contemporary poetry, and much of it left no impression on me at all, but from time to time I came across a poem that moved me deeply and I felt a faint but familiar prick of ambition.

Then one day I pulled a half-empty notebook from the leather trunk that held my trousseau. I placed it on the table and parted the pages. It had been a long time—many weeks—since I'd stolen away to write a poem. I realized that for the first time in my life I could write whatever I pleased. On a whim I slid a cartridge of green ink into my fountain pen. I started scribbling so fast that at first it didn't seem like writing at all, just chasing my thoughts across the page, cramming words up and down the margins. Then I went over what I'd written and revised it. I read the verses aloud, only to cross out so much that only a few words remained. I did this many times. When I finally looked up from my work, the sky outside my window had turned dark. It was already night and I hadn't realized how much time had passed.

The next day I read over what I'd written. I managed to startle myself with the rough, raw anger of those poems. As a girl I'd hidden my poems under my mattress for fear my mother or—worse—the Colonel might read them and punish me for what I'd written. But I knew my father would never see these poems, and every day it mattered less and less to me what Parviz might think if he read them. So why shouldn't I just write what I wanted? Why shouldn't I write about what I really thought and felt?

When I think back on this period of my life, I remember it as having the intensity of a love affair. The green ink with which I'd written the first poems pleased me so much that I gave up writing in black ink and composed all my poems in green. For the first time, I wasn't following a model but working directly from my own emotions and sensibilities. Parviz had shown me a different way to write, but now my work was becoming truly my own. There was still a gap between what I wanted to say and how well I managed to put my ideas into words, but slowly the gap began to narrow, if just a little.

I didn't intend to share these new poems with anyone, at least not at first. I wrote for myself, and that was enough. More than enough. In those hours, I was happier than I'd ever been, happier than I imagined I could be. I was alone in a room, and one by one the poems were setting me free.

When I gave Parviz a copy of one of my milder poems, which I'd inscribed with gratitude for his encouragement, he said nothing. I'm not sure that after our marriage he ever read a single thing I wrote.

Fine, I thought. *That's just as well. My poems really are my own now.*

Back then there was still a strict division between a "poet" and a "poetess." No matter how skillful her writing, a woman was invariably given the feminine moniker. This, apparently, was where I now belonged, among the so-called aspiring poetesses. But ambition had got hold of me. I squirreled away money from my housekeeping allowance to subscribe to a few prominent publications. Thumbing through these journals, I saw that the addresses of the publishers were printed on the inside flaps. Somehow I thought if I went in person to the office of one of these publications I might fare better than if I sent my poems by mail. It was an idle thought, and one I quickly dismissed. Why would an important literary journal want to publish a sixteen-year-old housewife from Ahwaz?

I was long accustomed to hearing discouragement from others, but now I was discouraging myself. I hated myself for it. True, I was terrified, and I had no real sense of what I was doing, but when, after many days, I couldn't come up with a reason that didn't stem from fear, insecurity, or shame. I finally asked myself why I shouldn't try for something more.

We'd leave. That was my plan: Parviz and I would leave Ahwaz. I'd find a way out for both of us. I'd think of some way of making money and we'd move to Tehran together and then we'd set up our own house, however modest. I could pursue my poetry and maybe, beyond the reach of his mother, Parviz could return to his own writing, as well. We'd be happy if we moved away—or at least in Tehran we'd have a chance at happiness, a chance we'd never had in Ahwaz.

Then, one day in the early months of our marriage, life took a turn that made my plans impossible. I set out for the marketplace early in the morning, a green woven basket under my arm. A few doors from the house, I suddenly felt weak and light-headed. I stumbled toward the old stone wall to steady myself, but before I could reach it my knees buckled under me and I fell to the ground. My first thought when I came to was that I must have forgotten to eat, which happened often in those days, but the next morning and the morning after I still felt so queasy that I could barely bring myself to drink a glass of water. At noon I went into town and called on a local nurse for a poultice to help settle my stomach. The nurse, a tiny old woman with gray eyes, tipped my chin up, peered into my eyes, and then, without comment or explanation, pressed her hands against my stomach. I watched her face as she massaged me with determined fingers. "May God grant you a son," she said at last. I was confused, which she must have noticed, because then she added, "You'll be a mother soon."

II.

IT WAS AUTUMN, THE EERILY STILL KIND OF AUTUMN DAY that sometimes precedes the season's first hailstorm in Ahwaz. My legs and ankles had swollen up terribly in the last weeks of pregnancy, which made walking a torment, but I thought that if I went out for a walk it might hasten the delivery. With a kerchief wrapped tightly about my head and my hands buried in the pockets of my coat, I set out down the road that led to the river, away from town.

The streets were deserted; it was late in the day and even if anyone was down by the riverbank, I was so distracted I wouldn't have seen or heard them. I had no idea where I was going, only that I had to keep walking. I walked until exhaustion stole over me, until my sides began to ache, my fingers turned numb, and my cheeks smarted from the cold air. I'd been gone for over an hour when I felt the first contraction, and only then did I finally head back to the house.

The labor was quick, a blessing for which I knew to be grateful. When the midwife swaddled him in a cotton cloth and handed him to me, I clasped my baby to my chest and breathed in his scent. Kamyar—my Kami. His small face was bright red and he had a shock of black hair. I traced his forehead with my fingers, then kissed his eyelids, his palms, the sweet downturned petal of his lips. Later, when the room was dark and Kami had fallen asleep, the midwife sat with a bowl of ashes between her knees. Working quickly, she rubbed the ashes into my wounds to stanch the bleeding, and when she was done she wrapped my belly tightly in gauze.

That night Parviz sat in the chair beside Kami's crib, watching him with quiet joy. I slept deeply, as deeply as if I myself had turned into a child, and together we three made a warm enclosure.

I woke the next morning to the sound of a cry tearing through the air. I sat up and looked around the room. Parviz was gone and Kami's crib was empty. My heart lurched. High and distant, the cry grew louder and higher as I listened. My first thought was that Kami was hurt and crying out in pain. I leapt to my feet. The binding around my waist was tight, and I felt light-headed as I made my way down the hall. In the foyer I stopped to catch my breath and listen. The house was quiet, which only made me more frantic, but after a minute I realized the crying was coming from outside.

When I flung the door open, I saw a crowd had gathered by the house, stretching from our door to the end of the street. Khanoom Shapour was standing near the gate, holding Kami in the crook of one arm. He seemed to be sleeping soundly, but I felt I had to get to him, I had to hold him in my arms. Before I could make my way outside, Parviz appeared and threw his coat around my shoulders. "You can't go outside," he told me, pulling me back into the house. "You're too weak. You need to rest."

I pushed my arms through the sleeves of Parviz's coat and forced my way past him. The temperature had dropped in the night and the ground was pebbled with hail. Fumbling and slipping in my bare feet, I made my way frantically through the courtyard toward the gate.

"In the name of the All-Mighty, the All-Merciful!" a voice called out.

Everything stilled. For a moment I stopped and searched the crowd to see who'd spoken. It was a tall, heavyset man. He stood with a lamb at his feet, his large hand clasped over its mouth so that it could make no noise. It was a small creature, months if not weeks old. Its thin, spindly legs were bound together with rope and its ears were rigid with fear, but otherwise it was silent now. With one hand, the man jerked the lamb back by its head, and with the other hand he lifted a knife to the creature's neck. The lamb twisted under his grip, but then in one swift gesture he plunged the blade into its throat. It made a small soft bleating sound, then its limbs folded and its eyes turned glassy.

Nausea flooded me, but I managed to push past the crowd and make my way toward Khanoom Shapour. Her eyes narrowed when she saw me approach. I must have been a sight, hobbling barefoot in the street, my hair unkempt and my swollen stomach protruding from under Parviz's long winter coat. "Blood brings good luck," she said as I came near. The words made no sense, but I said nothing, only wrenched Kami out of her grasp and turned back toward the house.

"May God protect you and your child!" a woman called out, clutching my arm as I tried to pass.

"May God give you ten more sons!" cried another.

Crossing the courtyard with Kami clasped to my chest, I let my eyes fall to the slaughtered lamb. Blood had soaked its white coat, making first a bright collar of red around its throat and then pooling on the flagstones. Fixated by the blood as it ran in the street, I slowed my step for a moment but then quickly turned away and willed myself not to see the ground reddening at my feet.

"But why?" I asked Parviz, who answered me by saying, "It's a custom, Forugh. They say it brings good luck."

Whether from the exhaustion of giving birth or from the spectacle in the streets, I suddenly felt dizzy and couldn't walk any farther.

"Careful, Forugh!" Parviz said, taking my arm and guiding me back to the house.

Within the hour the lamb had been skinned, carved into pieces, seasoned, salted, wrapped between sheets of newspaper, and handed out as alms for the poor. A sacrifice for my child and my husband's house. There would be a serving for us, too, cooked in a pot of herbed stew for dinner, but I pushed it away and refused to eat even though I knew there would be nothing else.

The year 1953 would later be remembered as the Year of the Coup. The country was divided over the nationalization of oil, a movement spearheaded by Prime Minister Mossadegh and opposed by the shah and his Western supporters. In August, the whole city of Tehran poured onto Avenue Pahlavi. The shah sent his soldiers and police marching through the streets, pounding drums and blasting pistols into the air as they swept across the capital. The king's supporters brandished gigantic posters of His Majesty. "Down with Mossadegh!" they shouted. Meanwhile, the other contingent distributed hand-printed leaflets denouncing the shah, and they met their opponents' cries with "Iran's oil is ours!" and "Down with the monarchy!" Men clambered onto the roofs of cars, and armored tanks barreled down the streets. Lampposts announced the names of those to be hanged there the following day. Children broke loose from their mothers' hands and were instantly swallowed up by the crowds. Husbands and uncles and cousins disappeared in those days; no one knew, at least not for a while, if they were alive or dead.

By summer's end, five thousand people would be dead in the streets or shut away behind prison walls. The CIA's first successful covert overthrow of a foreign government drew to a close. Iranian oil was again firmly in foreign hands.

But all this was happening in the capital, far removed from the walled compounds and empty sun-scorched streets of Ahwaz and certainly not in my world. I was eighteen years old, a wife, a mother, and a woman in the grip of fate.

Whatever they said about me later—that I was a bad mother and that I abandoned my child—the truth is that I loved my son. From the moment he was born to the moment he was taken from me, I loved Kami.

It's true that at first I didn't know how to take care of him. I had no experience with babies, so I'd have to teach myself everything about motherhood. Kami's cries unsettled me. My hands shook when I reached for him, and when

I held him I felt as though I might drop him at any moment. Worse, despite many tries, I failed at nursing him. Whenever I put him to my breast, his tiny lips locked into a tight line. He wouldn't latch on. Within a week of his birth, my breasts were as hard as rocks and hot to the touch. When he finally began to suckle, the pain was excruciating; as soon as he took to my breast, it felt as though my nipples were being pinched with tweezers.

"You're not holding him properly again," Khanoom Shapour told me, snatching Kami out of my arms. "Do it this way!"

I flinched when she put her hands on me, but after many nights of sleeplessness and exhaustion and Kami's hungry cries, I was too tired to protest and I let her guide me this way and that. When she set out large plates of chopped chives to increase my milk, I ate them, and when she handed me poultices of cabbage leaves, I pressed them against my breasts to ease my engorgement.

But no matter what I did, my milk still wouldn't let down. "The child needs nourishment," my mother-in-law told Parviz one night. "And it's obvious she can't nurse him."

The next morning she nudged a bottle of goat's milk into his lips. The liquid was faintly green and smelled sour.

"Don't!" I told her, slapping away the bottle and pulling Kami out of her grip.

"Would you rather he starves?"

When she tried to take Kami from me, I yanked him away so hard that his head jerked back. His crying pierced me, but I wouldn't let him go. I took him to my bedroom, where I pulled my blouse open and guided him to my breast. Again and again I coaxed his lips open with my finger, but they stayed locked shut. Eventually I gave in and allowed him a bottle, but I insisted on being the one to offer it to him. He drank greedily and slept for several hours in a row. Soon his complexion brightened and he grew almost plump.

"Will you ever leave that child alone?" Khanoom Shapour said. "You'll ruin him with your fussing and fawning." She criticized me for holding Kami too much and too often. I was too indulgent with him, she said, which was maybe true. I'd had little tenderness from my mother and knew love only from Sanam. I was determined to be a good mother. I wanted to understand Kami's every cry and meet it with a kind, calm efficiency.

In the mornings on the first warm days of the year, I bathed him in the courtyard by the *hoz,* and in the afternoons I took him into the garden to sit under the persimmon tree. The fruits swung like small glowing lanterns in the breeze, and I sang him whatever snatches of song I knew. "I'm a flower carved in stone. What should I say of my forlorn heart? Without you shining on me like the sun, I'm cold and colorless." I would set Kami's bassinet in the shade of the tree and sing him all the songs I remembered from my own childhood, songs from the nights when I couldn't sleep and my nanny had slept beside me in my bed. I recited every rhyme and riddle I remembered and many more that I invented just for him.

Agha Shapour had brightened with Kami's arrival in the house. Whenever he saw me lift the latch off the fence that divided the house and the garden, a smile crinkled up by his eyes. Some days he laid Kami against his knees and rocked him with his old legs, from side to side, and Kami would grow quiet and fall asleep. Kami was growing fast now. Each day brought some change in him, and I didn't want to miss any of it. Remember this, I thought when I sat in the grass, spreading my skirt in a circle around me, looking up at the sky, and savoring the warmth of the sun on my skin while Kami slept nearby. Remember this, I thought when the fruit trees ripened in the summer and Kami tasted his first fig. Remember this, I thought when I held him to my chest, burying my nose in his soft black curls.

But Khanoom Shapour was determined to claim my son as her own. She bought him rattles and balls. A stuffed monkey in a red suit with large brown beads for eyes. At the New Year holiday she'd pressed golden coins into his small fists. One day, without telling me, she took him to be circumcised, and when she returned she had tied a tiny blue amulet around his wrist. "To protect him from the evil eye," she said, knotting it so tightly that it cut into the soft folds of his skin.

I was furious. "How could you let her do that?" I demanded of Parviz.

"He had to be circumcised, don't you know that?"

"Yes, but why didn't you tell me beforehand? So that I could have been there to hold him. To comfort him."

"I thought it was better this way. I mean, look how you're acting now. . . ."

"How do you expect me to act? He's my son! *My* son, not hers!"

I had only one picture of myself with Kami and it was one I would carry always. One day Parviz and I had gone to a photographer's studio in town. Kami had fussed the whole way there, but when we entered the bright room and the photographer took his place behind the tripod, Kami suddenly settled down and we were able to sit for a portrait.

What did I see later, when I held the photograph of the three of us in my hands? A young woman with painted lips and unruly curls. The Forugh who existed for the briefest time: a wife, a mother. The pearls that looked too tight about my throat. The lost look in my eyes. And next to me, with a hand placed hesitantly on my arm, a husband in a three-piece suit and bow tie. Despite the eleven years' difference in our ages, with his smooth brow, shy smile, and jacket that was much too big in the shoulders, Parviz looked younger than me.

On those spring days, I spent hours away from the house, pushing Kami's carriage down the mud-packed alleys of Ahwaz. "The cold will be the death of that child!" Khanoom Shapour shouted after me when I left the house, which only further stoked my desire to be outside. One afternoon I tucked him into his stroller and headed for the river. There was the scent of fires burning in the town and smoke snaking into the sky. Usually dozens of people stood begging for alms outside the mosque, but the day was chilly and I saw only one old woman there. She wore a thin shawl pulled around her shoulders and a kerchief knotted tightly under her chin. I dug into my pockets, pressed a few coins into her palm, and continued toward the river.

I'd left the house without a coat, and Kami was dressed only in pajamas. The wind snapped against my skin and Kami's cries grew louder and louder, but I didn't really hear him. At some point I began to run. Soon I was running so fast that my blood beat against my ears and the stroller was jerking and bumping wildly under my hands. I became aware of a voice calling out to me, telling me to slow down, to take care, but I couldn't stop running. I remember there was a slamming of brakes and the furious screech of wheels, and then I woke as if from a dream and saw that I'd managed to steer Kami's stroller straight into the throng of cars. Panicked, I looked down into the stroller. Kami's face and his small hands had reddened from the cold, but he was fast asleep.

A strange force was gathering inside me. I'd expected motherhood to temper my desire to write, but the less time I had to devote to it, the more the idea of writing consumed me. When summer finally came and the afternoon heat became unbearable, I would take Kami to my bedroom, pull him to my chest with his face toward me, and close my eyes, falling into sleep with the curtains fluttering and the wind whispering through the trees outside. Sometimes I was too restless to nap and would place Kami in his crib and putter about the room. Once, I caught sight of myself in the mirror and wondered at how much I'd changed. When I was a girl, Sanam was forever trying to fatten me with sweets and oily stews. I'd been knobby-kneed and flat-chested. Well into my pregnancy, even as my belly grew round and high, the rest of my body stayed thin. It was only now, as a mother, that I'd at last acquired a woman's body. I stood in my pale silk slip before the mirror and traced the slight swell of my hips and belly, of my newly full breasts. When Kami stirred, I lifted him into my arms and pressed my lips to the top of his black-haired head, humming some half-remembered song.

It was the only peace I would ever know in that house, and it was in these hours that I again began to plan my escape.

12.

I am the progeny of trees.
Breathing stagnant air wearies me.
A dead bird advised me to
bear the flight in mind.

The ultimate end of all forces is connection,
connection with the luminous source of the sun,
and flowing into the intelligence of light . . .
Why should I stop?

—from "Only Voice Remains"

I TOLD NO ONE WHERE I WAS GOING OR WHOM I PLANNED
to meet. It was a Monday, and Kami had just settled down
for a nap and my mother-in-law retreated to her room
as she did each afternoon for her prayers and siesta. I set
Kami's bassinet in the living room, where his cries could
easily be heard when he woke. I smoothed his blanket and
kissed his forehead. I'd been planning this day for months,

but all of a sudden I felt panicky. It was wrong to leave Kami. I shouldn't go.

The light through the curtained windows seemed thin and stifled. I think if Kami had stirred at that moment, I would have abandoned my plans, but he was fast asleep. I checked my wristwatch. A quarter past noon. There was only a sliver of time before Parviz would return from town to take his lunch. I'd have to go now or stay trapped in the house with no way of leaving. "I've gone to visit my mother," I'd scribbled in my note to Parviz. "I'll be back Friday." There'd be arguments when I returned, that and days of Parviz's dark, silent moods, but I forced these thoughts from my mind as I grabbed my pocketbook and trench coat and stepped into the streets.

Once at the train station, I paced the platform, looking constantly about me for fear that someone would recognize me and ruin my plan. Any minute now my mother-in-law would wake up and find me gone. I was the only woman at the station and also seemingly the only person to board the train, but there were few passengers that day and thankfully I didn't encounter anyone I knew.

The trip to Tehran would take twenty hours. I'd purchased a third-class railway ticket—the best I could afford even after weeks of putting aside money from my household allowance. The seat was hard and did not recline. With my forehead pressed to the cold rattling glass and my chin cupped in my hand, I watched the low, wide buildings of Ahwaz, the marketplace with its tented roof, and the mosque's blue dome gradually disappear. All at once the desert was everywhere, and I was overcome with a feeling of relief. Sand, rocks, hills—the whole landscape was tinted the same shade of orange as the sky. A soft glow encircled the distant mountains, and slowly I felt myself breathe again.

I unclasped my purse and pulled out a folded notepaper on which I'd written an address: "Zand Alley, Number 22." I didn't recognize the street name and I had only the vaguest idea how to find my way to it. I slipped the note back into my purse and checked again for my poems. I didn't dare to look at them just then, and they stayed sealed in the envelope inside my purse.

The uncertainty, the heedlessness, and, most of all, the excitement with which I left Ahwaz for Tehran the first time—later it would all seem to me the mark of true innocence: the innocence of throwing myself headlong into the future and thinking I might escape without consequences or regrets.

I woke in a panic several times that night. Was Kami all right? Did he cry out for me when he woke from his nap, had he taken his bottle, was he fussing and whimpering in his sleep? It was wrong of me to have left him. Selfish and wrong. I nearly didn't disembark when the train pulled into the Tehran station at eight o'clock the next morning, and I might have turned back right then, except there'd be no train back to Ahwaz until the next day.

But then, as soon as I stepped into the streets of Tehran, I felt it, that unshakable sense of having returned home. It was autumn, the season of pomegranate and quince. The scent of roasted nuts and barbecued corn from the street vendors, of mud-packed alleyways, gasoline fumes, and concrete roads—I hadn't known, until I encountered them again, how much I'd missed the city. I drew a deep breath and steeled my nerves. Outside the train station, a man with a black fedora pulled low over his face pointed me out to his companion, and the two men exchanged a look and then turned to stare at me. The area down by the railway was notoriously rough, and the only women I saw were old, kerchiefed street peddlers. As I approached, the man in the fedora told his companion something that made them both laugh, and then he raised his hand in a slight wave. I wrapped my shawl around my neck, dug my hands deep into the pockets of my coat, and walked on.

I crossed from the railway station and onto Avenue Pahlavi. Farther uptown, the streets grew more crowded. Vendors were setting up their trestles for the day's work, their carts laden with fruit and long loaves of freshly baked sesame flatbread. I realized I was famished, so I stopped and bought myself a paper cone of hot chestnuts, the first of the season, and ate them as I walked.

In the distance, just beyond the city, I saw the ring of the Alborz Mountains. The snowy peaks glowed faintly pink with the morning sun. When I was a girl I'd climb up to the roof just to stare out at these same mountains. I'd look clear across the rooftops to the highest one, the volcano called Mount Damavand. Sanam had told me the story of the Simorgh, the magical bird that made its home there. Damavand seemed as distant to me then as another country, but even as a small child I didn't doubt I would one day make my way to it, and farther even than that.

Now I was a woman, a wife, and also a mother. I'd only come as far as Tehran, the city of my girlhood, but no distance seemed greater than the one I was traveling today.

I continued to draw looks as I walked, but it eventually occurred to me that here—in this district, at least—no one knew me and I myself knew no one. I held my head higher, walking faster and with longer strides. The buildings were taller than I remembered, but two years had passed since I'd moved away, and in that time Tehran had been busy making itself over into a Western-style metropolis. Here was a boulevard crowded with buses and automobiles, an alleyway thick with exhaust plumes; there was a street with boutiques, cafés, and restaurants. Eventually, the city and its bustling streets absorbed me, and as I walked I ceased to think or to care about what people thought of me. I walked on, exhilarated and wide awake, despite the sleepless night I'd spent on the train, and it wasn't long before I found myself on Zand Alley.

Halfway down the street I stopped in front of a worn wooden door and studied the small glazed tile toward the top. It was painted with the number 22. I'd expected something grander for a publishing house, but the building was run-down—nearly derelict. I riffled through my pocketbook and again checked the note. The tile was a faded blue, and the black numbering had cracked with age, but this seemed to be the correct address.

The door opened onto a narrow stairwell. After checking over my shoulder to see if anyone was watching me, I climbed the stairs and proceeded down a dark, dim hallway. The building seemed deserted, and I again worried I'd come to the wrong place, but gradually I heard the sound of voices at the end of the hall, and then I came to a door with a small metal placard inscribed PAYAM MAGAZINE.

I sucked in my breath, pushed the door open, and found myself in a large room with several desks, all but one of them unoccupied. A wiry man in shirtsleeves and a loosened collar sat pounding on a typewriter. When the door swung open, he looked up at me, and then for a moment his hands rested in the air. His expression was not so much one of annoyance as of confusion.

"*Kh-Khanoom* . . ." he stammered, rising from his chair. "Have you lost your way?"

I shook my head and asked, "This is the headquarters of *Payam,* isn't it?"

"Yes, but—"

"And the office of Mr. Pakyar," I continued, "the editor in chief of *Payam,* is also here?"

"Yes, but—"

"Well, I've come to see Mr. Pakyar."

At this he looked more puzzled, but he said nothing more, only led me to a chair in the foyer and directed me to wait there. I thanked him, then sat down with my pocketbook on my lap.

After some minutes, two men appeared from a room toward the back of the office. The older of the two was bald and portly and wore no jacket. *So that's Mr. Pakyar,* I thought, and sat up straighter in the chair. The second man was perhaps thirty, with a charcoal-gray coat draped on his arm and a hat in his other hand. The two men exchanged goodbyes, the older man clapping the younger one on the back as they made their way toward the entrance.

I stood up. I felt the weight of the younger man's eyes as he approached—and then he gave me an appraising look that ran the length of my body. He raked a hand through his hair. If it surprised him to see a young woman in such a place, however, he gave no show of it—only placed his fedora on his head and tipped it to me as he passed.

The men exchanged a few more words and then the door creaked shut. The visitor was gone, whoever he was.

"And who is this?" Mr. Pakyar asked the assistant.

He hadn't addressed me, but I stepped forward anyway. "Mr. Pakyar, I've come to speak with you about—"

He looked at me, face to feet and back again, then said, "If you've come for work, miss, I'm afraid we don't need a receptionist just now."

I shook my head. "I haven't come for a job. I'm here to give you these." I pulled the envelope from my pocketbook and held it out to him. "They're poems. My poems."

"Ah," he said slowly, glancing at the envelope, "a poetess."

"Poetess"! My dislike for the word was instant and irreversible. Whenever I heard it afterward, I returned to that moment and saw myself as that editor saw me that day: a simple housewife from the provinces who carried handwritten poems in her pocketbook. Not a poet but a mere "poetess."

"Have you published anything?" he asked.

When I confessed I hadn't, he smirked.

I lifted my chin and crossed my arms over my chest. "Read one poem, sir. Just one."

Mr. Pakyar opened and then closed his mouth. With his eyes still on me, he slit the envelope open with his index finger, and the seal tore in a long, ugly rip. He pulled the pages from the envelope, and I watched as he glanced at the first poem. This he did so quickly that he couldn't possibly have read anything more than the title. "Your interest here is misplaced," he said, lifting his eyes. "You're better off going back home," he said, his eyes drifting to my wedding band. "Back to your husband, *khanoom*."

————

Tears pricked my eyes and I moved as if in a daze, following the crowds toward an open-air market. A group of boys careened past me on bicycles, nearly knocking me over. Women gripped their veils between their teeth so as to leave their arms free for their bundles and packages and the children who tripped alongside them as they made their rounds. I sat by the side of an old stone fountain, watching the crowds. The pungent fragrance of roasted meat wafted from a kabob shop. I felt sick in the pit of my stomach.

After all the trouble of traveling to Tehran, leaving my Kami behind, I'd been dismissed in the space of five minutes. I'd been so upset I'd left without retrieving my poems from Mr. Pakyar. *He'll toss my poems in the trash,* I thought; *he's probably thrown them away already.* Suddenly I wished I hadn't come to the city at all, and I buried my face in my hands.

"Miss?" came a man's voice.

When I looked up, he was there. The man from the office, the one with the gray coat draped over his arm. He wore it now with the collar turned up to the cold, and the fedora was pulled low over his brow. He was smoking a cigarette and watching me.

I could have refused to answer him. I could have cast my eyes down, squared my shoulders, and walked down the street and clear away from him. I knew equally well how to repel a man's gaze or to encourage it. That's the sort of cunning a girl learns early.

So, I might well have looked away. Instead, I met his gaze. "Yes?" I said, wiping my eyes quickly with the back of my hand.

"You were just in the office in Zand Alley, weren't you?"

"I was."

"Forgive me, but you look a bit lost here," he said.

I raised my chin. "I'm not."

He was silent, drawing a thoughtful drag on his cigarette. "Nasser Khodayar," he said, and extended his hand.

It took a moment for me to react. For all my attempts at sophistication, I'd never before shaken a man's hand, but then I quickly held out my hand and let him clasp it between his.

"Forugh," I said.

"So, Forugh," he said, letting go of my hand and sliding beside me by the fountain. "No luck with Mr. Pakyar?"

He'd made the connection between my hurried meeting and my distraught state—a further humiliation. I was quiet, and then said, "He barely looked at my poems. He'll throw them away. I bet he's done it already."

"That's probably true."

I stared at him. "You think I'm silly and stupid."

"Not at all."

"But you agree it's useless. He won't publish my poems."

"Look, Forugh," he said, "twenty new journals spring up in this city every day." He flicked the ash from his cigarette and continued. "Tehran's full of poets, and when they can't find someone to publish their work, they set up their own presses, throw in a few of their friends' poems, and congratulate themselves for their bold new contributions to Persian literature."

I tilted my head and narrowed my eyes. "How do you know so much about all this?"

He reached into his breast pocket and pulled out a card. NASSER KHODAYAR, it read, EDITOR IN CHIEF, ROSHANFEKR.

I looked from the card in my hand back to him. *Roshanfekr—The Intellectual—*was a popular magazine, one I knew well. This man in a fedora was its editor. For a moment I couldn't think what to say.

He took another drag of his cigarette and then said, "Why don't you show me some of your poems? That way I could get a sense of your style and tell you what I think."

"You'd really do that?"

One corner of his mouth lifted in a smile. "Why not?"

"But I don't have any more copies with me." I thought for a moment. "I could send you some if you give me an address?"

He looked quickly at his watch and then back at me. "Tell you what," he said, grinding his cigarette with his shoe. "Why don't you meet me here Thursday morning? You can bring your poems and I'll let you know what I think of your writing."

"Thursday? I don't know if—"

He touched his tie and tightened the knot. "Come if you like, and if you don't, well, then that will be your choice entirely." He gestured across the street, nodding toward a small teahouse at the corner. "Half past ten. I'll meet you there. If I had to guess, I'd say our literature will be all the poorer if you don't come," he said, "and so, maybe, will I."

With that he flashed me a smile, cut across the street, and was gone.

That night I made my way to Amiriyeh, back to a house to which I would never have imagined I'd return. Not alone, in any case. After the encounter with Nasser Khodayar, I walked for hours with little sense of where I was going. Even if I could spare the money, no hotel would rent a room to a woman traveling on her own, so I had no choice but to spend the night at my mother's house. Truly, there was nowhere else to go.

"You've come by yourself, Forugh?" my mother asked as soon as she saw me at her door. She looked at my unbuttoned coat and my messy hair. It was past eight o'clock and my arrival had clearly startled her. She bit her lip nervously and peered over my shoulder. Then she placed her hand on my shoulder and hustled me inside.

"Did Parviz send you away?" she asked as soon as we were in the house.

"No," I said, setting down my purse and shrugging off my coat.

"Thanks be to God," she sighed. "But he allowed you to come all the way to Tehran on your own?"

When I didn't answer, she asked me something I'd never heard from her before: "Are you all right, Forugh?"

The worry in her voice gave me pause. Did she think he'd cast me out? Or hurt me in some way?

"I missed home," I said. It was, I realized in that moment, the truth.

"I see," she said quietly. "It's sometimes that way. In the beginning especially." As she said this I watched her hands, twisting and untwisting one corner of her apron. She seemed to want to tell me something more, something of her loneliness as a young bride, perhaps even of her loneliness now, but instead she drew her shawl tightly about her shoulders.

"Yes, it's sometimes that way," I echoed vaguely, gathering up my things and following her up the stairs. When we reached the door to my old bedroom, I turned and studied her more closely. Her waist had thickened since I last saw her at my wedding. Wrinkles fanned out at the corners of her eyes, and her lips, which she'd always painted a deep red, were bare and faintly cracked. She also seemed to me sadder than I remembered, but then I'd left her when I was very much still a child and now I'd returned more grown up and could see her differently. Yes, I thought as we parted that night, there was something different about her, something she wouldn't confide and I couldn't yet guess.

"I knew something was up when he turned up in the neighborhood and I heard him humming to himself," Sanam told me later that night. My mother had retired to her room, and now Sanam and I sat in the kitchen, drinking cardamom-spiced tea and nibbling on chickpea cookies.

"Humming?" I said, confounded by the vision of the Colonel in such a carefree mood.

She nodded, folded her hands across her chest, and launched into her story. He hadn't been to the house in weeks and he looked so different that she hadn't recognized him at first. He'd grown stout and his walk had taken on the jaunty gait of a bachelor, but as soon as he pulled a cucumber from his pocket she knew it was him. "To mask the scent of liquor on his breath," she explained. "An old trick of his." She watched as he smoothed the tips of his thick mustache with his fingers and then screwed his face into the scowl with which he always greeted my mother. "The next day he disappeared," she said.

He'd been gone for close to a month when word came that he'd set up another woman in her own house. Since then, my mother had been crying as she stood before the samovar in the morning, pouring the tea. Crying as she shelled fava beans, trimmed parsley and basil for the stew, and rinsed the day's rice. Crying as she embroidered in the parlor in the afternoons and as she stooped over our best carpet in the *mehmoon khooneh* to smooth and straighten its tassels. She spilled too much salt in her stews and tipped too much saffron into her rice. Pots fell from her hands and onto the kitchen floor. She dropped to her knees to mop up the mess, but her eyes were absent and she did a very poor job. Her *tahdig*—crisped rice—burned to brown and sometimes even to black. My mother, who'd always been fastidious, grew inattentive and slatternly. She grew tired and gaunt. She grew old.

No one in the family had been formally introduced to the Colonel's other wife, but Sanam passed her in the streets a few times by chance. The new wife was slightly plump and pretty, and she had a large mole on her right cheek. From the neighbors, Sanam learned that the Colonel's second wife was just sixteen years old when my father married her. No one seemed to know anything of the girl's family or of the nature of her courtship with my father, but as Sanam spoke that night I imagined her as a merchant's daughter, maybe the youngest in a tribe of pretty sisters, the one who'd given the most trouble and the one her parents were most keen to marry off and make a husband's worry.

The Colonel moved his second wife into a house a few streets away from our home in Amiriyeh, and after that he never again passed the night with my mother. Day by day, he continued to grow younger. His stomach, however, strained inelegantly against his military uniform, and the fabric of his jacket now puckered and its buttons threatened to pop loose. The neighbors reported that the new wife was an unusually good cook and that the Colonel was especially fond of her sweet saffron custards. He'd also purportedly outfitted his second house with smart new furnishings and appliances for his new bride. He was so besotted with her, the neighbors said, so entranced by her grins and her giggles, that he refused to let her leave the house on errands my mother had routinely performed since the first days of their marriage.

Now in the afternoons my mother no longer lit the charcoal brazier for the tea, nor did she entertain guests in the parlor. Instead, she sat at the *korsi,* under piles of quilts, staring down at her hands or gazing absently at the embers. When the flame died out, she didn't call for Hassan to replenish the coals, and at night, when the house was quiet, Sanam often came upon her sitting alone in the dark kitchen; if Sanam approached, my mother looked up with an expression so confused that it seemed she didn't know her at all.

I didn't sleep that night or the next. I was exhausted, and it was useless to lie there in the dark, but I couldn't drift off to sleep. I missed Kami and I knew Parviz must be frantic about my disappearance, but my mother didn't have a telephone and there was no way to contact him. On top of that, I couldn't stop thinking about my mother. It had never occurred to me to wonder what was in her heart. She had been married to the Colonel for more than twenty years. How many times in those years had she gone to sleep wondering if he would return to the house in the night? Sometimes he would disappear for whole weeks, only to reappear without telling her where he'd been or how long he would stay before leaving again. For her, marriage had always been an act of faith. All her rituals, habits, and devotions shaped themselves around that faith. The house where she had arrived as a young bride and brought up seven children, the garden that had once been her refuge and that she forced herself to forget—all these things had surely taken on a new meaning now.

My siblings and I never learned the name of our father's other wife, just as we did not know him except as the Colonel. We called her his *zan,* a word denoting both "wife" and "woman." As for my mother, for the rest of her life she retained the same title, though we understood its meaning now as I think she herself did—a lie, a betrayal, and a disgrace.

I set out from Amiriyeh at ten in the morning in my beige trench coat and with my hair pinned up in a chignon, which I hoped would make me look older and more sophisticated. The night before I'd copied ten poems from memory and tucked them into my purse. I was lucky to know them by heart, but of course this morning I was so nervous that everything I'd written seemed to need revision. I'd painted on lipstick and run a stick of kohl around my eyes. My heart was knocking against my chest, but despite my nervousness, my hand was steady and sure as I winged my eye makeup in the corners. In the end, I had settled on just three poems and removed the others from my purse. He'd like them or he wouldn't—there was no use second-guessing myself now.

When I reached Zand Alley I lingered by the entry to the teahouse, peering inside and searching the men's faces. Then, out of the corner of my eye, I saw a silver sports car parked on the street. Nasser Khodayar poked his head out from the window, gesturing to me with his gloved hand.

"Where should we go?" he asked as I approached.

I was prepared for a cup of tea, perhaps a quick lunch in a nearby restaurant. I told myself before setting out that I'd meet with him just long enough to give him the poems and get his opinion of where I might send them.

I stepped toward the car and set one hand on my hip. "I thought you'd tell me where I can send my work," I said, "not drive me around the city, Mr. Khodayar."

"Nasser—please call me Nasser," he said, smiling. "Isn't it easier to talk privately rather than surrounded by all these people?" He waved in the direction of the streets.

I glanced up. He was right. Just by standing next to a man's car, I'd already attracted the attention of several passersby. I asked, "Where can we go?"

"Anywhere you like."

The prospect of this "anywhere" thrilled me. I thought for a moment, seeking in my mind the most exotic destination I could imagine. "How about Karaj?" I said, naming what I'd heard was a picturesque spot an hour outside the city. I was sure he wouldn't want to go as far as that, but to my surprise he pushed his sleeves up, turned the ignition key, and patted the seat beside him—all while keeping his eyes on mine. "Let's go to Karaj, Forugh," he said.

"You're not serious?"

"Why not?" he asked. "I know a little coffeehouse up there. A nice spot in the hills where we could talk comfortably."

"Well, for one thing, I have to catch the train back to Ahwaz this afternoon."

"Ahwaz?" he asked, lifting his eyebrows. "I guessed you didn't know the city well, but I didn't realize you'd come from as far away as that! So how does a young woman from Ahwaz get as far as Tehran on her own?"

Afraid it would lead to further questions, I ignored the comment and instead asked, "Will you really tell me what you think about my poems?"

By way of answer, he leaned over and opened the passenger door.

I return to this moment often because it was when everything that came next in my life was decided. I knew that if I entered the car, I would become a certain kind of woman. A "cheap woman." If anyone were to see me now, whatever was left of my reputation would be gone.

I pushed the thought from my mind and slid into the passenger seat.

As Nasser started the engine and steered into traffic, I stole a sidelong glance in his direction. He was the handsomest man I'd ever met and certainly the most sophisticated. His hair was combed back with brilliantine and he smelled of tobacco and clove-scented cologne. When he shifted the gear, his hand brushed my knee, and I realized I'd never sat in such close proximity to a man who was not related to me. A hank of hair fell into his face and he pushed it back in a swift, practiced gesture. I trained my eyes on the road and stared hard ahead.

After some minutes he opened the windows, and a chilly but pleasant breeze filled the car. As we drove, he talked about the journal he edited and his connections to various other literary magazines in the city. He'd started out as a reporter for one of the large Tehran newspapers, writing about art and literature. He'd been *The Intellectual*'s editor in chief for a few years already, but lately he'd become interested in bringing more contemporary writing into print, including work by emerging poets and writers.

Ten or fifteen minutes, the city gave way to quieter, tree-lined streets and I felt myself relax. The farther north we traveled, the air turned cooler and carried the moist, clear scent of the pines. The wind was soon whipping against my hair and face, and I pulled a kerchief from my purse and knotted it under my chin.

He asked a few questions to draw me out, all of them simple and polite, but all the while we shared a more intimate, wordless exchange. I'd entered his car. I'd let him drive me away. By these means I'd told him much about who I was and what else I might be willing to do.

Karaj had the simple prettiness of the provinces: wide green fields and orchards broken up by the occasional cottage or barn. The road became winding, and with each plunge and swerve I had the sensation of falling. My heart pounded and lurched, and I gripped the edges of the seat. Nasser parked along a hillside, and we walked down a narrow mountain path and then cut across onto an unpaved road. Street vendors were selling bright copper bowls and bushels of white mulberries.

We came to a quiet side street and he placed his hand on the small of my back, steering me off the path and into a passageway. The coffeehouse was small but airy, with low banquettes covered in cushions and kilims. White tents had been strung up through the trees, and the patio looked out across a small stream.

"Don't your days belong to anyone?" I asked him once we'd settled at a table.

"No."

That stopped me—not what he said so much as the coolness with which he'd said it. "You're very lucky, then," I told him.

"Yes," he said slowly, "I suppose by that measure I am."

"And by that measure I'm not."

A waiter approached the table, setting a gurgling water pipe and two small glasses of tea before us. He was a young man, thin and wiry. I watched as his eyes slid from me to Nasser. I stiffened and looked away.

"Here," Nasser said when we were alone again. He held the wooden nozzle of the pipe up to me, offering me a smoke. When I shook my head, he shrugged and then drew a deep puff. The scent of tobacco and mint filled the space between us. I plucked a sugar cube from the bowl, tucked it into my cheek, and took a slow sip of tea.

"Who do your days belong to, Forugh?" he asked.

He was watching me closely, waiting for my reply. I turned the question over in my mind. Who *did* my days belong to? I wish I could have made some clever answer, but I could only laugh a little and pretend to study the view.

Afterward we walked for a time along the stream. Once, when I stumbled over some rocks, he took my hand and steadied me. A few steps on, when we stopped to admire the view, he reached over and placed his hand on the small of my back. I felt my heart kick against my chest.

"You're glad you came now, aren't you?" His eyes danced across my face.

"Yes," I said quickly, and allowed myself a smile.

We continued up the path. "I've decided something," I told him when we made our way up from the riverbank. "I've decided this day belongs to me."

Tilting his chin, he blew a plume of smoke up in the air, and then he smiled.

"I missed my family," I told Parviz when I returned to Ahwaz.

I'd been gone five days by then—gone and free for five days. I had been reluctant to return home, though the feeling fell away as soon as I held Kami again.

"You should have told me you were going, Forugh. Do you know how it looks, you running away like that? Spending nights away on your own? Leaving Kami behind?"

He went on like that for a long time, but I heard his words as if from a distance, like an echo. That night, I didn't reach for him or try to soften his mood with explanations or apologies, and after he fell asleep, I sank even deeper into my thoughts. In my head, I replayed every detail of the afternoon I'd spent with Nasser. Again and again my mind returned to the moment just before I'd stepped out of his car. He'd placed one hand on my bare knee and another against the back of my neck. "Meet me again," he'd said, and brought his lips to my mouth. In my haste to catch the train back to Ahwaz, I'd forgotten to give him my poems. *Yes*, I thought now, *I'll meet him again. I'll meet him again very soon.*

13.
_____

IT WAS SO MANY YEARS AGO, BUT I CAN STILL SEE MYSELF making my way to him. I conjure the apartment: spare, hushed, and dark. A ceiling fan spins overhead, throwing slivered shadows against the walls. The rooms are barely furnished. I close my eyes and I see myself standing before him. I see myself pause, unpin my hair, and slip my feet free of my heels. He looks at me and smiles. Do I smile back? Do I greet him? What I remember is this: I unclasp my pearl necklace, take off my blouse, step out of my skirt slowly and deliberately. I play the part of a woman for whom gestures like this come naturally. I play this part for him but also for myself.

I stand before him in just my silk stockings and slip. He uncrosses his legs, leans forward. Waits. He knows what I want—that's his power over me. I'm sure if I'd been less determined to appear experienced, he would have been more forceful, but he knows how to calibrate his advances.

He knows I'll yield more readily if I'm given the chance to make the first move—yes, he's known that about me from the beginning.

"The poetess," he calls me, and it reminds me that to him I'm not really a poet, just a girl who thinks she can write poetry.

I pull away a little and cross my arms over my chest.

He grabs my wrist and pulls me back toward him and down to the bed. "Maybe you'll write about this," he says, catching my face with two hands.

It's more a dare than a question, but I answer it all the same.

"Yes," I say gamely, and begin unbuttoning his shirt.

"Everything?"

"Everything," I answer, and then grin.

He loosens his trousers, kicks them free. As he comes close I smell clove, the same scent that filled the car on our drive to the mountains. I close my eyes. His hands are on my breasts now, his breath against my skin. His fingers move down toward my stomach and then between my legs. My breath catches. I climb on top of him, my knees on either side of his thighs, and then the room fades and falls away.

I will write about it later—"everything," just as I promised now. With Nasser, I'll forget all sense of propriety and modesty until it is too late, but on this day there's no knot of memory to untangle, undo, and rearrange, no history yet for either of us to betray. I know hardly anything about him, and he knows nothing at all about me, nothing apart from my name and the fact that I write poems, but this not knowing is necessary to the story; it makes me brave enough to begin.

Alone afterward, I rise from the bed and start to dress. As I bend to hook the garters to my stocking, I catch a glimpse of myself in the mirror above the dresser. What do I see exactly that draws me closer to my own reflection? I hook my other stocking, straighten my slip, and walk toward the mirror. I push my hair from my face and study myself. There is, of course, still much of the old me there, the girl with the full lips and dark eyes, but my hair is in tangles and my cheeks are flushed. I step closer. Look more carefully. Wine, pleasure, heat: My face still holds their trace.

Something else about me changes that day, but it isn't a matter of appearance or even of experience. Standing before the mirror for those few minutes, I take the first true measure of my body and decide that it's shame, not sin, that's unholy.

Tuesdays and Wednesdays. Those were the only days he was free to meet, or the only days he chose to set aside for me.

From now on, as often as I could manage it—about once every month or so—I took the train from Ahwaz to Tehran. A third-class ticket cost close to nothing, which was lucky since I had little money to spare. I never asked permission to go or announced my plans to anyone before leaving. I simply packed a small bag and got on a train.

"She goes to visit her family," I once overheard Parviz tell his mother.

"It makes no difference! She shouldn't go alone," she told him. "I knew she'd bring us nothing but shame. You need to control your wife, Parviz. They're talking about her all over town."

"She only goes to see her family," he answered weakly, then added, "Her mother isn't well, you see."

And for all Parviz knew, that was true. I spent more and more time holed up in the house with Kami, and eventually it must have seemed I was truly in the grip of a terrible homesickness, because I no longer went into the streets of Ahwaz by myself or took Kami out for long walks. I was far from free, but soon I discovered that as long as I found my way to my mother's house and passed the night under her roof, I could travel to Tehran once and sometimes twice a month.

Now when I set out from Ahwaz by train, it was still always in secret but anticipation completely displaced my nervousness. I'd never outrun my guilt at leaving Kami, but as soon as I reached Tehran my doubts and indecision receded. I always headed straight for the tangle of buildings where Nasser kept an apartment, my heels clapping against the pavement, pausing every so often to switch my small valise from one hand to the other. I was learning to walk the Tehran streets as though I had always belonged to them, and as I discovered the pleasure of looking out upon the world, I realized the prohibitions of my girlhood had been meant not only to hide us girls from others but also to hide the greater world from us.

Once on my way to meet Nasser in the city, I caught a glimpse of myself in a storefront window. I'd recently bought a pair of black cat-eye sunglasses, and now I watched myself pushing them up onto my head, opening my pocketbook, and painting my lips. The girl I'd been was gone. Growing up I'd been forbidden from stepping foot outside my father's house or showing myself to men, but now I had as little shame as the European and American women I glimpsed from time to time in the streets. I drew my sunglasses back onto my face and made my way to a little café squeezed between a bakery and a bookshop. It was Nasser's favorite meeting place. Sitting in the back room of the café, waiting for him to appear, I lit a cigarette, brought it to my mouth, and slowly let out a stream of smoke. I smiled to think of myself doing what I'd been forbidden to, and when I drew stares from others, from men as well as women, I met them evenly.

We'd spend an hour together in his apartment, sometimes two—not much time, but enough to forget what I'd left and what I could lose by continuing to see him. I remember the steadiness of his gaze, how easily he could make me yield to him. He always left without offering any apology or explanation except to tell me we shouldn't be seen leaving the apartment together. He'd rake his fingers through his hair, tuck his shirt into his trousers, and remind me to lock the door when I left. I didn't say when I would be back, but we both knew I would.

Often, I wandered through those two rooms hoping I might find some trace of him to bring back with me. The walls were empty of photographs, the shelves free of mementos. I riffled guiltily through his drawers and closets, searching for some old picture of him or maybe a note written in his hand. But there was nothing intimate or personal in that apartment, nothing for me to find and take. He never asked me to spend the night and I never brought it up. Still, I would have stayed there until he returned, waiting hours or even days, and it was only my love for Kami that led me from Tehran and back toward the dusty, barren streets of Ahwaz.

From time to time I couldn't help but see the trouble waiting for me. I remember one day when I climbed the stairs to Nasser's apartment, I met a woman carrying a large bunch of white tuberoses toward her apartment. "How pretty!" I said to her, and reached my hand toward the bouquet. I only meant to compliment her on their loveliness, but she flinched and pulled away. The woman's eyes met mine, and she glanced across the landing to Nasser's apartment and then back at me. I stiffened and let my hand fall to my side. In that moment I not only understood the woman's estimation of my character but also began to realize that other women had been to visit Nasser before me and that there would be others when I no longer made my way here.

Meanwhile, Kami was now a toddler. His hair had grown in thick and he had my black eyes and his father's high forehead. He'd been a quiet baby, but he now screamed and cried if I so much as made a move toward the door. I was always exhausted in those days but also distracted and restless. One day were sitting outside in the garden together. I was wearing a red skirt, which was long and flared, and I'd spread it out so that it made a circle on the ground. Kami sat across from me, rolling a ball toward me. I'd made up a game of sometimes grabbing the ball and hiding it behind my back. Each time he'd toddle toward me and snatch at the toy, I'd lift it out of reach, then suddenly let him grab it with his small, chubby fists.

We'd been playing that game for a while when I noticed a small stain at the hem of my dress. Something strange came over me then. The stain seemed to swell before my eyes and, even more inexplicable, I felt sure that it would somehow contaminate Kami. I dropped the ball and began frantically wiping at the stain with my sleeve. Kami started to cry, which thankfully freed me from my crazed attempt to scrub the stain on my skirt. I lifted him up and held him to my chest. He settled down almost at once, but from that moment I held the terrible knowledge that I didn't have full possession of myself.

Months passed. I knew it was a mistake to continue meeting Nasser. Worse, I missed Kami so much when I went to Tehran. With each trip it seemed he was adjusting himself to my absences. Now, if he fell and cried when toddling around the house on his unsteady legs, he sought comfort from Khanoom Shapour, not me. She'd heft him onto her hip and disappear into another part of the house. Maybe soon he'd forget me altogether? It was an awful thought, but it didn't stop me from going. Not then.

I told myself I'd go to Tehran just one more time, and maybe that's what I really believed—that I could see Nasser once more and then stop altogether. I could never explain the power he had over me, my lack of concern for consequences, except that my body had lost all interest in reason. Despite the shame I'd already brought my family, I had little real experience of men. Before, when I was alone with Parviz, I'd wanted so much to please him, which is, of course, a longing of a kind, and one sufficient to pitch a young woman into restlessness and unreason, but it was pure desire that shot through me now, desire that made me both brave and weak.

But there was something else that bound me to Nasser. Even if I knew we had no chance for a life together, being with him gave me the notion I might yet break into Tehran's literary scene. He was my one connection to that world, and that wasn't a connection I could easily give up.

The affair with Nasser was the only experience in my life I'd ever truly regret, but despite all it would cost me, it also gave me much for which I later felt grateful.

Nasser did what he wanted and never apologized for it. I'd had that quality myself once, but it seemed a long time since I'd let myself be guided by my own needs and desires. Nasser gave me this quality back—had, in fact, given it to me the day he drove me up into the foothills outside Tehran: the sure, quiet confidence of simply taking what I wanted from life.

And I can say this without hesitation: Without him I wouldn't have become the talk of Tehran. For all Nasser refused me in our love affair, he encouraged me not only to write but also to publish exactly those most candid, revealing poems I might have kept for myself.

It happened only gradually. Every time I came to Tehran, I brought along some new poems. Each one confessed something true about my life, offered some revelation about marriage or motherhood. One day it had occurred to me I might submit a few poems to a small literary journal by mail. "The Rebellion" and "The Wedding Band" were accepted, which gave me the courage to send others out. If my poems didn't exactly attract the attention of the literati, I knew no better pleasure than undoing the brass clasp of my trousseau to add a new publication to the small collection I kept there.

Nasser's response to these first publications had been warm but short of enthusiastic. "Push yourself further," he told me. "Write about yourself as you are here with me, in this room, in these hours."

One afternoon we sat at the table in his apartment with a cup of coffee before each of us, and he read through a sheaf of new poems I'd brought him. I remember sitting across from him, watching him as he read. More and more, I was not merely writing about love in the abstract but writing to Nasser, seeking him out through my words and hoping to insinuate myself in his mind. Whatever I couldn't tell him in person, I put into verse.

I was nervous to have him read them, intensely so. I felt an urge to leave the room, but I forced myself to sit still and wait for him to finish. To distract myself I fiddled with the pearls wrapped round my wrist, worrying the beads. I was so anxious that when I finally remembered my tea and brought my cup to my lips, it had already grown cold. When I put it down with a clatter, he didn't look up but continued to read in silence. He read quietly, slowly, taking his time with each poem, reading some of them two or three times before moving on to the next one, sometimes mouthing the words quietly or tracing the cadence with his finger on the page.

"That's the one," he finally said, placing it before me on the table. It was a poem I'd titled "Sin," which closed with the lines:

> I've sinned a sin of pleasure
> beside a body trembling and spent.
> I don't know what I did, Oh God,
> in that quiet empty darkness.

There was no dedication, and I hadn't included his name in any of the lines, but every last detail would have been recognizable to Nasser. It was his poem—his and mine.

"You're sure?" I asked. I'd worked on the poem for many hours, fretting every word, every pause, revising the lines until they finally satisfied me, but even as I wrote it I knew such a declaration of passion by a woman was not permissible. It could never be published.

But Nasser would not give up. "Don't you want to be part of something new? Something bigger?"

"Of course, but—"

He frowned. "This is your best poem by far and also the most daring. You *must* publish it, Forugh."

I was silent, considering his words.

"We'll run it in next month's issue," he continued. "There's time, though just barely. Everything's already been sent to the typesetter, but I think I can rearrange things to make room." He stood up and was pacing the room with "Sin" still in his hand. "But you really should take a pen name," he said. "Especially with a poem like this."

A pen name? How, I reasoned, could I tell the truth about myself if I couldn't even call myself by my name? I knew that when women published poetry, they nearly always did so under pen names. It was as if they thought that by taking a pseudonym they could simultaneously protect and liberate themselves. Most male poets took pseudonyms as well. But writing under a false name would only make me feel like a coward.

"No," I said. "I want to publish under my own name." I hadn't planned it exactly, and despite Nasser's prediction I had little sense I'd just chosen the name and also the poem that would soon carry me into a new life.

14.

MINE WAS A COUNTRY WHERE THEY SAID A WOMAN'S NA-
ture is riddled with sin, where they claimed that women's
voices had the power to drive men to lust and distract them
from matters of both heaven and earth. Yet, when I leafed
through magazines and opened volumes of poetry, I found
that men had always described their love and their lovers
with utter frankness and freedom. For thousands of years
men had compared their beloveds to whatever they pleased,
voiced all manner of amorous petitions and pleas, and described all the states to which love delivered them. And
people read this poetry with complete equanimity. No one
screamed out in protest. No one cried, "Oh God, the foun-
dations of morality have been shaken! Modesty and purity
are about to collapse! This writer is dragging down the
morals of our youth! We're doomed to perdition!"

Because I was a woman, they wanted to silence the
screams on my lips and stifle the breath in my lungs. But I
couldn't stay quiet. I couldn't pretend to be modest or pure

or good. No. I was a woman and I couldn't speak with the voice of a man, because it was not my voice—not true and not my own. But there was more to it than that. By writing in a woman's voice I wanted to say that a woman, too, is a human being. To say that we, too, have the right to breathe, to cry out, and to sing.

❧

"Sin" arrived by post one afternoon.

For several days I'd contrived to time my visits to the marketplace in Ahwaz to coincide with the postman's arrival. As soon as I lifted the parcel and felt its pleasing heaviness, I knew what it was. I debated taking the magazine into the house, where I could read it in my bedroom, then thought better of it and headed outside. I hid the package under my shirt and hurried to the garden, behind the chicken coop. Sitting down with my back against the wooden slats of the building, I tore the parcel open and freed the journal from the wrapping. Knees drawn up, I opened the magazine and began to read. I must have been smiling as I thumbed through the pages. My eyes searched hungrily for my own name, and there it was—" 'Sin,' a poem by Forugh Farrokhzad." Then, directly above my poem, I found this editor's note:

> In this issue of *The Intellectual* we introduce a daring new poetess, Forugh Farrokhzad, a young wife and mother. In "Sin" the poetess repudiates our country's traditional strictures and confesses the explicit yearnings of her sex. With this poem, Forugh promises to be the voice of the new Iranian woman, a

spokeswoman for a new, uncensored brand of femininity.

My hands were shaking. I read the words a second time and then a third. "The explicit yearnings of her sex"? "Sin" was a sensual poem—there was no denying that—but it was neither "explicit" nor was it a confession on behalf of womankind. And what was the point of announcing my status as a wife and mother? To punish and shame me for what I'd written? If this wasn't enough, what I saw next stopped me cold. On the page opposite my poem, there was a silhouette of a woman's naked body. I turned the page and there, on the next page, beside another one of my poems, was an interview with Brigitte Bardot, along with a photograph of the actress in a bikini. She stood with her head thrown back and her glossed lips open.

Three days later, back in Tehran, I confronted Nasser. "Why did you do this?" I said, holding up the magazine to him and blinking back angry tears.

He looked at me with disbelief. "We only emphasized your daring—nothing more. No woman has ever written a poem like this, Forugh. Not even close! It was bound to attract attention. Surely you realized that when you agreed to have it published."

I threw my hands in the air. "If I only wanted to attract people's attention, I could have done it with much less effort!"

"The point is not that you have people's attention," he said. "You do, and you would have had it no matter what.

The editor's note and illustrations only announce your relevance as a modern woman writer. The only question is, what will you do with this attention now that it's yours?"

All the next week I swung from regret at having published "Sin" to a grudging acknowledgment of Nasser's justification for presenting my work in the manner he did. Eventually I reasoned that "Sin" was a testament to my efforts as a poet and also to trying for a life on my own terms. Even if I only just barely knew who I was and what I wanted, that poem was part of my refusal to be silent and small, and I wouldn't regret having written it.

That, in any case, is what I told myself as I prepared to attend a celebration for the new issue the following week. *The Intellectual* was a thriving magazine, and I knew that much of Nasser's work as its editor in chief was to cultivate relationships with other editors, writers, and arts patrons. Still, I'd been surprised by his suggestion that we attend the event together. We'd been out together in public on just a few occasions, and even then we'd only frequented places where it was unlikely he'd meet anyone he knew. The coffeehouse in Karaj, the little café by the bookshop—these places had been chosen by him for discretion as much as for their charm. This party, on the other hand, would be hosted in a large private house, and the guests would all know him well.

"You need to get out and mix with people," he told me when I voiced my hesitation. "You need to be seen out in society if you hope to have a career as a poet."

I guessed the invitation was consolation for having published "Sin" in the way he had, but even so I wasn't prepared for the ease with which he slipped his arm around my waist and led me into the gathering.

"Won't they wonder if we're together?" I whispered as we made our way toward the drawing room.

He laughed and drew me even closer. "Do you think we're the only ones here with secrets?"

At first, nervous as I was, I didn't really see anyone at all, but as we walked through darkened rooms filled with cigarette smoke and conversation, my worry quickly gave way to fascination. With their black cocktail dresses and beehives, the women resembled models from the latest European magazines. We passed a couple kissing passionately in a hallway, another caught in a heated argument by the bar. And then there was the music streaming from a record player outside. Jazz. I heard it for the first time that night and loved it at once. This, I thought, was music to loosen your limbs and quicken your heart.

I slipped my hand free from Nasser's grip and he drifted in another direction. I was halfway to the terrace when I noticed a black-haired woman in a bright-blue dress. Cinched tight at her waist, it flared out in a circle and brushed the floor. Her dark hair was pulled off her face with a scarf in the same shade of blue as her dress. She had porcelain skin and large black almond-shaped eyes, which she'd accentuated with kohl. She was encircled by several men, all of whom seemed engrossed in her conversation.

I was so busy studying the woman in the blue dress that I didn't notice Nasser until he stood behind the podium at one end of the drawing room. "Ladies and gentlemen!" he shouted over the din. After a few words of welcome, he introduced some of the honored guests: a longtime publisher of one of the city's major newspapers, a celebrated poet who'd recently returned from a visiting professorship abroad, and a celebrated novelist who looked to be a young man of no more than twenty. One by one he gestured to them and they tipped their heads in acknowledgment. Then he lifted his arm in my direction. "It's now my honor to introduce a writer whose poetry embodies the bold voice of the new Iranian woman." Leaving his place at the head of the room, he walked toward me. "Miss Forugh Farrokzhad," he announced, taking my hand. "Would you do us the honor of sharing your poem 'Sin' with us tonight?"

I stayed fixed in place, so stunned I couldn't move. Nasser hadn't so much as hinted that he wanted me to recite a poem that night, much less this one. He hadn't asked beforehand because he knew I would likely refuse, but if he asked in front of others I'd have no choice but to recite the poem for them. I felt my face redden, but how could I demur without looking cowardly? I walked toward the front of the room and took my place before the crowd. When I saw all the faces that were turned my way, I almost faltered. A camera popped and flashed. There were coughs and then silence, whispers and what I imagined was laughter, but then I noticed that the woman in the blue dress was watching me. Her look of compassion and encouragement across that room steadied and emboldened me.

I took a deep breath and began to recite the poem. My voice sounded flat and hollow even to my own ears, but I fought to keep my declamation clear and even until the last line. When I finished, many eyes had fallen to the floor. No one clapped or said a word. But then I saw that the woman in the blue dress had tipped her head and was studying me with interest. Eventually there were murmurs from the back of the room, followed by a faint, scattered applause.

Afterward, there were other recitations and readings, but I couldn't concentrate on them. All the anger I'd felt when I'd first seen "Sin" published in such a sensational way surged through me again now. I'd been such an idiot to let myself be used in this manner. I made my way to the back of the drawing room, desperate to be away from Nasser, and it was then that I came across her again, the woman I'd been studying earlier, the one in the blue dress. She was sitting on a banquette, and when she saw me, her face broke into a smile of unexpected sweetness.

"I enjoyed your poem," she said, making space for me to sit beside her. "You write very well, you know. And you're brave."

"You're very kind," I said, as I sat down next to her.

"But it's not kindness," she answered. "Your work is . . ." Here she paused, considering her choice of words. "Simple."

"Simple?" I asked, and felt my face color again. "Do you mean stupid?"

She laughed. "Not at all," she said. "I meant unaffected. Natural."

I nodded. "In that case I'll call you kind again."

She smiled again and tilted her head. "So may I kindly call you Forugh?"

"Of course."

"In that case you'll call me Leila," she said. She slid slightly closer to me. "How old are you, Forugh?"

"Nineteen."

"And from your poem I gather you're married?" When I

bristled, she said, "It bothers you that I've asked. I've made you uncomfortable with my forwardness."

"Not at all, it's only that I'm asked that whenever I'm asked about my writing," I said, remembering my encounter with the editor at *Payam* magazine.

"People treat you differently when they hear you're married. As if you don't have the right to do what you do. To write what you write."

Her directness startled me. "Yes," I answered, "that's just how it is."

She placed a hand on my shoulder and dropped her voice. "Your writing interests me, Forugh, and I think we have a lot to talk about." She reached into her pocketbook. "Would you be free to visit me later this week?" she said as she handed me a calling card. "At, say, three o'clock on Friday afternoon?"

I'd have to stay at my mother's house longer than I'd planned, but already I knew I had to accept. That I wanted to accept. Flustered, I sputtered a quick yes.

At that moment, Nasser approached with two wineglasses. Leila's eyes flicked up in recognition and she returned his greeting with a nod. She rose, plucked a wineglass from his hand, and then she was gone, a flash of bright blue and black curls parting the crowd and then disappearing into another part of the house.

"Looks like you've made something of an impression on Leila Farmayan," Nasser said after we'd both watched her make her way across the room.

"Actually, she asked me to visit her."

His eyes quickened with interest. "You're not serious?"

"What do you mean? Why shouldn't she ask me?"

"Do you have any notion who that woman is?"

I'd been so distracted by our exchange that it hadn't occurred to me to wonder. "A writer?" I guessed.

"A writer?" he said, and laughed. "No, she's not a writer, though I do remember she produced some translations years ago. French poetry, I think it was. Anyway, she's something much better than a writer, Forugh. Leila Farmayan is a Qajar heiress and also one of the city's most influential arts patrons."

Walled with stones and hedged with honeysuckle and jasmine, the garden estate stood under a canopy of plane trees. The air here was cool and redolent. I had hired a taxi to carry me up to the northern suburb of the city, and as soon as I stepped into the lane, I was glad that I hadn't taken a chance and walked instead. I would have arrived late, if I'd managed to find my way here at all.

I lingered for a moment outside the gate, then pushed it open and walked toward the house. The door was the old-fashioned type: hand-carved and painted a pale turquoise, with a gleaming brass knocker set up high. For a full minute I stood and looked at it. I'd never called on a woman before, which made me strangely shy. I straightened the collar of my dress, smoothed my skirt, and knocked. After some minutes a figure appeared in the doorway. "Miss Farrokhzad?" the woman asked, and when I said yes, she smiled and opened the door wide to let me pass. She led me through a passageway lined with ornate tiles and decorated with geraniums spilling out of antique pots, and from there we proceeded into the house. Fine paintings lined the walls.

The silk carpets shone. We passed through a spacious parlor where an entire wall had been overtaken by leather-bound books. I peered at the covers. There were many titles in French and what I guessed was Russian.

Until I met Leila, I'd never had any contact with a member of a Qajar family, the dynasty that preceded the current one. My knowledge of the clan didn't extend much beyond what I'd overheard at my father's gatherings, and that could be summed up as this: Even after Reza Shah had stripped them of their titles and much of their lands, they were still rich beyond imagining. What I saw now confirmed that and more.

Eventually we came to an exquisite courtyard that looked as cozy and inviting as a scene from a gilt-edged Persian miniature. Carpets covered the floor, and, in the shade of a jacaranda tree whose branches dripped with bell-shaped purple blossoms, there was a round silver table laden with fruits and bowls of wild mulberries and green almonds.

"You found me!" Leila called out as she saw me approach. She was sitting with her legs crossed on a *takhteh*, a wooden daybed piled with cushions, but as I came close she stood up, took my hands in hers, and smiled with genuine warmth. She was a little younger, I saw, than I had taken her to be the first time we met. That night I had thought her nearly thirty, but now I guessed her to be twenty-five at the most, and if anything I found her more beautiful. There was something so fresh and unusual about the silver clasp with which she gathered her hair atop her head and the rows upon rows of golden bangles at her wrists. She wore a red flounced skirt and a simple white tunic that fell loosely over her shoulders, and she was barefoot.

I settled onto the *takhteh* across from her.

"Well, Forugh," she said, her eyes sparkling, "you've really caused a stir."

"But what does it mean? Am I a curiosity or something more than that?"

She didn't answer right away. She took a sip of her tea and her lips lingered on the rim of her glass. "I think it's both," she said slowly. "For the moment you're a curiosity, but I do think there is, as you say, 'something more' to your writing."

"Which is what precisely?"

She leaned forward in her chair. "You've offered something in your poem that many people would not be willing to give: yourself. That's an exceptional gift."

"Not everyone shares your opinion. One of them called it"—here I searched my mind for the precise phrase I'd read in a review just the day before—"'a spurt of narcissism.'"

"These so-called literary critics of ours!" she said with a laugh. "Their stupidity is matched only by the flair with which they flaunt it!" After a pause, she leaned closer to me and said, "And, anyway, they're wrong. Your poem isn't only about you. It's about what we women feel in the act of love. What we forbid ourselves from confessing to anyone—even, sometimes, to ourselves."

"I'm beginning to wonder if it's worth it, confessing one's real feelings and experiences."

She pressed her lips together. "Think about the writers you've most admired. What has given you solace in their words? What has given you courage? I can guess that when you have been moved, it's been by a writer who has risked honesty."

As she spoke, I thought of the thrill of discovering contemporary poetry. "Yes, that's exactly what I'd like to do."

"But you've done it already, Forugh! There's an exceptional unity of form and feeling in your writing. It's a new Iranian poetry." She peeled the skin from an almond, revealing the creamy white nut at the center, and held it out to me.

I smiled and slipped it into my mouth.

"You're curious about what people think about your work," she continued. "That's understandable. But do you think reading these reviews will make you a better poet?"

"If anything it makes me worse."

"Exactly! Besides, there's no easier way to dismiss a woman's achievements than to call her dishonorable, and that, Forugh, is no less true in these uptown literary salons than it is in the most pious corners of the bazaar. They want you to regret writing anything in the first place. That's their objective. To shut you up."

"But I don't regret publishing my poems."

"Of course not! We never do regret our own accomplishments, even though we may put them off or avoid them altogether." She took a sip of tea and continued. "I have to tell you, Forugh, that I'm sick to death of all these self-appointed 'masters' mimicking the poetry of seven generations past. I'm ready for something else."

"So what," I asked, "do you think poetry should be now?"

"That's a question you'll have to answer with what you write. *How* you write." She paused to peel another almond, which she then ate. "Tell me, do you plan to publish more poems?"

"There will be three more in the next issue of *The Intellectual,* and *Khandaniha Magazine* has accepted four others." I paused. "Also," I said slowly, "I've just had an offer from a publisher here in Tehran to collect some of my poems into a new volume."

This news had come just that week. I'd wavered at the proposition, uncertain whether putting together a collection would stoke the controversy sparked by "Sin," but now my misgivings fell away and I found myself talking excitedly about the project. "I'm thinking of calling it *The Captive,*" I told Leila.

"But that's excellent, Forugh! You must send me all your future writing."

After a time, our conversation turned to her own work. Nasser had made it seem as if Leila had given up working as a translator, but I discovered that the stacks of papers on the table beside her were translations of a six-hundred-page novel by an Algerian writer, a project that had absorbed her for more than a year and was still at least a year from publication. I marveled at what I guessed were hundreds, perhaps thousands, of hours represented in those pages and at the calm, steady state of mind necessary for such an undertaking. The various other surprises of our conversation—that my poems impressed her, that she saw them as skilled, vivid, and lasting—all this had the effect of not only bolstering my confidence but also deepening my curiosity about her life. I had the feeling she lived alone and that she had an unusual degree of independence for a woman, but just how this had happened was a mystery to me.

"Forugh," she said as she accompanied me to the door at the end of the visit. We walked shoulder to shoulder, so close that I could smell her perfume, a blend of roses and something else I couldn't place. She stopped and turned to face me. "There's another reason why I asked you here. Besides your writing, I mean. You see, some lessons I've learned too late and others I haven't learned at all." For a moment she seemed to be far away, entangled in a memory, but then she returned her gaze to me. "Anyway, that doesn't matter. What I want to tell you," she said, dropping her voice to a near whisper, "is that there's a lot of speculation going around about the lover you write about in your poems."

I stiffened. "What sort of speculation?"

"Everyone's saying that 'Sin' is autobiographical, and they're dying to know the identity of your lover."

"Everyone, including you?"

She shook her head. "I don't go in for gossip, Forugh, but I think that just now you're up against more than you realize."

"How do you mean?"

"Tell me, how well do you know Nasser Khodayar?"

Later I'd marvel at my complete inability to comprehend what Leila was warning me about and why. At the time I thought she was merely telling me to guard my heart. She'd spoken to me as a woman of the world, and I was eager to match her confidence. I think I even smiled.

I saw at once that my attempt at nonchalance didn't persuade her. She pressed her lips together and her eyes darkened with worry. "Take care with him, Forugh. Just take care."

15.

"YOU HAVE TO STOP."

I was absorbed in a new book of poems by Ahmad Shamlou when Parviz entered our bedroom and issued this demand. I smoothed the cover of my book closed and lifted my eyes. He pulled up a chair next to the table, set his briefcase on the floor, and sat down.

"Stop what?" I asked.

He leaned toward me, his elbows on his knees and his hands folded together. "Stop going to Tehran on your own."

"Your mother's been talking to you again, hasn't she? Going on and on about what people think about me, what they're saying in town."

He lifted his briefcase to his lap and unclasped the lock. As soon as he drew out the newspaper and thrust it before me, my mouth fell open. There, on the front page of Tehran's leading paper, was my poem "Sin," accompanied by a picture of me and a lengthy review of my new book, *The*

Captive. Nasser had predicted I'd attract publishers, and he was right. There'd been no want of editors eager to publish my poems after "Sin." Letters came weekly, soliciting my work. Journals to which I'd been submitting work for years without any success now reached out to me for poems. Still, this was a major newspaper, with a readership that went far beyond the literati.

He slid the newspaper onto the table, smoothing the pages flat. I'd anticipated this moment. I'd even rehearsed a defense for myself, but now that the time had come to deliver it, I sank farther into the chair. I read as quickly as I could, skimming the first paragraph. "This woman," it began, "this Forough Farrokhzad, believes that it's through the basest of desires that she can liberate herself."

I couldn't stand to go past that sentence.

"Read it, Forugh," Parviz said. "All of it."

I forced myself to finish the review. The writer went on to call me "uneducated and uncouth." What people now called poetry, he claimed, was not poetry at all, and for this there was no better proof than my writing. I was a woman. I had only been educated to the ninth grade. I'd clearly read nothing of importance. But these weren't the most damning claims. "Miss Farrokhzad uses sex in her poetry to gain notoriety," the author wrote. "She is one of these women who think that by cheapening themselves like Western women they will become free. We regret that voices like hers will likely only increase with time."

I finished in a daze. I had achieved notoriety, just as Nasser had predicted, and now I'd have to pay for it.

"It's just one review," I managed to say when I finished the piece. "One review by some hateful critic—"

"But it isn't one review! You're the talk of Tehran,

Forugh! Imagine when an old classmate wrote to ask if my wife was a writer—the one writing those poems everyone's talking about—and I said, no, you must be mistaken. I told him, 'Forugh writes sometimes, she always has, but not that kind of poetry.' "

My cheeks went hot. "What do you mean, 'that kind of poetry'? What kind of poetry do you imagine I write?" When he didn't answer, I asked, "Have you even read anything I've published, or does your mother forbid you to do even that?"

"I don't need to read your poems to know your complaints against me, but did you think I've been so distracted by my happiness that I wouldn't notice what you do? Over the last few months you've sought every opportunity to leave this house." A pained look crossed his face, but he cleared his throat and continued. "When you went to Tehran all those times before, I defended you. I made excuses. I lied for you. Over and over again I said you were going to see your mother."

"I was!"

He shook his head. "But she wasn't the only reason you went to Tehran, isn't that true? And these poems you've written, they're not about me, are they?"

There was, of course, no answer to this.

Parviz pressed on. "Do you remember how you asked me on the night of our wedding if I'd wanted to marry you?"

I nodded, but I couldn't understand why he was bringing this up now. We'd been married for three years, and the memories of our early affection for each other, our flirtation, had faded long ago, overrun by the months, years, of silence, resentment, and loneliness.

"I *did* want to marry you," he continued. "Despite everything, I was glad to be married to you. All this time I've tried to understand you, but it's you who hasn't been content with the concept of marriage."

Watching him as he spoke, it occurred to me that he wasn't so different now from when we'd first met. He was as thoughtful in his manners as he had always been, and he still had the sad eyes and slight build that made him seem younger than he was. The same uncertain posture and his slightly unkempt hair. I was used to his habit of trying to calm and counsel me, but I was shocked to hear him speak now with such determination.

"Do you hate me?" I asked, my gaze on the table. It was the first time we'd spoken about the circumstances of our marriage, and now I was the one who was unable to meet his eyes.

"No," he said quietly. "I don't."

The air in the room was stifling. I crossed the floor and cracked the window open. For some moments I stood staring out at the ivy trailing the wall. "But now," I said, turning to face Parviz again, "you're asking me to stop? Stop writing, stop going to Tehran, stop—"

He raised one hand in the air, interrupting me. "If you decide to go to Tehran, I won't stand in your way."

I couldn't have been more perplexed. "You mean won't prevent me from going there alone?"

"I will not. But I also won't accept a marriage on the terms you've set up for yourself."

The surprise passed out of me, replaced by a new awareness. "Are you planning to divorce me?"

"I'm telling you what I can and cannot accept."

I drew a breath. "If we were to divorce . . ." I said slowly, setting down each word carefully. "That is, if I wanted a divorce, what would happen with Kami?"

He looked at me calmly. "I've told you I won't prevent you from going to Tehran, and I won't. And if you want a divorce I'll give you one." Until now his voice had a certain soft brokenness to it, but here his words turned decisive. "But whatever you choose to do now," he went on, "Kami will always belong here in Ahwaz."

From there everything unfolded quickly.

The scandal over "Sin" had morphed into speculation about my love life. People no longer wondered who my lover was but rather which one of my many lovers the poem memorialized. Every day some new man stepped forward with an article or interview claiming he was the one I'd written about. There was Massoud Gilani, with his boast that we'd been meeting secretly for years, which, by his calculation, meant that we'd been together even before my marriage. There was Shahriar Shekarchian, who claimed that I'd picked him up at a party one night last spring. According to Mr. Shekarchian, I had a wicked taste for champagne and poker. There was a certain middling poet who stated not only that he'd been my mentor but that our relationship had blossomed into an affair. And so the rumors spread.

The more speculation, the more attacks on my honor, the more I withdrew into myself. For a while I stopped traveling to Tehran. I think I disappointed people by not refuting the rumors, but actually it sickened me not to defend myself, and as furious as I was with Nasser, I had no plan to reveal his identity. I never mentioned his name to anyone, and so far as I knew, Leila was the only one who'd worked out the connection between us.

Then one day in July, I flipped through the pages of an issue of *The Intellectual* and discovered the first installation of a story called "Bruised Blossom." The author was listed as Nasser Khodayar. I remember thinking this was strange, since Nasser hadn't mentioned anything about writing a new story. Gripping the pages between my hands, I read faster and faster as I realized that this wasn't fiction at all. It was a story about me.

The plot was simple. A would-be poetess from the provinces travels to Tehran. Desperate to be published, she seeks out a celebrated editor and tries to seduce him. Her moods are volatile and her judgment childish, but her every move is calculated and cunning. The editor dodges her advances, but she eventually succeeds in seducing him and blackmails him into publishing her poems in his journal. The story closed with a love scene rendered in minute, near-pornographic detail.

"To be continued in the next issue of *The Intellectual*," read a note at the end.

I held the magazine in my hands for a very long time. I read it again, more slowly this time. Part of me was desperately searching for proof that this was a hoax or that I was only imagining the resemblance between the story and our affair, but it was unmistakable. Nasser had given his heroine my rope of pearls and my lipsticked smile. He'd given his character my ambition to become a writer, which came off not only as opportunistic but as grossly misguided since she had no talent whatsoever. The illustration that accompanied the store bore an uncanny resemblance to the one of me that the magazine had printed alongside "Sin." Worse than

all this, in his crude rendition of our story, Nasser had embedded dozens of lines, images, and metaphors he'd lifted
straight from my poems.

When I finished reading "Bruised Blossom," I pressed
my forehead to the page, closed my eyes, and wept. All this
time we'd been meeting, I'd been leaving behind my husband and my child, which Nasser had known, even if we
didn't speak of it. He could have guessed what it would cost
me to have our affair confirmed in print. He must also have
known I'd see the story; he knew I read every issue of *The
Intellectual*. But how long had he been plotting to reveal
his identity by writing this story? From the very moment he
suggested publishing my poem? And what else would the
next installations of "Bruised Blossom" reveal?

I wanted to shut myself up in my room, close my eyes,
and not speak to anyone, but if I didn't confront Nasser
after such a betrayal, what else would I accept? Who would
I eventually become?

I went to see him. I went the next day, still in a haze of
fury. I can't even remember how I made it there, as I was
completely unaware of anything except the necessity of
making my way to Nasser's apartment.

It was past eight o'clock when I arrived. I'd never been
to see him at this hour of the night. I climbed the stairs two
at a time, and I was breathless when I reached the second
story. Light spilled out onto the landing from his flat and I
could hear music from the apartment. I knocked on the
door. Hard.

He came to the door with a glass in his hand, his tie un-
done and his shirtsleeves rolled above the elbow. He didn't
smile or greet me. I glanced over his shoulder and into the
apartment. From the voices, laughter, and cigarette smoke,

I guessed he was hosting a party. Was that a woman's voice? I stepped forward, making to enter, but he pulled the door closed and led me by the wrist onto the stairwell.

"Why did you do it? Why did you write that story?"

"Why shouldn't I have written it?"

"It wasn't your story to tell!"

He raised an eyebrow. "Is it only your story? Does what happened between us belong only to you?" he said. He was still holding my wrist. "Is it only yours to tell in your poems, however and whenever you like?"

"But I showed you all my poems before I published them! If you objected to what I'd written, you could have said so."

"There was nothing to object to, Forugh." He was speaking to me in that slow, even way that one addresses a child. "You are free to write whatever you please. After all, I'm not your husband. I've never had any expectations of you."

It was true. He'd never laid any claim to me, but until now I'd managed to take this as proof of his feelings for me. But I didn't know him. Not at all. The realization, when it came, unmoored me. He'd learned nearly my whole life story through my poems, but in all the time we'd been together he'd told me almost nothing about himself.

Another thought streaked through my mind. "How much money did they give you?" He didn't answer, which was answer enough. He'd been offered a price and he'd taken it—it was as simple as that. Simple but also unforgivable. I wrenched myself from his grip and lurched toward him, pummeling my fists against his chest. "How much did it take to sell me out, to make me look ridiculous, to—"

He grabbed my arm, his hand tightening on my forearm. For some moments we stood together in the landing, staring at each other with an almost calm regard. I wanted to curse him, but then, before I could stop them, tears welled in my eyes. "Nasser," I said, struggling to control my voice. "Please don't publish any more of that story. I beg you!" What crossed his face in that moment was something I'd never seen from him: pity. He let go of me very quickly then. He walked toward the door and reached for the doorknob, then hesitated and turned back. The pressure of his grip had left a throbbing welt, and I lifted my hand to my face so that he wouldn't see my tears. "You don't own the stories that happen to you," he said. It was the last and also the most honest thing he'd ever say to me.

I never found out afterward whether Nasser meant to write "Bruised Blossom" from the very start—whether he'd intended all along to publish my poems and subsequently profit from them—or whether he'd made the choice to betray me only after my poems sparked such controversy.

While his intentions eluded me, there were two immediate consequences to his story's publication. First, "Bruised Blossom" undid the spell under which I'd lived for more than a year. I was furious at myself for not having anticipated Nasser's betrayal. All sorts of things became clear to me now. I'd followed his advice and accepted his decision to sensationalize my work. I'd let him make a spectacle of me, which I'd justified to myself as part of his vision for my career. But I was done with that now. In one instant I was in thrall to him, and in the next moment his betrayal, and my own stupidity in trusting him, completely ended my infatuation.

The second result was more complicated. Without the publication of "Bruised Blossom," the scandal surrounding my poems might have been confined to Tehran's literary scene. Instead, it found a much wider audience. Each installation of the serial was more salacious than the last, which boosted sales and spurred criticism. Emboldened by the public's anger over the loosening of morals under the shah's regime, especially among young women, editors were on the lookout for controversial—or, even better, inflammatory—stories about the "New Iranian Woman." The details of "Bruised Blossom" were soon repeated, but without the pretext of fiction, in a story that ran in the city's major newspapers under the headline FARROKHZAD'S SHOCKING AFFAIR. Until then the Farrokhzad name had been associated only with Colonel Farrokhzad, but it was precisely this fact that drew so many readers to the piece. The writer made much of my father's brilliant career as a colonel and his inability to control his teenage daughter. As for my writing, he dismissed "Sin" as "a parable of ruin to which the nation should give heed."

FARROKHZAD'S SHOCKING AFFAIR appeared on the front page of one of the city's most widely circulated papers, along with a photograph of me wearing a sweater that accentuated my breasts and a skirt that barely skimmed the top of my knees—a shot that I realized had been taken in the street just a week before without my knowing it. It made me uneasy to think that I was being watched. I stared at the picture for a few moments, then read the article's concluding lines:

Ms. Farrokhzad has betrayed her husband, denouncing both marriage and motherhood. She has taken up with a man who we can only hope will eventually disentangle himself from the sins into which she has led him. One can only wonder how much damage she has inflicted on her son. A mere child now, he will grow up and one day learn of his mother's shameful actions. She has left her child no legacy except the unintelligible babbling of a woman who lives only for herself and her desires. Worse, she has usurped the idiom of faith only to mock our cherished customs. These may seem like the isolated indiscretions of a single misguided young woman, but it is in this way that the finely wrought tapestry of our culture fades and frays.

It was, in short, an onerous argument against women's liberty. Laughable, yes, but also dangerous, as soon became clear. One day, when they were making their way from the marketplace back to Amiriyeh, my mother and Sanam were attacked by a gang of teenage boys in ragged clothes. The boys had given chase, cursed at them, and pelted them with stones. It was impossible to imagine how a group of teenagers could harbor such hatred toward a pair of women as old as their own mothers, which raised the more alarming prospect that they'd been dispatched by a larger organized faction. Then, not a week later, we discovered the brass knocker of the house pried loose and tossed in the gutter. A note had been hammered onto the front door with this message: "The daughter of this house is a whore."

Shortly after Parviz delivered his ultimatum, I returned

to Tehran to clear my head. That's when I learned what had happened to Sanam and my mother in the streets. What would stop these people—whoever they were—from entering the house and attacking them again, or worse? Now under siege, the house fell quiet. Except for my little sister, Gloria, my siblings had all left home. Puran lived on the other side of Tehran with her husband and couldn't easily get away, and all but one of my brothers were still studying abroad. Hassan, the old manservant, ran all the household errands now. I spent long evenings with Sanam in the kitchen, while my mother shut herself in her room or paced the hall, her hands clasped in front of her and her unbound hair hanging down the sides of her face.

I'd planned to stay a few days, but now I couldn't go back. It was too dangerous and, besides, I couldn't abandon my mother, sister, and Sanam. It was no longer possible for me to walk in the streets, even with a chaperone. I couldn't even go to the public bathhouse, so every other day Sanam would heat some water and I'd bathe at home. For once I didn't complain. At first I'd managed to shrug off worries about my own safety, but fear now seeped into the whole house, and I was loath to cause more trouble.

According to Hassan, who'd heard the news from some neighborhood gossips, the next thing to happen was that a bundle of newspaper clippings appeared on the doorstep of the Colonel's other residence. These were articles from the so-called "progressive" journals that had reprinted my poems alongside pictures of barely dressed women, as well as fundamentalist publications decrying my poems and asserting that in failing to control his daughter, the king's trusted colonel had shown the true face of the regime. Mine was a cautionary tale of lust, licentiousness, and the so-called "emancipation of women" at the cost of the nation's cultural and social decay.

Then, one day, a second anonymous note was tacked onto the Colonel's door. It read: "Silence your whore of a daughter, Colonel Farrokhzad, or one day soon you'll come home and find your house burned to the ground." The note stayed up for several hours, plenty of time for the neighbors to see it and start gossiping. I don't think he actually believed anyone would dare make good on the threat, but now his name had been sullied, and that he wouldn't stand for.

Early one morning the Colonel marched into the house in Amiriyeh and asked Hassan to summon me to his library. He hadn't set foot here for many months, yet this was as much his house as it had ever been, no matter where he now chose to spend his nights or whom he called his wife.

I found him pacing the room with his back toward me. He was still wearing the jacket of his military uniform, which told me that he didn't plan to stay long, and that whatever he planned would happen quickly. When he turned around, I dropped my eyes in deference without willing it—the habit of a lifetime, and one not easily shed.

He didn't bother with a greeting. "You've dishonored me," he said, stepping toward me and pointing his cane so that its tip nearly stabbed my chest.

It was as if two of me stood before him in that moment. One was the young girl who lived in a state of dread, fearful of his blows and harsh words. The other was a woman who had taken risks and stripped away her fear. It was this second me who answered: "And this time you can't save face by marrying me off."

His eyebrows arched up and his face reddened. "Marry you off?" He raised the cane above my head as if to strike me, but then he dropped it to his side. "It was only through my efforts that you retained some measure of dignity after that business with Parviz, and now you come back here as a wife who's been turned out by her husband."

"But I haven't been turned away by my husband! I chose to come to Tehran on my own."

"Parviz knows you're here now?" he asked with a surprised look.

"Yes."

"And he's read these things you've written?"

"He has."

"Then he's more of an idiot than I reckoned. No man would allow his wife to publish such poems. Never."

"I'm proud of the poems I've written. I'd publish them again."

"What you write isn't poetry, Forugh. It's filth. Filth and nonsense."

"What would you have me do about it now?"

"I would have you put an end to all this and return to your husband in Ahwaz."

"And if I won't?"

The words stopped him. For a moment he neither moved nor said a word. Only looked at me. "I will allow you to stay here for a fortnight—by which time the worst of this sordid business should be over," he said. "During this time you won't so much as write your name on a piece of paper or set one foot outside this house. You will stay in the *andaroon* at all times and you are forbidden to leave for any reason."

"But you can't stop me from going to see Kami—" I said, faced with real terror at the prospect. I hadn't left my son for more than a week before, and a fortnight seemed an eternity.

"If you wish to see your child, Forugh, you'll straighten yourself up and return to Ahwaz, where you can resume the responsibilities to which marriage and motherhood bind you. Otherwise—"

"Yes?"

"There is no other way."

Oh sky, if one day
I want to fly from this silent prison
what should I say to my weeping child?
"Forget about me,
for I'm a captive bird"?

I'm that candle that illuminates the ruins
with her burning heart.
If I choose darkness,
I'll destroy everything around me.

—from "The Captive"

A fortnight. Fourteen days, thirteen nights.

It must have been quite clear, when my father left the house, that something serious had transpired, but neither my mother nor Sanam chose to press me for details afterward. I'd told them that I'd come to Tehran because I needed a rest, and they continued to understand this as a temporary period, a time for me to gather my strength before returning to my husband and my son.

My mother spent most of the time in her own room, and the few times she came to check on me she was strangely calm. She didn't put up her hair, make up her face, or dress in anything but an old housedress, and she showed an uncharacteristic lack of interest in my plans. Sanam's response was much less muted. Days, she sat at the foot of my bed, her hands working her worry beads and her lips silently saying prayers. She cooked my favorite foods—thick saffron puddings, pomegranate stew, barberry rice. In the evenings she prepared pots of burning rue, circling the smoke over my forehead to ward off the evil eye. It had always made me happy, that fragrance of crackling wild rue—something to do with feeling safe and loved—but I barely noticed it now.

At night I dreamed of Kami and woke to the feeling of his body against me only to realize I was alone and back in my father's house, reaching for something that was not there. Each time I left him, it took longer for him to ease into my arms and for his eyes to lose their fear of me. How long would it be before he completely forgot me? As the days went by, loss took hold of me, and it would not let go. There were times when that loss was so great, so suffocating, that I thought I'd die of it.

Anxious, overwrought, I sprang from the bed and paced the floor. I would go back to Ahwaz, I told myself; I'd go back to my child. I told myself that if I returned I'd have a decent life. I'd have a husband who'd maybe forgive what other men would never have forgiven of their wives. Parviz hadn't divorced me, and I guessed that he would accept my decision to return so long as I consented to his terms: no more publications or trips to Tehran. The scandal would ebb, the newspapers and gossips would seize on some other story, and soon enough people would forget my name. I could make the best of my fate. I had my books, having acquired a decent reading library of my own in Ahwaz over the last few years. And I could write poems, if just for myself. I could watch my son grow up. It would be what many considered a good life, maybe even a better life than I had any right to expect after what I'd done.

But just as soon as I decided to go back, all my old worries returned—the frustration over my seclusion, my mother-in-law's disapproval, and the endless arguments with Parviz. All of it would start again if I returned to Ahwaz—again and again. How could I stop writing? And what would it mean to stop? Under all these thoughts lurked the worst fear of all: *You don't know how to be a mother. No, it's worse than that: You can't be a mother. You're incapable of it.*

I hated myself for it, but I knew I couldn't return to my life in Ahwaz. I'd tasted freedom, and my sense of the world and of myself had changed because of it. I'd learned that life was harsher, but also more varied and pleasurable, than I'd imagined. I'd traveled to Tehran on my own many times. I'd made my way through unfamiliar streets, had let the city's chaos, danger, and promise become part of me. Sure, I'd fallen for a man who'd betrayed and humiliated me, but I was making a name for myself as a poet. Writing had cost me so much, but it was also the thing that saved me, that allowed me to live. I wasn't the woman I wanted to be yet, but I was beginning to resemble her now.

And yet I'd never heard of a woman surviving away from her family, without a father or husband to protect her. It wasn't just beyond hoping; it was beyond imagining.

The longer I was confined to my room, the deeper I sank into confusion and despair. Often I wouldn't wake until afternoon or only in the night. I stared at the darkness for hours. Every night I closed my eyes and watched myself as if through a mirror, my reflection so close that I felt if I could just touch it, sleep would enfold me, but night passed into day and then again to night.

One morning something urged me to pull the linens from the mattress and pile them in the center of the room. I dropped to my knees and started to tear them with my hands. It made a harsh, ugly rip that startled me at first, but then I wanted only to hear that sound again and again. I remember looking at my shaking hands at one point and feeling that they were not really mine. They seemed disconnected from my arms, which in turn were disconnected from my body. I was unable—or perhaps unwilling—to stop myself from what I was doing. It was the work of hours, and it took all the strength I had, but evening found me on the floor, nestled among a pile of shredded bed linens. When Sanam came to the room that night, I saw in her expression what I had done. What I had become. Mad. Crazy. I closed my eyes and let her fold me into her arms. "Oh, my daughter, my darling daughter," she murmured, smoothing my hair and rocking me softly against her chest as she cried.

The fifteenth day arrived and with it the man in the lavender cravat.

I'd received no further word from my father and he'd

made no more visits to the house. How would he answer my refusal to return to Ahwaz? What would he do with me now?

I didn't have to wait long for the answer. At the beginning of September, a loud knock came at the bedroom door. Before I could rise to open it, one of my brothers entered the room. "My beloved sister," he said, greeting me with the graciousness of a stranger. He'd recently completed his university degree in Europe, and there was a certain glossiness to him now, an authority and swagger he hadn't possessed before.

Two men followed him into my room. One wore a gray suit and lavender tie and carried a small black valise. My brother introduced him as Dr. Rezayan and the man with him as his "associate."

I shuffled to my feet. I'd spent days in the room without bathing or changing, and although it was already past noon I was still in my nightgown and my hair was unkempt.

Dr. Rezayan cocked his head and studied me through heavy-lidded eyes. He took a long time just looking at me, his eyes traveling from my face to my feet and then back.

"The Colonel tells me you haven't been feeling well," he said eventually, snapping the two brass locks of his valise open, "and that you need a rest."

I remember how calm and flawless he looked, leading me to the edge of the bed, guiding me down, standing over me. I remember his gray suit and the glint of the diamond pin in his silken lavender tie. I remember the quiet in the room as he filled a syringe from a small glass vial. I remember how my brother held me against the mattress by my shoulders, firmly but without much force, because

I was so listless and weak that it took nothing for him to restrain me. I remember that in those moments no one spoke, and I remember watching the needle plunge into my arm until I swam into darkness and I remembered nothing at all.

16.

I speak from the depths of night.
From within darkness
and out of the depths I speak.
If you come to my house, dear friend,
bring me a lamp and a window
to gaze out at the fortunates,
at the ones outside.

—"The Gift"

IN ANOTHER TIME—BUT ONE NOT SO DISTANT FROM MY own—a woman like me, a woman who lost her reputation, a woman who persisted, despite various punishments, in bringing shame to her family, might have been taken to Tehran's public lunatic asylum, the *timarestan*. Built in the last century, the *timarestan* housed the city's most severely misbegotten: epileptics, opium addicts, and all those judged mentally defective or else *ravani*—psychotic. Once there, the wayward woman would've been shackled to a cot and locked away in a cell not much bigger than a coffin. Most likely she'd never be allowed to leave.

By a mere trick of fate, I wasn't taken to the *timarestan* but instead to the Rezayan Clinic. I didn't go mad there, or not for long, but my time at that clinic changed me in ways I could never undo.

The clinic stood in the lush, hilly hamlet of Niavaran, ten miles northeast of Tehran. Like other palaces built in the late nineteenth century, the main building boasted marble columns, intricately hand-painted tiles, and mirrored mosaics. Its three acres had been planned by a French landscape architect and included no fewer than four formal gardens ringed by plane and cypress trees. The shah's summer estate, with its sprawling formal gardens and grand pavilions, its hunting lodges and park of pine trees, was less than two miles away.

People had lived here once. A nobleman and his many wives and children; maids, chamberlains, houseboys, grooms, and gardeners. But that was all a very long time ago. The nobleman left for France and, except for those left to sleep undisturbed in a nearby mausoleum, his family followed. The house withdrew into itself, moldering in neglect, until one day Dr. Faramarz Rezayan, an esteemed and enterprising doctor of psychiatry, happened on the property and decided it would make a perfect home for the privileged insane.

In what had once been vast guest parlors and majestic private quarters, there would now be dormitories, communal showers, isolation chambers, examination rooms, and an operating theater. At the Rezayan Clinic, order replaced dereliction and the tortures were called "treatments," but the secrecy that governed the old *timarestan* not only survived but flourished here. From the outside, the clinic was

wholly indistinguishable from any of the other splendid
mansions in Niavaran, and, surrounded as it was on all sides
by high stone walls, its purpose was hidden from those who
passed, with no sign or other marker to betray what went
on there.

  If for some reason you should have come looking for me
at the Rezayan Clinic you would never have found me, I'm
sure of it. But let's say you somehow made it as far as the
three-foot-thick asylum walls. You can be certain that you
wouldn't have been allowed past the clinic's iron gates.
From your vantage point under the canopy of plane and
cypress trees, only the grounds would have been visible to
you, and those grounds, you would have discovered, were
not merely lovely. They were perfect.

The sky had been cut into pieces. I remember the feeling
of terror as I opened my eyes and saw the strangeness of a
blue sky sliced by thick metal bars. Images came in quick
succession—the Colonel, my brother, the man with the lavender tie—but when I tried to remember how I'd gotten to
this place, I couldn't conjure anything.

  I lifted myself up slightly onto my elbows and looked
around. The room was about ten feet square, with bare
walls and no decoration except a single ceiling light. The air
was stiflingly hot and smelled of bleach and lye, which only
intensified my nausea. A second narrow metal-framed bed
was pushed against the opposite wall. That morning it was
empty, but I could make out the impression of the body
that had lately occupied it.

  No sooner had I swung my legs over the bed than I felt

the room shimmy and tilt, and I collapsed back onto the mattress. When I finally focused my eyes, I saw that I was wearing a hospital smock. The front was smeared with fresh vomit, and I made an effort to wipe it away with the corner of a sheet, but my fingers felt strangely heavy and I soon gave up.

I stared up at the ceiling and tried again to remember how I'd come to this place, but there was something wrong with my head. I couldn't think properly.

After some time, I made a second attempt at standing up. The bed in which I found myself was covered in a plastic sheet that made a hissing sound as I shifted my legs. I discovered I could make it, if just barely, to the window. Holding the wall to steady myself, I peered outside. There was a small courtyard below with a fountain and some shrubs, but I couldn't see over the garden wall.

Legs quivering and head spinning, I staggered out of the room and made my way down a long, wide corridor. Here the ceiling was punctuated with skylights, and light fell like a soft crystal dust onto the bare tiles. My head had cleared up a little, but I thought I might be sick again. The hall was empty and still, but as I proceeded I could make out voices coming from an open door.

At first I thought I'd stumbled onto a party of some kind, but even in my strange, disoriented state I quickly understood that this was no ordinary gathering. I braced myself with one hand against the wall and looked more closely at the women in the room. A few seemed like ordinary housewives, dressed in simple skirts and dresses, but others wore hospital smocks and were extremely disheveled. They straddled stools, sprawled on couches, leaned against the walls. Some walked about aimlessly, some screamed and shouted, while still others stared into the distance. I saw an elderly woman with thickly rouged cheeks and heavily made-up eyes. I saw a girl not much older than me pacing the room in circles, swaying her hips as she went. She swept past me and for a moment her gaze fastened on mine. I saw an older woman of perhaps forty or fifty sitting on a divan with her hands folded demurely on her lap, her face fixed with an immovable smile. I saw a large woman in a purple dressing gown sitting cross-legged on the floor, rocking back and forth. Her sobs and screams garnered no reaction from any of the others in the room.

My gaze was drawn up to the ceiling. Judging from the scale, the room was, or rather had once been, a large guest parlor, but aside from a few gold-footed settees, all the chairs were plastic and had been scattered around the room so that they stood at odd angles from one another. Still, something of the room's original grandeur survived in its architectural details: the intricate woodwork along the walls, the chandelier dangling from the ceiling, the ceramic tiles set into the walls, and the five large carved doors, all but one of which was now shut.

I felt a hand grip my shoulder and then a voice say, "Forugh? Is that you?"

I flinched, swinging around to face a woman with wire-rimmed glasses, bobbed hair, and startlingly clear blue eyes. A foreigner, European most likely, but I wasn't sure from which country. She was perhaps thirty, with the slender figure of a teenager but the assured manner of a much older woman, and she wore some sort of nursing costume: an all-white ensemble consisting of a collared blouse, long flared skirt, apron, and peaked white cap.

"We didn't expect you'd be up for a while, but here you are, Forugh!"

She pronounced my name with a distinctly foreign accent, so that it ended in "k." She spoke with a clipped but not unfriendly manner, but how did she know my name? I still had no notion of how I had come to this place, and yet it was clear from the woman's familiar manner that I was known here.

I wrestled my arm away. "Where am I? Why am I here?"

At this a few of the women in the room lifted their eyes. The attention seemed to annoy the blue-eyed nurse, and she quickly linked her arm under mine and pulled me away and back into the corridor. "You've been sick, Forugh," she said when we were alone, "and you've come to stay with us so that you might feel better."

Her Persian was awkward and half the words she spoke were English, but I understood her well enough.

"I'm not sick!" I snapped, but as soon as I pulled away I felt dizzy, and without her arm to steady me I felt I would collapse. If I could just speak to her in English, if I could only keep my words clear and sensible, but I felt so sick that even in my native tongue the words came out thick and staggered. Worse, I was seized by a ferocious thirst, which I'd later realize was an effect of whatever medicine I'd been made to take.

"I don't want to stay here," I managed to say.

"But, my dear!" she said, taking my arm again and guiding me down the corridor. "You're very fortunate to have found your way to us. What is it you say in Persian? 'This is your own home.'"

Fragments of memory returned to me as she led me

down the hall. The black valise, the needle. I stopped walking and gripped her arm. "There was a man in a lavender cravat. He was a doctor, I think. . . ."

"Dr. Rezayan!" she said, her eyes brightening as she turned to face me. "But of course you would have met him already! He pays a visit to all his patients before they come to stay with us." We'd reached the room I recognized as the one I'd recently fled. "He took his degree in England, at Oxford. You're familiar with Oxford, yes?" She didn't wait for me to answer before continuing in the same breathless manner. "After obtaining his medical degree, he practiced at some of the most prominent private hospitals in Europe. I was a nurse in a clinic he directed, you see. He gave up many opportunities abroad in order to return to his homeland. It's really rather extraordinary how—"

I grasped her forearm. "I want to speak to him! I want to know why I was brought here!"

"And so you will, Forugh! But you will want to rest and shower before you meet with Dr. Rezayan. You will want to be at your very best."

She stripped off my soiled smock and pulled a new one over my head. My body was sticky with sweat, and my hair stuck to my head and my neck, but even as I perspired I felt cold and I couldn't stop shivering. Little black specks flickered before my eyes and I realized I was probably going to faint. I let the woman guide me back to the bed and pull the bedsheets over me. Then I closed my eyes, shaking miserably until sleep overtook me again.

I woke to a hand shaking me roughly by the shoulder. My eyes flashed open. The blue-eyed nurse was gone; a differ-

ent woman was standing over me. Her hair was arranged in
pigtails like a girl's, but wrinkles lined her eyes and the corners of her mouth. She wore a smock identical to mine, and
it dawned on me that she must be my roommate. Just beyond her shoulder I saw the barred window and slivers of
sky, tinged now with the blush of dawn. I rubbed my eyes
and forced myself to think, but before I could speak, the
woman pulled me up by the arm. The next moment, her
sweaty hand was in mine and we were in a brightly lit corridor, surrounded by many other women hustling down the
hall.

"Where are we going?" I asked, but her soft answer was
swallowed by the noise.

We continued down the corridor until we came to a
large chamber with a tiled fountain in the center. A bathhouse. The fountain was empty, but steam filled the room.
"My name is Pari," my companion said as she let go of my
hand. "Forugh," I answered, and fell into line behind a row
of women. Along one wall there were several open showers,
to which the women were being herded one by one. I
watched as an orderly pushed an older woman in a wheel-
chair toward the stalls, wheeled her under the spray, and
shouted, "Clean yourself!" The orderly was a large woman
with powerful shoulders and thick arms as strong as a man's.
When it was my turn to step forward, she took a long look
at me, slowly, from head to toe, arranged her mouth in a
smile, and said, "You're the poetess."

I must have looked startled then, which only increased
her pleasure in calling me out in this way.

"I've heard about you," she said. Her arms strained
against her sleeves, and there were rings of fat around her
neck. She came closer, and I was assaulted by the sour odor

of an unwashed body. "You've had an easy time, if you ask me. I'd rather see any daughter of mine in her grave than shaming herself as you've done."

For a moment she hesitated, and I realized she didn't want to touch me. In her eyes I was tainted and unclean. In the end, she seized my wrist and thrust a sliver of grayish soap and a *kiseh* into my hand. "Well, now you're here, and you'll clean yourself up sure enough."

The room started spinning again, only faster now. "I can't," I said.

"'I can't,'" mimicked the woman, then pulled me forward by the collar of my smock and yanked it clear over my head. Out of an instinct for self-protection, I tried to cover my naked breasts with one hand, my pubic area with the other. "You're ashamed of yourself now, are you?" she said, and slapped away my hands. Her breath still short from the labor of pushing me into the stall, she held me under the water and began to soap and rub me with the *kiseh*. At times her eyes looked away and at other times not, and I didn't know which was the greater humiliation. The water was scalding hot, but each time I flinched she caught me by my neck and forced me back under the stream.

That afternoon I was taken to Dr. Rezayan's private office.

He sat behind a large lacquered desk, cradling the phone with one hand and writing with the other. His charcoal-gray suit was immaculate, his tie the same delicate purple shade of my memories. My body still remembered to fear him, but there was nowhere to go. I reminded myself to breathe and to keep my face arranged in a serene expression as I scanned the room.

We were alone in what looked like a gentleman's study. The room was vast—many times larger than the other rooms I'd so far seen. From the plush silk carpets to the fully stocked library and immense, gleaming desk, the room stood in stark contrast to the shabbiness of the rest of the clinic. Here everything was perfect—gleaming and grand.

I turned my attention back to Dr. Rezayan. His eyes were hazel, he had a straight, narrow nose, and his top lip was slightly fuller than the bottom one. If it weren't for his perfectly accented Persian, I would have mistaken him for a foreigner.

A clock drummed away in the corner of the room and a bird sang from the tree outside the open window. I shifted awkwardly in my chair. After the bath, I'd been made to wear a plain long-sleeved dress, and my hair had been clipped back from my forehead with metal barrettes. They were digging into my scalp and itching terribly now, but I sat still, with my hands folded on my lap.

"Doctor, I don't want to be here," I said when he finally looked up from his desk. My only chance, I told myself, was to speak in a measured and clear manner. To be sensible and calm. "I want to go home."

For a moment he peered at me as if I were a puzzle he was seeking to solve, then he said, "When you are better, Forugh, you will be able to return home."

"Better?"

"Calmer."

"I'd like to see my father," I blurted out, thinking that since my father had sent me to this place, he could also get me out. Perhaps if he came to visit me, if he could see what it was like here, he would take me away.

That hope was immediately dispelled. "The Colonel

wants you here in our care," he said, adding, "To keep you from harm."

He reached for a pad of paper and began to make a few notes. For a moment my eyes strayed to the books on the shelves—they looked to be medical texts, mostly in English but a few in French. Numerous framed diplomas decorated the walls, all of them in foreign languages and stamped with ornate golden seals.

"Does my husband know I'm here?"

"Indeed. Both he and your father have consented to your admission and treatment."

"Can I write him a letter?" I asked, watching his pen move across the page.

"I don't advise it," he said, setting down his pen and paper to look at me. "Not in your present condition."

"My condition?"

"You're agitated, Forugh. You're disturbed." He uncrossed his legs and leaned forward. "I'm told," Dr. Rezayan continued, lacing his fingers together on the desk, "that you're often in the streets, that you go out at night alone. Unaccompanied."

"And that's why I've been brought here?"

"You do realize that if you persist in such behaviors you could be molested or hurt?"

"But I haven't been—"

He cut me off. "I understand you have a son," he said, walking around the table to stand close to me. "That you are a mother."

Was it the panic in my eyes that showed him? Was it my stammer when I asked if I could see Kami? Something in that moment told me he'd found my weakness, and he wouldn't let it go now.

"Would you really wish for your little boy to see you as you are?"

I looked away.

"You do know, Forugh, that you're not well enough to take care of your son. You know that I'm right?"

I didn't answer.

"Perhaps," he continued, "it will help you to know that your condition is a disease of the body. You see, all mental disorders originate in the body, in this case the brain. Really they're no different from physical diseases. No different at all."

"And if this is true," I said, raising my gaze, "that I'm sick in the way you describe, what can be done for me?" My voice was shaking, not from fear now but from anger. My resolution to stay calm had deserted me and I felt capable of violence, of striking or biting or scratching him. "Is my 'condition,' as you call it, something for which you have found a cure?"

"There are indeed interventions for someone with your . . ." He paused, measuring his words. "Needs," he said finally.

"And if I don't want to be treated?"

He lifted his chin, drew a long breath, and then looked at me squarely. "Your father has put you in my care," he said. "When you are calmer, perhaps you'll have visitors. Maybe you'll even be able to see your son. All this depends on your cooperation. And you will cooperate, won't you, Forugh?"

After a lunch of watered-down kidney bean and beef stew, Pari and I filed back into our room and the lock was bolted shut behind us. Steel-gray bands fell from the barred window across my bed and down the bare tiles. I looked over at Pari. Her eyes were large and restless, and she had a nervous habit of working her lips into a pout and then relaxing them. She sat cross-legged on her bed, unbraiding and rebraiding her pigtails. That hair, its thickness and luster—it was clearly her pride.

"How long have you been here?" I asked.

She stared at me blankly, then looked away. I thought she hadn't heard me and so I repeated my question.

"Been where?" she asked dully.

I didn't ask her again, but after a few minutes she began to speak. "I used to play the piano," she said as she twisted locks of hair between her fingers. "I learned when I was very small. Bach, Rachmaninoff, Mozart. Before they made me stop, I could play anything." For a moment her expression was bright and her face opened in a smile. She dropped a braid, let it fall and loosen on her shoulder. When she held up her hands for me, I saw that they were mottled with brown spots but her fingers were indeed long and tapered in the way I imagined a pianist's would be.

"Who made you stop playing?" I asked.

A strange expression crept across her face, and her hand wandered to her throat. "The tongues," she said, her eyes fixed on a point in the distance. "One day instead of black keys there were rows of tongues on the piano." Her eyes flashed to me, she leaned forward slightly, and she asked, "Can you guess who they belonged to? The tongues?"

I shook my head.

"*Deev!*" she said with strange excitement. "They were demons' tongues!" She moved again, this time returning to her cross-legged position. She explained that whenever she sat at the piano, a demon rose from the keys to pull her deep into its belly. She told me this part of the story casually, as if it were something she'd heard someone say somewhere, a story that had nothing to do with her, but when she finished she said, "Do you believe me, Forugh?"

I tilted my head and studied her. Her expression had changed and she now looked fearful, haunted. She started braiding her hair again, only more furiously. "I don't know," I said. "I mean, I'm not sure I believe in devils and all that . . ."

Her face fell but her fingers continued to fret her braids. It was clear I'd disappointed her, but I didn't know what else to say. Silence closed over us.

Then, in the late afternoon, when thin rays of sunshine shone through the window, I tried to coax her out of her restless trance. "Sit in the sun with me," I told her, patting my cot and gesturing for her to take a place beside me.

"Don't you know that demons enter your head through the sun?" she answered, though she lifted her eyes and laughed as she said it.

❦

Years later I'd hear that the mansion's original owner, the Persian nobleman who'd long since left Iran, made his mark on the village of Niavaran. Sometime in the 1920s he commissioned hundreds of wrought-iron streetlamps to be brought over from France, and ever since then the narrow, winding roads of the village had been graced by the same faintly green glow of Parisian boulevards he'd admired on his European tours. I'm not sure the story was true, but my memory of the Rezayan Clinic would always be wedded to the green-tinged sky I saw on nights when I stood in bare feet by the window, too beaten down and too frightened to imagine I'd ever again be free.

In my first days at the clinic, I would sink into memories of Kami and weep for hours. All I could think about was how I could get back to him. Nothing mattered but figuring out how to leave this place. I thought if I paid attention to the patients who were told they were getting better, the ones who'd likely soon be discharged, I would be able to figure out how to get myself free. I noticed that the best-behaved patients always took their pills and spent their days in a state of mute torpor. That's what I had to do to free myself, I thought: not fight back. Instead, I'd pretend to be obedient, pleasant, and calm.

At night the nurses floated from room to room with trays full of pills. Large white pills that always got stuck in my throat, tiny orange pills that blurred my vision and set my hands shaking, red pills for sleep—a true mercy in this place—oblong pills, round pills, bitter pills, sugar-coated pills, pills without a hint of flavor: I took them all. Mornings I jerked awake, sweaty and shivering; by noon I was dim and disoriented. Nights I fell into a thick sleep from which only more pills could release me.

Eventually I learned to hold the pills under my tongue and then spit them into the toilet when no one was looking. I spent days in my room, where I turned to the wall and began silently reciting all the poems I knew. At first I couldn't remember anything—the poems were gone, and nothing, not even a line, remained—but then the verses rose up like a silent chant. I'd have to hold fast to them or they'd disappear again.

But gradually I came to understand that I was here precisely because my father had sent me away and that there was therefore no home to which I could return. I'd reached a place where I was no longer a wife or even a daughter but a child. No one would come and take me away. At this realization, my temper flared. It was no use trying to be good—it simply didn't matter. So whatever the nurses demanded, I refused to do. I stayed awake when they told me to go to sleep. I wouldn't eat and I wouldn't speak. I spat out the pills they forced into my mouth. I sat in my small dark room and refused to come out, not even when the others walked in the garden in the late mornings, even though I knew I'd cry for joy if I felt the breeze on my skin or saw the sun again.

At the Rezayan Clinic I learned there are many types of madness. Pacing, ambling, running, and wandering—I was surrounded by women who couldn't be still. Even in the night they paced in their rooms and banged against the walls. From behind my door I could hear the shuffle of their feet and their voices calling, screaming, singing, and crying to themselves. Others sat in a stupor, their eyes glassy and dull. I learned that their stays at the clinic—and also my own—were described as "holidays."

As if we'd all come here to enjoy the gentle climate of the northern foothills. As if we could rest and this was a place where rest could be found.

She was always there, the girl. Her breath, her footsteps—soon they sounded louder to me than my own. She was a girl I'd seen in the parlor on my first day in the clinic, the one who always walked with a flirty swing to her hips.

Wherever I went, to the common room, to the toilet, to the bathhouse, she followed me with that walk, though she never spoke to me, not a word.

This went on for days. I tried to ignore her, but one day I couldn't stand it anymore. "Go away!" I shouted. She lunged forward and her hands went to my face. Her nails dug into my cheeks, and with all my force I pushed her back and away from me. She lunged toward me again, and this time I bit her in the neck, breaking the skin so that blood began to flow in a thin trickle down her throat.

The girl gave a long, loud cry. Two orderlies sprang into the corridor and pried us off each other, yanking me by the hair and pinning my arms behind my back. The girl stared at me, her eyes huge but also strangely calm. Blood streaked down her neck and onto the collar of her dress. Her hands went to the wound on her neck, and then she held her hands to her face. There was a tenderness with which she regarded the blood—a quality of complete absorption— and before I was carried away I saw a small smile play on her mouth.

There are rooms in this world where you can scream until your voice grows hoarse and eventually dies. One curse or one pinch and the nurses take you into the deepest reaches of the asylum, into a room without windows or fresh air. Isolation.

Here you have a small metal bowl for drinking water and a toilet with rusted pipes and a mildewed string. A single lightbulb encased in plastic in the center of the ceiling. Nothing else. You lie down on the ground and press your cheek against the cold tiles. You entertain yourself with all the stories you remember, with the pattern of the tiles, with the rhythm of your own breath. You say your name over and over, as if such incantations might return you to yourself.

Hours pass. Days.

In a room like this you watch yourself from a distance. A thin glass wall separates you from yourself, but you won't be able to make your way to the other side. You are divided. Split. Sometimes this feels like true freedom, to be so unburdened from what you once were; other times it will terrify you. At certain moments you recognize the ridiculousness of your situation. You'll begin to laugh, then to cry, and sometimes you'll do both at once.

You are a woman alone in a room. You've always been here; you've never been here. Which is it?

When you're finally released from this room you'll be told you can't read any books and you can't write any poems because your brain is sick. You're told that reading and writing will make you sicker. If you can even form a thought after all the tranquilizers you're made to swallow in the morning, at noon, and in the night, you're told you must stop yourself from thinking, because it's thinking that landed you here in the first place. But it's impossible. You want to stop thinking but you can't.

You are a woman who's been disowned by her father and cast out by her husband, a woman whose son knows her less each day and very soon won't know her at all. You are a woman living in a room with locks for which you have no key, with windows that cut the sky. You are one of many women, young and old, who've been turned out of their homes for reasons you'll never really know, much less understand, and like them you've been shut up behind the walls of a mansion in a district famous for its fresh air and the genteel glow of its French-imported streetlamps.

And beyond this there are other rooms still. One day Pari showed me a room where no one ever came out. "There are things that happen here, Forugh. Bad things. Sometimes they come at night and take you like they took her."

"Took who?" I asked softly. Pity, not curiosity, spurred me to ask her to tell me more. I thought her tortured mind had conjured this story and that if she could take me to this place and I could show her that it was not frightening, it would calm her nerves. "Who did they take, Pari?"

She dropped her eyes and didn't answer.

"Please show me where they took her," I said, linking her arm with mine.

The clinic was a dark, rambling place, with long passages and unexpected chambers. We were quiet as we slipped from the ward, even quieter as we climbed to the second story and then to the third floor. Pari gripped my arm as we mounted the steps together. At the end of the corridor we came onto an open door. Together we peered inside.

"There," said Pari, and lifted her hand in a small wave. In a corner of the room, a woman sat on a chair. Her hands were on her lap and her legs were crossed at the ankle. On her head she wore a brightly patterned kerchief that stood in strange contrast to her gray smock and the neglected and stifled look of the room. Though we were less than ten paces away, the woman gazed at us as if she didn't see us at all.

"Who is she?" I whispered.

Pari shrugged, her eyes still pinned to the figure in the

room. "Her room was across from mine. I saw her some-times in the bathhouse. She cried a lot, but she was . . . nice."

"What happened to her?"

Blinking nervously and working her mouth, Pari said, "They took her away. It was early in the morning, when everyone else was asleep. They took her away and they shaved her head. Told her to close her eyes. She closed her eyes. Told her to sing a song. She sang a song."

"And then?"

"They drilled a hole in her skull and then they started cutting the sick part of her out with a knife. 'Keep singing,' they told her. She sang as long as she could. When she stopped singing, they knew it was done and then they stopped."

The woman inside the room gazed ahead in a still, unset-tling way. She was so close and yet oblivious to our pres-ence. "The nurses talked about it later," Pari continued. Her voice was smaller now. "Late at night. That's how I know what happened. She couldn't walk or talk after what they did to her. Just stared at the wall and picked at the bandages on her head. Her hair was brown when she first came here, but it grew back in patches, some white and others black, and then one day the nurses started covering her head. Not because it bothered her. No. Because it bothered them." Her eyes darted across my face. "Do you believe me?"

It didn't make sense, not exactly, but when I felt Pari's hand slip into my own, I gripped it and whispered, "Yes."

She nodded, then continued with the story. "She was empty. Gone. A long time passed like that. Then a strange thing happened. Her husband came to visit her. She hadn't spoken or shown a reaction to anything for weeks, but when she saw him she sprang to her feet and bit his finger right through to the bone. He didn't come again after that, and then they took her out of the ward and moved her here."

"She never leaves this room?"

Pari shook her head.

Suddenly it seemed wrong to watch the woman anymore. I dropped my eyes to the floor, only to look again. "And no one comes to visit her?" I asked.

"Nobody knows she's here."

One day, not long after this exchange, I returned to my room after bathing and found a newspaper on my bed. It had been folded to a photograph of me, the same one that had accompanied FARROKHZAD'S SHOCKING AFFAIR. "Rumor has it that Ms. Forugh Farrokhzad has gone insane," the article read. "Let's pray this is only a rumor, or that she'll soon recover, but woe be to the daughters of Eve who spurn God's will and take up their pens to write. This is the fate that awaits them."

I sank onto the bed and read the piece through to the end. My marriage, my writing, my affair, my comings and goings between Tehran and Ahwaz—every detail was explained as an essential part of the story of my madness.

I kept the newspaper, folded it neatly into one square and then a smaller square, and then I hid it under my mattress, just as I'd once hidden poems as a girl. It was a cruel, hateful piece of writing, but it was also proof—my only proof—that people knew I was still alive.

17.

IMMODEST. IMPETUOUS. DISRUPTIVE. DEPRESSED. SLOV-
enly. Excitable. Impertinent. Dishonest. Obsessive. Secre-
tive. Erratic. Nonsensical.

Some ten years later, in an attempt to make sense of that
time of my life, I acquired the medical records from the
weeks I spent in the Rezayan Clinic. It was a thin file, held
together by a rubber band, and in its pages I met the
cramped but meticulous handwriting of Dr. Rezayan for the
first time. They were terse entries, none longer than a paragraph. His notes from our first meeting, on September 5,
read:

> The patient admits to having left her husband and
> infant son on many occasions. She indulges delu-
> sions of pursuing a literary career and shows no in-
> sight into her present condition or the consequences
> of her actions for either herself or her family. Her
> behavior has been more stable since her admittance,

although she is still rather high-strung. She has an arrogant attitude and appears to live in a fantasy. The clinic has obtained copies of the patient's writings, and upon careful review these documents support the conclusion of a disordered mind.

I was struck by both the brevity of the entry and its assuredness. At the time of its composition Dr. Rezayan had seen me on two occasions, the day he came to my father's house and the day he interviewed me at the clinic. Each occasion had lasted less than fifteen minutes.

Riffling deeper into the file, I encountered a medical certificate. Under a column dedicated to NATURE OF ILLNESS, I read the words "mental defectiveness." I read this calmly—almost without feeling—but when I came to the section denoted PROPOSED COURSE OF TREATMENT, I felt my heart drop. There, in the same terse hand, was written "electro-shock."

It always began with the blinking of a red glass bulb set into the wall. A red light blinking and shapes shifting in the darkness, then the smell of rotten eggs mixed with the smell of bleach.

I was taken away early one morning by two men in white smocks and white trousers. In all the time since I'd come to the clinic, I hadn't seen any men apart from Dr. Rezayan, and many days had passed since then. One of them grabbed my shoulder and gave it a rough shake. They marched me to a part of the clinic I hadn't seen before. The pills made me sleepy and I had no fight in me. We continued to the end of the corridor, past the bathhouse. The rooms were silent now, the faucets still, the only sound the slap of my rubber slippers and the men's heeled boots against the tiled floors.

"Miss Farrokhzad," came a voice as I was led into a dimly lit room.

Another man in a white smock. It took me a moment to realize it was Dr. Rezayan, as I had never seen him without his suit and lavender tie. I was lifted onto a high table, and the men tied my arms and my legs to the bed. The blue-eyed nurse appeared and snapped on a pair of black rubber gloves. She smeared a gel on my temples, and I remember watching her hands with a slow fascination. I remember my gown sliding up my bare thighs, the heaviness of the restraints at my wrists and ankles, the nearly tender smile with which the nurse readied me for what would come next.

The red light pulsed on and off. From the corner of my eye I saw a pair of long metal clamps, and then I heard the snap of the rubber against my head. Fear shot through the fog and all at once I was awake. But it was too late. When I opened my mouth to scream, a piece of black rubber was thrust between my teeth. The blue-eyed nurse bore down on me with her hands, pushing my legs against the table. I heard a strange clanging noise, and then a steady electric whine started up from somewhere behind me. The red lamp blinked on and off frantically, the first jolt of electricity ripped through my skull, and the room filled with the scent of my body's burning.

That night I witnessed my own burial. In my dream I was lowered into a grave and covered with soil. The dark squelching earth shifted and heaved around my body; dirt filled my mouth and worms crawled over me; the hairy roots of the trees encircled my neck and entangled my arms and my legs. I jerked about, desperate to free myself, but with each movement I only buried myself deeper into the earth, deeper into death and decay. Then the dream changed. All at once there was no earth, no worms or roots, only my body caught in a vast white expanse.

I woke to sheets wet with perspiration, my gown twisted in my legs, and four pairs of bright red welts encircling my wrists and my ankles. I was gasping for breath. Pari was gone, though it would be days before I registered her absence. The first effects of the treatment—anxiety and jitteriness—only confirmed the need for more treatments. Whatever my reaction, stupor or violence, it ensured only more-frequent sessions of shock and heavier doses of pills. That dream burial came again and again, haunting me all day and flooding me with dread. Too scared to even close my eyes, I lay in bed, the shock reverberating through my bones. I studied the walls, the textures of light, the now-constant trembling and twitching of my hands.

"You're better," the blue-eyed nurse told me with the gentle smile reserved for the insane. "Much calmer. Much more at peace," she said, patting my hand. "It won't be long now until you're well enough to go home."

Home? The word snagged in my mind. Did she mean back to Ahwaz or to the Colonel's house in Tehran? I had no idea.

I couldn't rid myself of my nightmares, but I'd lost my memories. I didn't remember the treatments. I simply had no recollection of what had been done to me or even of how many days had passed since I'd been brought to the clinic. Faces that were familiar to me—Pari's face, the face of the blue-eyed nurse—became unrecognizable. Worse, I could remember hardly anything from the time before I'd been brought here. I forgot that I'd been married and that I'd left my husband. I forgot the words to every poem I'd ever learned, including the ones I'd written myself. I didn't forget Kami—something in me held him fast—but for a time I did forget his face and, I think, even his name.

When my memory started coming back, with it came the worry of where I would go if I were ever released. Not long after the shock treatments began, I received a letter from one of my older brothers—a short, cold letter, asking and admitting nothing but stating that I should be grateful for his help. "I am sorry you have been ill, sister," my brother wrote. "I am pleased to know, however, that you've made such good progress in these last few weeks. I have spoken with Parviz and he does not forbid your return. It has been difficult to prevail over his mother's objections, particularly after so long a separation, but I am hopeful you'll be able to return to Ahwaz whenever it's determined that you've fully recovered."

I pushed away my thoughts of home and turned my attention to one question: Who else besides me was getting shock treatments? It suddenly felt very important to figure it out. Maybe if I knew that, I could figure out how to make it stop. At first I thought only the women who caused trouble were punished, the ones who cried at night or screamed in the halls, but then I saw it was also the women who never spoke. I knew it from their hands. The woman who painted her eyelashes with thick coats of mascara, two circles of rouge on her cheeks, and the bright pink lips of a doll—she got them, too. Limbs could be still or restless, expressions mild or anguished, but we all had the same shaking fingers.

Apart from the time I bit that girl, I hadn't been violent, but one day I thrust my hand between the metal bars and punched through the window of my room. I didn't feel the pain, not when the glass shattered and not when shards cut my hands. I wanted to see the sky. That day I was taken to the chamber to be stripped of my gown and confined for two nights in the isolation chamber, the only torture worse than shock. After that I learned not to scream, because when I screamed they came with their needles, their pills, their restraints, and by then I knew it was better to hide my fear than to cry out.

One day in October, just after two o'clock in the afternoon, two women slipped through the gates of an old mansion in Niavaran and into a car parked under the shade of the plane and cypress trees. One wore a blue coat draped over a plain white nightgown, the other a green silk dress and high-heeled shoes. They walked shoulder to shoulder, arm in arm. When they reached the courtyard, the one in the nightgown looked up at the sky, shading her eyes and working out the last time she'd seen the sun.

Most of my memories of the Rezayan Clinic would return to me as memories often do: splintered and strange. Others I'd lose forever. But my memory of the day Leila came for me would always be whole, perfect, and true.

She appeared at the foot of my bed one morning. I was alone in the room—Pari was gone and I hadn't been assigned another roommate. Leila leaned toward me and smoothed her gloved hand over my forehead. I woke to her dark eyes watching me. I had the feeling she'd been standing there for some time. It must have startled her to see me so changed—my puffy face, my bloated stomach—but when she spoke she said only, "You're leaving this place today. I've arranged everything, Forugh."

She pulled open the closet and found it bare except for one skirt and a pair of shoes. I was drowsy, my movements heavy and slow, and when I stood I had to lean on her arm to steady myself. When she saw that the zipper on the skirt wouldn't close, she pulled the skirt off and hung it back in the closet. She took off her coat and dressed me in it, pulling my arms through the sleeves and straightening the collar for me. Next, she placed my shoes before me. When I stepped into them they felt strange on my feet—tight and bulky. Leila took a comb from her purse and pulled it through my tangled curls, unloosened her scarf from her neck, and used it to tie my hair back in a low ponytail. All this she did with a quiet and sure touch.

When she finished dressing me she took my arm, hooked it under hers, and led me from the room. In the hallway, a few of the women lifted their eyes to watch us as we made our way down the hall together. When we passed her, the blue-eyed nurse looked up for an instant, then turned quickly away. I was sure someone would try to stop us, but no one did.

Outside, the light was so bright I had to squint. I lingered for a moment by the door, staring at the mottled yellow leaves at my feet. Later I worked out that I'd been at the clinic for a month, though at the time I couldn't have said if days or years had passed. That morning all I knew was that I'd missed the first days of autumn. The plane trees were bare, and it wouldn't be long before the year's first snowfall. I threw a glance over my shoulder for one last look at the clinic, but Leila pulled me away, gently but insistently. I followed her. We'd met only twice before this day, but I never questioned the conviction in her voice when she said, "I've arranged everything, Forugh." She drew me close, and I bent toward the balm of her voice. I had no idea how she managed to secure my release or where she'd take me from here, but it didn't matter. My brain still hummed from the force of the electric shocks, the terror of the isolation room, and the vast quantity of tranquilizers and sedatives, but I wasn't too far gone to know that by taking me away, she was doing something no less astonishing than saving my life.

PART THREE

Reborn

18.
_____

I'll greet the sun again.
I'll greet the stream that flowed within me,
the clouds that were my tallest thoughts,
the aspens in the garden
that endured seasons of drought with me,
the flock of crows that brought me
the scent of the fields at night,
my mother who lived in the mirror and
reflected the face of my old age,
the burning womb
my lust has filled with green seeds.
I'll greet them all again.

—from "I Will Greet the Sun Again"

YEARS AGO, WHEN SPRING CAME TO TEHRAN, THE GYPSIES walked down from the mountainside with their arms full of branches from the white mulberry trees. Even the little ones came with the branches balanced on the tops of their heads or clutched against their chests. The gypsies had black eyes and wore bright patterned kerchiefs and flounced skirts that skimmed the ground. Their feet were always bare. The mulberries they brought down from the mountains were sweet, round, and hard. When people in the city saw the gypsies approach from the distance, they went down to the street to greet them, and the longer and more bitter the winter, the greater people's delight in their return. From street to street, alleyway to alleyway, everyone pressed fat coins into the gypsies' palms because it was the New Year, the time for generosity, forgiveness, and hope.

When spring came that year, anybody passing through Tehran would have looked up toward Mount Damavand and seen it, the promise of a new beginning. The meadows in the foothills were thick with poppies, tulips, and hyacinth; the plane trees were heavy with new leaves; the winds that came down from the mountains cleared the smoggy air. I'd lost my husband, my son, and, very nearly, my life. All that was left, the one thing that survived, but also the thing that pulled at me most fiercely, was my desire to write. I was sad and I'd never be rid of my sadness, but I wasn't frightened anymore.

❦

"Here we are," said Leila as she led me into the room.

After we left the Rezayan Clinic together, Leila drove me to her house. She'd prepared a room for me across the hall from her own bedroom. It was a small but bright room with a wooden platform bed, a chest of drawers, a small desk, and a chair. In an armoire I found a new green silk dressing gown and a pair of matching slippers; soon a row of pretty dresses, blouses, and skirts would hang there, too. From the window I could see past the walled garden and over the trellises and trees. Beyond that, there were mountains.

That first night, Leila stayed with me until I fell asleep. When I opened my eyes again, it was completely dark. I made my way to Leila's room, where I stayed awake long enough to hear her tell me I'd been sleeping for two full days, and then I fell asleep again.

One afternoon, when the pills finally began to wear off and I started to feel stronger, Leila took my arm and walked me through the house, showing me all the rooms one by one, from the parlor to the kitchen, until we reached the library. I followed her inside. Books were everywhere, spilling off side tables, heaped in stacks on the couch, piled in every corner.

I could feel her looking at me as I took in the room. "I hope you'll be comfortable here," she said. "The bathroom is just down the hall. My housekeeper will come down in a little while, and if you're hungry or thirsty you can ask her to bring you something. I'll be back at four, sooner if my appointment ends early. All right, Forugh?"

I nodded. "This is perfect," I said. "Thank you."

I sank into a leather armchair by the window, and for a long time I just listened to the quiet. The only sound was the soft breeze brushing against the windows. This was a different silence from the Rezayan Clinic. There the silence was oppressive and heavy with terror and pain. Here the silence was pleasing; it soothed me, eased my fears.

"Hungry?" said Leila when she appeared in the doorframe later on, stretching her arms above her head with the lush movements of a cat. I wondered why a servant didn't prepare her meals, but as soon as she struck a match to the stove it became clear how much she loved to cook. I watched her from my perch on a kitchen stool. The shelves were piled high with bowls and pitchers, jars of honey, herbs, and spices, along with jugs of wine. From time to time she looked over her shoulder to make a point or to gauge my response to some story she was telling. I felt shy in her presence, and mostly I was quiet, listening and watching her.

Dinner was a simple meal of whitefish and a rice pilaf with fresh herbs. I devoured two plates. It was strange to be waited on, but Leila did it so offhandedly, with so little ceremony, that it seemed like a natural extension of our conversation. Afterward, we sat cross-legged beside the fire, and then, with each of us cupping a large glass of sugared tea in our hands, she told me something of her history.

"My father was a Qajar prince," Leila began. "One year he went south to put down an uprising on his family's ancestral lands. When he came back, he brought my mother as his new bride." She tucked a cube of sugar into her mouth, took a sip of tea, and continued. "He was sixty-three, husband to nine wives, father to several dozen children, and his father's heir. She was a thirteen-year-old, black-eyed, olive-skinned Bakhtiari girl from the provinces."

As she spoke, I looked around the room. The brightly colored knotty wool carpets, the two thick rows of gold bangles on her wrists, her bare feet and mass of dark curls—I now understood that all this had come to her through her mother's tribe.

"What was she like, your mother?"

"Sweet-tempered and quiet, but brave in her way. When the other wives snubbed her, she didn't make a fuss. She always did as she pleased and gave me freer rein than the other girls. My brother, Rahim, and I were the only twins in the harem. I made a pet of him when we were little. He followed me everywhere, which was a problem when the time came for him to begin his studies."

"Why was that?"

She smiled. "Whenever a tutor came for him, Rahim refused to leave my side, so I just went along with him. I think I learned more than he did—I definitely enjoyed the lessons more, especially the poetry lessons. There was a period of time—about a year—when I copied all of Sa'adi's poems by hand. My father's other wives thought it was ridiculous, educating a girl as if she were a prince, but I think it pleased my mother to shock the older pious wives."

"And your father indulged her in allowing you to study?"

"In a way. He was so old by then that he barely noticed what she was up to. And then, when we were thirteen, he died." She hesitated, furrowing her brow. "My mother passed away a year later. She was quite young. It didn't make sense. It still doesn't." She shook her head slightly, and I saw that the pain was still alive in her. She cleared her throat and continued. "Rahim was sent abroad to boarding school. It seemed cruel, sending him so far from home, but the family had decided, and there was nothing for it."

"What did they decide for you?"

"Marriage," she said. "What else?"

"And did you marry?"

She shook her head. "No, though I suppose I wanted to get married, or at least be courted. The trouble was that none of my father's wives took much interest in arranging my marriage. For one thing, they had their own daughters to worry about. Anyway, a year went by, then another . . ."

"How did you wind up living here?" I cleared my throat and added, "On your own?"

"Well, I'd never felt close to my father's other wives, and with my mother gone and Rahim in England I was truly on my own. When we turned eighteen, my brother and I came into some money. Mostly it was his money, but . . . well, that's a story for another time. Anyway, he also inherited this"—she gestured to indicate the house—"and since he doesn't have any use for it, here I am."

She took a last draft of tea and then explained that when she didn't stay in the palace compound and instead chose to move away—and without first taking a husband—her family called her selfish and impudent. For a woman to live alone was a bold decision, one without precedent. Leila's behavior galled them; her answer was to ignore them. She was so preoccupied with her translations and her literary causes that she barely registered their disapproval, which amounted to her most audacious rebellion.

"I could live for them or I could live for myself," she concluded. "The choice wasn't hard."

I wanted to ask her more questions about her life, but for the moment I settled for asking how long she'd lived in the house.

"Eight years."

"It's a very beautiful spot."

"Yes. It still feels like a village in this part of Tehran, doesn't it?"

I nodded. The remoteness of her property had struck me the first time I'd called on her, but I saw the advantages of this more clearly now. If you wanted to live on your own and had the means to do it, this was just the sort of place you'd choose for yourself.

She poured us each a fresh cup of tea, and I realized it was my turn to speak. I had the feeling Leila knew or could guess much of what had happened to me in the last year—there'd been so much written about me in the papers, and even if much of it was nonsense, some parts were undeniably true. But where should I start?

"I left my husband," I said. Then, after a moment, I added, "And my child."

"Yes," she said softly. "I'd heard as much, but I didn't know how much to put down to gossip." She leaned toward me, placed a hand on one of mine, and closed her fingers over my hand. "Tell me how it happened."

For a moment I hesitated, but then I cleared my voice and began to speak. I told her everything, about my marriage and separation from Parviz, about Nasser's betrayal and Parviz's refusal to let me see Kami if I didn't stop writing and return to Ahwaz. I described the Rezayan Clinic and what had happened to me there.

She was the first person to whom I confided absolutely everything. It took a long time to tell her my story. Sometimes I hesitated. At one point, when I spoke about Kami and the pain of missing him, I had to stop. Leila quietly slipped into the kitchen, returning with a bowl of white mulberries. She listened without judgment, asking a question now and then, but mostly she just let me speak, and when I couldn't speak she was also quiet.

"You're brave," she said when I finally finished.

"Even if what I've done costs me my son?"

I watched her carefully, anxious for her answer. I think what I wanted was for her to take my hand and tell me, yes, even if it cost me my son. I could be forgiven for leaving my marriage. I wasn't heartless or crazy. But she neither agreed nor disagreed with me. She just listened.

In that moment, it was almost enough.

Still, a question was nagging at me, and it seemed I now had a chance to ask it. "Ever since I got here, I've wanted to know something."

"Yes?" she asked, arching an eyebrow.

"When you came and took me away from . . ." I searched my mind for a word to describe the clinic. "That place," I said finally, "how did you manage it?"

She smiled slightly and shrugged. "There are always ways. Even in our country—no, *especially* in our country—there are always ways."

"Money?" I asked.

She didn't answer, which confirmed my guess.

"In that case, I'm in your debt."

"You're not, so please don't speak of it. The only thing I want to know is what will you do with yourself now that you're free?"

When I opened my mouth, nothing came out. What *would* I do with myself now? I had no idea. I had no home and no family—at least none that would take me in. Even if I had the money for it, no landlord in the city would rent an apartment to a single woman. I lowered my head and buried my face in my hands.

She took my wrists in her hands, pulled them gently away from my face, and leveled her gaze to mine. "You'll rest, *azizam,*" she said, laying her hand on my shoulder. "For now you'll stay here and you'll do nothing but rest."

On the fifth day, Puran came to visit.

"Oh, Forugh!" my sister said as soon as she saw me, and gave a cry.

She rushed toward the chair where I was sitting, bent down, and hugged me hard. When she drew back and lifted her hand to wipe away her tears, I saw the pretty wedding ring on it, and when she pulled off her coat I noticed an unmistakable bump.

"How are you, then?" I asked her.

"Well, as you can see, I'm pregnant," she said, as she took off her hat. "I've been tired, but it's wonderful."

I smiled. "I'm so pleased for you, Puran."

"Thank you, Forugh *joon*," she said, sitting down and arranging her coat across her lap. She tipped her head to the side and studied me. "And you? Are you . . . ?" She hesitated, as if weighing her words. "Better?"

"You mean less crazy?"

Her cheeks flushed. "No, I didn't mean that. It's just . . . we were frantic when you were sent away. We didn't know where you'd gone. I think Mother was the most worried, and she was heartbroken when we came to visit you and you didn't say a single word to her the whole time we were there."

"You came to the clinic? You and Mother?"

Her forehead wrinkled. "Don't you remember?"

I shook my head. "How were you able to get in?"

"They tried to turn us away," she said, "but Mother wouldn't budge. I've never seen her so determined. She was terribly upset, you know. Sanam, too. They took it very hard when you were taken away. Anyway, when we got up to your room you were in an odd state."

"They gave me shock," I said quietly.

"Shock?"

"Electric-shock treatment."

"Oh." She gazed very sadly at me, and the room grew still. After a few moments she held a hand out to me and I took it.

"Mother thought you were angry at her and that's why you wouldn't speak to her. She thought it might upset you if she came today, but you will see her, won't you?"

I nodded dumbly, but I still couldn't understand what Puran was telling me. I had absolutely no memory of their visit, and it made me desperate to think she and my mother had been there, right in front of me, and I hadn't known it.

But Puran seemed eager to move on from the subject. "Well," she said, "here you are now, Forugh. Miss Farmayan has been so kind and generous. When she called me to tell me you were here, my heart nearly burst."

"I missed you," I said. "So much."

"Yes. Me, too. I thought of you all the time, every day."

I nodded. "Tell me more about your life now. I want to know everything that's happened."

"Well, there's the baby, as you know, and . . ."

"Yes?"

"I've started publishing a few articles—"

"Publishing?" We'd both loved books growing up, but this was the first I'd heard of her writing.

"Oh, just little things. Reviews here and there, and I've started working on a play. . . ." She seemed suddenly uncomfortable, as if she regretted telling me her news. She stopped and looked at me hard. "Are you going to be all right?"

This seemed, at that moment, an impossibly difficult question. I looked away.

"You must . . . you must miss Kami?"

I swallowed and felt my eyes well up. I'd already written

Parviz three letters since leaving the Rezayan Clinic. "Please let me see Kami. You can bring him here, to Tehran. Just an hour. Please."

When I told her about the letters, Puran pressed her lips together and peered at me. "You're sure you don't want to go back?"

I looked at her, her pink cheeks and round belly. She no longer looked like a pretty girl; she looked like a lady. She had permed her hair, her eyebrows were thin and arched, and her face was made up. Her skirt-suit had brass buttons and a wide lapel. It looked new and expensive. But that wasn't the real change. I'd gotten stuck—I was still stuck—but she'd been living her life and it had changed her. She wasn't timid anymore, and she had an air of wisdom and authority now. Also, she was writing and I was not.

I winced. "What do you mean, go back?"

"To Parviz. Was he so awful that you won't consider it? Not even for Kami's sake? A child needs his mother, Forugh."

Her hand was still in mine, and I shook her from me.

"You don't understand anything that's happened to me. Nothing."

"What's happened to you, Forugh? Tell me. Please."

But I couldn't. I was smarting from what she'd said, but what struck me the hardest was the distance between us. She seemed very far away just then, and I'm sure she felt the same. We sat there in silence until finally she gathered her things and rose from her chair.

"You'll come visit me as soon as you're feeling better?" she said as she buttoned up her coat and placed her hat onto her head. Her expression was pleasant, her tone bright. "I'd like you to see my house, and the baby, when it's born."

"Yes," I started to say, and felt my throat catch.

After my sister left, I was tired. I had a headache and I felt nauseated—more so than when I had first left the clinic. I stayed up all night, my head throbbing and the night mocking me with its stillness. What would it all be for in the end, my rebellion? What would it be like for Kami, growing up without me? Could I continue to live without him? And even if I chose to return to Ahwaz, would Parviz take me back after all this time?

Every morning after breakfast, Leila retreated to a small cottage in one corner of the property, where she worked during the day. At Leila's, I had everything I needed. Soon the rooms of the house began to feel familiar, and I had, if not yet a feeling of being at home, a feeling of being safe. Leila had given me refuge in her beautiful house. She had given me time. I wasn't writing yet, but my hours were given over to reading and thinking. I slept late and took long walks. She had a camera, a small silver Leica, which she sometimes used to take photographs when we went out walking in the countryside, and when she saw how much I admired it she spent several afternoons teaching me how to take pictures. Soon I was spending entire afternoons poking around the lanes and meadows beyond the house, snapping photographs. I began to take the solitude and freedom for granted. To think of them as mine.

Sometimes I heard voices in another part of the house and knew she was entertaining a guest there, and I thought maybe it was a lover. I didn't disturb her, nor did she impose on me. Many people came calling. There was, for example, the publisher of the Algerian novel she was translating, as well as poets, writers, and playwrights she supported in various ways. They brought her books and gossip, took tea or drank a glass of wine. Leila let me know I was welcome to join them, but most often I politely declined the invitation. There were times, though, that Leila and I passed an evening discussing poetry or talking over her literary projects, the progress of her translations, as well as the work of other writers she'd pledged to support. We'd stay up chatting against the backdrop of music from her record collection. Ella Fitzgerald. Miles Davis. Billie Holiday.

When Leila drove us into the city, I'd marvel at all the changes in the capital. If you stood on the corner of the Avenue of the Tulip Fields, you'd go dizzy watching all the taxis and buses riding up and down the streets. Electricity had arrived in Iran, and at night whole sections of the city shimmered and glowed with it. Leila took me to parts of Tehran where I hadn't been before, neighborhoods where women walked breezily with their beaus and everything felt new. Together we went to Café Naderi where writers and philosophers nursed coffees and argued late into the night. We went to dance halls that played rock and roll. Few people understood this new American music, with its strange twang and foreign words, but they didn't need to. It was the spirit that mattered, its promise of freedom and of elsewhere.

On those drives through Tehran I felt fearless and unfettered, as if all the old constraints and prohibitions no longer applied to me. Of course, I was wrong. Since leaving the Rezayan Clinic I'd become, once again, a fixture in the gossip columns. My breakdown, so public and so notorious, was a topic of endless debate. Some people insisted I'd faked madness, while others claimed I'd always been mad. My poems were forgeries; my poems were filth. I was said to have taken a dozen lovers since my return to Tehran—more, by some accounts. Men who'd sneered at me and wouldn't meet my eyes just a few months ago now wrote about our purported love affairs.

These fictions were also seasoned with rumors of what looked to be an unnatural friendship between the daughter of a prominent and wealthy Qajar prince and me. Everyone knew that Leila Farmayan had taken me in, that we were living together at her garden estate outside Tehran, and more than once we were seen riding through the foothills in her car, the city to our backs as we climbed northward toward Damavand, stopping alongside meadows and creeks to share a picnic and take turns drinking from a flask of wine.

While a woman of her class was freer than most women, Leila's standing didn't completely shield her from gossip. Our names were never explicitly linked in the papers, but I guessed that even people who sought Leila's patronage spread rumors about us. A male lover was one thing, but two women living together? That wasn't just sinful; it was downright deviant.

Leila shrugged it all off. "Actually," she told me one day, "I should thank you. You see, all this gossip has deflected attention from a messy breakup that would otherwise be the talk of the town."

"You mean," I said, picking up on her teasing tone, "that you didn't realize how useful it would be to befriend a reprobate?"

She tossed back her head and laughed. "No, but I won't take it for granted from here on out. I promise you that."

We were never lovers, not in the way people assumed. It

would seem to me later that Leila's tenderness toward me was an expression of the warmth and openness that were her nature, and yet there were nights when, sitting on a stool beside the footed tub and chatting with her as she bathed, the air heavy with the scent of rose water and music streaming from the record player in the next room, I felt joy surge through my chest. When I ran a washcloth along her shoulders and then down the slope of her back toward her waist, it was nothing I hadn't done hundreds of times for my sister, but with Leila these gestures lost their innocence. A soft moan escaped her mouth, she shifted her legs in the soapy water, and it became impossible to ignore her pleasure, which was nothing less than the pleasure of being alive.

19.

————————

OUR IDYLL CRACKED APART ONE DAY IN JANUARY.

"A letter's just come for you," Leila said one morning at breakfast. She pulled it from the pocket of her skirt and slid it across the table. It was a pale-blue envelope, thin as tissue paper and stamped with an official seal. The return address listed a government ministry in Tehran.

"Here," said Leila, handing me a clean knife to tear the seal.

I could sense her watching me. "Do you want me to go?" she asked.

I lifted my eyes and shook my head. I took a long gulp of tea and then turned the envelope over.

Inside I found a single sheet of paper in the same shade of blue. It was very thin and the edges were crisp. A legal notice—brief, conveying only and precisely what was necessary. I read it once. Felt my heart drop, blinked hard, and read it again.

"What is it, Forugh?"

It took me a moment to get the words out. "The divorce has been finalized and . . ."

"Yes?"

"Parviz has been granted full custody of Kami."

Leila parted, then closed, her lips.

My head was whirring. Children belonged to their fathers—everyone knew that. It was both custom and law. Parviz might have allowed me visitation rights, but of course his mother would have persuaded him against that. He'd pressed for full custody of Kami and now he had it. There'd been no hearing and there was no redress; it all happened quickly and as a matter of course.

We sat for a while without saying anything. It was one thing to accept the divorce—Parviz and I had been separated for months and I understood that divorce was inevitable—but it was quite another thing for me to accept the consequence it entailed: to be separated permanently from Kami. Despair was sinking into my bones. I thought I might be sick. I slumped down in my chair and raised my eyes to the ceiling. I was staring up in a daze—how long, I don't know—when Leila pulled her chair closer to mine. Tears filled my eyes and then fell hot and fast against my cheeks.

"Do you think there's anything I can do?" I managed to ask her after a time.

I was still holding the letter, though it now was crumpled and smudged. I held it out to her and then watched as her irises flicked from line to line. "I think," she said slowly, her eyes on the notice, "that maybe your father could contest this."

"He'd never do that."

She looked up and nodded. "In that case, from what I know, there's nothing we can do."

"Because I'm a woman? Is that why?"

"I'm so sorry, Forugh. If there was any way I could help you fight this, you know I would, but I don't think there's anything you—or anyone, for that matter—can do."

I knew that I had to change. A few weeks following the divorce letter, a package arrived from Parviz. It was filled with what I'd left behind in Ahwaz. The little bits and pieces I owned were mostly worthless. A few hand-sewn dresses and a pair of secondhand high-heeled shoes; a cake of soap and a half-used jar of face cream, two tubes of lipstick; some pictures of Kami and my family that I'd kept taped to the bedroom mirror. Down toward the bottom of the box I found a stack of old diaries and copies of my first published poems. I sat down cross-legged on the floor and spread the diaries out in front of me. I paged through them, remembering so clearly the hours I'd spent writing down my thoughts, my memories, my hopes for the future. I'd scribbled letters and poems to Kami in those journals. Even so, it was like gazing at someone else's past. I thought for a moment of holding on to the diaries, but instead I put them back into the box along with the other things. I kept only the poems and the photographs. Everything else I threw away.

On my way from the trash bin, I slipped downstairs, rummaged in a storage pantry, and eventually found what I needed: a pair of brass scissors. They felt cold and heavy in my hands. Back in my room I stood before the mirror and looked at myself: blotchy skin, eyes purpled with shadows, long, scraggly hair. I looked miserable and afraid. My father had done this to me, I realized. Parviz and his mother had done this to me. But for the first time in many awful days, I thought, *I won't let them do this to me anymore.*

I raked my fingers through my hair to unloosen the tangles and then lifted the scissors. I cut one inch, then another. When I stepped back and looked at myself, what I saw encouraged me. With this chin-length bob my eyes looked bigger, and my square jaw was more prominent. I was much less feminine like this, but it was as if I'd come into focus, and as I turned my head one way and then another, hope flickered in my heart.

Day by day pain slackened its grip. It would never stop hurting—I knew this—but eventually I sought refuge in a quiet vow: somehow I'd figure out a way to see Kami again. Until then it was vital that I make something of myself. And this, now, was my chance to do it.

I had no concrete goals yet, but I'd started making notes in my journal for some new poems. I could stay up writing long past midnight, if the urge struck, and then sleep until noon the next day if I wanted. I could go into the countryside and take photographs. I spent long hours in the sun by the window, staring at the foothills of Damavand. Alone in the library, I ran my hands along the rows of books there. Rousseau, Molière, Dumas. Colette, Sand, de Beauvoir, Verlaine. My English was bad and my French was even worse, but there were several shelves of Iranian poets— Khayyam, Sa'adi, Hafez, and Rumi—and some days I'd pull down a thick gold-embossed volume and settle onto a couch for an afternoon of study. A whole week could pass without my speaking to anyone; Leila's quiet presence was the sole interruption of my reading and writing. I didn't have to answer to anyone but myself. I was alone and on my own for the first time in my life.

"I sent out some new poems today," I said as I helped myself to another portion of saffron pudding one night.

Leila smiled. "What are they about?"

"The divorce," I said. "Kami. What's happened to me these last few years. Sometimes I think I'll never be done with the past, or at least this part of it."

"You're finished with bothering what your husband or family thinks about your writing, that's the main thing. Now, write the poems you're meant to write."

I did. Not long after I left the Rezayan Clinic, the publisher of my first book contacted me to inquire about a new collection. I got to work immediately.

"What will you call it?" Leila asked when I was preparing the book for submission. It was far from complete, but as I held the manuscript in my hands now, it felt substantial. I handed her the title page. *"The Wall"* it read, and under that, in the same bold font, my name, "Forugh Farrokhzad."

> This is the last lullaby I'll sing
> at the foot of your cradle.
> May my anguished cries
> echo in the sky of your youth. . . .
>
> I've cast away from the shore of good name
> and a stormy star flares in my heart. . . .
>
> A day will come when your eyes
> will smart at this painful song.

You'll search for me in my words
and tell yourself: my mother,
that's who she was.

  —from "A Poem for You" (Dedicated to my son,
    Kamyar, with hopes for the future)

20.

_____

I REMEMBER THAT FIRST NIGHT, WHEN HIS EYES SOUGHT me out from across the room. His trim dark suit, his eager, handsome face, the almost careless way he gestured with his glass as he talked. It was nearly sunset, but heat still rippled the air and sharpened the scents of cigarette smoke and perfume in the room. I knew I should turn away, that I shouldn't give people more reason to talk, but it was impossible. I watched as his gaze skimmed the guests, drifting past a group of women in full flounced skirts, past their looks of pretty, practiced boredom and their French cigarettes encased in long-stemmed silver holders, and landed, finally, on me.

To celebrate the summer solstice and the first warm days of the season, Leila always opened her house to her wide circle of friends. Two years had passed since I first came to live with her, but I hadn't felt up to attending last year's solstice celebration and had spent the night alone in my room. I was feeling much better this year—I was back to my previous weight, my skin was brighter, and my bobbed hair was thick and glossy, with a saucy flip—though even now my hands still trembled from the shock treatments and my headaches sometimes lasted for days.

I made my way downstairs a little after five in the evening, stopping on the landing to admire a vase of massive pink peonies. The house looked particularly beautiful that night. All the windows and French doors were thrown open; lanterns were hung from the trees in the garden; smoking pipes were lit and scented with rose water; albums were stacked by the record player. At dusk there was a distant ring of the doorbell—the guests had begun to arrive. Save a few, they were all men, and the ease and confidence of Leila's conversations with them fascinated me. I observed her from a distance, slowly sipping a glass of wine. She could sit listening quietly for a long time and then suddenly utter the most piquant comment. Just now she'd tossed her head back in laughter, exposing her perfect creamy throat.

All of a sudden a hand gripped my forearm. "Are you the infamous Forugh?" asked a man. I wrenched myself free and told him I was. He wore one of the skinny black ties that were fashionable then. Between puffs from a thin cigarette, he told me he'd just come from Paris, where he'd been completing his degree at the Sorbonne and working on a translation of some French avant-garde poet. When I admitted I hadn't heard of the poet, he looked annoyed and launched into a lecture about this "god of letters."

I begged off, slinking back into the drawing room, where I caught parts of a heated conversation. There was talk of the streets. Protesters. *Shoolooqi*—trouble. Just that morning a riot had broken out in Tehran. Windows had been shattered in one of the wealthier quarters of the city, where many Europeans and Americans lived and worked.

All night I'd been aware I was being watched—a sensitivity I'd never be fully cured of—but for the moment the men were too embroiled in their argument to pay me much mind. I took a few steps closer so that I could make out more of their conversation.

"It's the Tudeh," said a man. "Those communists. They're stirring up trouble again."

"And why shouldn't they?" someone else chimed in. His hair was white and long, almost like a dervish's. Despite the warm weather, he wore a brown nubby-looking three-piece suit.

"How do you mean, Mr. Kamaliazad?"

"I mean that trouble's precisely what we need. It's 1957. It's been four years since the coup, and look at where we are! The king's nothing but a puppet for the West." He shook his head. "What other chance do we have for ending imperialism and the shah's dictatorship? And who else is better positioned to do it than the Tudeh?"

"But by supporting the Tudeh, we'd only trade one tyrant for another. Instead of the British and Americans we'd have the Soviets forcing the shah's hand, and then you can forget about democracy."

"That's true," came a voice. "Look what happened in China and Cuba."

A contemplative silence fell, followed by the assertion: "We've made a grave mistake basing our economy on oil."

"What choice did we have, exactly? How could we have made any progress toward modernization without selling our oil to the West?"

"You mean *giving* it to them," said the man with the wild white hair. "The men who brokered all those deals with the English and then the Americans have never been on the side of the people. They never planned to share the profits with the rest of the country, and they haven't. But who is there to blame but ourselves? We were foolish enough to think they'd act in the people's best interests."

"Well, for better or worse, oil is Iran's best hope for the future."

"No. A revolution is Iran's best hope."

"Even if it brings bloodshed?"

"However much we want to deny it, nothing can change in this country without armed opposition."

"But a revolution can't happen here. Not on the West's watch."

"Open your eyes, gentlemen. Look around. It's already happening."

At this the air in the room tightened and the conversation ceased. I hung back, taking a long sip of wine, watching the men and thinking about what they'd said. The talk of armed insurgency and revolution startled me. I'd been working almost constantly on *Rebellion,* my third book, and these last weeks I'd been oblivious to what was happening beyond Leila's garden walls.

I'd soon come to know the group and their theories well: the leftist philosopher Reza Kamaliazad, with his wild white hair and brown three-piece suit; the avant-garde writer Mansour Javadi, who bullied his way through debates, continuously pulling at his thin mustache and pushing his rimless round glasses farther up onto his nose; and the film director Darius Golshiri, the one who spoke the least but whose authority no one, not even the most sarcastic mem-

bers of the group, challenged. The Lion—that's what people called him. I'd seen photographs of Golshiri in the
newspaper and I placed him right away. I saw now how well
the nickname suited him. He was very tall, with broad
shoulders and an athlete's build that were perfectly accentuated by his tailored suit. Handsome, almost absurdly so.
The set of his jaw, his way of holding a glass of whiskey, the
cigarette pressed between the tips of two fingers—I took in
each detail.

Eventually the talk started up again, but now the subject
turned to literature and books. Someone mentioned a new
French translation of Sadeq Hedayat's *The Blind Owl*.
Glasses were refilled with whiskey and wine, emptied and
then filled again; ashtrays overflowed; and verses from
Hafez's and Rumi's poems peppered the conversation.

Then, during a lull in the conversation, Darius Golshiri
glanced in my direction and caught me looking at him. I
felt a rush of nervousness. I wasn't ready for him; I was totally unprepared. He stepped forward and extended his
hand as he introduced himself. When he came close I noticed the roughness of his cheek, the fullness of his lower
lip, the tiny lines that fanned out from the corners of his
eyes.

Smile, Forugh, I told myself. I held out my hand.
"Forugh," I said quickly. "Forugh Farrokhzad."

"Ah," he said. "I know your name. I just saw a few of
your poems in the recent issue of . . ." He narrowed his
eyes, straining to place my work.

I supplied him with the title of the journal that had recently run some of my poems.

"Yes, that's it. Those were the purest, most original

things I've read in a long while." He took a drag of his cigarette, then added, "Stunning, really."

"Stunning," he'd said. His exact word. He fixed me with his hazel eyes and said it again: "Stunning."

At this all eyes turned toward me. Even the man with the round glasses looked my way, his indifference punctured by Golshiri's compliment of my work. "Have you published a book?" the man asked loudly.

"I have. Two, actually."

He raised his eyebrows. "Is that so?"

"Yes," I continued, careful to keep my mouth set in a smile. "And I'm putting together a new manuscript just now. It'll be out next year with Amir Kabir Press."

He drew on his pipe and tilted his head to study me, and I watched his eyes narrow behind the round frames and then disappear in the hard white glint of his spectacles. "I see," he said, and then turned to his companion. "It's truly extraordinary how many women have taken to scribbling poems these days, isn't it, gentlemen?"

The smoke from his pipe enveloped me in a spicy, acrid odor, and I gave a cough.

"A true mark of progress," answered Javadi with a barely muted smirk.

I felt myself bristle, but already they'd introduced a new topic.

"We were just discussing the new film by Max Ophuls. Have you seen it, Miss Farrokhzad?" Javadi asked.

"I haven't."

"The lady is a writer," Kamaliazad interjected. "She can't exactly be expected to follow the latest European cinema!"

"But surely she takes an interest in other artistic forms?"

Golshiri said. This last part of the discussion had unfolded as if I weren't present at all, but now the men turned to face me. "Wouldn't you say, Miss Farrokhzad, that a broad interest in the arts is necessary to the development of one's poetic sensibility?"

"Absolutely. An artist should expand her education beyond her own discipline, but such an education doesn't come easily to everyone, and to most women it doesn't come at all."

Javadi narrowed his eyes. "Are you a feminist, Miss Farrokhzad?"

"Don't harass the woman!" Kamaliazad said, presumably in my defense.

"You do read fiction, though, don't you, Miss Farrokhzad?" said Javadi, amused behind his spectacles.

"Of course—"

"Then perhaps you can offer us your opinion of a recently published work."

"Which one?"

"*The Void*. Do you know it?"

I was worried he'd bring up an unfamiliar title, but I recognized this one immediately. Touted as the season's must-read, the story wasn't even a story. It was an obscure and rambling philosophical meditation, the work of some pretentious hack whose name I couldn't recall.

I turned to Javadi. "While I haven't had the opportunity to attend university or familiarize myself with foreign films, I've always thought that in a work of art the audience matters much more than the artist. *The Void* fails on that count."

"Do tell us more, Miss Farrokhzad," Kamaliazad urged.

"Well," I started, "it seems to me the only point of that story was to prove the reader's stupidity, and to me that's an arrogant and hollow gesture."

A strange silence fell over the group. "Mr. Javadi," said Kamaliazad, addressing the man in the round spectacles, "you must thank this young lady for offering you such an honest critique of your work."

I looked at Kamaliazad, then at Javadi, desperate to know if this was a joke. It wasn't.

"I'll forgo the thanks," Javadi said, his eyes locked on mine, "but I do have a question for you, Miss Farrokhzad."

My face burned. "Yes?"

"What if people *are* stupid?"

"I beg your pardon?"

"Let me put it this way: Should an artist reduce himself to the lowest level of intelligence of the people around him—or indeed of those in front of him?"

The hostility of these last words erased my embarrassment. "By insulting people's intelligence you lose any chance to educate them, and in refusing the validity of their perspective you've denied yourself the main purpose of making art."

It was Darius Golshiri who spoke next. "Which is what?" he asked.

"You surely have your own theories, Mr. Golshiri."

"But if you were to say, Miss Farrokhzad?"

"Connection," I said. "Not just between one idea and another, but between people."

He nodded just slightly, then smiled in a way I took as assent. Perhaps even admiration. I lifted my chin, drew a deep breath, and smiled back.

Whatever force it was that had led me so far from where I should have been, from the sort of life I was supposed to be living—well, I hadn't left that part of myself behind. It was still inside me and now it was pulling me in a new direction.

The party ended hours after midnight, when darkness began to give way to the tint of dawn. "Tell me about Darius Golshiri," I asked Leila when the last of the guests had left. "Do you know him well?"

She was well past tipsy and her eyes shone. With a glass of wine still in one hand, she slipped her other arm around my waist and together we climbed the stairs. "Our families were close, so I've known him for years, but nobody really knows 'The Lion,' which of course only convinces people of his genius. He started out as a stringer for American news outlets. Now everyone's saying he's the first really important Iranian director. International audiences and all that."

When we reached the landing, she paused to fix the strap on her dress. "I've heard he likes hiring people with very little—sometimes even no—experience making movies. Poets and writers especially."

"Poets and writers? Why's that?"

"Don't you know, Forugh? Ten years ago everybody wanted to be a poet. Now everyone wants to be a film-maker. They imagine it's the surest route to fame." She rolled her eyes. "Darius Golshiri started off as a writer himself, actually. The difference was, he was quite good at it. I don't really know why he gave it up. Anyway, since opening his own film studio he's been fetching up writers from all over town and setting them up with work. I heard he just hired Sadeq Chubak to work for him as a screenwriter."

"And what's he like?" I asked as we crossed into her room. "I mean, apart from his films."

"Arrogant," she said, and sat on the edge of her bed. "Uncompromising." She unclipped her earrings, stepped from her shoes, and started rubbing her feet. She looked up at me and studied my face. "Why do you ask?"

"I've been thinking of looking for a job," I said. The words came out quickly. I had no particular plan and it hadn't occurred to me to ask this question until just this moment, but I felt the argument take on more weight and conviction as I spoke. "If he's hiring writers, maybe I could find something there. What do you think?"

Her features creased with worry. "You know you can stay here as long as you like? That you don't need to worry about work for now?"

"I know. It's only that I want to. To work, I mean."

She tipped her head to the side and studied me. "And you want to work at Golshiri Studios?"

"I think I might."

She hesitated, and I braced myself for the questions and protests I guessed were coming, but when she spoke she said, "I think that's a splendid idea."

21.

I pulled up in front of Golshiri Studios in a trim blue sports car. It had been a gift from Leila, the most generous gift I'd ever received. "So you can get back into the world," she'd explained when she bought it for me a year ago, waving off my protests, "and not have to depend on anyone." She'd delighted in teaching me to drive. We'd spent a week practicing on the winding back roads behind her house. I loved it at once—loved the feeling of freedom and the momentum pushing me forward, that excitement when I downshifted perfectly, the feeling of the car as an extension of my body, coaxing it through the twisty mountain lanes, getting pushed back against the seat as I floored it down a straight stretch of road.

Still, that morning I was so nervous that my hands shook as I gripped the steering wheel, and I drove so slowly I was nearly late to work.

"So you're the poet Forugh Farrokhzad!" said a slim-hipped young man named Amir, who met me in the studio on my first day.

"I am."

He looked me up and down. I was dressed in a trench coat, a flared black skirt, and a polka-dot blouse. My heels were low and red. When he was done looking me over, he flashed me a smile and said, "I've read your poems."

"Really?" I said, shrugging off my coat. "Which ones?"

"All of them! We used to pass them around at school. The girls were crazy about them. They could recite every single one by heart."

I'd heard rumors that "Sin" and some of my more recent poems were circulating among high school– and college-aged girls, but this was my first outright proof of it. I grinned. "How about you? Did you share their enthusiasm?"

"Oh, I knew more than a few myself. They were very good poems. I bet I could still recite one for you. Would you like me to?"

"Maybe when we know each other better," I said, and smiled.

I expected him to laugh and he did, which told me we'd get on fine.

I followed Amir to the front room, where he pointed out a bare desk and explained that I'd be working as a receptionist. In the slower hours of the day I'd also be typing out film treatments and synopses. This last part made me nervous. I had no skills, strictly speaking. I wrote my poems by hand and had no occasion to use a typewriter.

"You'll catch on soon," he said when I told him my misgivings. "By the way," he asked offhandedly, "do you know anything about making movies?"

"About as much as I know about being a receptionist and much, much less than I do about writing poems."

"Well, if your writing's any indication, you're more than qualified for this job," he said. "But why waste your time here?"

I laughed. "How many poets do you think survive on what they make from their writing?"

He didn't answer.

"Exactly, Amir *jan*. None."

I spent that first morning before a small desk in a badly lit, poorly ventilated room, struggling to make sense of the switchboard. The most junior-level assistant in the studio, Amir was also the best copywriter. He worked with furious attention and for most of the day he barely registered my presence, which I understood as the freedom it was. I was lucky to be employed at all; most women rarely worked outside the home. If anyone else at the studio took notice of me at all, they expected me to be barely literate, at best a decorative element, and they didn't engage me in conversation.

In the afternoon I ventured in the direction of Darius Golshiri's office, holding my breath hopefully as I poked around. I hadn't seen him since Leila's party, but I'd cast my mind back to that night at least a hundred times. I couldn't stop thinking about him. Couldn't stop my thoughts from returning, again and again, to his wry smile, the gleam of his hazel eyes. Couldn't stop trying to guess what his attentions meant, if they meant anything.

At four o'clock I screwed up my courage and asked Amir when I could expect to see our boss. There was a charged silence in which I felt as if everyone in the building could hear our exchange.

"Mostly he's out shooting footage," he said, and continued marking up some press materials. "Otherwise he's in his studio in Darrus, up in northern Tehran. He edits everything himself by hand. He's meticulous. Tireless. Sometimes he stays up there for weeks at a time and we don't see him around here at all." He looked up from his work. "Why do you ask?"

"No reason," I answered, casting my glance down and pretending to study the file in my hands. I didn't see Golshiri at all that day—nor would I see him on the second or third. I imagined that after the warmth of our connection at the party he'd be eager to find me at his office, even seek me out, but he didn't. When he did finally appear at the studio, nearly three weeks later, there was little indication he even knew I'd started working for him.

One afternoon, I arrived home from work and mounted the steps to Leila's room hurriedly, peeling off my gloves as I went. Amir had solicited my help editing a new script, and I was eager to tell her about it. As it happened, I didn't get to talk to her at all. Stepping onto the landing outside Leila's bedroom, I stopped abruptly. Voices were coming from her room. Was it crying I heard? The door was ajar and I peered in cautiously. I caught sight of the back of a man's long torso, the shine of his black hair. He was young—I guessed about twenty-five or thirty—and tall, with his shoulder blades jutting out from under a thin shirt. Leila was sitting on a chair, her hair covering much of her face. Her palm was flat against her forehead, and tears wet her cheeks.

I thought if I moved they would see me. I had a vague

idea the man might be her lover, and from the whispers and urgent low voices it sounded as if they were arguing. For a moment I stood in the hall, wondering what it all meant. I waited another few seconds, then backed away, my steps muted by the thick carpet that ran down the hallway.

I found her in the kitchen shortly after six in the evening, chopping cilantro and parsley for dinner's stew. Her eyes were red-rimmed from crying, but she didn't mention her visitor. Instead, I told her about Amir's offer to let me help edit a script and she listened generously, asking me about the story and my opinion of it.

But she was distracted. Quiet. Working through a pile of herbs, she dropped her knife and it clattered to the floor. She bent down and picked it up, only to fumble it and cut the heel of her hand with the blade.

When I grabbed a towel to stop the blood, her eyes flicked up. For the first time that night, she looked right at me, and I realized then that she knew I'd seen someone in her room.

"My brother, Rahim, was here," she said. "You see, he's gotten himself mixed up with the Tudeh Party and—"

"Your brother's a communist?" I broke in. From what I'd heard, communists were impoverished young men who gathered in dark, dingy basements to read forbidden foreign books, though I couldn't have said what those particular books were or why they were banned. I tried to imagine Leila's brother as a bearded revolutionary in tattered shirt-sleeves, but it didn't make sense.

She caught my confusion. "About half the communists in this country must be from prominent, if not titled, families, Forugh. Who knows their excesses better than their own? The coup changed him, but he's always been idealistic, uncompromisingly so. He wanted nothing to do with his inheritance or with this house."

"And now he's in trouble with the government?"

"I think so. He's been going off about the shah for years—the corruption at court, the need for change. Of course he's right about all of it, but ever since the coup there's been a crackdown against dissidents. And not just against communists, but nationalists and Islamists. Anyone who opposes the monarchy is being blacklisted."

"Do you think he's in danger?"

"He says he isn't, but I don't believe him. Why else wouldn't he tell me where he was staying?" She closed her eyes, drew a long breath, and then looked back at me with a worried expression. "Forugh?"

"Yes?"

"You can't tell anyone he was here. I shouldn't have told you, only—"

"Only we can never have secrets from each other."

She didn't answer.

"No secrets," I repeated. "Do you hear me?"

"Of course not," she said. She smiled a little and let me take her hand in mine, but she'd turned quiet again and her eyes were fixed on a place I couldn't see.

"Mr. Golshiri needs a woman's voice." I'd been working as a receptionist at the studio for more than six months and by now I'd discovered I could do my work in half the time, which left me plenty of time during the day to work on my poems. I was struggling with a new composition when Amir poked his head into the reception area and summoned me. I had no idea what he meant about Golshiri needing a woman's voice, but I shuffled my poem under a stack of other papers and then followed him down a corridor and into the recording studio.

I'd stopped thinking about Golshiri—well, not entirely, but at least that's what I told myself. Now, as I approached the studio and heard his voice, I felt a tinge of anticipation. The room was dark and filled with cigarette smoke, and at first I couldn't even see him. As my eyes adjusted to the dimness, I saw there was a long table toward the back of the room, and Golshiri was sitting there with his brother, Shahram, and several other men. I walked toward the table and eased myself into a chair. When he finally looked up from some papers, Golshiri nodded at me but didn't smile.

"Would you please read this for us, Forugh?" Shahram said, motioning to a script on the table and handing me a set of headphones. He had the same olive-toned skin and hazel eyes as his brother, but his manner was light. Friendly.

I smoothed the page and leaned toward the microphone. The room was completely quiet. I drew a deep breath and began to read aloud. Once or twice I stumbled over a line and had to start again, but after a while, I realized it wasn't so different from reading a poem. I forgot the others were watching and my voice grew steadier. When I finished, I looked over at Golshiri and saw that the others were looking at him, too—everything here was up to him. Someone played back the recording. My voice sounded soft but also more assured than I recognized it.

"That's all, then," Shahram told me. "Thank you."

I rose from my chair, but Golshiri waved for me to sit.

"I'd like to have your opinion on something, Forugh," he said.

He motioned to someone in the screening booth. The room went quiet, the only sounds the hiss of the projector and the beating of a film reel, and then some images flashed across the screen. Long shots of the desert, the land, the face of a child. The images were black and white but sometimes tinged with watery colors. In several shots, a character stood off-center or in the background, looking away. It was unlike any movie I'd seen before.

"What did you think?" he asked when it was over.

I was surprised he asked me, and it took me a moment to respond. "The images are exceptionally vivid, but there's a kind of cold authority to the voice-over," I said. "It sounds as if it were narrated by God—or somebody's idea of God."

"And how would you do it differently?"

I knew I was treading close to danger, that I could easily offend him, but why not tell the truth since he'd so pointedly asked for my opinion? "Make the voice-over less authoritative," I said. "That would open a space for a viewer to enter the story. If the voice is warmer, people will feel more sympathy and engagement."

He said nothing, but when I left the room a minute later I could tell he was still turning the idea over in his head.

Was I wrong to have told him what I really thought? Later that afternoon, I got my answer. It came by way of an invitation.

"He's traveling to Abadan with his brother and a few assistants for a new project," Amir told me. I could tell from his expression he was as astonished as I was by the message he'd been asked to relay to me. "He wants you to join him."

"Join him? Me?"

"That's right."

At first I didn't grasp what he was saying, but once I did I felt my face flush and asked, "What's in Abadan?"

Amir's brow furrowed. "You really don't know?"

I shook my head.

"Oil," he said. "Oil and a whole lot of trouble."

22.

———————

FOR THOUSANDS OF YEARS, IRAN'S OIL WAS THE EARTH'S secret. Whenever the Zoroastrians—the ancient Iranians for whom fire was the essence of life—came across oil, they took it as a sign of fire flaring underground and built temples to their god, but the oil itself was only useful to them when it cooled and hardened and could be used to carve statues or as caulking for ships. When the English descended on the country in the early 1900s, everything changed. No sooner did they discover oil in the southern provinces than they designed and built the machines to extract it and sent overseers to guard and ship it. In Abadan alone, three hundred thousand barrels were now loaded onto tanks and shipped every year to nearly every major city in the world. "Fortune brought us a prize from fairyland beyond our wildest dreams," Winston Churchill would write of the discovery of Iranian oil.

Then came Mohammad Mossadegh. The Iranian prime minister looked like a man who'd entered the world brooding and indignant—and so far as anyone knew he had. Ever since his youth, he'd been consumed by the idea of Iranian independence. Eventually the obsession turned into a conviction that Iranian oil should belong to Iran. In London and Washington, politicians called him a madman, to which he coolly replied: "Iranian oil belongs to Iran."

For a time it nearly was, but the 1953 coup ousted Mossadegh, propped up the shah, and tightened England and America's grip on Iran's oil. Still, in the 1950s, oil was everything. Every conversation, no matter the subject or speaker, circled back to oil: how it was extracted from the earth, who was allowed to export it and sell it abroad, what it would mean if the country ever finally gained sovereignty over its oil wells and the subsequent profits. Subterfuge, accusations, and, above all, greed—they raged and raged until one day in 1958 the earth itself answered with fire.

The train sped southward, the engine plowing past the darkened silhouette of the Zagros Mountains. Inside my cabin it smelled of leather and camphor and all was quiet except for the rattle of the wheels against the rails. I wore a pair of khaki pants and a loose cotton blouse I'd bought especially for the trip, my feet tucked into a pair of soft canvas espadrilles. My bag held a fresh notebook, Leila's camera, and several rolls of film. When I settled into my seat and drew back the curtain, I could just make out the valley through the window. Then, half an hour outside the city, the train reached a spot overlooking the Salt Desert. Rimmed by the snowcapped peak of Mount Damavand and the valleys of the Zagros Mountains, this was the only remnant of the sea that had once covered all of Iran. Farther on I saw the blue-domed shrine of Fatima and abandoned villages crouching against the hills. And then there was only sand, stone, and sky.

It was a long trip. I slept, woke, read from a book, wrote notes to myself, wondered how the others were passing the time. There were six of us on the assignment. For Golshiri, this was just a scouting trip, so there was no need for a full crew, just his brother, Shahram, a camera operator, two assistants, and me. I was the only woman, which was why I had my own couchette; the others shared two compartments in another part of the train. My feelings for Golshiri at this point were a confusion of curiosity and frustration. I'd heard he only put together a full crew when he began to shape a film and knew for sure the story was worth pursuing. Later I'd find out he already knew there was a story in Abadan—a big story connected to much bigger stories. As for me, I'd accepted the assignment with little sense of what my role would entail, but I had a lot to prove, not just to the others because I was the only woman there, but also to myself, to my sheltered past, to the life I'd left behind.

We reached Khorramshahr the next day. Outside the station, I shielded my eyes with one hand and looked out at the horizon. The sun was white and swollen. At eight in the morning, the air was already scorching hot and I could feel the perspiration pooling in the small of my back.

It was clear the driver was confused by my presence. A woman traveling with a group of men? No veil or wedding band in sight? As the driver stood staring at me, mouth agape, Golshiri opened the front passenger door and motioned for me to sit. He handed me my bag, which I set under my feet. The seats were leather, already hot from the morning sun, or maybe they'd never cooled off from the day before.

We set out in silence, me in the front and Golshiri and two assistants in the back seat. Shahram and the cameraman traveled by another car. A small, narrow island of mudflats, Abadan lay at the extreme southwestern part of the country, close to the border with Iraq. A few miles from the train station, a grove of palm trees rose up, and then, closer to town, I saw smokestacks and flares in the far distance.

Bumping across a railroad track and onto a smoothly paved road, we reached a street with many small white houses. Each house was exactly like the one next to it. They all had window boxes, though they were empty of flowers, and the windows were tightly shuttered. The streets were quiet and empty, though once or twice I saw another car slide past, a driver in the front and the dark shape of a passenger in the back seat.

We drove on, past more shuttered cottages. Eventually the dusty roads broadened into paved avenues shaded by palms. There were signs, written in English, for a country club, and then we turned up a private road with the words HERTFORDSHIRE MANOR engraved on a wooden sign. "There's the production house," I heard one of the assistants say. From a distance it seemed beautiful: a large terraced home with a veranda, garden, and tennis courts. As we got closer, though, I saw that the swimming pool was empty and cracked; the lawn was rutted with patches of dirt, and the grass had turned yellow and dry as straw.

The air inside the house was still and thick with humidity and dust. My room was a large suite on the lower level; the others were lodged on the second story, and Golshiri took over the carriage house. I stripped the bed down to the bare mattress. Tomorrow I'd wash the sheets, setting them in the sun to dry on the terrace outside my room, but not now. The heat was unbearable and my head thrummed with a headache. In the morning we'd hike out to the oil fields to see the fire. All I could do now was collapse into the bed with my shirt and slacks clinging to my skin, my shoes still on my feet.

"This used to be a village of five hundred people," Golshiri said the next morning as we set off together for the fire. He was freshly shaven, the comb tracks visible in his damp hair. He wore a canvas jacket and carried a leather satchel bulging with camera equipment.

I pulled the Leica from my bag, then lifted the strap over my head with one hand and followed him out of the house. The others had gone ahead already. Outside, the road shimmered with heat, and the asphalt felt pliant under my shoes as I fell into step with Golshiri. It was strange and thrilling to walk beside him, and it occurred to me this was the first time we'd ever been alone.

The sky was a white haze. Gulls wheeled overhead. The road followed a corrugated metal wall, and in the far distance stood a long row of oil wells, their strokes stilled now by the fire.

"What happened to turn it from a village into this?"

"Iranian oil is unlike any other in the world, and the English knew it as soon as they got here. Back in the twenties an average well in most parts of the world extracted four and a half gallons in a day; here nearly ten thousand barrels gush from the earth each day. The British found they could skip the extraction process—that's how readily oil gives itself here—and it wasn't long before they brought their journeymen, wells, and equipment. Four years ago, BP—that's British Petroleum—took over. They've turned these wells into the most lucrative British enterprise anywhere on the planet. All they need, all they've ever needed, is workers. Iranian workers."

We crossed over a clearing and continued our walk on an unpaved road lined by a row of desolate storefronts. Two small boys crouched under a tree, tossing a marble back and forth in the dirt. Behind them stood a large billboard balanced precariously on rickety wooden stilts. COCA-COLA was written in Persian and English on the bottom, and the picture showed a pretty girl raising a green bottle to her lips.

"They call this the Paper City," Golshiri said, pointing toward some hovels fashioned from rusted metal and dried mud. Small flies swarmed around us, and I tried to swat them off. It was no use. I covered my nose with a scarf and tried to breathe through my covered hand. It was nine o'clock and already ninety degrees; by noon the temperature would rise to nearly 120. The stench of oil filled the air. Later that night I'd rub myself raw in the bath, but when I went to sleep I would still catch the sulfurous scent, though I wouldn't be able to tell if it was my skin or the air in the room.

"Before this there just were warehouses," Golshiri continued. "Four thousand people crammed together inside. No bathrooms. Each family had a blanket and that was where they lived, confined to those few feet on the warehouse floor. Then BP came up with the idea to let the workers build shacks for themselves out of discarded oil drums. The men work eighteen-hour days in the oil fields. They're paid fifty cents a day. There's no spring season here, only winter and summer. In the winter the earth floods, and all around the mud's knee-deep."

"Where did all the workers come from?"

"When word got out that the English were hiring, villagers came from all directions. BP built everything here. All these shanties"—he gestured with his hand—"but also the country club and the tennis courts. Iranians aren't allowed over there, not even to use the drinking fountains."

"Two separate worlds," I said.

"Exactly."

Everything turned dark as we approached the oil fields. Smoke from the flames curtained the air and blackened the sky. Through the black plumes, fire shot like a geyser, and the force of the flames turned into a choking wind. Heat licked my face, and the only sound was the fire whipping in the wind. I followed Golshiri farther toward the wells, but the gusts were strong and walking was almost impossible. We staggered on. We didn't speak, because there wasn't anything to say. My eyes smarted from the fumes and the grit. I yanked my scarf from my neck and shrouded my face. Through the tall waves of heat, I could make out overalls and hard hats, then dark bodies and blackened hands. The workers. The heat obscured their faces, and I strained to make out their words over the din.

I looked back toward Golshiri. "How did the wells catch fire?" I shouted.

He brushed his hair back from his eyes. Already a layer of soot covered his face. "All anyone knows for sure is that a spark lit the air. Some people say the workers did it, but that makes no sense. Those wells are their livelihood. There's nothing else for them. Nothing. Anyway, the oil company can't afford that theory. Who else could they find to fight the fire? The locals are the only workers they've ever had around here."

"How will they put it out?"

"That, really, is the question," he said, his eyes fixed on the burning wells. "You see, a fire, especially a fire of such scale, won't be easily extinguished. It either dies down slowly, over the course of months or even years, or else—"

"Yes?"

"It's killed."

By the time we reached Abadan, the fire had been burning for many weeks. Oil-well fires were notoriously difficult to put out, and the fire here had already burned through May and June, spreading from the wells into all directions. Instead of oil, the wells now carried water from the Karun and blasted it into the flames, but that hadn't lessened the blaze. The gases were noxious, and there were dozens of stories about workers passing out from the fumes. All the foreigners had left for the gulf; any Iranians with the means had left town, too. With thousands of workers idle and the city at a near standstill, word was going around that there would be riots if the fire wasn't extinguished soon.

In late June, a call was placed to Myron Kinley in Houston, Texas. The undisputed international authority on oil-well fires, he was a short but powerfully built man, with a limp and a scar-ravaged body he'd earned over the many years he'd spent practicing his profession. Having accepted the assignment, Kinley got on the first flight to Iran—an eight-thousand-mile journey.

Now it was July. Myron Kinley had been in Abadan for several weeks, but he and his men had not managed to put out the fire. And now he was faced with the problem of what to do with me.

"Get that woman the hell out of here," he said as I approached. He pointed at me but addressed Golshiri, speaking in English. Until I came closer and could see his pale-blue eyes, I mistook him for one of the workers. He wore a hard hat, and his face and arms were totally black from the soot.

Golshiri strode forward. He answered Kinley in English, and I struggled to make out the exchange that ensued. "As you know, Mr. Kinley, we have permission from the authorities to film the fire. This woman is part of my crew, and I insist she stay with us."

"Listen here, Mr. . . . ."

"Golshiri."

"Golshiri," Kinley repeated, though it came out in a thick Texas drawl. "I got a hundred-man crew here." He wiped his brow with the back of his hand and then spit into the sand. "Three men have died already trying to put out this fire, and I call that lucky. Real lucky. I don't care who all gave you permission to film here, but I'm not taking responsibility for that woman's safety, so if you don't get her out of here, your whole crew leaves."

That's how I found myself banished to the tent city, a makeshift camp on the other side of the oil wells. The women would be there, Golshiri told me, and suggested I take a look around.

The tents were a brilliant white, billowing faintly from the fire's winds. As I approached, I could make out veiled figures. I knew it would be impossible to earn the women's confidence bareheaded, so I unknotted the scarf at my throat, unfurled it, then tied it over my head to cover my hair. Inside the encampment the women wore long crimson veils over crimson dresses. Their eyes were heavily smudged with kohl and they had dark skin and tattooed hands. Arab blood. I hung back, but I was intensely thirsty and I had no drinking water with me. One of the women stood before an iron pot, cooking over a naked flame in the already agonizing heat. I stood there for some minutes, unsure how to approach her, but then she set down her ladle and walked toward me.

"Yes, lady?" she said. Her stomach was round and high and her red veil nearly brushed the ground. Like the others, she had coppery brown skin and black eyes. She was very beautiful, with a heart-shaped face and dimples, but what astonished me was her necklace. From a distance it looked like it was made of silver coins, but as she came closer I saw it was fashioned from Coca-Cola bottle caps.

"I'm sorry to bother you, but I've come from Tehran and—"

Her eyes widened and she clucked her tongue. "Tehran!"

"Yes."

At that moment an older woman approached. She had the same heart-shaped face and the same kohl-lined eyes. This, and the familiar manner with which she placed her hand on the younger woman's shoulder, told me they were mother and daughter.

"We're here to make a film about the fire," I told them after I'd greeted the elder woman.

The woman's face gave nothing away. I waited for what seemed like ages, and when she did finally answer, she only said, "Why?"

The question took me aback. I'd taken it more or less on faith that what was happening in Abadan should be documented, but the woman was shrewd. She wouldn't be satisfied with a glib reply.

"To show how the fire's affected you," I said.

For another moment she was silent, but then she gestured for me to enter the tent.

I followed her inside, unwound my camera from my neck, and sat down on a faded, threadbare carpet. There were three other women in the tent, and they regarded me with a calm curiosity. One of them rose and prepared some tea, which she served to me heavily sugared and in a small copper cup. At first I couldn't make out much of the women's talk, since their dialect was so unfamiliar. I listened more carefully and spoke less, which maybe endeared me to them, because they began to make a place for me in their conversation.

"Where is your husband?" one of the women asked.

I waved with a vague gesture that could indicate he was at the fire with the rest of the crew or on the next continent.

"Food is scarce here?" I asked before they could press me for more details.

"Yes," the younger woman said, her eyes on the ground. "And water."

"They drove us away from the village," the mother explained, "and told us to stay here, in these tents. The foreigners are gone now, but our men still go out every day to the wells. They work fourteen hours at the fire, and they come back at night half crazy from heat and exhaustion."

"Since the fire started," the young woman said, "the babies are always coughing, and the older people are weak and sickly."

"Twelve of our goats have died already. The only ones left have gone mean and wild."

I took a gulp of tea and set down the cup.

"Mina!" the older woman called. Almost at once a small girl scampered into the tent. Her arms were thin as twigs, but she was dressed as a miniature version of the women, with a crimson veil, and her large brown eyes were rimmed with kohl. "Show the lady what you found yesterday!"

The child's eyes went wide at the sight of me in my pants and with my camera around my neck. I could tell she was unused to strangers, but she did as her mother told her. When we ducked out of the tent, she walked ahead of me, looking over her shoulder from time to time to make sure I was still following behind. We walked away from the encampment, and after some minutes we came to a clearing shaded by a very large palm tree. The trunk was gray and desiccated, its bark prized open and its fruits shriveled and blackened by the heat. The child squatted down and pointed her finger at something barely visible in the sand. I bent down and looked closer.

A bird—it was a bird. The wings were spread open, and it lay with its beak pointed up at the sky like a tiny arrow. I touched it with one finger. The bones were frail and brittle and its feathers were pressed into the earth, stuck in oil and silt. It looked as if it had been trying to fly when it died. I felt my eyes begin to smart. When I looked up, the girl pointed to another figure and then another. There were at least a hundred dead birds embedded in the ground.

Back in the tent, I pulled the lens cap off my camera and flipped the shutter open. At first the women raised their hands to cover their faces or drew the edges of their veils to hide themselves, but eventually their shyness and vigilance eased and then fell away. I found the young woman with the heart-shaped face and the bottle-cap necklace sitting by herself at the edge of the encampment. The sun was on her face and her whole throat seemed to glow with it. I raised my camera to my eye. The light was pure and plentiful. I could feel the woman waiting for me on the other side of the lens, and then I focused the camera and clicked the shutter.

That night, as I stood in the dark inner courtyard pinning up my just-scrubbed bed linens, I heard heavy boots against the tiles. I turned around to find Golshiri watching me.

"How was it at the camps?" he asked. I couldn't tell if he really wanted to know or if he was just making conversation.

"Sad," I replied. "But beautiful, too. The women are doing their best to care for their elderly and their children, but so many people are getting sick. Everything's getting sick here. I took some photographs—"

"They let you photograph them?" he interrupted, surprised.

He came closer, so close that I could feel the warmth radiating off him, could detect the sweat from his own day in the fields. I tucked the pins in my pocket and stepped back from the clothesline. "Not at first. We couldn't make much sense of one another in the beginning. They think it's strange, a woman coming from Tehran to ask them questions. It didn't help that I don't understand their dialect very well, but eventually some of them began telling me about the fire."

"What did they say about it?"

"They say it's made the children sick, that they can't stop coughing. The old people, too. No one tells them what's going on, but the women say the air's been poisoned by the fumes."

"They're right. But you know that."

"I don't think they understand why we're here, what we're trying to do by making a movie about the fire."

"You explained it to them?"

"As well as I understand it myself," I said. "It doesn't seem enough to help them, somehow. Making a film."

"It's a record. A testimony."

For a moment we were silent, then I asked, "What happened out at the wells today?"

"The workers poured cement in the sand. The desert out there's covered in cement. They've rigged up the oil pipes so that they reach all the way to the Karun River. Tomorrow they'll start blasting the fire with water. Kinley thinks he's got it figured out this time."

"Does he?"

"We'll see."

I pressed my lips together. "I think I could convince them to be filmed—the women, I mean."

"For the documentary?"

"The fire displaced them. No, it's totally disrupted their

lives. It seems to me that's part of what's happening here, too."

His eyes narrowed—my only encouragement. He was calculating, thinking through what I'd said. "See if you can take more photographs," he said finally. "If you think you can convince them to be in the film, I'll go out there and take a look around myself." He cleared his throat and continued. "You'd need to come along." He turned to me. "Would you want to?"

Was he really asking for me to collaborate with him on the documentary? I bit back a smile. "Of course," I said quickly, my heart hammering against my chest.

23.

IN THE END, IT WAS A BOMB THAT PUT OUT THE FIRE. IT
was dropped from a helicopter and straight into the flames.
The winds were ferocious above the fire, and for nearly an
hour the helicopter struggled to right itself. It circled the
sky and then returned, only to bob and buck against the
wind, but finally it steadied long enough to finish the task.
When the bomb fell into the fire, the earth trembled with
the force of an earthquake and then everything went very
still. I was in the encampment that day. The children were
accustomed to smoke and fire, but the force of the explo-
sion terrified them and they began to cry. Cries rose up to
God, turning into frantic prayers and then more silence. A
second blast exploded the stillness, and when I looked out
to the horizon, the sky was a riot of flames and black smoke.

The next day, in place of fire, gases shot from the earth.
The air was rank with the stench of burning oil and smol-
dering steel. The sky went from black to gray and then
white. This went on for three days, and when it stopped,

Myron Kinley left Iran. I was free now to walk out by the wells, to pick my way through the rubble alongside the other members of the film crew. I took photographs as workers hauled charred ladders, pumps, and hoses onto trucks and then dumped them into the gulf, where the refuse from the fire was turned into another of the sea's secrets.

Other than Kinley and his crew, there hadn't been a foreigner in Abadan for weeks, but now they were returning. The streets filled with the noise of their cars and the cafés filled with their voices. Soon the workers and their families would return to the Paper City and to their work at the wells. The fire had burned for ninety-one days, and now it was gone.

We stayed in Abadan for another week after the bomb fell. During the daytime, while Golshiri and the other men were out shooting footage by the oil wells, I walked around Abadan, alone. I set out at dawn, in the coolest part of the day, stopping to photograph the tall grasses that had somehow survived the fire and the deep heat of summer. For all the calculated, manicured order of the colony, the wells themselves were ugly, but I saw now what drew Golshiri to this part of the country. The bare earth, the rough silence of the men, the violence of the fire, which was matched only by its indifference to the world around it. In Abadan, the bleakness of the landscape threw beauty into high relief, but you only saw it if you knew how to look carefully.

The days seemed to slide by swiftly now. The women in the encampment never complained about my presence. They were used to me, regaling me with stories about the times before the wells, when they lived as nomads and their lives were set to the rhythm of the seasons. After the fire they were busier than ever. They'd have to move everything back to the Paper City, which was hard work in the blazing heat.

For days I was still forbidden to go near the fire, which made me furious, but I realized none of the men could have experienced what I did: the encampment, how the women made a life even there, the moments of laughter, how they sometimes spoke in songs. Their resourcefulness moved me deeply. I also felt a delicious anonymity at the camps. No one knew anything about me here. I was a stranger from the capital; that was all. In Tehran I'd become a spectacle, but all that felt very far away now. It wasn't my poems that marked me, or the fact that I'd been divorced or even that I was on my own. In Abadan I was different, but no one particularly cared.

A woman could see herself better where she wasn't known, I decided.

A vague plan began taking shape in my mind. Until now poems had been the medium through which I communicated ideas and feelings. With my camera, my work was still to observe and record, but writing poems depended on solitude, while this work was taking me outside myself. There was something so appealing about this. Coming to Abadan had not only given me a feeling for my own possibilities but also launched me into the world and initiated me into a community. I didn't think, yet, that I could make films by myself—that was past imagining—but I wanted to learn all I could.

I could watch Golshiri work for hours, and I think that's how it really started between us, with admiration. So far as I could see, there was no fear in him, none. He did everything with a cool authority, including teaching me how to work. I learned everything from him: How to scout a location, how to angle a camera, and how to operate it. How to look into the viewfinder, select a target, and press down the lever. His own assuredness gave me confidence, and soon I realized I could capture an experience or a place with pictures as well as with words.

In the evenings we sat in the courtyard, swatting at mosquitoes and smoking cigarettes. He'd talk about his life and I would quietly listen. I learned he came from a wealthy family in Shiraz, the city of poets in the south. The Golshiri men were learned aristocrats who spent their days in leisurely contemplation, but it was his mother, a woman unable to write even her name, who'd most shaped his education. One day she took Golshiri's hand and headed for the closest school. She was determined to become literate—so determined that when her husband objected by saying her plans would compromise her maternal responsibilities, she'd simply taken her son along with her. He was four years old.

He'd taught himself English by sitting in his father's house in Shiraz, listening to BBC Radio and American Forces Network broadcasts, a fat dictionary on his lap. "What use is that?" his father and grandfather demanded to know. America was *yengeh donya,* the tail end of the world. He'd been taught to think of Persian poetry as the world's highest artistic achievement, though mild concessions were made for certain works of French and English literature. The Iranian upper class was still looking to Europe for its models, but he set his sights on a newer New World.

At thirteen he discovered American literature, Hemingway in particular. He couldn't believe a story could be told with so little ornament or that he should find in these American novels and stories a spirit so like his own. Eventually he began to translate these books into Persian, but what came out didn't seem like Persian at all; now spare and sharp, his mother tongue had been made over by English, just as he himself was being remade from a knobby-kneed boy into a man in the mold of his heroes. That's when he took up writing short stories.

Why, I asked, didn't he keep writing fiction? "It was useless," he said after a pause. He frowned as he said this, and his voice took on a hard edge. In a country still riddled by illiteracy, he explained, what he was doing was basically meaningless to most people. No, he wouldn't be a writer. He never gave up his love of books, but he trained himself to see the world through images and sounds, adapting the features of the novels and stories he admired into cinematic techniques. By temperament he'd always been independent, and from what he told me I guessed he was unencumbered by the necessity of making money from his films. As a director he could work alone for long stretches of time, which suited him, and he was free to pursue a project for as long or as little as he liked.

Golshiri saw the whole history of the country in the Abadan fire, but something more essential drew him here and to this work. Making a movie called for control. For mastery. It had to do with the way a film enveloped the viewer. As we worked together, it occurred to me what he did with such assurance and effortlessness was capture the whole world. To direct a film was to say "Look, this is how I see the world," and then to say "See it as I do."

Golshiri—Darius, as I came to know him—used to say we'd always loved each other, even before we met. He'd recite Rumi's couplet, the one about lovers not suddenly meeting but being in each other all along. "I've been waiting for you," he said. "I've always been waiting for you." But he had his story, and I have mine.

In my version, our love story began the night I crossed the garden in Abadan. I remember the lush heat as I made my way to the carriage house, the square of light in the darkness that told me he was still awake. He was sitting with one leg crossed over the other, his sleeves rolled up to his forearms and his collar loose, a glass of whiskey in one hand and a book in the other. When he looked up and saw me standing in the doorway, his face softened with recognition, then pleasure.

I sat down in the chair opposite his and folded my legs under me. My dress, a simple shift, skimmed the tops of my knees and revealed skin tanned from days in the sun. My hair, shiny, black, and bobbed, was tucked untidily behind my ears.

We looked at each other for a long time. The gleam of his hazel eyes, the glow of his skin. His presence. His intensity. It was hard to think what to say.

A strand fell over my eyes, and he pulled his chair closer, reached over and pushed the strand away. Our knees were almost touching. "You—" he said, his hand lingering near my face.

"Yes?" I said lightly.

"You're brave. You don't fear the things other women fear."

"Maybe not, but it hasn't earned me much praise in the past."

We both fell silent for a moment, watching each other.

"But your past doesn't matter to me," he said, lifting his glass. It was beaded with moisture, the whiskey burnished gold by the lamplight.

"Excuse me?"

"Everything that happened to you. Your marriage, your divorce—you don't need to feel ashamed for anything in your past."

"Well, I don't feel ashamed about any of that. I never have."

At this I caught a slight register of surprise. We were quiet again, studying each other.

"You're married," I blurted out. If I expected an explanation, he didn't give me one.

"Yes," he said. There was nothing in his tone that invited a response, so for the moment I left it at that.

I looked away. When I looked back I saw that his gaze had fallen to the rope of pearls knotted between my breasts. His chair scraped against the tiled floor and his body slid toward me. I watched as he touched the pearls around my neck and then traced his fingers along my collarbone. It was the moment between not having something and having something, the moment between desire and deed, and then he took a last draft of whiskey and set down his glass.

❧

My whole being is a dark chant
singing you into the dawn
of eternal growth and bloom.

In this chant I conjure you with a sigh,
I graft you to the trees, to the water, to the fire.

—from "Reborn"

All at once: That's how I first saw the Caspian Sea. Later, I'd travel the road to Chalous many times, but never without remembering my first view of it, on the day Darius took me there. It would seem impossible that it could have risen before me suddenly, so long is the approach to the beach in that place, but the first time I traveled to the Caspian it felt as if we shot through a forest of pines and straight toward an endless line of blue.

I thought he'd forgotten, or didn't choose to remember, what had happened between us. The kiss, the urgent fumbling, the sound of voices in the courtyard, and how we'd sprung apart just before his brother knocked at the door. But then there was this: a suggestion, almost casual, to drive north together and spend a week by the sea before going back to Tehran. The others would go directly to the city, he said, but he would hire a car and drive us to Ramsar.

Now the backseat was piled high with cameras, tripods, and canisters of film. He'd handed me a map when we set out from Abadan. A line had been traced to mark the route north. It bypassed Tehran and ran past the jagged lines of the Alborz Mountains, where pale yellow gave way to bright green, then looped round and round so many times that it made me dizzy just to follow the route with my eyes. From Chalous we would continue north until we reached the Caspian.

All along the way, turquoise domes beckoned in the sun,

their stones a blue so pure it encapsulated the earth's long-ing for the sky. We approached the coast in the late after-noon. Though I was tired from the long drive, the magnificence of the countryside rejuvenated me, and I craned my neck out the window. The road opened onto endless green fields, mountains shrouded in mist, vast dense woods, rolling green hills, and, finally, the sea.

"The Caspian," he said, gesturing broadly once he'd parked the car.

I stepped outside, dazed. He turned to study me and I could see he was clearly pleased with my reaction. The wind picked up, tossing my hair across my face. For a moment I forgot Darius. It was just past four o'clock, and the beach was completely empty. I shaded my eyes to study the view. The sea was vast and blue here, not the tin gray of the gulf. Orange groves rimmed the coast, and in the distance pine trees stretched up to the sky.

I broke away from him and made off for the sea. The air was moist on my skin, and the steady surge of the waves filled my head. Even from here I could see the shore was dark and wet. I had an urge to feel the water against my bare feet. I slipped off my shoes and then continued down the pebbled shore. When I reached the water's edge, I glanced back toward him and then watched as he lifted his arm to wave. I waved back. Aware of his gaze now, I turned again toward the waves, lifted my skirt, and stepped into the water.

The joy of it. Walking into the sea that day gave me a feeling of freedom I loved and had always loved. Suddenly I was a child crouching under a honeysuckle bush in my mother's garden. A young girl sneaking up to the rooftop to gaze at a sky thick with stars. I could not remember the last time I had felt so carefree and happy. I closed my eyes, inhaled deeply, tasting the salt in the air, and thought, *I want to be of the sea.*

Leaving the beach, we held hands as we walked to the car. We drove to his villa, in a small village on the beach. Tucked above a citrus orchard and draped in bougainvillea, the villa faced the Caspian. Inside it was large but spare and plain. It would be ours for a week. As soon as we entered, Darius threw open the windows, and a soft, damp breeze, smelling of rain and cypress, filled the room. I stepped toward him and he reached around my waist, found the zipper of my skirt, then undid the buttons of my blouse and slipped it over my head. I had one brief moment of self-consciousness, but then he kissed the hollow of my throat, my neck, the inside of my wrists, and I could think of nothing. In the honeyed evening light, I bent toward him. In that room, I forgot hesitation and doubt. "You're beautiful," he murmured, and knelt to kiss my breasts, and the next words were lost against my skin.

The next morning, as I took in the shining brass bed, the crisp cotton sheets, and the aroma of Turkish coffee wafting from the kitchen, I understood that this was a very different happiness from any I'd known. We spent hours walking on the shore and along the mountain trails and came back to the villa for dinners of whitefish, fresh greens, walnuts, yogurt, and figs with cream. At night we talked by the fire and drank red wine. We slept late and made love twice a day. It was a true heaven.

One such afternoon, I learned the meaning of my name. "Forugh," he murmured, his head resting on my navel, his warm stubbled cheek brushing my skin. "Do you know what it means?"

"My name?" I said, laughing.

"Yes."

"It means light," I said.

He raised his head. "No, not light. Or not quite," he said. "It means luster—the glow that circles light."

Those days by the Caspian Sea were the only ones that were ever completely ours. A world separate from everything and everyone else. When I wrote about them afterward, the words carried me back there, back into the thrill and sweetness of a love beginning:

> We found truth in the garden,
> in the shy glance of a nameless flower,
> found eternity in the moment
> when two suns faced each other.
>
> I'm not talking about
> fearful whispers in the dark.
> I'm talking about daytime
> and open windows and fresh air
> and a stove where useless things
> are left to burn,
> a land fertile with different plantings:
> birth and evolution and pride.
> I'm talking about how our loving hands
> built a bridge forged of scent and breeze
> across the night.

—from "Conquest of the Garden"

24.

"It seems I'm in disgrace," I told Leila. It was a balmy summer morning on the terrace, and I was sitting on the grass with my legs drawn all the way up, my chin resting on my knees. Only a few weeks had passed since Darius and I returned to Tehran, but already it was clear everyone knew or could guess we were now lovers.

"Shocking," she said teasingly. She lowered the record onto the turntable and dropped the needle in the groove. There was a hissing and crackling and then the song started up. Ella Fitzgerald.

"You're falling in love with him," she said after we'd listened for a while.

"Fallen," I corrected her. "It's already done."

"I see." She tweaked the volume down a notch and studied me quietly.

"You're not going to warn me off him?" I asked.

She arched an eyebrow. "Would it work?"

I shook my head. "No, but I do remember you trying to steer me away from someone before."

"Nasser?"

"Yes."

"He wasn't worthy of you. Not even slightly."

"And Darius is?"

"Possibly," she said, "but only possibly."

"He's arranging a place for me to live in the city."

"Oh," she said, looking surprised. For a moment she said nothing. "Is that what you want?"

"Yes."

Her face went very still. "If things don't turn out quite as you want, promise you won't be too proud to come back, will you? You'll remember you always have a place here with me?"

I felt a stab of sadness, and I could only nod and say, "I will, Leila *joon*. I promise you, I will."

Love is another country. No, I'd go further than that. The difference between foreign countries is never so great as the difference between being in love and not being in love. Not only does the world around you seem changed when you are in love—bright where it was once dull, lively and varied where it was once routine—but people are different, not least of all you yourself, though the difference might be that you've returned to your native self.

Falling in love with Darius brought forth my old impetuousness but also a warmth and hopefulness I had lost. The wisest thing to do would have been to stay at Leila's, at least until I had some clear notion of where I stood with Darius. But I didn't do the wisest thing. In those days, I thought he was my future, that everything was just beginning, and for a while so much was.

My new home was in a part of Tehran I hardly knew, a bustling district that felt a world away from my childhood home in Amiriyeh. I loved the little grocery at the corner, loved all the cafés, boutiques, and bookshops down the street. The apartment itself had two bedrooms, and one of them I made into my office. Darius had the apartment furnished before I moved in, and what little decoration there was pleased me, with simple, modern lines, the overall impression elegant but not ostentatious. Right away I began to rearrange the furniture and to unpack the few things I'd brought from Leila's house. She'd given me a carpet, a lovely red kilim. "For good luck in your new house," she said. There was a terrace with a small garden, and until the weather turned cold, I laid the kilim on the ground outside and worked there. It was the first time in my life I had a home of my own, and I relished the feeling of pulling the door shut behind me and knowing I wouldn't be disturbed. I was living in Tehran, earning a living, and, for the first time, I was in love.

Darius wasn't perfect—far from it. He could be remote and arrogant, but I admired him in spite of those qualities, maybe even because of them. We spent hours talking about poetry and films. These were the kinds of conversations I'd never had with a man. He wanted to know my opinions about everything, and of course he shared all his ideas with me. He talked about his plans for the studio, all the films he was burning to make. I'd never known anyone so intense—so ambitious and alive.

What attracted me deeply, perhaps most of all, was his lack of sentimentality, his refusal to be ruled or defined by the past. Darius couldn't be bothered with tradition, and he had no use for nostalgia or even for remembrance. "We only lose ourselves by looking back," he said, and he was a man who would never be lost. Everything in his world was deliberate. He was free on the terms he'd decided for his life. What others called "fate" was to him an ancient mindset that stunted people's thinking and kept the country choked and subservient. He didn't care for the old Iran, with its notions of a destiny inscribed across one's forehead, and he laughed at the ignorance in which people chose to live. Iran was surging toward modernity, albeit unevenly, but his countrymen lived as if it were still the fifteenth century. It was unintelligent. Unfathomably so.

Talking to him, I realized that until now my life had been haphazard, as had my education. All that would change—I was determined it would and so, too, was Darius. He hired a tutor so I could improve my English. He set up accounts for me at the city's best booksellers. T. S. Eliot's poems and essays. George Bernard Shaw's plays. Hemingway's stories and novels. I bought these books by the armful and began to read my way through them. He liked to hear my reactions to the writers he loved. He'd ask me to read my poems aloud to him, and he was content to just listen, his tall frame spilling from the chair in the corner of the living room, which seemed so small when he occupied it.

Every time I turned the lock and passed through the front door, I wanted to know he would be waiting for me in that chair, wanted to know he'd pull me into his arms, walk me backward into the bedroom, and stay with me until the next day and all the days after that. But just because I wanted these things didn't mean I could have them. He'd stay over some nights, but most of the time he drove back up to Darrus before morning, to his house there. I should have let myself understand what I was in for—he was married, after all. If I were honest, I would have to admit I knew exactly what I was getting myself into from the moment our affair began. I just told myself it didn't matter.

A Fire was my first film project at Golshiri Studios, and while it didn't find much of an audience in Iran, it would win an international prize, and that launched my cinematic career. Not long after the trip to Abadan, I started working in the editing department. Until now, money—or a lack of it—had been my torment, but my new salary was three times what I'd been paid as a receptionist. I loved the feeling of freedom a steady salary gave me, but most of all I loved the work. In editing films, I was inventing a visual rhythm and syntax, translating my ideas into a medium that felt fresh but consonant with my writing. I'd come home from the studio late at night and go to bed with my mind still buzzing with ideas. As I advanced at the studio, I joined Darius at gatherings of esteemed intellectuals and their pleasant, lovely wives. *Look how well you're doing,* I'd say to myself. I was meant to be in Ahwaz—or else locked up in an asylum—but instead I had found my way to this new life.

Through Darius, I came to know the painter Sohrab Sepehri, the poet Ahmad Shamlou, the architect Bijan Saffari. Every one of them knew we were lovers, but this was a new era—or an era some Iranians wanted to see as new—and people in our circle pretended not to notice or care we were together. For a time, too long perhaps, I pretended the same.

Darius had been careful to tell me very little about his wife, but I began to piece together parts of their story. When we met they'd already been married for fifteen years and had two children, a boy and a girl. So far as I knew, he had only one complaint against his wife: boredom. He'd solved that easily enough by building a separate house for himself.

I called it "the glass house," on account of all the enormous windows. It was a large modern structure, set on a remote property in Darrus, far from the city and with nothing but trees and mountains all around. The drawing room had lacquered white walls and a polished white parquet floor with fine silk carpets scattered here and there. A painting of bare tree trunks by Sohrab Sepehri hung above the mantel, and the chairs and couches were all covered in buttery white leather. The house had a cool but stately emptiness. The stone tiles were mostly bare of carpets, the walls decorated with a few modernist paintings of exceptional caliber. One had the feeling here of entering a world without women, which it was.

He made it sound as though she—he only spoke of his wife as "she" or "her"—was content with their separation. That it had been in place long before I came along. That they were married in name only. He told me in such a way that I believed him. Especially in our first few years together, I think the two things really were separate—his marriage and his feelings for me. Maybe he also thought it would hurt me to hear a different version of the story, but he treated the subject as though it had nothing to do with me, and instead of voicing the questions flooding my mind—*Do you mean you're permanently separated? Are you planning to get a divorce?*—I held my tongue. I never kissed him, never touched him, never said an intimate thing when there was anyone to glimpse or overhear us, and if my head and heart chafed at the secrecy of our arrangement, I told myself I had to stifle them. We'd struck a bargain of a kind. I had to love him within the limits of his life, or I wouldn't have a chance to love him at all.

Photographs of us cropped up in the papers all the time. I could tell it unnerved him. Whenever somebody pointed a camera in our direction, he opened a distance between us, but there was always a look, a gesture, or some slight movement between us of which we were unaware. Later I would look at those photographs, the grainy images blurred and softened by time, and I'd see it—how our bodies were drawn together as if by an invisible thread. One picture showed me with a long-stemmed cigarette holder, sitting on a couch with my feet tucked under me, and him with his head bent toward me, leaning close to listen to something I was saying. Another caught me holding two wheels of film while he pointed his camera up to the sky. His linen trousers were white and slightly creased by the heat, and I was squinting against the sun, following his directions and learning to sharpen my vision beside him.

That first year we were together, with the first flush of spring, he planted a row of saplings in the terrace outside my apartment, tucked them one by one into the ground, patted the earth above them, and encircled them with smooth stones for safekeeping. *See?* I thought. *Roots. We're putting down something solid here, something that will last.*

❧

"Forugh was a still, feminine pond without waves or movement. Darius Golshiri has now fallen into that pond like a bright stone and replaced the calm and quiescence with vibrant waves."

The idea for a party came to Darius on the day one of the big Tehran papers reviewed some of my recent work. This was in 1961. We'd spent a rare night together in Darrus, and I was lingering in bed with a mug of sugared tea when I picked up the newspaper and noticed the review.

Now, it wasn't as if I was wholly unprepared for what it said. These latest poems had inspired a round of familiar screeds: "Forugh's poems showcase a fascination with matters of the body and continue this woman's campaign to corrupt our nation's youth. . . ." Usually, reviews of my work were linked directly to some scandal or other in my life, but for the first time a small number of critics voiced praise for the poems, focusing on the writing itself rather than using my poems as an occasion to generate more gossip. "While they are as fully impassioned and embodied as we've come to expect from Forugh," wrote one, "these new poems demonstrate not only a greater range of philosophical and political subject matter but also an ever-stronger technical finesse."

I'd also started receiving notes and letters, most of them from young women, telling me how much they admired my writing. "You express what I can't say, not even to myself," and "You write with the soul of Hafez, but in a voice that's completely of our time." The letters were full of intelligence, curiosity, and rage, the very things that had drawn me to poetry in the first place, and it gave me a strange but wonderful feeling of kinship to read these women's words.

I smoothed the newspaper over my knees. It was my habit now, as I drank my tea in the mornings, to sit up in bed, flatten the paper across my lap, and read it front to back. This morning, I opened the arts section and saw my name linked to Darius's. What I read unhinged me: Darius, the author claimed, was writing my poems for me. That, he insisted, was the only thing that accounted for the strength of my latest work.

"Take a look at this!" I said and handed Darius the newspaper, stabbing the offending article.

He took one look at the byline and refused to read it. "The man's a nobody," he said. "How can you take anything he writes seriously?"

As usual my stubbornness and rage were no match for his pride. I envied his cool, constant refusal to be even slightly annoyed by the gossip surrounding us. He was not one to read reviews of his own work, and he always seemed oblivious to people's opinions of his films. On rare occasions he'd dismiss some journalist or another with a cutting remark; more often, he acted as if his critics and enemies just didn't exist—no, as if they couldn't exist.

"I'm throwing you a party," he said. "And they can all go to hell."

The dress for the party arrived by courier in a red-ribboned box. Later it would seem impossibly stupid, but for days all I could think about was what I should wear to the party Darius had decided to throw in Darrus. He never made any apologies for his wealth. He dressed impeccably and, while he never said it outright, he expected the same of me. For my birthday he'd given me a necklace of pavé diamonds, and from the moment he fastened the clasp and called me beautiful, I knew how much it pleased him to see me dressed up.

I spent a whole day in uptown boutiques with carpeted floors and mirrored walls, boutiques where beautifully turned-out shopgirls praised my narrow waist and slender legs, bent down with tape measures and pins, and laid all their prettiest and finest garments at my feet. The dress I finally settled on was truly exquisite: raw black silk with a fitted bodice and flared skirt. Refined but alluring. Perfect.

I tipped the courier and carried the box to the bedroom. Bags and boxes lay splayed open on the floor. The bed was scattered with other purchases from my shopping spree: seamed stockings, two-inch satin heels, a cashmere wrap. I loosened the red ribbon from the box, pulled off the lid, and then stripped down to my slip. I bathed and made up my face before the mirror. Cat eyes and crimson lips. The flash of diamonds at my throat set off my eyes. I flipped off the bathroom lights and crossed into the bedroom. The silk gleamed and rippled as I lifted the dress from the folds of faintly perfumed tissue paper. I shimmied it down my waist, zippered up the back, and straightened the skirt. The lining was silk and cold against my skin. It was only when I turned to look at myself in the mirror that I realized I was holding my breath.

"You're magnificent," Darius whispered when I arrived in Darrus later that night. He placed his hand at the small of my back as I walked through the door, and for a few moments we lingered in the foyer. He was dressed in navy trousers and matching sports jacket with a wide lapel, and his white shirt was opened at the neck. He'd started wearing his hair longer and he looked very tanned, as if he'd just come back from several weeks at the seaside. He leaned forward so that I thought he might kiss me, but then there was the sound of footsteps approaching and he quickly stepped back and drew away his hand.

The glass house glowed with the light of hundreds of candles. Determined that this night would rival the best parties in Tehran, Darius had ordered crates of English whiskey and French champagne and pounds of the choicest, costliest Iranian caviar. Gardenias and roses perfumed the air. A four-piece band, on tour from America and summoned here with an enormous fee, was playing Latin jazz in the great room.

Talk quieted as I entered the party, only to resume at a higher pitch. I didn't know many people in attendance, but nearly everyone knew my face well enough to whisper and nod in my direction. I caught fragments of conversation—comments about the currency rates, an article someone had published in one of the undergound communist papers, a new art-house cinema, some scandal at court. It had become fashionable for men and women to mix at social events, but even in this smart set there were limits, and many old ideas survived. Looking out at the guests, I saw that the women fell into the usual groups: wives and girlfriends. When the wives took my hands in theirs and congratulated me on my latest publication, it seemed to me it was really their own graciousness and generosity that stirred them.

I was more comfortable talking with the girlfriends. Most of them didn't seem to know who I was, which made it easier somehow, but I knew from experience I'd likely never see them again. That, I knew, was the strange, sad economy of love in our milieu. But where, exactly, did I belong?

If only Leila were here, I thought miserably. She had canceled at the last minute—the second time she'd canceled plans in the last few weeks. "I don't feel up to it," she'd said. "I'm so sorry, Forugh, but I just can't come."

I drifted away, down a corridor and past a pair of tall doors into the library. Here a stack of my books stood mostly untouched on a side table. Darius had said the party would be a celebration of my latest poems, but it was the scandal that captured people's attention, the fact that I was Darius's mistress, and they'd come just to see us together. They didn't care about my writing—not really, and maybe not at all.

Darius must have anticipated all this, because he didn't stay at my side or hold my hand that night. Which was fine—no, it was even understandable. But I didn't expect that he'd greet me and then disappear. Within an hour my head was swimming with wine and jazz, I'd reached a state of bored restlessness, and I couldn't find Darius anywhere. *Where is he?* I wondered.

On the dance floor, someone elbowed me in the back and I lurched forward. The band was playing Tito Puente, the tune bright and loose and very loud. I couldn't see much other than a mass of bodies and a cloud of smoke hovering in the air. I threaded my way across the room, ducking between dancing couples, and at last found him chatting among a group of men. I lifted my hand in a small wave, but when I caught his eye he only nodded very slightly and then carried on with his conversation.

I had no expectations of him, but his dismissal gnawed at me, and I felt myself tense. Briefly, I thought of marching over to him, but instead I shouldered my way through the room and stepped out onto the veranda.

Outside, the cool air cleared my head. My feet were hurting from the new satin heels, and I slipped them off, careful not to snag my stockings on the flagstones.

"This whole country's diseased," I heard someone say.

I followed the voice to where a group of about a dozen people had gathered. Seated on a large wrought-iron chair in the garden, Bijan Bazargan, the intellectual-of-the-moment, was holding court before a circle of acolytes.

I eased myself down on a nearby bench.

"Diseased," he repeated. He was a portly man, with a heavy beard. "We watch American soap operas, wear blue jeans, drink Coca-Cola, and call ourselves open-minded. But that's not open-mindedness. As Al-e-Ahmad teaches us, it's a disease we've contracted over decades of imperialism, and it's called Westoxification."

Westoxification. I had heard the phrase before. The new rallying cry among Tehran's intellectuals, it stood for everything wrong about modernization and consumerism, about an Iran that saw its way forward by angling toward the West. The cure, presumably, was a return to tradition.

"And nowhere is this pathetic aping of foreign manners and gross consumerism so rampant as among today's Iranian women."

I'd been listening absentmindedly to Bazargan's lecture, but this last part caught my attention.

"How do you mean?" I called out as I stood up.

It took a moment for him to place me, but once he did, he smiled with what seemed like delight. "Forugh Farrokhzad, the poetess!" he said, gesturing broadly in my direction. "I'd think of all the women at this party, you'd understand my meaning best." He turned to his audience, which I now noticed was made up entirely of men. "These days, young Iranian women seem to think that just by styling their hair differently and wearing short skirts, they're suddenly free. In fact, these women have only prostituted themselves to foreigners and imperialists."

He meant it as provocation and I took it as that. "I wonder, Mr. Bazargan, if you'd rather have us women shrouded and sequestered in our homes?"

"Whatever their shortcomings, the ways of the past were at least our own. Our customs are our identity, Miss Farrokhzad, and by giving them up we've lost sight of who we are."

"What do you mean, 'our own'? It doesn't seem to me that women have had much freedom in choosing the traditions that govern their lives."

He smiled and shook his head. "Your trouble, Miss Farrokhzad, is that you imagine all women share your discontent. This is, of course, a typical mistake among our country's new would-be feminists. Tell me, what can you possibly understand of the lives of most Iranian women?"

I nearly managed to bite my tongue, but now he'd goaded me and I couldn't back down. "Maybe very little, but I do know that it wouldn't cost you much to return to the past, whereas, like any other woman in this country, it would cost me a great deal."

He rose from his chair and stepped closer to me then—close enough that I could smell the sour odor of alcohol streaming from his breath.

"Madam," he said loudly, "how can you stand in this fancy house with this fancy garden, in your fancy dress, and with the rank of . . . what? A mistress? A half wife? How can a woman like you lecture us about the value of custom and tradition?"

The next thing happened quickly.

It was his hot, sweaty fingers I'd always remember. The way he gripped my shoulder with one hand and reached back and fumbled with the other one against my neck and the collar of my dress until I heard something tear.

The label—he'd ripped it clear off, and he was now holding it up for everyone to see.

"Without her fancy label," he announced, "the notorious poetess is just another simple, modest Iranian woman!"

It took me a moment to realize it, but when he tore the label, my dress split open at the back. I scrambled to yank the zipper up, but it had ripped and wouldn't budge. People now went quiet and looked away. I felt a hand pull me back, but I surged forward, grabbing for the label, which Bijan Bazargan was still brandishing in the air. "You idiot!" I screamed. "You jackass!" He laughed and lifted the piece of cloth higher, waving it over my head in some imitation of a folk dance.

Still shouting, I let myself be led off the veranda by Darius. He covered me in his sport coat, took me into another room, and spoke to me in a cool and reasonable tone. But everything he said—that Bazargan was obviously drunk, that he was famous for his outrageous gestures, that he'd left and I should return to the party now—only infuriated me further. I needed air, water, something. I needed to get *out*.

I grabbed my purse and made for the door before Darius could see the swell of my tears. His jacket was far too big for me, but I clasped it tight at the throat as I brushed past the knots of whispering women. The pebbled drive was silver in the moonlight, and it was only when my feet hit the ground that I realized I wasn't wearing any shoes. I'd left them on the veranda. For a moment I considered going back for them, but then I decided against it. I winced and picked my way down the path toward my car, and I was already half-

way down the driveway when I glanced in the rearview mirror and saw Darius waving and shouting something I
couldn't hear.

It was past midnight, and the road from Darrus was deserted and dark. Tears stung my eyes, blurring my sight. I
cranked down the window and let the night in. I had broken out in a sweat without realizing it and the cool air
against my skin made me feel clammy, but as I drove toward
Tehran, too fast and too recklessly, the tight, cramped feeling in my chest gradually eased.

Then, just outside the city, I turned onto Avenue Pahlavi
and hit a wall of light. I braked hard, swerving to the side of
the road and sending my purse flying from the front seat to
the floor. I blinked, blinked again, then flipped off the headlights and rolled down my window. Lifting my hand to
shield my eyes from the glare, I craned my head outside to
see what was going on.

An army tank was blocking the road. A figure cut through
the brightness and moved toward my car. I glanced in the
rearview mirror. Smeared lipstick and raccoon eyes. I was
wiping my face with the back of my hand when the soldier
beamed his flashlight into the car, ran it from my face to the
men's sport coat I was wearing.

I cut the engine and dropped my hands to my lap.

"Where are you headed?" he asked, not unkindly.

"Home," I said, and gave my address. From a distance, I
heard the long whine of a siren. "What's happening in the
city?"

He looked out toward the city and then back at me.
"There's been an assassination," he said. "We're under martial law."

25.

WHAT HAD HAPPENED WAS THIS: ON HIS WAY TO PARLIA-ment earlier that day, a high-ranking government minister was ambushed in an alleyway. A pistol was shot once and then again. The first bullet pierced the minister's forehead, the second his heart.

It was a communist plot. A British plot. An American plot. An Islamist plot. Every conceivable and halfway-conceivable scenario was advanced, which left most every-one sure of nothing—nothing apart from their own helplessness and the certainty that worse was coming. And worse did come. Another night of riots, this time close to the British Embassy, followed by several days of sirens, raids, searches, and arrests. The sidewalks were vacant, haunted only by police and soldiers patrolling the streets.

The situation, while unnerving, provided the solitude I needed. For the first time, I wanted to be away from Darius. With Tehran under martial law, no one could travel in or out of the city, and the phone lines had been cut off, so I had no word from him, which suited me just fine.

I was lucky I'd gotten to Tehran when I did; an hour later the whole city was sealed off. With checkpoints at nearly every intersection, it had taken me more than an hour to make it back home. As soon as I walked through the door, I shrugged off Darius's jacket, slipped out of my dress, and unpinned my hair. I was exhausted but strangely calm. In the frantic haste of getting ready for the party, I'd left the house a total mess. Now I went from room to room, picking up stray clothes, tidying the tables, clearing the sink. By the time I was finished, both Darius's jacket and my once-perfect, now-ruined dress lay in a crumpled heap at the bottom of a dustbin, but I could still taste the humiliation every time I thought about the party and what had happened that night. Whatever his feelings, Darius was too ashamed, or too frightened, to defend me, much less acknowledge our relationship. Everything between us now seemed based on a massive lie—a lie I'd told myself. Even after all that had happened with Nasser, I'd let myself be misled. I'd let myself be fooled into thinking our relationship was more than it was. I hated Bijan Bazargan and I hated Darius, but even more I hated myself.

I spent the next few days pacing the house with the wireless radio turned on. *Leila*, I thought at every mention of a Tudeh conspiracy. She must be frantic for her brother's safety. Again and again I picked up the phone to dial her number, only to find the line dead. I felt a stirring of unease that grew stronger by the hour. Then, on the third night, my phone rang near midnight, shrill and electrifying. I flipped on the light and reached for the receiver.

"Leila?"

But it was Darius. "Are you all right?" he asked as soon as I picked up.

I sat up in bed and rubbed my eyes. "I'm fine."

"Why'd you run off like that?"

I took a deep, steadying breath. "You know why."

"Because of Bazargan? I told you, he's a show-off. You can't let him get to you."

"It's not only him. It's everyone. Everywhere I go. Do you know that behind our backs people call me your—"

"My what?"

"Whore." The word sounded terrible. I hadn't said it before and had not known I would until now. I raked my hand through my hair and stared up at the ceiling. "People read the newspapers and see pictures of me and say, 'Oh, she's not actually talented, she's just managed to attach herself to someone who can do things for her. She gets all her ideas from him. I hear she doesn't even write her own poems.' "

"Come on, Forugh. Does it really matter to you what people say?"

"I don't want it to matter. I've really tried not to care, but I can't help it. People would never talk about you the way they do about me, and they would never dare suggest I influence your films, much less make them for you."

"The real issue," he said, his voice softening, "is that no one has a right to any part of our relationship. What we have belongs only to us."

"But I don't like this feeling of secrecy. I don't like to pretend. I had to do that for so long, before."

"It's not an ideal arrangement—not at all—but that's the fault of this small-minded country and all these idiots around us. There's nothing either of us can do to change their way of thinking."

"No, I suppose not." I paused for a moment and rubbed my forehead with the heel of my hand. All at once I felt a piercing loneliness, and despite myself I asked, "When do you think you can come down here?"

He coughed and cleared his throat. "You know they're not letting anyone in or out of the city right now."

"But you'll come as soon as you can?"

"I'll try, Forugh. I've got to sort out a few things. Just wait for me, okay? You can do that for a little while, can't you?"

When I didn't answer, he sighed into the phone and said, "Please wait."

Please wait. I screwed my eyes shut. A sense of rage welled up inside me, and I felt myself begin to sweat, hot with frustration. "But haven't I already been waiting? Haven't I been waiting all this time?"

It was clear from my first glance at Leila—sitting in her unmade bed, still in her nightgown at two o'clock in the afternoon—that something was very wrong. The shades were drawn, and I blinked hard as I walked toward her in the airless room. "Forugh," she said, much too quietly, and I knew at once that she was not at all her bright, unflappable self but rather a hazy approximation, all slender wrists and frantic eyes and unkempt hair.

With Tehran under martial law, almost another week had passed before I could get up to her house. That morning the government had declared the assassination a communist plot. "Members of the Tudeh Party are traitors," an official announced over the radio, "enemies of both king and country, and they will be rooted out one by one until we are rid of their pestilence."

I settled on the edge of the bed and put a hand on her shoulder. Her bones felt thin under her cotton tunic. "Have you heard from Rahim?" I asked.

She lifted her eyes. "Nothing."

"Is there any chance he might be angry with you?"

Her eyes snapped to attention. "Why would you think that?"

"Well, do you remember that day when I saw the two of you? A few years ago? It seemed like you were arguing. Were you?"

I could see her hedging, weighing what she shouldn't tell me against the urgency of my questions and her own need to unburden herself. "I'd gotten him a passport under an assumed name. And cash. I wanted him to leave the country, at least for a while."

"But he wouldn't go."

What she said next, she meted out carefully. "He said too many people were counting on him. Something had happened and he couldn't leave Iran." For a moment she was quiet, wrapped in some dark thought. "Have you heard what happened up by parliament?"

"You mean the assassination?"

She nodded.

There'd been no other talk in Tehran for days and days. I nearly asked her how she could possibly imagine I hadn't heard the news, but then I stopped. It was clear she wasn't thinking straight.

"Yes," I said. "I've heard."

"God help me, Forugh, but I can't let myself think he'd be involved in something like that."

"You don't know if he was."

She bit her lower lip and looked down at her hands. "That's true."

"Do you have any idea where he could be now?"

"There was a place he stayed once near the university, a safe house. A few times I've gotten as close as the campus gates. I wander around, poking my head around the coffee shops and bookstores, hoping I'll run into him. But so far I haven't had the nerve to go find him."

"Why not?"

"He made me promise not to. He said it was just a matter of time before I was followed by SAVAK—if I wasn't already being followed, that is."

SAVAK. The shah's secret police. I'd heard there were thousands of them in the city, a vast network of agents and informers, and that they were as brutal as they were stealthy.

"Do you think that's possible, that someone's watching you?"

She answered with a helpless shake of the head. "Some days I think yes, and I see them everywhere—in the street when I go into town and even out in the fields around the house—but then I think no, I'm imagining it, there's no one there, I'm being crazy . . ." Her voice trailed off and her eyes were round with panic.

"But without a passport and money he'll never get out of the country, right?"

"I don't think so, no."

"Then I'll go," I said. Even if I didn't fully understand what he'd done or been accused of, I knew the effect of Rahim's disappearance on Leila, the fear and hopelessness that had gripped her. If I could at least reassure her that her brother was alive, perhaps I could ease her distress. I owed her so much and here, finally, was a way I could help her.

The rain fell hard the next morning, and runoff from the old waterways flooded the streets. I parked several blocks away from Tehran University. For some minutes I sat in the car, listening to the rain drum against the windshield and steadying my nerves. Leila and I had gone over the plan several times. No one could see the car and connect me to Rahim. I'd have to be quick, and if anyone stopped me and asked me why I was here, I'd say I'd come to visit a cousin. I did, in fact, have a cousin at the university. I hadn't seen him in years, but it was something, a connection. An excuse.

I pulled a dark-blue scarf over my head, tightened it with a knot under my chin, and pulled on the loose black overcoat that Leila had bought from one of her housekeepers. When I stepped from the car, I held my umbrella so that it obscured part of my face.

The neighborhood around Tehran University was a honeycomb of densely populated streets, lanes, and alleys. It was Sunday and the bookshops and publishing houses were quiet, but I passed several coffeehouses in which I glimpsed students sitting together in pairs and small groups, their heads wreathed in cigarette smoke.

I crossed the street, darting past the occasional umbrella, and ducked into a side street, only to find myself standing in several inches of water, my shoes and stockings soaked. The wind picked up and snapped my umbrella so that the fabric sagged and flapped. I was fumbling with it when I saw that there was a man standing across the street in a long black coat, looking my way. I thought I had seen him before, over by the university gates. He was watching me closely and now he suddenly started in my direction.

I turned on my heel, picking up my pace, crossing one street and then another. After a while I paused, looking over my shoulder. To my relief, the man was gone. I was close now—nearly there. I scanned the building numbers but couldn't find the address. *You must not panic,* I told myself. *Keep your head, you'll find it.* I doubled back and eventually came upon the correct address, a two-story apartment building bordered by a grocer and publishing house, both of which were closed for the day.

Inside the building, the ceilings were low and the warped wooden floorboards creaked. Toward the end of the hall I saw a door. It was painted mustard yellow, just as Leila had described. There was no answer when I knocked, but I heard a shuffling of feet and then scraping of chairs against the wooden floor, and so I knocked again.

"Yes?" came a voice as the door opened a crack.

The boy—he would seem to me immediately a boy, not a man—was nervous and unshaven. I pushed the scarf off my forehead. My coat was trailing water onto the landing, and I felt the cold water leaking into my sleeves. I dug in my pocketbook for the papers: a counterfeit passport, some letters and banknotes, tied together with string. I passed it all to the boy, through the narrow opening, then watched his eyes scan the passport and gauge the heft of the envelope with his hand.

After a moment, he pulled the door open. As I entered the flat, I caught the smell of bodies pressed into cramped rooms for many days, shuttered away and hidden. There were three figures in the first room. They were sitting cross-legged on the floor, and one of them was smoking a cigarette. The windows had been papered over and the room was in near darkness, but I could make out their surprise when they saw me.

"Did anyone see you come into the building?" the boy asked, guiding me toward a hallway.

"I don't think so."

He stopped and turned to look at me. "You're not sure?"

I shook my head.

He stared at me and seemed ready to say something more, but instead he continued walking down the hall. I followed him up a staircase, which led to another door and then finally to a small room without a window.

Stepping inside, I first saw a cot and then a figure underneath the sheets. Rahim. I moved toward him. I thought he'd resemble Leila, but his features were so disfigured with bruises and swelling that I could see nothing of her there. His eyes were blackened and swollen, the lids welded shut. A charred black scar ran down one side of his face. His hair was longish and matted to his scalp. He was shirtless, the skin of his chest pale, nearly hairless, and crosshatched with fresh lashings.

I took a deep, shaky breath and grabbed the boy by the elbow. "You need to take him to the hospital. These cuts must be disinfected and stitched up or they won't heal. And he may have more-serious injuries, broken bones . . ."

He shrugged out of my grip. "Do you have any idea what's going on these days? One look at him and any doctor in this city would call the police."

"But he's bleeding, he's—"

"Listen," the boy said. "There's no way we're going to let them make a martyr of him."

"A martyr?"

"He's as good as dead if he leaves here."

"But there has to be somewhere you can take him! He'll die if you don't get him some kind of medical attention."

A groan rose from the bed, and the boy and I both turned toward Rahim. He was hooking a finger in my direction. "It's all right," he said when I came closer. His voice was ragged and nearly inaudible. When he opened one eye, his gaze didn't meet mine but hovered somewhere above it. "I'll be all right."

I crouched closer and caught the scent of blood. The gashes on his chest were wet with it.

Minutes went by before he spoke again. "Tell Leila I'm safe and . . ."

"Yes?"

"Be careful, Forugh."

I nodded and placed a hand gingerly on his arm. "Your sister sends her love. She wants you to be safe. She wants to help you." I'm not sure he heard me, as his eyes drifted closed, but already the boy was leading me from the room and I had no choice but to leave.

Outside, the pavement gleamed with the rain from the downpour. My kerchief was soaked through, but I pulled it low over my head and knotted it tight. I had done what I was supposed to do. But what could I tell Leila? Her brother was not all right. Nothing was all right.

"Be careful, Forugh," Rahim had said. It wasn't until later, when I'd left the safe house, climbed into the car, and driven back home, the image of Rahim's ravaged body before my eyes the whole way, that I realized I hadn't told him my name. He knew it already. I'd never discover how he found out, but he knew not only my name but that I would come. That I'd help him escape. He'd only been waiting for me to appear.

Rahim was smuggled out of Tehran hidden under a tarp among ten thousand potatoes on the back of a truck. His convalescence took place in a village of less than fifty people and lasted three weeks. From there, he traveled by foot with nothing but a rucksack on his back. Usually it took five days to walk to the border from that place, but he was weak and fevered and it took him eighteen. He followed a narrow, winding mountain pass until he reached the border between Iran and Turkey. A Kurdish goatherd guided him over to the other side. Six more days of walking. His fever had not come down, his lungs were weak, and he developed a cough that would stay with him until he died, many years later, in a small bungalow in Berkeley, California. He got to Istanbul by train. In all, the journey took two months, and it would be another month before a cable reached Leila, telling her he was out of the country.

Not long afterward there were rumors that Rahim had been granted asylum in America and was making noise about the shah's regime. Human-rights abuses. Tortures and murders. After that Leila lost track of him, but for a while it was enough to know he'd made it out of Iran. She was calmer, sinking back into her translations, but she never fully recovered. He was her only family, the only one who'd mattered, anyway. Now he was gone and she knew—I felt sure of it—she would never see him again.

26.

"DO YOU WANT TO DIRECT YOUR OWN MOVIE?" DARIUS asked by phone from England.

He called the studio one afternoon when I was at work. The operator connected us and there was a lot of interference on the line. My God, it was good to hear his voice. How was it possible that I missed him so much?

When martial law had ended and I returned to the studio, I hated how much I wanted to see Darius again. Though I'd craved time on my own, he was never far from my thoughts. But when I went back to the studio, I found out he'd flown to London for an extended trip. It hurt me to know he'd left without telling me he'd be gone. Weeks had passed since then and I wouldn't tell him—I couldn't tell him—how lonely I'd been. Working and working, the empty apartment no longer a refuge but a taunt.

"What do you mean, my own movie?" I asked now, all brisk professionalism. I was sure he'd catch the strain in my voice, but if he did he chose not to make a point of it.

"A new documentary. The director's dropped out, and I was about to scrap the project when I thought of calling you."

"But what happened to the director?" I said, twirling and tightening the cord around my finger. It seemed strange that someone would just abandon a project. Maybe he'd gotten into some sort of trouble with the government? You heard more and more stories like that these days.

"Who knows?" said Darius. "He's probably strung out on opium somewhere. It wouldn't be the first time." There was a loud buzz, and for a moment it seemed we'd been disconnected. "Anyway, there's a crew waiting up in Tabriz." He waited a beat, then said, "Do you want to step in and direct it?"

Of course I did.

"We've got some support from a government organization," he went on, "but you call all the shots. It's all yours."

"Who's on the crew?"

He rattled off some names, only one of which was familiar to me. "Obviously they won't be expecting you."

"You mean they won't be expecting a woman."

"Nothing you can't handle," he said, and then paused. "It's wonderful to talk to you, Forugh. I've missed you." The line went silent for a moment. "Are you still there?" he asked.

I wanted to tell him how much I missed him, how much my body missed him, but there was a choked feeling in my throat and instead I said a quick goodbye and hung up the phone.

The next morning, I packed up the company jeep with a camera, tripod, and film and drove to Tabriz. Once there, I met up with the crew that was waiting for me. Before leaving Tabriz we stopped for two canisters of fuel—there'd be no service stations the rest of the way—and then we settled in for the hour-long drive to the Bababaghi Hospice in a small village to the north. I had a crew of three men, a budget of nearly nothing, and twelve days to make a documentary on a subject about which I was almost totally ignorant: leprosy.

Bababaghi was encircled by a tall fence, the wood worn and cracked with age. Walking through the colony the first time, I saw faces without mouths, hands without fingers, legs without toes or even without feet. As a child I'd been taught to think leprosy was contagious. A half hour of research the night before my trip taught me this wasn't true. But no matter what doctors and scientists said, the mere mention of the condition still terrified people. Most of the people at Bababaghi had been forced to live their whole lives here, and their children, even the healthy ones, were prisoners as well.

Everything I saw when I arrived at Bababaghi confirmed the necessity of documenting this place and its people. And yet I felt myself falter. The sufferings of these people seemed indescribable, unspeakable, inexpressible. That first day I sat by myself under the shade of a tree, working out some plan for how to proceed. A small girl with black eyes and pigtails tucked her doll in a wheelbarrow and pushed it past me. In the distance a man cried out, and there was no answer, anywhere, to his cry. For him, for all the people here, the world ended at that tall, decrepit fence. The colony wasn't just a symbol of imprisonment; it was the essence of imprisonment, a thing so immovable, so cruelly relentless, that I realized it could never be shown in any way other than what it was.

I had just twelve days to finish the project—there wasn't money or time for an extensive shoot. Still, I decided the first few days should be given over to learning the rhythms and rituals of the leper colony. Once I'd established some measure of trust with the people, I'd devote the next eight days to filming the documentary. It was maddening, thrilling, and exhausting work, and when it was done I called it *The House Is Black.*

❧

"I've barely recovered from my astonishment at your poetry, Forugh," Bernardo Bertolucci confided as we stood together in the crowded amphitheater, "and now you've brought that same talent and vision to your work as a filmmaker."

It was the night of my directorial debut. Gloved to the elbows, I was dressed in a black satin sheath and three-inch-high sling-back pumps. The film world had been buzzing about Bertolucci ever since *La commare secca* came out earlier that year. Darius had sent him an advance copy of *The House Is Black* and invited him to travel from Italy for the premiere. The auditorium was bright and hot, filled with the usual mix of the prominent and the up-and-coming, the old guard and the avant-garde. There were a good number of foreigners in attendance, as well. A journalist from Argentina, another from Israel, a large group from the American Embassy. Leila was also somewhere in the room, looking resplendent in a raspberry-red dress and matching lipstick.

My sister and her husband had come, as well, and they'd brought my mother along with them. We saw each other infrequently, so I was surprised when they'd accepted my invitation but grateful, too, and I told them so. When she saw me, my mother took hold of my hand and squeezed as hard as she could. Then my sister stepped forward and kissed me on the cheek. "Oh, Forugh," she said, eyes brimming. I'd never stopped feeling she disapproved of my divorce. Nevertheless, she called every few weeks, visited me several times a year. I'd gone to see her first play when it debuted and had attended the others she'd staged since then. Each time I published a book of poetry I sent it to her, and she'd always call to thank me. Whenever she wrote an article for a magazine, she would set aside a copy and give it to me when we saw each other. And now, standing together in the foyer, I felt her pride in me, and it just about crushed me with happiness.

I'd chatted with my family briefly before someone pulled me away, leading me toward Bernardo Bertolucci. Gracious introductions, followed by compliments and more compliments. People were watching us. They were leaning close to hear.

"You're a true artist, Forugh," Bertolucci declared.

"It's hard to accept a compliment like that from you, Mr. Bertolucci."

"Bernardo," he said and smiled.

"Bernardo," I echoed. As I said this I stepped a little too close, smiled a little too long. But I didn't care. I'd worked hard on the film and I knew it was good. This was my night, and I was determined to enjoy every minute of it.

"Nonsense, Forugh! You're truly an exceptional artist. I can see that your work comes from your own life. I want my films to do that, always. I'm against censorship of every kind, and I think I know something of the challenges you face as an artist here in Iran. Our countries are not so different—the history, the corruption, the struggles. Wouldn't you agree?"

I started to respond but then stopped. Not twenty feet away, Darius stood with a woman's arm laced in his. I'd never seen her before, but I knew immediately who she was.

I felt sick, light-headed, and I couldn't look away. Bertolucci's gaze followed mine. "Ah, I see Darius has arrived." He turned back to me and held out his arm. "Shall we join him, Forugh?"

I wanted to escape, to turn on my heel and flee, but already Bertolucci had tucked his arm around mine and was leading me through the crowd.

I felt Darius's eyes on me as we approached, but I couldn't trust myself to look at him. I was still trying to catch my bearings when I heard him say, "And this is my wife."

Wife. Of course she was his wife. What else would he call her? Still, it floored me to hear him say it aloud.

I could tell from how she raked me over, forehead to heels and back again, that she knew exactly who I was. Pretty and petite, she wore a flawless powder-blue suit with white piping and elbow-length sleeves. A gold wedding band flashed on her ring finger. Her eyes lingered briefly on my décolletage before settling back on my face with a pleasant expression.

"It's wonderful to finally meet you," she said, reaching out to shake my hand.

All at once, I felt gangly and awkward, and my cheeks began to redden. I'd imagined her as fragile, lusterless—had

I really imagined her at all?—but this was a woman in full possession of herself. Certainly more so than I was at that moment. I was so flustered I barely managed to choke out a hello, but when she said, "I'm so looking forward to your film," it was with a look of complete graciousness that nonetheless managed to convey a note of pure loathing.

And suddenly I understood who I was to Darius—or, rather, who I was not. He and Bertolucci had fallen into conversation, something to do with a mutual acquaintance in Italy, and I fumbled with the clasp of my purse, desperate for a cigarette. I had none. When I looked back up, I saw that Darius's wife had cocked her head to look at her husband, in a way that signaled both tenderness and respect. There was something else there, an unspoken familiarity, a history translated through their bodies, a something I stood completely outside of. They belonged to each other, and I belonged to no one.

I was grateful when, a few minutes later, the doors to the theater swung open and the lobby lights blinked on and off. Bertolucci, Darius, and his wife began to walk toward the theater, and I mumbled a hurried apology and broke off in the opposite direction.

I was pacing the foyer when Leila found me. I must have looked a mess, because as soon as she saw me she said, "What's happened?"

"Darius's wife . . ." I stammered.

Her eyes widened and she gripped my wrist. "She's here?"

I nodded.

"What do you want to do, Forugh?"

I flicked my eyes around the room. The foyer was nearly

empty, and the film would start any minute. *My* film would start any minute.

"I want to go inside."

"Then that's what you'll do."

She slipped a hand into the crook of my elbow, and together we made our way into the auditorium and down the carpeted aisle to the front row. Whispers rippled around us, but my mind was flitting wildly and I was oblivious to the looks and stares. The seats were almost full and we had to stumble over several pairs of legs to reach our seats. I sank into my chair, which seemed very narrow and hard. Darius and his wife were just a few seats away to my left, but I willed myself not to look in their direction.

This was not the entrance I had imagined for myself, not at all. I hated Darius for bringing his wife, for not knowing— or caring—what it would mean for me to have her there. Of course I was bound to meet her eventually, but this night was my debut, not to mention we were in the company of nearly five hundred guests. But maybe that was the point. Maybe he wanted every one of those five hundred guests to see him on the arm of his wife.

"Look up there," Leila whispered. There was something strange in her voice. An uneasiness. She gestured with her head toward two figures in the gallery. Their faces were in shadow, but I knew them by the glitter of their tiaras, their impeccable posture, the diamonds encircling their long-gloved arms—Empress Farah and the Princess Ashraf, the shah's twin sister.

"Did you know they were coming?" she asked.

I shook my head. Suddenly she looked grave and her face began to pale.

"What's wrong?" I leaned closer, taking her hand in mine, hoping to ease her fear.

Before she could answer, the theater darkened, the curtains slid open, and then the opening shot filled the screen. A man ran a ravaged hand along a high stone wall, chanting numbers until they became a kind of song. When he reached the end of the wall, he turned back, performing the ritual again. The sun beat down cruelly, beading his forehead with sweat, but he went on with his chant. I heard the sound of my own voice, weaving scripture and poems in the voice-over, and the first image gave way to other candid shots of people in the colony. The film was like a poem, like a rendering of a dream. Mangled hands without fingers, legs with no feet or toes, faces without eyes or mouths. The bright eyes and unblemished face of a small boy. A woman before a window, brushing the silken black sheet of her hair. A man in prayer, raising two handless arms to God. The hidden things of this world. The beauty that shadows despair.

I knew by the silence all around me that I'd made people see it.

Later, at a reception at the prime minister's mansion, Darius pulled me into a dark portico.

Whatever upset Leila in the theater had seemed to pass, and after the screening she insisted we go to the reception together. We were standing in the courtyard when her eyes fastened on something over my shoulder. I turned around and saw Darius making his way toward us.

"Can you give us a few minutes?" he said to Leila as he approached.

She looked at me. I swallowed hard, then nodded.

"I'll be in there," she said, tossing her head to indicate the house.

As soon as she was gone, he took my hand and led me into the portico.

I yanked my hand back from his grip and folded my arms across my chest. "You could have told me your wife would be here!"

"Would you have shown up if you knew?"

"What do you think?"

"You see! I didn't want to risk your not coming."

"Then you shouldn't have come yourself. Not with her."

"Everyone expects to see us together at these sorts of formal events. You understand that, don't you?"

"No. I don't."

"Look, she knows we're together and she's made her peace with it, but I can't—" His voice broke off.

I saw it all then, understood it all: the hesitations, the separations, the silences. He was bound to her. He'd always be bound to her.

"You can't divorce her." I heard my voice go hard and bitter. "That's what you wanted to say?"

"It would devastate her, Forugh. She's not like you. Respectability is everything to her."

I wish I could say I made some cutting remark then or that I told him how much he'd hurt me, not only tonight but at the party in Darrus and all the times he'd pretended I was no one to him and there was nothing between us, but all I did was turn away. Darius called out something that sounded like "Please," but I didn't turn back or stop. I stumbled toward the house and found a door.

Inside, the salon was overheated and teeming with pe ple. I was used to wealth by now, but I'd never been pa a crowd like this, the men in tuxedos and silk cravats, the ladies with their gowns and heaps of jewels. People drifted past me, a whirl of perfume and cigarette smoke. I had a vague notion Darius was following me, and I quickened my pace. I shouldered my way through the crush of people, stumbling and cursing. "Miss Farrokhzad!" called a voice, but I didn't turn my head, only walked steadily onward, searching for a glimpse of Leila.

I turned down a long hall and found myself in an even larger salon. Here a waiter approached with champagne, and I plucked two glasses from the tray. Champagne always made me sick and light-headed, but I knocked back the first glass in one long gulp.

"Forugh!" Darius called from somewhere behind me. Before he could stop me, I'd drunk the second glass.

The champagne hit fast and hard. In a minute the room was tilting. Darius grabbed the empty glasses from my hands and muttered something I didn't catch. From behind my eyes I felt a hammering in my head. The glittering ceiling and mirrored walls splintered the light into thousands of pieces, throwing specks of color against every surface. And then I saw it: the brilliant tiara bobbing between the guests. The princess was coming toward us, parting the crowd as she approached.

On her arm was a tall, silver-haired man in a dark suit with a boutonniere on his lapel. "Eskandar Gerami," the man said, bowing ceremoniously as he introduced himself as the princess's adviser. His hooked nose put me in mind of an eagle.

"Your Highness," said Mr. Gerami, "may I present to you Miss Forugh Farrokhzad, the director of *The House Is Black,* and its producer, Mr. Darius Golshiri."

I gazed at the princess. Her hair was blue-black, cut in a straight bob. Her white mink was draped over her evening gown and hung almost to the ground, and her gloved hands were stacked with rings, one of them a turquoise the size of a robin's egg.

As Darius bowed to kiss her hand, I watched her lower her lusciously fringed lids and smile. Her perfectly painted lips, her mole—which I was fairly certain had been penciled in—the deft flick of eyeliner that accented her slightly wide-set eyes: She had a cold but ravishing beauty.

Uncertain what to do, I extended my hand. The princess's shake was slight and unconvincing. Her eyes narrowed as she took me in, and she flashed me a strained smile. "I have always had the highest hopes for our country's women, and it gratifies me to learn of your work with Mr. Golshiri."

"Thank you," I said. A little too late I added, "Your Highness."

"I'm deeply touched by your film," she said, turning to Darius. "How movingly you've shown the plight of these poor people!" As she said this, her eyes teared up a little. Mr. Gerami instantly produced the handkerchief from his breast pocket, and she dabbed the corners of her eyes very gently with it a few times before continuing. "I feel it's vital that we extend our charitable works to help such unfortunates. You do know, Mr. Golshiri, that it has been my particular calling to provide refuge and comfort to the dispossessed and to bring the issue of human rights to the attention of the king. I wonder, have you heard about my new projects in the south?"

"I have heard something, yes."

"I'm glad to know it—so very glad. You've been quite

difficult to reach lately, Mr. Golshiri. I would have so loved to enlist your talents to showcase some of our recent successes. I do hope," she said in her velvety voice, "that you'll be more accessible as we continue our work on behalf of the people."

Far away, across the room, I saw a flash of a raspberry-red dress and a tumble of dark curls. Leila. She saw me, too. Her eyes slid from me to the princess and then back to me. For just a moment she held my gaze, then she disappeared into the crowd.

"Thanks to the princess's unbounded generosity in advancing civil and human rights," Mr. Gerami was saying, "and of course to the monarch's own great vision for our country, the regime has never been more popular than it is now."

I felt the heat rise to my face. I'd been too full of my own bitterness to notice it earlier, but all at once I understood: it was Rahim whom Leila had been thinking of just before the film started. Her brother's fate was linked, even if tenuously, to those two figures in the dark. I felt hot and weak-kneed. Maybe it was all that talk of human rights or maybe it was an effect of the champagne, but Rahim's prostrate, battered body came back to me with amplified clarity.

I cleared my throat. "I wonder, Mr. Gerami, how much of this popularity depends on gratitude and how much depends on fear?"

Darius shot me a sharp look.

"Fear?" said the princess, her penciled brows arching up. Her eyes lingered over me for a long, odd moment, and then she raised her chin and spoke. "It may be that in the past certain parties have offered false counsel or acted improperly on the monarch's behalf, but the shah himself has only ever been guided by his deep love for the country."

"As his loyal subject," Darius said, "Miss Farrokhzad shares the shah's devotion to Iran, as do I."

Mr. Gerami looked from Darius to me. "Your work on behalf of these unfortunate souls is admirable, Miss Farrokhzad, but is it possible you've spent disproportionate time dwelling on these rather grim stories? Are you aware of His Highness's campaign against illiteracy, the new legislation supporting women's rights, his generous land reforms? May I suggest that in the future you focus on the monarchy's many historic advances? It seems a far greater use of your talents, Miss Farrokhzad."

"Indeed," said the princess, and smiled.

"Wise counsel," Darius said, bowing his head.

"Don't say anything," he hissed, his words hot against my ear. "Not a word until we're in the car."

"Leila's waiting for me in there and she—"

"Call her in the morning and tell her we had to talk."

"But she—"

"I have to speak to you now, Forugh. Alone."

The moon was set low in a navy sky, bright and swollen as a lantern. From behind the tall stone walls that enclosed the mansion there came the sound of laughter, conversation, and music—the sounds of a reckless, glittering world.

Inside the parked car, Darius turned to me, breathless. "You can't go around talking like that." His face tightened, and his grip on my wrist was as firm now as when he'd marched me to the car. "It's dangerous and you're being stupid."

"That's what you dragged me here to say? You humiliate me by bringing your wife to my premiere, and on top of that you want me to keep quiet? Maybe it doesn't faze you, but I can't stand all that smug self-congratulation, all that preening and phoniness. They put up hardly any money for the film, and now that it's out and there's talk of foreign prizes, they want you to work for them? Never mind that they call it 'your' documentary because they can't stand the idea that I made it!"

A car flashed past and its headlights swung around, flooding the car with light. For a moment, Darius's face was caught in the glow and then the darkness slid over his features again.

"Do you honestly think that's the first time they've made me an offer to work for them? That I haven't spent decades dodging their patronage so that I could build something of my own?"

"But what's the point if you can't ever say what you want, what needs to be said?"

His eyes scanned my face. "If we all say what we want, in the way we want, who do you think will be left to make art in this godforsaken country?"

"That's it, then? We shouldn't say anything? Not even when—"

I stopped myself.

"When what, Forugh?"

"Do you know what happened to Leila's brother?"

"Rahim?"

It startled me to hear him say Rahim's name. Leila's family had been close to Darius's, so he must have known

Rahim, and likely very well, but we'd never spoken of him. I'd never told Darius—or anyone else—that I'd gone to the safe house and seen Rahim before he disappeared from the country.

I bit my lip and stared ahead. A bird trilled noisily somewhere outside. "Forget it," I said. The air in the car was humid and heavy. I started to roll down the window, but he reached over and stopped me.

"Tell me what you know about Rahim. Every last thing."

I took a deep breath. "He was beaten so badly he couldn't stand, he couldn't talk."

"When was this?"

"After the assassination."

"And you helped him?"

"Yes."

His silence was sudden. He stared ahead, working out what I'd said. When he was done, he turned back at me. "From now on, figure out a way to put what you want to say in your poems and your films, but don't go around criticizing the regime directly. There are some decent people in there"—here he jutted his chin in the direction of the prime minister's mansion—"but there are also certain people who will peg you as a dissident and then it's over. Writing poems, making films—it all stops."

I stared into his face: the tanned skin, the hooded hazel eyes, the hard set of his jaw. For a moment I tried to imagine what I would have made of him if our lives hadn't become entangled. His massive self-confidence, his fierce independence and pride—part of me was already detaching itself from him, snapping into a different awareness about who he was and what we'd be to each other from now on.

"So that's your idea of freedom?" I said hotly.

"What are you talking about?"

"You've asked me to say nothing about our relationship, and now you want me to keep quiet about what's going on all around us. Don't say this; don't say that. Is this what freedom is to you?"

He shook his head, as if the question pained him. "It's my idea of survival," he said.

I looked at him for the space of a few heartbeats, then I jerked the door open and swung my legs out of the car. This time he didn't try to stop me.

"I love you, Forugh," he said just before I slammed the car door shut. "I'm trying to protect you. I'm trying to keep you safe."

27.

"Have you ever gone swimming in Amir Kabir Lake?"

"No," I told Leila, cradling the receiver between my ear and shoulder, the cord stretching from the jack in the hallway to the kitchen. "I've been out that way a few times, but I've never gone all the way down to the lake. Why do you ask?"

"I'm really so sick of Tehran. Aren't you?"

"Well, sure, but—"

"Listen, I'm staying up in Karaj through the end of May. I have this place up here. An old family house. About an hour from the city at this time of night. Why don't you come up and join me for a while?"

"I would, but I'm writing," I told her. This was true and not true. I'd been holed up in the apartment for five days straight, working through a new cycle of poems, but the words weren't coming. I was working from home, avoiding Darius. He called me once after the premiere, but I'd hung up as soon as I heard his voice. He hadn't called again after that. I kept trying to put him out of my mind, but it was no use.

"So come do your writing up here! It's early in the season; everything shuts down in the middle of the week. We'd practically have the lake to ourselves. I bet you could use the time away from the city, and the swimming's perfect here, Forugh. The water's a little cold in the mornings, but by noon it's perfect. There's a kitchen at the cottage and I can cook for us . . ." She rattled off a list of dishes. "Pomegranate and walnut stew, crisped rice, saffron pudding, baklava."

I laughed. "Are you sure that's enough food?"

"Listen," she said with mock seriousness, "if you don't come up here yourself, I'll have to drive all the way back to Tehran and kidnap you. You know I'm capable of it, Forugh *joon*."

"Fine," I said, and laughed again, which brought me, very briefly, back to my old self. "When shall I come?"

"Are you free tonight?"

When I opened my eyes, all I saw was a shuttered window and a weak thread of light. Arriving in darkness the night before, I had seen a scattering of small cottages set against a dark hillside. It wasn't until the morning, when I threw open the window, that I saw how beautiful it was here. The cottage was part of an old hunting lodge that had belonged to Leila's father. Surrounded by acres of woodland, an orchard of pomegranate trees stretched from the terrace toward the mountainside, and in the distance I could make out poplars dancing against the sky.

I pulled on a dressing gown and went looking for Leila.

"You're a real gypsy," I said when I found her in the kitchen. There was the scent of bread baking, the fresh fragrance of herbs and of cumin and coriander and saffron.

Wearing a white cotton dress, her curls pulled back with a scarf, she was standing by the stove in bare feet. The windows streamed with condensation. Rings of fire blazed under all the burners. I watched her move between the kitchen counter and the stove, a spatula in one hand and a wooden spoon in the other. She looked over her shoulder at me. "Better a gypsy than a princess," she quipped.

She poured me some tea, in a pretty but chipped china cup, and I sat down at the table. When she turned back to the stove, I took in the room. The polished oak armoire that stood at one end of the kitchen might have been transported from regal quarters, but the floors were covered in colorful tribal rugs, and everywhere I looked there was an impression of warmth and simplicity.

"Now that you're finally awake," she said as she set an iron mortar and pestle and several cinnamon sticks before me, "you could help out a little."

I took a sip of tea and began grinding the cinnamon. When I finished I took a pinch of the spice between my fingers and began dusting the top of the saffron pudding with it. I arranged the slivered almonds on top, making a star at the center of the bowl.

I glanced over and saw she was watching me.

"Not bad," she said, and I pulled a face.

"You're looking well, Leila."

The corner of her mouth lifted in a slight smile. "You say that as though you weren't expecting it."

"That's not true," I told her. "It's only that I know you don't go out much anymore. And"—I swallowed—"you seemed upset that night. At the premiere, I mean. Just before the movie started and then later when we were at the party."

"Nerves," she said, and shrugged. "It happens sometimes. Because of Rahim, because of what happened."

I swallowed. "Any word from him recently?" I ventured.

She shook her head. "He's out of the country. He's safe. That's all that matters." She ran the back of her hand against her brow, sighed, and stirred the pot. "It's getting so hot. What time is it anyway?"

I checked my wristwatch. "Half past eleven."

"Already?" She lowered the heat on the stove and set down her spoon. "In that case, let's go for a swim."

We changed quickly and set out for the lake. Following the narrow footpath through the woods, we tramped past dense columns of silver-leafed birch until we reached a clearing, and from there we looked out across dales and ridges to where the landscape was punctuated by a small blue-green lake.

On the beach, Leila wriggled out of her summer dress and let it drop to the sand. She was wearing a turquoise bathing suit with a halter top and a high-cut bottom. Her skin was very fair and there were freckles on her shoulders and chest. Even without a stitch of makeup, she was about as beautiful as I'd ever seen her.

I pulled my tunic over my head and kicked off my pants. My faded black tank suit was too big in the chest and the fabric sagged. I tried to straighten the straps, but it wasn't much use. "Honestly, Forugh," Leila said, as a smile crept onto her lips and her eyes took on a familiar gleam, "for such a famous temptress, you sometimes show a remarkable lack of style."

I couldn't help but laugh. "I've missed you so much, Leila."

"Me, too," she said. "I'm so happy you came up. I love the quiet, but it's much better with you here."

She slung her arm around my shoulder, and together we made our way down toward the water. On the shore she stopped to tighten the tie on her halter. I was still picking my way gingerly over the large rocks that lined the shore when Leila surged past me and dove under the water with a fierce kick. Waist-deep in the warm water, I squinted against the sun and watched her. She swam beautifully, with strong, steady strokes. You had to be confident to swim like that, I thought; you had to have done it for years. All your life, maybe.

"Don't tell me you don't want to get your hair wet!" she called out a few minutes later when she saw me dog-paddling with my head high above the water.

She swam over to me and then dove down under the water, and for a minute I couldn't see her, though I could feel her leg brush against mine once and then a second time. She bobbed up in front of me a moment later, splashing me so that water streamed down my face and soaked my hair.

Afterward, when we were done swimming, we spread our towels on the beach. I sat cross-legged, looking out toward the lake and sifting the warm pebbled sand through my fingers. She slipped on her sunglasses and stretched out on the towel, her dark wet curls splayed around her. When I looked over at her, I thought she'd dozed off, but then she suddenly said, "So. What's going on with Darius?"

"What kind of question is that?"

She lifted herself up onto her elbows and looked at me. "A direct one. A simple one."

"He's not planning on divorcing his wife, if that's what you're asking."

"Things aren't how they used to be. People are getting divorces now. It's happening more and more."

"I've been divorced already, remember? I know all too much about it. And if the point of his getting a divorce is that we'd get married, well, I'm not sure I want that just now, or ever, really."

She shifted on her towel, pushing her sunglasses onto the top of her head so that I could see her eyes. "All right," she said, softening her voice. "Forget marriage. What I want to know is, are you happy with this arrangement?"

"I'm fine."

"That's really all you want? To be 'fine'?"

I was quiet for a moment. "Maybe it's better to want less for a change."

"Oh, Forugh. Listen to you! You wouldn't have said that a year ago. Or when you first moved back to Tehran and had far fewer choices than you do now.

"You know I put as little stock in public opinion as you do," Leila continued when I didn't answer, "maybe even less, but that's not the point. What matters is what you think, Forugh, and what you feel. You don't conform to anybody's ideas of what you should do with your life, but it's not that you don't care how you're treated. You're never going to be like that, however you try to pretend."

I pressed my lips together and stared out at the water. "Well," I said finally, clenching fistfuls of sand and then letting them sift through my fingers, "it doesn't matter. My feelings aren't enough to persuade him to make some sort of change."

Her answer was quick. "They should be," she said, pulling her sunglasses back over her eyes and lying back on her towel.

We'd walked back from the lake in silence, both sleepy from sunbathing, tangled in our own thoughts. At dinner Leila tried to draw me out of myself, to tease me in the old ways, but I couldn't shake loose what she'd said about Darius. She was right, of course, but I couldn't tell her that just then. I slipped away to my room early that night, but it took me a long time to fall asleep, and I was still in bed when a screen slapped against the front door and I jerked awake. There were noises coming from the other room, a shuffling and then the sound of a door banging closed. A crash, as of furniture overturned, and rapid footsteps. But then the noises suddenly stopped. Just a servant tidying up the cottage, I thought. I sank back under the covers, drifting off to sleep, and woke to a noonday heat, the sheets damp and twisted around my legs.

"Leila?" I called out, pulling on a robe and stumbling into the kitchen. A chair had been knocked to the ground. I picked it up and called out to Leila again. There was no answer, but I saw signs of breakfast—the little metal coffeepot sat on the stove and next to it was a cup, half full and with lipstick coating its rim.

I rinsed out the coffeepot, made a fresh brew, and carried a cup from the kitchen to Leila's bedroom. The door was closed, but a sliver of light showed through at the bottom. I knocked quietly. "Leila?" I didn't hear an answer. I knocked again, then turned the knob and poked my head inside. Her bed was made, the pillows neatly fluffed and the quilt folded. I set down the coffee and sat on the edge of the bed. *She must be down by the lake,* I thought, but then from the window I saw her turquoise bathing suit hanging on a line in the garden, alongside our towels and my own black suit.

I checked my watch—12:37. Maybe she'd driven into the village, not wanting to wake me? I walked outside but found her car parked beside mine. She must have gone for a walk. I went back to my room, dressed, and then poured myself a cup of coffee. I read for a while, nibbling at a piece of flatbread she'd set out on a plate for me. I couldn't concentrate and kept reading the same page over and over. The quiet in the house was maddening. I checked my watch again—2:12. Finally I put down my book and scribbled a note and tacked it to the front door: "Down at the cove. Looking for you."

The first part of the walk took me past a row of pomegranate trees, the boughs heavy with deep-red fruit. I thought we had walked diagonally toward the lake, but we must have walked straight. I tried to work out the way Leila had taken me, but the footpaths all looked the same and I couldn't find the birch-lined path from the previous day. Eventually I saw what looked like a wider trail and made my way in that direction. After wandering for ten minutes, I came to the cove where we'd swum together. The lake was still, like a sheet of glass reflecting a cloudless blue sky. I sank to the ground, knees to sand. The water near the shore was a clear pale green, dappled with sunlight. Overhead, birds circled the air, and there was the relentless buzz of insects in the trees. I looked out at the lake. On the opposite shore, I could see two boys fishing. I watched them angle their rods and cast their lures into the water. A few times the ends of their poles fluttered and dipped, and then they yanked them back to set their hooks. Once, one of them caught what I guessed was a trout, though from a distance it was hard to be sure.

There was a sound then, a hawk's scream.

An instinct turned my head to the left. I clambered to my feet and dusted the sand from my skirt. I noticed another footpath leading from the shore into a copse of beech trees. The path was narrow, uneven, and studded with rocks, but I continued down the trail. Eventually the path grew thick with tall, leafy bushes that scratched at my bare legs. Twigs snapped under my feet; roots tripped me. I was running now. The lake disappeared and reappeared behind the trees, and then suddenly the trail opened up into a clearing, from which I could see another small cove.

She was there, in the lake, not ten feet out from the beach. She was wearing her white sundress and a shoe on one foot. Her mouth had been gagged and her hands had been roped together in front of her. Her long black hair floated around her shoulders, and her still eyes were open to the sky.

I stood there at the lip of the lake, not moving, not blinking, not breathing. I don't know how long I stood there, staring at her dead body, but at some point I turned and ran back up the footpath, back to the house and to my car. When I reached the village, I was screaming unintelligibly and I could not stop.

28.

_____

And this is me
a woman alone
on the threshold of a cold season
on the verge of understanding
the earth's polluted existence
and the simple sadness of the sky
and the weakness of these hands. . . .

I'm cold,
I'm cold and it seems
I'll never be warm again . . .
I'm cold and I know
there's nothing left of the wild poppy's dreams
but a few drops of blood.

—from "Let Us Believe in the Dawn
of the Cold Season"

LEILA'S DEATH CUT MY LIFE IN TWO: BEFORE AND AFTER.

After Leila died I became a different person. I drove to Darius's house the night of her murder, half crazed, desperate, and afraid. He made me sit down and tell him what had happened. I could barely get the words out, choking on them through my tears. Taking it all in, his face turned pale and serious. For once, he didn't seem to know what to do or what to say. Toward dawn, when light began to bleed through the window, I took three sleeping pills and slept for fifteen hours. When I woke, he was still in the room. He was sitting on the edge of the bed and his eyes were soft and kind, which made me remember what had happened and start to cry.

BODY OF QAJAR HEIRESS FOUND IN AMIR KABIR LAKE, read the headline a few days later. The story ran in the last pages of the newspaper. It was three paragraphs long and revealed more or less nothing. Leila's relatives had buried her quickly and quietly in the family mausoleum, and if they were planning any sort of memorial, I hadn't been invited to attend, nor had anyone I knew. The authorities, meanwhile, refused to offer any sort of explanation for her death, apart from the assertion that she'd drowned.

"Leila did not drown," I told Darius. Tears blurred my eyes as soon as I said her name.

"I know."

My body stiffened, then began to shake. When he reached for me, I buried my face against his shoulder. We sat together for a long time like that. My voice, when I drew back from him, was a whisper. "But why . . . ?"

He looked pensive and uncomfortable. It took a few minutes for him to answer, but then he said, "I think they wanted Rahim. He's been making too much noise, and too many people have been listening."

"But what did any of that have to do with her?"

"Maybe they thought he'd come back if he knew she was in danger."

My chest had tightened and I couldn't get air inside. "He didn't come back."

"No."

"I don't understand. It doesn't make sense."

"They probably wanted to send a message to his comrades. Who knows?"

"We need to do something."

"Do something? What do you think you can do?" He shook his head. "Work, Forugh. Write your poems. That's all you can do, and it's more than most anyone can accomplish these days."

"It's not enough."

"Nothing's enough. Do what you can."

But I didn't write. I couldn't write. I went back to Tehran, and for the next several weeks I lived in a blur of grief, rarely leaving the house, rarely bothering to shower or change my clothes. Night after night I found myself up late, unable to sleep, pacing the room and thinking, *It can't be, it can't be, it can't be.* But it was.

Her death was my fault. No matter how much Darius tried to convince me later that it wasn't, I'd always believe I was to blame. Not that I could have saved her. No— I couldn't have done that. But if I hadn't stayed up so late the night before, I would have woken up earlier. I would have seen when they—or was it he?—came for her. I couldn't have stopped what happened next, but she wouldn't have died as she did. Alone.

Despite what Darius told me, I felt as if I needed to do something, but I didn't know what. I smoked endlessly and barely ate at all. A menacing presence seemed to lurk behind every window and every door. I no longer trusted anyone, not even people I knew. I hardly talked to anyone anymore. The longer this went on, the more difficult it became to imagine living any other way. It was as if I had never had a different life than the one I had now.

Whenever I did go out and come back alone to the empty house, I'd walk in a hurried zigzag, looking over my shoulder every few steps. Once I made it inside, I'd search every room to make sure no one was there before bolting the door shut and barricading it with a side table and two chairs. Darius came by a few times, but the long silences between us made me miserable and I wanted to be left alone, in the darkness of my own thoughts and memories.

Once, when I was a small girl, I saw a man hanged. We'd spent the afternoon at the bazaar, my mother, Puran, and I. It was a warm spring day, and all up and down Avenue Pahlavi the trees had started flowering. I remember the air was thick with the scent of cherry blossoms.

By the time we neared Toopkhaneh Square, the streets grew busier but also strangely more quiet. All of a sudden a small gasp escaped from my mother's mouth. "May God kill me!" she whispered. She dropped her packages and clapped her hands over her mouth. Peaches and plums tumbled to the ground and rolled toward the gutter.

I traced her gaze, standing on my toes for a better view. Some hundred yards away, a dais had been erected over the fountain in the center of the square. A length of rope dangled from a post, and under it stood a chair. Two hooded men were leading a third man to the dais. A black handkerchief had been tied around his head, covering his eyes. *A prisoner,* I thought. His hands had been tied behind his back, exposing two dark circles of perspiration under his arms. His clothes were soiled and tattered, his collar was awry, and he wore no shoes.

I scanned the crowd. Hundreds of people, almost all of them men, stood together in pairs and in clusters, their eyes focused on the platform. A few feet from where we stood, a father had hoisted a small boy onto his shoulders, and here and there I saw a few women, mothers and grandmothers with children. There were many policemen and soldiers, as well.

I turned back toward the dais. I didn't quite understand what was happening, but even so I couldn't stop myself from looking. The prisoner had been dragged to the chair and forced to stand on it. The length of rope was thrown around his neck and then yanked tight. One of the hooded figures kicked the stool aside, and the prisoner's body jerked up and then swung heavily through the air.

"*Maman,*" I whispered. I tugged at my mother's dress, but she stood quiet and unblinking. For some minutes the square was silent. Long after the man's body stilled, the crowd neither dispersed nor stopped gawking at the figure hanging from the rope. They stared on and on. They couldn't tear their eyes away. I couldn't tear my eyes away.

And then all at once the shouting began. First came one call from the far end of the square closest to the platform, then a chorus of curses from all directions.

"Death to the traitor!"

"Long live our king!"

"Long live Iran!"

Child that I was, I could neither understand nor describe what happened that day, and in time the memory fell away. But I remembered it now, after Leila's death. At night, in a dream, it came back to me. I woke trembling and clammy, but I had the words to say what I'd seen. I hadn't written anything in months, but now, just when I was sure I was done with poetry, a hot, restless rage surged through me, displacing my bewilderment and fear. Grief had quieted and hardened me, but now it also made me reckless. I got to work. Poems about the feeble threads of faith and justice, the law's black kerchief, fountains of blood, my country's youth cloaked in a funeral shroud—these new poems were strange and dark and free. And they were hers. Every one.

> The sun was dead.
> The sun was dead and "tomorrow"
> was an odd, antiquated word
> children no longer understood.
> They drew it as a black blot
> in their notebooks.
>
> My people, a fallen people
> dead-of-heart, dazed, lonely,

wandered from exile to exile,
dragging the burden of their own corpses
and the murderous thirst of their hands.

—from "Earthly Verses"

June of that year, 1963, was a month of martyrs and bloody days. Resentment over the shah's alignment with the West had reached a fever pitch. An increasingly large contingent was pushing for a return to traditionalism, an embrace of Islam and the teachings of the Koran, yet so many others embraced the changes under the monarchy, saw them as part of Iran's renaissance, its chance for modernization and growth, its chance to be consequential on the world stage. Artists, intellectuals, and students forked in opposite directions: toward communism or democracy. In answer to the cries of "Down with the shah!" and "Down with imperialism!" the holy city of Qom had been set ablaze. Seminary students were shot dead in the streets; clerical robes and religious texts were heaped onto bonfires; minarets and golden domes were turned to ash. In Tehran, pictures of a cleric named Khomeini were papered in every corner of the central bazaar. That was the first time most Iranians had heard of him, but in sixteen years he would lead the country into revolution and Iran would become an Islamic republic. A year after that, the shah would be dead.

It seemed impossible, back then, to trace the fits and machinations of kings, presidents, and politicians to an obscure cleric, but those three days of bloody riots presaged all that would come. "I can summon a million martyrs," Khomeini said, and the first several thousand came forth now. It was Ashura, the annual day of mourning for the beloved Imam Hossein. Incensed by the regime's assaults on Qom and emboldened by memories of Imam Hossein's martyrdom, men flooded the streets, whipping chains against their bare chests. In the city, I heard them. They marched until their bodies were ripe with gashes and the streets were stained with their blood.

The fires, the murders, the riots, the marches—all seemed part of some progression. Every death was telling some part of our story, which was Iran's story, but no one could tell how the story would end. We were driven by forces we couldn't understand, moving toward a destination we couldn't see. Those were bitter and black days, full of prophecy and dread, and every face seemed disfigured by grief, confusion, and rage.

I remember those days, and the months that followed. The secret police and government informers were everywhere, their numbers ever increasing. When you heard they were eight thousand strong—twenty thousand, sixty thousand—you thought, *impossible*. How could the estimates vary so wildly? But that was the point. Not knowing how many there were, we imagined them everywhere. They might be anyone, everyone.

Mullahs were rounded up, imprisoned or exiled. Leftists, with whom the religious right shared little apart from their hatred of the monarchy, met the same fate. A playwright I knew disappeared and was found dead weeks later at the edge of the Salt Desert. Books were censored, and newspaper after newspaper shut down. Any mention of democracy or social justice was deemed subversive. Treasonous. People scattered into the countryside or left the country altogether.

In prison cells and dark basements, in warehouses and along stretches of barren roads, there were bodies that would never be claimed or tended or buried. We would never witness those tortures and deaths, nor read or hear of them, but they were there, in our silence and our fear.

One particular afternoon, as I was making my way back to my car from a bookstore near Tehran University, where I'd spent most of the morning, I noticed that a large number of students had gathered near the university gates. Between the protesters and the onlookers I guessed there were about three hundred people in the crowd. There were still scattered protests about town, watched over by phalanxes of heavily armed security forces, but a gathering this large was unusual enough to make me stop and stare.

"Our oil is ours!" the students chanted. "Death to the dictator!" and "Democracy for Iran!" I pushed past the onlookers and managed to read the demands inscribed on their posters: political reform, greater civil rights, freedom of expression.

A young man in an olive-green canvas jacket and longish hair had made his way onto a sort of platform. The crowd seemed to know him. There were shouts and whistles, and before these had quite died down I made my way toward the front. "Fighting imperialism is a national, moral, and religious duty," he began, speaking through a bullhorn. "All those who can contribute to Iran's independence and do not are part of the plot against our country," he declared. "There is no compromise or middle ground in this struggle." He was repeatedly interrupted by people shouting out their assent, and he fought to be heard over their cries. I stood listening for a while, but eventually people began to shove and jostle one another, and all the shouting made it impossible to hear anything more.

I shouldered my way through the crowd and crossed the street. My bag was heavy with books, and I stopped on a corner to switch it to my other arm while I fumbled inside for my keys. When I looked back up, I saw that several cars had stopped alongside the university gates. A dozen men were clambering onto the sidewalk and running toward the protesters, their guns drawn. With the first shot, my heart gave a kick. Later, everyone reported screams, but I remember there was a long silence before the chaos started.

For a moment I stood transfixed by fear, and then I felt myself snap and tingle with life.

I tore into an alleyway, my bag thumping against my thigh as I ran. I was nearly to my car when the earth cracked and threw me to the ground. The world went silent. When I opened my eyes the air was thick with smoke. From somewhere behind me I heard the sudden rattle of machine-gun fire, followed by panicked shouting.

I had to get back to my car; somehow I had to find it. I sprang to my feet and started running again. I'd lost my bag by then, but I'd managed to hold on to my keys.

When, finally, I found the street where I'd parked, I hurled myself inside the car and sat gripping the steering wheel, desperate to catch my breath. My wrist was bleeding, but the sensation was far from me, like something I'd left behind in the streets. I peered over the dashboard for signs of life. Nothing. A minute passed and then I heard shouting and the hard pop of a pistol. I glanced in the rearview mirror and saw them—dozens of men running in the street, the scream of sirens at their backs.

I started the engine and nosed the car forward, but then there was a hammering against the hood and I slammed on the brakes.

Three men stood in the street, blocking my way. The one in the middle had a wide, wet circle of blood on his chest, and the two others had each grabbed him under the arms and were half carrying, half dragging him toward my car. They looked young—not older than twenty, I guessed. One of them had the beginnings of a beard, and another wore glasses with thick black frames.

"Please, miss!" shouted the bespectacled one, rapping against the hood of the car.

If I had a moment of doubt it was then, sitting inside my car and staring at the three men from behind the windshield. Who were they? How could I trust them? It was at this point that I might have chosen to do something very different from what I actually did. But I couldn't see this moment for what it would mean later—for me or for those men. Instead, I shook myself loose from the daze that had stolen over me and pulled the back door open by the latch.

They crammed into the back seat, a confusion of arms and legs. Except for their labored breathing and the low, constant moan from the one who'd been shot, they were silent. My hands were shaking, my knuckles bone white as I gripped the steering wheel. Already the air in the car was thick with the tang of sweat. The radio struck up a tune—an airy love song—and I slammed the button off.

An afternoon in Tehran, a bright sun in a blue sky, street-cars, ice-cream vendors, plane trees, a city busy with other stories. I swung left, then right again and into a main thoroughfare. I had no idea where I should go; my only instinct was to keep driving. It took me a while to work out where

I was. It was a relief to fall into traffic, to find myself surrounded by so many other cars and people, and after a few minutes my grip on the wheel loosened, just slightly, and I forced myself to breathe.

At Avenue Pahlavi a car swerved in front of mine, coming to a stop at a crooked angle. One door slammed, then two more, and three uniformed figures emerged, their faces in shadow and their batons raised and ready.

In prison there were things I tried not to think about but couldn't.

Like the three young men as they were dragged from my car and into the street. How they were beaten, even the one who couldn't stand, the one with the circle of blood on his chest. Their bloodied faces, their torn clothes, their broken bones. Their fear.

Like Leila in the lake. Her screams before they gagged her and tied her wrists with rope. The hands that grabbed her by the shoulder and marched her down to the lake. Her struggle, if she could still struggle, when her head was forced under the water. Her terror when she realized she would die. That she *was* dying.

In the cell: a metal cot, a basin, and a stool. The stones were damp and stank of urine and rot, and there was a high concrete wall with a square window no wider than an outstretched hand. I looked down at my clothes. My blouse was splotched with blood, and the blood had dried to a burnt brown.

Later—much later—rumors spread that Leila was a traitor, a communist operative just like her brother, but what did not change was the part of the story where they said she drowned in the lake. That she was a poor swimmer, that she'd swum too far out and then didn't have the strength to swim back. That it was an accident and nobody was to blame.

"It's not true," I told the prison walls over and over again. "It's not true, not true."

A key rattled against the lock, interrupting my mad sing-song.

The guard was young, maybe twenty—the same age as the protesters at Tehran University. He stopped in front of me and my gaze traveled from his boots, up the length of his uniform, to his chiseled jaw, and finally to his eyes. I remember thinking, *What does he want from me? A woman sitting cross-legged on the floor in a torn dress and no shoes, a woman who converses with walls and holds her palms up to the sky as if in prayer? What could he possibly want from me?*

"You're that woman," he said coarsely. I watched his grip tighten on his baton. "That poetess."

I winced and inched away toward the wall.

He lifted the corner of my dress with the baton and then ran it very slowly from my ankle up to my thigh.

"My father is Colonel Farrokhzad—" I started to tell him, but before I could finish I was kicked, low and very hard, in the stomach. It knocked the breath out of me, that kick, and the room went black.

When I came to, I saw I was alone in the cell. There was a searing pain where the guard's jackboot had struck my abdomen, and I couldn't pull myself up from the ground. My whole body hurt. Not as badly as it would tomorrow, or the day after that, but badly enough that all I could do was lie with my eyes on the ceiling, clutching my sides.

They kept me separated from the other prisoners in the women's section of the jail, but I heard them—their voices, the shuffling of their bodies, their cries and their whispers—and I shored it all against my despair.

That night, memories passed through my mind in the space between one hour and the next, yet each was rich, vivid, and complete. Entire scenes and conversations surfaced without the slightest omission or abbreviation. Mostly they were very early memories—my mother's garden, our big old garden in Amiriyeh, as it used to be before it was destroyed. I saw it so clearly, with the lovely tiled fountain, the high walls draped in honeysuckle and jasmine, the many trees under which my sister and I had once played when we were girls.

In the morning there were voices and the beat of boots against stone tiles, and when I woke I saw my father before me with the glint of a tear in his eyes.

Poetry could tell every story. I had believed that once.

The day my father came for me in prison and took me back to my old house in Amiriyeh, I slept for three hours, woke up, and started to write. It wasn't a poem but a letter addressed to every country that was not my country, and it was Leila's story, Rahim's story, the story of the prisoner, the three protesters, and every other story I couldn't tell in a poem, because a poem was a world and it took time to understand a world and now there wasn't any more time.

I wrote for ten hours straight. The dread and desolation that accompanied me for weeks hadn't dissipated or disappeared. They grew, they changed shape, they evolved into these words. I had never worked so hard on a piece of writing, and it was the only thing to which I didn't sign my name.

The next day, I drove to the university. Every part of me hurt, but I managed to make my way to the mustard-yellow door and to the scared boy inside.

He was confused, but I saw he remembered me.

"Don't open it," I whispered when I pressed the envelope into his hand. "Not yet. Wait until one of you is out of the country. Then tell them what's happening to us. Tell everyone you can. Do you understand?"

"Yes," he said, and closed his hand over mine.

"We should leave," Darius told me. "We should just take off." We were driving in the foothills outside Tehran, climbing up toward Damavand. He gripped the wheel with both hands, eyes narrowed at the tunnel of branches through which we wound our way.

"Take off?"

"Leave the country. We can disappear."

"What makes you think I want to disappear?"

"Don't you? What's left for you in this country?" He didn't wait for me to reply before saying, "Nothing. There's nothing for you in Iran anymore."

I didn't answer. Not at first. He turned left and then drove down a long, narrow road. The sun was setting, the shadows of the trees lengthening in the dusk. I hadn't been this way before, and all of a sudden I realized it was already happening. He was already making me disappear.

"Where are you taking me?"

"Nowhere," he said as we crested the hill. "Anywhere." He eased the car to the side of the road, turned off the ignition, and turned his face to me. "Listen," he said, "I've given this a lot of thought, and I think we should leave the country."

"Where would we go?"

"England, America, wherever you want."

I folded my hands in my lap and sat very still. If we went abroad, he continued, we could live together openly, free from the eyes that followed us everywhere in Tehran. He'd already worked out where we would live: a big country house somewhere outside London. A house of our own— that's what he called it. If I didn't like it there, we could try New York or Los Angeles.

"What about your wife?" I asked when he finished speaking. "And your children? Will you leave them here or bring them abroad, too?"

"I don't know, Forugh. We can work that out. There's time for all that. The important thing is for us to leave. Forget about everything else."

I turned my face to the window. Forget about everything else. How would we ever do that?

My thoughts spun away from him, but when he laid a palm on my shoulder I turned and looked at him. "You need to think about this calmly," he was telling me now. "Rationally. If you wait much longer, we won't be able to get out. You do realize what the stakes are, don't you, Forugh?"

"Oh yes," I said. "Yes, I do."

29.

Will I ever comb my hair with the wind again?
Will I ever plant pansies in the garden again,
set geraniums in the sky outside the window
    again?
Will I ever dance on wine glasses again?
Will I ever wait expectantly for the doorbell to
    ring again?
I said to Mother, It's all over.
I said, Things always happen
before you expect them to;
we have to send word to the obituary pages
    now.

—from "Let Us Believe in the Dawn
of the Cold Season"

I DIDN'T LEAVE IRAN.

The years passed. My love for Darius never flagged,
yet our patterns never changed—what he wanted, what I

wanted. We were together and then apart more times than I could count. Again and again I went from his glass house back to my apartment, from the depths of intimacy to complete solitude. When people called me his mistress—or worse—I forced myself not to care, but each time I saw him with his wife, I had the stifling feeling of living behind locked doors and shuttered windows. I developed an instinct for navigating the labyrinth of streets and alleys of Tehran, for making my way alone. I traveled abroad, too, I saw other countries and discovered different customs. Invariably, I grew restless and uneasy. Invariably, I returned to Darius and to Iran. More and more I was a woman on her own, at home in my work—my poems, my films—but never truly settled in the world.

Then one day in February 1967 I went to visit my mother in Amiriyeh.

"They say there'll be snow tonight," she told me as I rose to leave. It had been a lovely visit, and I was reluctant to go. "Why don't you stay the night and leave in the morning? I can fix up a room for you and we'll have dinner together."

I glanced out the window. It was a little after three o'clock in the afternoon, and the sky was low and dark with clouds. I took my mother's hand and squeezed it. "I can't, *maman*," I told her. I had a dozen wheels of film stacked in the back seat of one of the studio's jeeps, ready to be delivered to Darrus. "They're expecting me and I'm already running late."

She gazed at me uncertainly and the wrinkles deepened around her eyes. "But the roads will be bad . . ."

Age had threaded her hair with white and softened her

features. She still lived in the old house in Amiriyeh, but she was alone now that Sanam had returned to her village in the south. The rooms around us lay still and lifeless, empty now of the seven children she'd raised, the husband she'd married, the servant who had become her closest friend.

I never saw the Colonel after he came to retrieve me from prison. I wrote him a letter once, thanking him for what he'd done to secure my release. In that letter I also asked that he try to understand me. "Will you ever see me not just as your daughter but as a human being?" I wrote. I could never have spoken the words to him. It was impossible. Even writing them to him took every bit of courage I had. But it was useless. He didn't answer the letter and I never wrote him another one.

I did see my mother, though. I stayed with her for several weeks after I was freed from prison. It was July, then August, and I remember how she would sit by my bed at night, her hands folded in her lap, and in the morning she would still be there. She was frightened for me, yes, but there was something else. It was the first time we had been alone together for any length of time, and those days changed something between us. "Forgive me," she said one night. We were sitting across from each other at the dinner table when she suddenly laid down her spoon and fixed me with a look so pained and pleading that I had to drop my eyes. I knew then that she understood what it had cost me to oppose my father all those years ago. Stuck in my resentment, I had interpreted her silence as cruelty. I thought she could never understand me, but even as I raged to be understood, I didn't know anything about her, nothing of consequence anyway. I was determined to change that.

"I'll be fine," I told her now, pulling myself out of her

embrace. We'd reached the door and I was tightening my scarf around my neck.

But her eyes were troubled. "Why are you rushing? Are you sure you're all right?"

"Of course. It's only that I need to get back to the studio before they close up."

"So stubborn," she said, and smiled.

"I'll come again next week. I promise." I took her hand and squeezed it.

"Yes. Yes, come next week. But come earlier so that we'll have more time together."

I ducked down and kissed her on the cheek.

"Goodbye, my daughter!" she called out when I reached my car, her voice echoing in the empty alleyway.

I looked up, smiled, and raised my hand in a wave.

Maneuvering my way through the late-afternoon traffic, I headed north on Avenue Pahlavi, past the rows of new gleaming high-rise apartments and overpriced boutiques that had sprung up in midtown. The city was closing up, readying itself for the snow. Metal shutters were drawn over the storefronts, blinds lowered. Everywhere people were rushing away. There was something strange about it. An excitement mingled with dread.

The city had changed beyond recognition. Wrecking balls and bulldozers had leveled the old buildings to rubble. The dust of construction hung permanently over the streets. Gated mansions reached up to the northern foothills, while slums fanned out from the city's southern limits.

I feared an age that had lost its heart, and I was terrified at the thought of so many crippled hands. Our traditions were our pacifiers, and we sang ourselves to sleep with the lullaby of a once-great civilization and culture. Ours was the land of poetry, flowers, and nightingales—and poets searching for rhymes in history's junkyards. The lottery was our faith and greed our fortune. Our intellectuals were sniffing cocaine and delivering lectures in the back rooms of dark cafés. We bought plastic roses and decorated our lawns and courtyards with plaster swans. We saw the future in neon lights. We had pizza shops, supermarkets, and bowling alleys. We had traffic jams, skyscrapers, and air thick with noise and pollution. We had illiterate villagers who came to the capital with scraps of paper in their hands, begging for someone to show them the way to this medical clinic or that government office. The streets of Tehran were full of Mustangs and Chevys bought at three times the price they sold for back in America, and still our oil wasn't our own. Still our country wasn't our own.

I'd said too much already, but I couldn't stop, not even when I began to suspect I was being watched. The letter I wrote after I left prison ran in the editorial pages of several prominent foreign newspapers—*Le Figaro, The New York Times, The Guardian*. The byline read "Anonymous," and for a time I was free to watch as my letter lit a fire under the regime. To the shah, who had promised the country two centuries' worth of progress in a decade, that letter wasn't just an embarrassment but a scandal, and it provoked a stark denial by the country's ambassador to America. Much, in particular, was made of the charges of police brutality at Tehran University. "These students," the ambassador asserted, "have incited aggression, and they must be brought to justice."

But by then the letter had circulated broadly and other people, mostly students and others living in exile, had come forth about the lack of civil liberties, the plight of political prisoners, the prevalence of surveillance and torture. If the allegations were believed or even half believed, it would compromise foreign relations and imperil international trade. A flurry of press releases and speeches followed, all eloquently asserting the regime's commitment to democracy and human rights. Then came the news that the three students had been granted a stay of execution and that their sentences had been reduced to life in prison.

When I read that news one morning in the paper, I sat very still, tasting something bitter at the back of my throat. THE KING'S MERCIFUL PARDON, ran the headline, accompanied by an especially flattering portrait of the shah. I'd wanted something else for those young men, for myself, for all of us: freedom. I knew now we wouldn't have it. I knew that by writing the letter I'd consigned those men to fates equal to, if not worse than, the swift executions that had been planned for them, and I knew, with complete certainty, that they would live and I would die.

The beech trees on the road from Tehran to Darrus were stark black against the slate-gray sky, their thin branches bending with the wind. The village was a sparse collection of dwellings, unspooling north toward the mountains. Just past a small roadside teahouse, I stopped at an intersection, looking left then right. I'd turned the heat all the way up but I was still cold, shivering. I rubbed my hands against my thighs to warm them. Winter always settled over this city so suddenly, and I was dressed in a skirt, with thin stockings, as if for a different season.

I heard the school bus before I saw it. Just as the signal turned green and I pulled into the intersection, the wheels screamed against the asphalt. Then, with a jolt, I connected the sound to a streak of color at the edge of my field of vision. I veered to the side of the road, missing the bus by a few feet before it rattled, then hissed, to a stop. Wheels of film flew to the floor. For a moment there was silence and stillness. My heart was beating hard. I was about to get out of the car and check if anyone had been hurt, but then the bus roared to a start. Their faces were silhouetted, but as the bus passed I saw that the children inside were peering down at me through the window, and all at once I felt a terrible sadness slice through me.

Kami, I thought. I closed my eyes against the memory, but it was useless, and I let my forehead drop against the steering wheel.

One day I'd gone to his school in Ahwaz. I covered my hair with a scarf in the hope that Khanoom Shapour wouldn't recognize me before I could even get to him. I stood by the gates to his school, working out what I should do when I saw him. So much time had passed. Year after year Parviz and his family refused to let me see him. Now a decade had passed. Would he even recognize me?

A bell sounded loudly and dozens of boys spilled into the courtyard. The children wore identical uniforms and carried the same brown leather satchels. I scanned every face, but I couldn't find my son. My heart was beating crazily. And then he appeared. Kami. He was a grown boy now. His torso and legs had lengthened and his black curls had been clipped off, but I knew it was him. My son.

"Kami!" I called out, pulling off my scarf so he could see me better. He must have known who I was. He must have felt it. I was suddenly sure of it. His face shot up in my direction and I stepped toward him, but already Khanoom Shapour was at his side. By then I was inside the courtyard, just a few feet from my son. I could almost reach out to him. But before I could come any nearer, Khanoom Shapour edged herself in front of Kami. "The bad woman's come to take you," she said, her eyes never leaving my face.

I held my head high and stepped toward them, but I stopped when I saw the fear in my son's eyes. All at once I knew what she had told him was something she had been telling him for years. That I was a dishonorable woman. That I was a bad mother. That I'd abandoned him. What else had Parviz let her tell him? What other lies had she told?

I let my mother-in-law move my son away then. She looked warily over her shoulder, and I thought Kami might turn to look at me, too, but he didn't. When he and Khanoom Shapour reached the end of the street, they turned left and disappeared. A sudden exhaustion stole over every muscle and bone in my body. I moved to the nearest wall and slouched against it, the stones cool and rough against my back. I'd been holding my scarf in my hand, but sometime in the last moments it had fallen to the ground. I didn't move to pick it up. The sound of children's voices floated from the courtyard. Laughter, high-pitched screams, the sporadic sounds of traffic. A bus clattered past and a woman walked by, leading a sulky little girl by the elbow. I was gazing at the back of the girl's blue-and-white checkered dress when I was struck by a horrible understanding. Kami wasn't my son. Not anymore. I could wait all my life and he'd never be my son again. The sadness I felt in that moment was stronger than any feeling I'd ever know. It was the deepest loss of my life, and it would stay with me until the end.

&

It happened a few miles outside Tehran, in the still-wild foothills outside the capital where concrete highways and high-rises gave way to gardens, orchards, and fields. I was so close to Darrus, practically there. A mile outside the village I stopped at a traffic light. The fog was thick, rising from the side of the road and obscuring my view. I had driven this way hundreds of times, but today it seemed as if I were heading into a strange and unmarked land. There were no shops, no people. A desolation I had never noticed before.

I glanced in the rearview mirror and watched as a car rolled up behind me. It was a black Ford sedan. It drew closer and closer, foot by foot, until it was so close I could make out the outline of the driver through the glass. His features were obscured by a hat, but for just a moment he lifted his chin and I could see his face. He saw me watching him and I caught what looked to me like a smile.

It was, I think, that smile that deranged me. Suddenly I felt sure I recognized the man. But from where?

The light was still red, but I peeled out of the intersection, my heart thudding against my chest, my palms slick with sweat. The car skidded and swerved, the tires whining against the dark road. A few seconds later, I glanced into the rearview mirror. The hood of the Ford was inches from my car, so close that I couldn't tell the screech of its wheels from mine. Coming onto a curve, I slammed my shoe down on the gas pedal and strangled a gasp in my chest. A concrete wall rose up before me, and it was then that I felt death had come for me here, on this road less than a mile from Darius's glass house. The thought hardened into knowing, and I gripped the wheel firmly with both hands. The seconds seemed to slow to minutes, and outside the landscape blurred, went white, and disappeared.

The jeep was upside down, its wheels to the sky, when Darius appeared. Someone recognized my car and ran all the way to find him and bring him here. The impact with the concrete barrier had flung me through the windshield. I landed in an embankment, my head colliding with the asphalt. My brain was drowning in blood, but my heart was still beating. I was alive.

Darius crouched beside me, screaming—"Forugh! Forugh!" I could hear him so clearly, and I tried to answer him but I couldn't. I felt my eyelids flutter, and when I opened my eyes again it was as if I were observing him for the first time, that very first time I met him at Leila's party, when he caught me looking at him and held my gaze. There was so much I wanted to tell him, so much I wanted to say, but there wasn't much time left, and even if there had been time, that somehow didn't matter anymore. My silence was part of the story. It belonged to it, was indistinguishable from it now.

He carried me to his car, cradling my head in the crook of his arm. It was night now and the road was dark. He never stopped talking to me as he sped back toward the city, not for a minute, and he was still talking to me when he carried me through a vast gleaming lobby and into the thin blue light of the hospital. My eyes closed. When they opened again, hours later it seemed, there was brightness and many strange voices. *We can't help her,* they said, one after another, the nurses, surgeons, specialists. *She's too far gone, practically dead, there's no point in operating.*

I don't know how long he held me. I don't know how long I lay there until all the others left and it was just the two of us in the room. *We can't help her,* they said, but what he heard then and would always hear was *We won't help her.*

He died with Forugh, people said afterward, and he never contradicted them. Not once. Not ever.

I see him there, in that last room where we were together, his hand clasped over mine and his face wet with tears. "I'm sorry," he says over and over. "I'm so sorry." He holds me as if it's the only place in the world he's ever wanted to be or belong. Sometimes he tells me we're on the beach by the Caspian, in Ramsar. It's the first day I see the sea, and he's watching me walk toward the waves with my shoes in my hands and I'm taking too long, the tide's coming in, but he lets me go because it's my moment and he wants me to savor it. Sometimes he tells me a story about a house tucked in a deep-green wood many thousands of miles away. It's our house, the house where we'll live together, and he says we'll go there tomorrow—no, we're already there, safe and free. Sometimes he whispers a poem, the most perfect love poem in the world, but the words slip loose from their meanings, fluttering in the air and tumbling down and down until silence closes over me and I am gone.

EPILOGUE

Maybe truth lay in those two young hands,
those two young hands
buried beneath a never-ending snow.
And next year, when spring
mates with the sky beyond the window
and green shoots of light burst from her body,
the branches will blossom, dear friend.

—from "Reborn"

THE GRAVEDIGGERS SET OUT WITH THE MORNING'S FIRST call to prayer. In spring, when the ground turned wet and loamy, or in summer, when it crumbled to dust, the job could be finished in as little as three hours, but it was now the middle of February, and with a hard snow falling and the earth so unyielding, the gravediggers would have to begin at sunrise and work long into the day.

It was the women—my mother, sisters, cousins, and aunts—who cleansed my body of sin. Starting with the right side of my body, they purified me limb by limb, from head to foot, three separate times. Though they spoke in whispers and glances, their hands were steady as they performed the ablutions.

Next they wound the white myrrh-scented shroud around my body, swathing me once, then a second and a third time. The ritual was repeated with a second *kafan,* and because it was winter and the snow was falling heavily, I was cloaked in a silk carpet.

At noon the men arrived and hoisted me onto their shoulders. A wintry haze had settled over the city. It would be dark by four. Trudging along icy pavements, their backs against the wind, they carried me into a white hearse and then drove me through the streets of northern Tehran. Hundreds upon hundreds of mourners followed in our wake. In the narrow alleyways surrounding Zahirodo'allah Cemetery, the cortege inched past teahouses and street vendors hawking roasted chestnuts, pomegranates, and sheets of flatbread, past the turquoise domes and minarets of Imamzadeh Saleh shrine, and through the tall gates of the cemetery.

All along the way, people on the sidewalks stopped to stare. The shah's police stood in their dark-blue uniforms and gold-edged caps, with their rifles and long swords. Watching—they were always watching.

The newspapers were full of pictures of me that day, February 15, 1967. Forugh, the Colonel's daughter, sitting on the stone steps of my childhood house with a white satin ribbon wilting at my crown and a blond doll posed on my lap. In the photograph, the Colonel stands over me in full military regalia and black boots half the size of my body. Forugh, the sixteen-year-old bride with arched eyebrows and a lipsticked pout that reads black in the picture. Forugh at nineteen, holding the son who would love, then fear, then despise me. Forugh, the divorcée, at twenty-two, my arms and ankles bare and a rope of pearls knotted between my breasts. Forugh, the notorious twenty-eight-year-old poetess, standing beside Darius Golshiri with bobbed hair and shy but smiling eyes.

Rumors drifted through the crowd. The roads had frozen up the night before, winter streaking the asphalt with black ice. I'd been driving too fast, at least twenty miles faster than was safe on that stretch of road, but for no known reason I hadn't pushed the brakes as I headed toward the embankment—there wasn't a trace of skid marks. Maybe I'd lost my head—hadn't it happened before? Didn't I have a history of madness? There was talk, too, of a school bus filled with children. Of a sudden swerve. Sacrifice and martyrdom.

There were other mysteries apart from the circumstances surrounding my death. "Golshiri," someone whispered, nodding toward a man who stood slightly apart from the other members of the funeral party. He was quiet, his hands folded before him. "Her lover."

"He bought this grave for her, you know. I've heard it's in his family plot, next to what will be his own grave."

At this, there was a perceptible intake of breath and a turning of heads.

Without a husband to claim it, my body belonged now to my father, the Colonel, so how had Darius Golshiri managed to bury me, and within his own family plot? And where would he bury his wife when she died? Next to me, his mistress? It was unthinkable. But no matter how carefully they studied him, no one could make out Golshiri's emotions, much less his intentions. Throughout the burial rites, his expression remained hard and impassive. He betrayed nothing that day—and he'd betray nothing for the next fifty years.

Except for what I'd written in my poems, in the end no one knew the truth about my death and no one knew the truth about our lives.

When I left my father and then my husband, I lost my name and I was no one. But there was freedom in this, to be a woman on my own. It made me strong, and it made me the poet I wanted to be.

I knew many poets whose lives had nothing to do with their poetry. They were only poets when they sat down to write. They'd finish a poem and then turn back into greedy, shortsighted, miserable, and envious people. Well, I could never believe in their poems, because I couldn't believe in them.

While I was alive, poetry was the answer I gave to my life. I didn't search for anything in my poems. I wrote to discover myself and to become myself. And I believed in being a poet in all moments, because to me being a poet meant being fully human. I tried to write and live with courage and also to die that way. Bravely. Honestly.

"There's nothing for you in Iran anymore," Darius had told me once. For days afterward I turned his words over in my mind. I wondered what it would be like to live in a place where a woman's life was less governed by shame and prohibition, a place where I could walk with my eyes straight on the horizon, a place where I could be free. I thought hard about leaving Iran, but if Darius couldn't fully choose a life with me, if he stayed married to his wife, what did it matter if we left Iran or went abroad?

But there was more to my decision not to leave the country. For so many years I wished I had been born somewhere else. I felt my life had been wasted in Iran. But the truth was I loved it. I loved Tehran's relentless sun and heavy dusks and dusty side streets. I loved sleeping on the rooftop on summer nights and waking to morning's call to prayer. When I walked in the streets, there was a memory at every turn, a rootedness I felt in my limbs and my heart. Whatever Iran wanted to be, I loved it. I'd found my life's purpose here. Every poem I'd ever written was entangled with my country's story. I loved its downtrodden, small-minded, generous people. I loved them; I belonged to them. They were my people, and I was theirs.

Many years after I died, a million books of my poems could be found throughout my country, hidden under beds and behind bureaus, crammed behind bookshelves and in the deepest reaches of drawers. A million books of poetry—it was a staggering number and unequal even to the ambition I'd had when I was alive. By then, the 1979 Revolution and war with Iraq had left very few families untouched by loss, and hundreds of thousands of Iranians had left the country and were now scattered all over the world. People read my work and claimed I'd foretold our country's destiny in it—the chaos, the ruin, the tortures, the silences. The sons who died, the daughters who disappeared. In Iran they read my

poems as auguries, and they called my death a blessing because it spared me from watching my prophecies come true,
one after another, for so many years.

Once, when my poems were banned by the new regime
and a publisher wouldn't stop printing them, his press was
burned to the ground. As if poetry could be destroyed like
a building or a body. But art wasn't like that. Art could survive; even when suppressed, even when outlawed, it could
survive far worse fates than fire.

There was a day in the new millennium when hundreds
of thousands of people gathered in the streets of Tehran.
People called it the Green Path—green for the Prophet
Mohammad as they knew him: humane, gentle, generous.
The faith in the streets was one reborn from our own roots.
People chanted my verses as they marched peacefully toward Azadi Tower that spring—"I Feel Sorry for the Garden" and "Let Us Believe in the Dawn of the Cold
Season"—but I wouldn't be there to see it, nor would I
witness the loss of so many young men and women along
the path of my country's bloody and aborted push toward
freedom.

"La elah ella Allah!"—God is the only God!—came the
cries as I was lowered into the ground.

The sun was a pale white circle above the Alborz Mountains; the wind blew faintly, stirring the sweet, smoky perfume of wild rue.

A ring of mourners encircled the grave. It was snow-
lined and banked with masses of white flowers. Tiny alongside the men in their forbidding black suits, three women

stood together, their arms interlocked. They wore Western-style dresses with straight skirts and collarless jackets under their coats, but each covered her hair with a heavy black veil. Two of them were my sisters and the third one my mother.

At last the funeral prayers began. *In the name of God, the Compassionate, the Merciful. Forgive those of us who are living and those of us who are dead, those who are present and those who are absent. Forgive us and forgive her.* I was turned to the right side, toward Mecca, toward the One who is the only One. Salutations on the Prophet, a supplication for the deceased.

A pause, a silence, and then the first fistfuls of soil fell upon my body.

I felt the earth calling me back to itself. I was ready now. Swallows would one day lay eggs in my ink-stained palms. Tender green shoots would force their way out of my grave and up toward the air. All this would happen later, in the spring, when the sun warmed the earth and the sky, but already I had reached a place where censure and suffering are meaningless, where courage has no boundaries, where hope lasts forever and does not fade.

AUTHOR'S NOTE

IN 1978 MY FAMILY LEFT IRAN WITH TWO MAROON leather suitcases. There'd been trouble in Tehran for a while, but that year the trouble suddenly got worse. We weren't sure how long it would last, but for now it seemed we should leave the country. There wasn't much time to pack, much less to plan. We flew to America, thinking we'd wait out the violence and chaos back home. The next year there was a revolution in Iran. The two maroon suitcases were unpacked and then cast off.

My family never returned to Iran. I never returned to Iran. But some things survived our exodus. Among the few cherished possessions my mother managed to bring to America was a slender book of poems by Forugh Farrokhzad. Growing up, I'd happen across the book every so often. I can still picture the bobbed-haired woman with kohl-lined eyes on the cover. Who was she and why had she followed us to America?

That image—its glamour, mystery, and modernity—

rooted itself in my imagination, but it wasn't until I was in college that I began to read Forugh's poetry and that my fascination with her truly began. At UCLA I had the great fortune to study with the late Dr. Amin Banani, a scholar of Iranian literature who'd been acquainted with the poet in the 1950s. No sooner had I read "The Sin" than I was possessed by Forugh's voice, its naturalness and immediacy. I was also bowled over by Forugh's audacity. This was a poem about desire written from a woman's point of view. Had Iranian women really once sounded like that?

Brought up in Tehran during the 1940s and 1950s, Forugh Farrokhzad, or "Forugh" as she became known, was the first woman to transcend the label of "poetess" without the support or patronage of a man, becoming a poet of tremendous accomplishment. She was not yet twenty when she wrote "The Sin," a poem so candid and daring that its publication in 1955 made her the most notorious woman in Iran. Her five books of poetry cemented her reputation as a rebel. An exile in her own country, as a filmmaker, she turned her lens on those banished to the fringes of society. Again and again she flung herself fearlessly into life, voicing passion and protest at a time when many still believed women shouldn't be heard from at all. She was simply too creative, too gutsy, and too ambitious to be silenced by the constraints others sought to place on her.

The risks she took cost her a great deal, but they also made her the artist she became. Her poems still offer an extraordinary reading experience more than half a century after they were first composed: The subject matter is daring, the language unfettered, and the point of view direct and unapologetic. More than perhaps any other writer, Forugh Farrokhzad gave Iranian women permission to be bold, fu-

rious, lustful, and rapturous. She ripped the decorous con-
ventions off women's writing, holding up a mirror for
women's hopes and pain. She cut a path through Iranian
literature with her courage and her honesty, and my mother
had been just one of a great number of women affected by
her life and work.

For me, a young Iranian American woman coming of
age in 1990s' California, reading Forugh's poems felt like
crossing into a different country, into a different idea of
what it meant to be a woman, into different possibilities for
whom I myself could become.

Her poems changed me. They stoked my curiosity about
Iranian women's lives, a curiosity I chased first as a literary
scholar and then as a writer myself. To write my first book,
a family memoir titled *The Good Daughter,* I spent several
years researching Iran before the 1979 Revolution. Even
after completing the project, so much about this time period still vexed and riveted me. Iran is a paradoxical country,
and those paradoxes were profoundly amplified in the fifties
and sixties. Women's lives underwent radical changes in
these years, yet many old prejudices and prohibitions endured. The ensuing tensions fascinated me. In addition,
since Forugh's day, women have become a vital presence in
Iranian literature, yet whether on account of cultural taboos
or outright censorship, it seemed that so much remained
unwritten, particularly about the decades leading up to the
revolution. What did it mean to be a woman in Iran at that
time? What were the rules? What were the possibilities and
encumbrances? I wanted to read—and write—a story that
answered these questions.

Eventually, my thoughts turned to Forugh. For many
years I'd continued to read all I could about her, not know-

ing it would lead me to write a novel. Then at one point I discovered she'd assisted some student activists during the turmoil that roiled through Iran in the early sixties. I set about learning all I could. I returned to her poems, then to scholarly sources. Discovery piled onto discovery. What I found astonished me, and eventually I thought, I have to tell her story.

As a poet, Forugh often drew inspiration from her life, and the outlines of that life—a troubled early marriage and divorce, the forced surrender of her son, her notorious union with a prominent filmmaker, and, of course, her death in 1967 at the age of thirty-two—form the novel's framework. Moving between interpretation and imagination, I embedded the novel with the images, tropes, themes, and rhythms of Forugh's poems and films. As I wrote, the ghost of her voice—its urgency and tenderness—was constantly in my ear. I wanted readers to hear it, too, so I steeped myself in her poetry, working from the Persian into English. By translating her poems for the novel, I gained a completely new intimacy with her writing, one of the most precious gifts that came from writing Forugh's story.

What I couldn't know I invented. In part this was of necessity. Unlike other novelists who've written about historical figures, I didn't have access to a well-stocked archive. When Forugh died in 1967, many of her papers disappeared. Friends and relatives, no doubt traumatized by the death of one so young and gifted, as well as by the ongoing turmoil in Iran, chose not to speak about the more controversial parts of her life. Her work, too, was silenced. After the 1979 Revolution her poems were banned, then heavily censored. When one press refused to stop printing her work, it was scorched to the ground. For decades Michael C. Hillmann's

A Lonely Woman, published in 1987, offered the only in-depth look into her life. Forugh's writing has been splen-didly illuminated by Professor Farzaneh Milani, yet Milani's full-length Persian-language study, *Forugh Farrokhzad: A Literary Biography,* was published in Iran shortly after I fin-ished writing this book.

Yet the gaps and fissures I encountered in the historical record opened a space for invention. "The historian will tell you what happened," E. L. Doctorow remarked. "The nov-elist will tell you what it felt like." In writing about Forugh, I wanted to go beyond what was known outwardly about her—what could perhaps ever be known about her, given not just the reticence of those who'd been close to her but the fundamental inscrutability of the human personality. I wanted to imagine what it felt like to be the woman writing those astonishing poems. To be the woman who created herself by writing those poems. And to do this I embraced the unique power of fiction to illuminate the past.

In writing *Song of a Captive Bird* I drew from Forugh's own poetry, letters, films, and interviews as source material but enlarged upon these in ways only possible in fiction. For example, the character of Leila Farmayan is based on a woman who befriended Forugh in the years immediately after her divorce, yet the novel expands her role so that she stands, finally, as a symbol for the untold number of Iranian men and women who have died under mysterious and not-so-mysterious circumstances over the course of the last cen-tury. I was unable to cover every aspect of Forugh's life in this novel, as some pieces of her story could be additional novels in themselves. For example, it is known that when she traveled to the Bababaghi Hospice in the early sixties to film *The House Is Black,* Forugh took a child from the colony under her wing, but I didn't want to invent threads where the record seemed particularly thin, nor intrude upon the memories of those loved ones who have survived her.

As I worked on *Song of a Captive Bird,* I found myself continually moved by Forugh's bravery, tenacity, and independence, pained by the slights, prejudices, and cruelties she faced, and awed by her talent, vision, and integrity. Through Forugh I found a way to enter the past and to return to the country I'd left as a child, but to my surprise I discovered that many of her dreams and frustrations echoed through the present. *Song of a Captive Bird* is the story of a woman who battled to create a life on her own terms, to balance conflicting roles and desires, and to survive in an often-hostile world. Her choices, when she had them, were hard; her independence and her career were achieved at significant cost, not least the surrender of her child and her own emotional well-being. Her love affairs both freed and entrapped her. She was a modern woman, and in her hopes and ambitions we can see our own.

Today Forugh's work is as significant as ever, and for the same reasons it has been for more than five decades. Forugh Farrokhzad is an icon in Iran, a gifted and spirited woman whose work and commitment to individual liberty and social justice resonate deeply across generations. Her poems have been banned and censored, but readers still manage to get ahold of them. There is perhaps no more touching proof of her legacy than the thousands of people who trek to her grave in Zahirodo'allah Cemetery every year.

Like those pilgrims, we can be enriched by seeking words for the inexpressible and expanding our view onto unfamiliar people and different worlds. We have today the same need to not just look at, but to truly see the struggles of those seeking justice and also to celebrate those who, like Forugh, show us the enduring importance of the arts to a thoughtful, free, and deeply felt life. "Remember its flight," Forugh famously wrote, "for the bird is mortal." My hope is that Forugh's story in *Song of a Captive Bird* will inspire and embolden readers, conjuring something of the magic that came with me from Iran to America in two maroon leather suitcases so many years ago.

ADDITIONAL READING AND VIEWING

Reborn and Other Poems. Forugh Farrokhzad. Trans. Hassan Javadi and Susan Sallee. Washington, D.C.: Mage, 2013.

Bride of the Acacias, Forugh Farrokhzad. Trans. Amin Banani and Jascha Kessler. Delmar, NY: Caravan, 1982.

The House Is Black, Forugh Farrokhzad. Golestan Studios, 1962.

Sin: Selected Poems of Forugh Farrokhzad, Forugh Farrokhzad. Trans. Sholeh Wolpe. Fayetteville, AK: Univ. of Arkansas Press, 2007.

A Lonely Woman: Forugh Farrokhzad and Her Poetry, Michael C. Hillmann. Washington, D.C.: Mage, 1987.

Veils and Words: The Emerging Voices of Iranian Women, Farzaneh M. Milani. Syracuse, NY: Syracuse Univ. Press, 1992.

"Icarus Reborn: Captivity and Flight in the Work of

Forugh Farrokhzad," in *Words, Not Swords: Iranian Women Writers and the Freedom of Movement.* Syracuse, NY: Syracuse Univ. Press, 2011.

Mirror of the Soul: The Forugh Farrokhzad Trilogy, dir. Nasser Saffarian. 2002–2004.

ACKNOWLEDGMENTS

MARY KARR ONCE QUIPPED THAT THE BEST PART OF WRITing is the company, and I agree. Writing this novel has put me in the company of some of the most gracious and brilliant people I have ever known, and my gratitude to them is endless.

For the woman she was, the poems she wrote, and the legacy she left, thank you, first and foremost, to Forugh Farrokhzad.

My agent, Sandy Dijkstra, cheered me on from the moment I first mentioned the idea of writing about Forugh. Her tenacity and dedication astonish me. Both she and the wonderful Elise Capron read endless drafts of this novel over several years. Andra Miller, my editor, embraced Forugh's story with love, enthusiasm, and unflagging attention. She has been my dream editor.

Enormously useful to my understanding of Forugh's life, work, and times was Michael C. Hillmann's *A Lonely Woman: Forugh Farrokhzad and Her Poetry*. I was honored

to participate in the conference Professor Hillmann organized at the University of Texas, Austin, in February 2017
to commemorate the fiftieth anniversary of Forugh's death.
The presentations and conversations of that day expanded
my knowledge and deepened my appreciation of Forugh's
exceptional body of work. I am also grateful to Farzaneh
Milani, who has written about Forugh with great insight
and eloquence. Forty years in the making, Dr. Milani's literary biography of Forugh has recently been released in Iran.
An English translation will be a tremendous gift to American readers, and I eagerly await its publication.

My former Washington and Lee colleagues Suzanne
Parker Keen and Lesley Wheeler continue to inspire me not
only with their devotion to teaching, writing, and scholar-
ship, but their all-around excellence as human beings. Early
drafts of *Song of a Captive Bird* were supported by several
summer research grants from W&L as well as a sabbatical
leave. A fellowship at the Virginia Foundation of the Hu-
manities and a "Rising Star" Outstanding Faculty Award
from Virginia's State Council for Higher Education allowed
me periods of uninterrupted time to research and write this
novel. My residency at Yaddo was a dream come true, not
least for the many gifted artists and writers I met during my
time there. I owe thanks also to the many mentors and
friends I met at the Bennington Writing Seminars: Amy
Hempel, Lynne Sharon Schwartz, Alice Mattison, and
Askold Melnyzuk.

For more than forty years Elaine Petrocelli and her crew
at Book Passage Bookstore in Northern California have
been creating one of the most vibrant literary communities
in the country, and I am grateful to have this exceptional
place as my home ground. As a teenager I used to get lost in

the store for hours and hours, holing up between the shelves and attending readings by a steady roster of literary luminaries. I've never stopped getting lost there and never will.

Beth (Bich) Minh Nguyen, Aimee Phan, and Juvenal Acosta have been my wonderfully supportive colleagues since I moved back to California. Each in her own way, my dear friends Persis Karim and Linda Watanabe McFerrin have been champions of countless writers, and I have been lucky to be one of them. Ashraf Mostofizadeh answered my questions about the Iran of Forugh's day. Michael McGuire provided not just technical support but loyalty and cheerfulness. My friend Rebecca Foust has supported me in innumerable ways over the years. Her friendship is a source of such joy and inspiration. A phenomenal poet in her own right, she focused her discerning eye on my translations of Forugh's poetry. They are much stronger for it.

From my earliest childhood, my mother fostered a love of Iranian culture and history in me. I am inspired by her fierce spirit and grateful for her love. I doubt anyone has such unstintingly kind and generous in-laws as mine, Penny and Stephen Reiter. The whole Reiter clan has embraced me as one of its own and now I'm not letting go. Thank you to my wonderful son, Kiyan, who can make me laugh like no one else. And finally, a huge and heartfelt thanks to my husband, Sean, who is always my most lucid adviser and loving supporter. I am beyond lucky to make my way through the world alongside him.

ABOUT THE AUTHOR

JASMIN DARZNIK was born in Tehran, Iran, and moved to America when she was five years old. Author of the *New York Times* bestseller *The Good Daughter: A Memoir of My Mother's Hidden Life,* she has been published in thirteen countries and recognized by the Steinbeck Fellows Program, Corporation of Yaddo, Library of Virginia, and William Saroyan International Prize. Her stories and essays have appeared in *The New York Times, The Washington Post,* the *Los Angeles Times,* and elsewhere. She holds an MFA in Fiction from Bennington College and a PhD in English from Princeton University. Now a professor of literature and creative writing at California College of the Arts, she lives in Northern California with her family.

jasmin-darznik.com
Facebook.com/jasmindarznikauthor
Twitter: @jasmindarznik
Instagram: @jdarznik

ABOUT THE TYPE

This book was set in Galliard, a typeface designed in 1978 by Matthew Carter (b. 1937) for the Mergenthaler Linotype Company. Galliard is based on the sixteenth-century typefaces of Robert Granjon (1513–89).